"Remember," said know we're Russian. He's got to be absolutely convinced that we're just a small counterfeiting operation for some underground group, probably the Mafia."

"I understand, Yuri, but . . . "

"I hope you understand," Vladislav shot back. "Because one small mistake and the whole assignment can fail. Ten years of technical development and training . . ."

Mikhail cocked his head to the side as he slouched down in the chair. Suddenly he looked more casual, more easygoing, more American.

"Wanna check me out, Mac?" he said in a heavy Brooklyn accent.

Vladislav lit another cigarette and blew the smoke up toward the hooded light. "What's your name?" he asked.

"Sal . . . Sal Barbieri."

"Where were you born, Sal?"

"Brooklyn. DeKalb and Clinton, 1937."

"Where'd you go to school?"

"P.S. 38."

"Dodger fan?"

"Whaddaya kiddin'?"

Robert Neidhardt

ROOT OF ALL EVIL

JOVE BOOKS, NEW YORK

ROOT OF ALL EVIL

A Jove Book / published by arrangement with
the author

PRINTING HISTORY
Jove edition / August 1988

ISBN: 0-515-09749-7

Jove Books are published by The Berkley Publishing Group,
200 Madison Avenue, New York, New York 10016.
The name "JOVE" and the "J" logo
are trademarks belonging to Jove Publications, Inc.

PRINTED IN THE UNITED STATES OF AMERICA

10 9 8 7 6 5 4 3 2 1

ROOT OF ALL EVIL

Prologue

In September 1943, the Germans were in imminent danger of losing the war. The German high command knew it better than anybody else and had urged Hitler to adopt a defensive strategy on all fronts. He would hear none of it.

Rather than admit defeat, he initiated a series of offensive measures. The boldest of these was Operation Bernhard, which was launched early in December 1943. The operation was responsible for the production of $630 million worth of counterfeit British pound notes, their purpose being to bring about the collapse of the British economy. An utterly demoralized England would be forced to surrender in a year.

Within a few months, distribution of the counterfeit pounds began to have an effect on Britain's economy, and the plan might have succeeded had the Germans not been forced to alter it after 1944. In order to combat an increased Allied military buildup, the money was used to pay off British spies and support underground activities rather than being directed into the economy.

Although the operation failed, the Germans recognized the feasibility of the plan and, during November 1944, began development of a perfect counterfeit U.S. hundred-dollar bill. When the war ended in 1945, they had nearly completed three different sets of plates.

The plates were never found.

1

Washington, May 21, 1990 (UPI)—

U.S. GOVERNMENT ECONOMISTS REPORTED TODAY THAT THE
ECONOMY HAD WEAKENED MORE THAN EXPECTED DURING
THE FIRST QUARTER OF THE YEAR. COMMERCE DEPARTMENT
FIGURES SHOWED A 4 PERCENT DECLINE IN THE LAST
QUARTER, AND THE GROSS NATIONAL PRODUCT WAS DOWN 5
PERCENT FROM LAST YEAR AFTER ADJUSTING FOR INFLATION.

ARTHUR BROOKS, PRESIDENT TURNER'S BUDGET DIREC-
TOR, SAID THAT "AN ECONOMIC STRATEGY BASED ON
GRADUALISM WAS DOOMED TO FAILURE." HE PROMISED A
"FULL-SPEED-AHEAD THREE-YEAR PLAN THAT WOULD JOLT
THE ECONOMY."

Hartford, Connecticut
May 21, 1990

THIS TUESDAY WAS no different from any other for Bob
Tompkins. It meant spending the afternoon doing the grocery
shopping, stopping at Pat's Amoco for gasoline, and picking
up Helen's prescription. He had to get the Valium once a week
now that her arthritic back had gotten worse. Damn doctors.
When it came to the back, it was amazing how little they knew.

It was nearly six o'clock when he turned his battered '74
Chevy into the Knollwood Shopping Center just outside of
Hartford. As usual, the parking lot was crowded at that time of
day. Ever since the new A&P had opened, finding a space near
the stores was impossible. Now he just automatically parked
on the outer fringe of the lot where there was always plenty of

3

room. The owner of a new Mercedes 450SL apparently had the same idea. Tompkins pulled in next to it.

He got out of the Chevy, slamming the slightly sprung door, and walked around the gleaming Mercedes. This was the car he had always dreamed of owning someday, only now his somedays were running out. He studied his reflection in the polished hood of the car. How he had aged over the past five years. At sixty-eight, his once erect frame was now hunched. The brown hair that had been his best feature at thirty was now a snowy gray. It had thinned in the front, revealing a freckled forehead that seemed too large for the rest of his features. He had always thought that his nose was too small and pointed. The mouth was thin and narrow. His whole face seemed too small to be sitting on top of his six-foot frame. He was so conscious of it, he had bought extra-large glasses to frame the small blue eyes that receded beneath gray, bushy eyebrows.

He hadn't needed the glasses until he hit fifty. By then he had put in thirty years working as an engraver for the government. How ironic, he thought. For years he had been surrounded by millions of dollars he helped to create, and now he had a measly eight hundred a month to live on. If they had allowed him to work until he was sixty-five, his retirement would have been at least two hundred a month more.

But instead, he was let go.

The art of engraving was changing, they told him. He wasn't needed anymore. The "old-school" type of engraver who worked on the entire bill was a thing of the past. Now they wanted specialists, men who were highly skilled in doing just portions of the work. "Selective engraving," they called it. He called it patchwork. Nevertheless, he found himself in early retirement with less money than he had planned on.

Well, the fella who owned this baby certainly didn't have any money problems. He glanced at the New York plates. The guy was probably some Wall Street type here in Hartford for a convention. Some people had life easy.

A few raindrops fell on the hood. He looked up at the darkening sky and decided he'd better get Helen's prescription and start home. She would be making him supper.

He hurried into the drugstore and picked up the Valium. The damn stuff had gone up in price again. But then, what hadn't?

As soon as he got back outside, the sky opened up into a downpour. It had turned cold. He pulled up the collar of his jacket and hurried along the protective overhang of the long building to the candy store. When he thought of it, he liked to pick up some chocolates for Helen. It was still one of the things that made her smile, and Lord knows, with the pain she suffered every day now, she didn't smile much anymore.

Inside the store, he searched the shelf for her favorite; the Whitman sampler with the cherry-filled centers. Instead, he found an empty space where they usually were, so he settled for a box of mixed chocolates, $3.25. Jesus, last week they were $2.85.

He went over to the checkout and handed the box to Ben Cummings, the owner.

"Has your little lady switched over to the mixed chocolates?" Ben said as he pointed to the box.

Tompkins took four dollars from his wallet and put it on the counter.

"Not really, but you're out of her favorite," he said.

Ben looked up and smiled, then reached down under the cash register.

"Me . . . out of Helen's favorite chocolates? Never."

He put a Whitman samplers in front of Tompkins.

"I've been saving these for over a week now. Where the hell have you been? I thought you'd never show up."

Tompkins looked at the chocolates, not knowing quite what to say. He really didn't know Ben that well. It was Helen who had gotten to know him about a year ago, when he bought the store. They hit it off immediately once she found that Ben was a match for her sharp wit. He stayed in the background while they swapped double entendres and puns. It was all too much for him. He didn't believe in playing with words, anyway. You used them to say what you meant, nothing more, nothing less. He simply said "Thank you" to Ben.

Ben put the chocolates in a bag and handed it across the counter.

"That's one terrific lady you've got there. Tell her I hope she's feelin' better."

By the time he got back to the car, he was drenched. He tugged at the sprung door to get in as fast as he could, then started the car and backed out of the space, noticing that the Mercedes had left.

As he made his way home it was difficult to see even with the wipers on full speed. The rhythmic sound of their patter against the windshield sent his mind wandering to the first time he and Helen had traveled over the road. It was just over eight years now. They had been on the way to see a new home that a real-estate agent said was perfect for them.

For thirty years they had lived in a large ten-room house in Suffolk, Maryland, from which he commuted to work at the Bureau of Engraving in Washington. When he retired in 1974, they moved to Hartford. Years earlier, Helen had fallen in love with the city when they vacationed there in a small cottage overlooking the Connecticut River. Also, they decided it would put them closer to their son Bill and his family, who lived just an hour and a half away, in New Haven. Now maybe they would see more of the children. Billy and Karen were both in high school and in just a few years would be off somewhere to college. So Bob and Helen had sold their house in Maryland and moved into the small six-room Cape-Cod on Walnut Street.

During the first two years Bill, Elaine, and the children visited regularly. The holidays were spent together and they enjoyed warm family gatherings. But gradually the visits came farther apart. Helen's condition grew worse, to the point where traveling was impossible. Soon the children became more involved with their growing circle of friends, and it became increasingly difficult for Bob to get everybody together for the trip to Hartford. Now they visited only three or four times a year, mostly on holidays.

Because of Helen's limited mobility, their social life was virtually nonexistent. He turned to an old hobby of his, photography. In less than a month he'd built a darkroom in the basement, complete with running water, an enlarger, the whole works. But he got little chance to use it. Most of his time was spent helping Helen around the house.

The Tuesday shopping trip was the only time they were apart except for Thursdays, when Mrs. Gilroy, an elderly widow who lived across the street, came to visit. Then he would either take a walk or do whatever errands needed to be done. This certainly wasn't the retirement he had looked forward to, but then again, it wasn't for Helen, either.

He turned into Walnut Street. The rain was coming down heavily as he pulled up under the carport of the small frame house. He got out, opened the trunk, and took out the two bags of groceries. As he slammed the trunk shut he looked up and noticed that all the lights in the house were off. Maybe the power was out. No, the lights were on across the street at Mrs. Gilroy's. Helen's pain must have gotten worse, and she'd gone to bed early. He fumbled for the back-door key with the groceries in his arms, opened it with his elbow, and went into the kitchen.

He turned on the light. There were some dishes in the sink, and the radio was on. It was tuned to a Yankee baseball game. Funny, Helen never really understood baseball. She had always thought of it as a rather silly game.

He set the groceries on the table and took off his wet coat. It was dripping, so he went into the bathroom and hung it over the sink. Returning to the kitchen, he decided that instead of putting the groceries away, he would check on Helen. Something was wrong.

He passed through the darkened living room, flipped on the hallway light, and started up the stairs. At the top he saw that their bedroom door was closed.

Slowly he opened it. The room was totally dark except for light filtering in from the hallway behind him. His eyes quickly adjusted to the dim light, and he saw that the bed was fully made. Helen's closet door was open, but the closet was empty. She was gone. Startled, he entered the room and went around the bed to turn on the night-table lamp. Just as he was about to, he heard the door close behind him. He turned and froze.

"Who's there?" he managed to say. His heart was pounding.

"Where's Helen?" No answer. He felt his body automatically retreating from the invisible intruder he knew was moving toward him. He couldn't go back any farther. The bathroom door was directly behind him. Maybe he could turn quickly, get into the bathroom, and lock the door.

Every muscle in his body tensed as he was about to whirl around. But suddenly the door opened and something was thrust into his back. The pain he felt was brief, but it surged through his shoulder blades and into his chest. Then he felt himself being pushed forward and he landed facedown on the bed. The last thing he thought before he lost consciousness was that he would never see Helen again.

The rain had stopped, and Mrs. Gilroy decided to take her dog, Penny, for a walk. The poor dog had been in the house all day and was scratching at the door, waiting to go out. As they came down the front steps Mrs. Gilroy looked across the darkened street and noticed a car in the Tompkins' driveway. It was the same car that had been there earlier in the afternoon. Three people were getting into it. Two men were helping a man into the backseat. Was it a man? She couldn't be sure with only the light of the street lamp. No, it must be Helen. The poor dear must have gotten worse, and they were taking her to the hospital. She wouldn't bother them now but would certainly call in the morning.

She started down the street with Penny and wondered why she had never met any friends of the Tompkins who owned a black Mercedes.

2

Washington, May 21, 1990 (UPI)—

IN A SPEECH BEFORE THE AMERICAN BANKING ASSOCIATION, JOHN CRISTALDI, UNDERSECRETARY FOR MONETARY AFFAIRS, SPOKE OF THE VULNERABILITY OF THE DOLLAR IN THE WORLD MARKET. MR. CRISTALDI POINTED OUT THE DANGER OF A FOREIGN NATION AMASSING LARGE AMOUNTS OF CURRENCY IN U.S. BANKS. HE WARNED OF A SITUATION ARISING SIMILAR TO THAT IN 1974, WHEN SWITZERLAND HELD OVER $10 BILLION IN SHORT-TERM NOTES ACQUIRED THROUGH BANKS IN THIS COUNTRY. "LIQUID ASSETS SUCH AS THESE," HE WARNED, "WHEN QUICKLY WITHDRAWN, CAN BE DETRIMENTAL TO THE VALUE OF THE DOLLAR AND RESULT IN SERIOUS CONSEQUENCES."

Zurich, Switzerland
May 21, 1990

IT WAS SIX-THIRTY in the morning, and traffic was light on Autobahn N-1 leading into Zurich, Switzerland. Karl Geisler shifted his Jaguar X41 convertible into fourth gear and felt the car leap forward. He glanced at the speedometer, eighty . . . ninety . . . a hundred miles per hour. Ahead was an S-curve, and then the Autobahn entered a tunnel cut into the mountainside. As the car sped into the first curve he turned the wheel ever so slightly, and the car responded by hugging the road at eighty miles per hour. A quick flick of the wrist in the opposite direction brought the car around the second curve, and it roared into the darkness of the tunnel.

Geisler felt the coolness inside as the wind blew against his face. He loved the power of the car, and he loved the fact that it wasn't what one would expect the chairman of the largest bank in Switzerland to be driving.

But then again, Karl Geisler wasn't typical of the men who ran Swiss banking. They were bald, overweight, conservatively dressed men leading conservative lives. At sixty years of age, he was in excellent shape. The long hours of exercising had paid off, and over the last three years he had lost nearly twenty-five pounds. At just over six feet two inches, his body was lean and muscular. His face was tanned from long hours of skiing in the winter sun. The dark color highlighted his blue eyes and contrasted against snowy white hair which he kept stylishly cut just over his ears. He was a man who had been handsome in his youth but now looked even better with age. And he knew it.

The end of the tunnel was ahead. He turned off the headlights and reached down into a compartment in the door for his sunglasses. Seconds later the car emerged from the tunnel, bursting into the bright sunrise coming up over the horizon. Ahead was a truck, moving slowly in the outer lane. He passed it at eighty-five miles per hour, honking the horn as he went by.

The power of the car exhilarated him because power was the most important thing in his life now. Since he'd become chairman of Union Suisse, a bank with over $3.8 billion in assets, money was no longer important to him; power was.

As he had grown older and accumulated more and more of it, he realized the effect it had on other people. When other seemingly powerful men were forced to come to him for funds either to save their careers or their companies, it gave him a kind of sexual pleasure to hold a part of their lives in his hands. Looking across his desk at men groveling, actually begging for funds to save their companies, on occasion caused him to have an erection. The sense of omnipotence was so overwhelming that he felt like a god with the power of life and death. Of course, the power had also led to physical sex. Ever since his wife, Elena, had died three years ago, he found it surprisingly easy to arrange an evening with an attractive woman and end up in her bed. Any one of them could have had a much younger, attractive man, but they chose him. Why? Because of power.

Power aroused them sexually, as it did him. He found his performance much more satisfactory now than it ever had been with his wife. She had taken his power for granted, and he had been unaware of what its effect might be on other women. Now he knew, and he wanted more of it.

He slowed the car down as he came into the outskirts of Zurich. The early-morning traffic had begun, and the streets were crowded with commuters. He made his way down Bahn-hofstrasse, passing the chic shops lining the street and pulled up in front of Union Suisse. The valet opened the door, took his keys, and he went inside.

It was just seven-fifteen, but the bank was humming with activity. Like most Swiss banks, Union Suisse officially opened at eight A.M., but Geisler's habit of arriving early had influenced the staff. He walked down a row of glass-walled offices, responding to a chorus of, "Good morning, Mr. Geisler." At the end of the corridor he entered the open elevator and took it to the second floor.

His secretary was waiting for him in his office with the agenda for the day. It included the usual Monday morning meeting with the senior officers of the bank, and oh, yes, he had forgotten about the luncheon meeting with Paul Welte. Welte was a gold dealer of questionable character with offices just a few doors up the street from the bank.

Rumor had it that the main source of his gold was the tiny sheikhdom of Dubai in the Union of Arab Emirates. It was suspected that Welte was buying gold smuggled across the Persian Gulf from India, loading it into British Airway cargo holds and flying it to Zurich. Once safely inside Switzerland, it was brought to Chiasso, a small town on the Swiss-Italian border where two major Swiss banks have gold refining facilities. There the gold was melted down into bars the size of building bricks and deposited into Welte's account. Since Welte was now considered a major importer from Dubai, and Dubai gold now accounted for one fifth of the free world's supply, the man was important.

Geisler had recently received one other piece of information concerning Welte; he was now doing business with the Russians.

• • •

At twelve o'clock Geisler walked into the Exchange Club, a private banker's club located in the heart of Zurich, across from the Schweig-Landsmuseum. He had always thought it rather stuffy and seldom ate there, but Welte had suggested it. The maître d' recognized him immediately and escorted him to a private room off the main dining room. There he found Welte seated in a large overstuffed chair sipping a martini.

Welte pushed the chair back from the table and stood to greet his guest. He was much heavier than Geisler had remembered him; probably close to three hundred pounds. His head was shaved, and he peered through thick, heavy glasses. Although his three-piece suit was of good quality, it looked like he had slept in it.

"Karl, how wonderful to see you." He looked Geisler over from top to bottom. "You look well. Bachelor life must agree with you."

Geisler shook his pudgy hand and looked down at Welte's enormous stomach.

"It does. In fact, we both seem to be enjoying our vices."

Welte chuckled and patted his stomach.

"I have only found *some* women to be irresistible, but never anything I could put in my stomach."

He laughed at his own joke and gestured for Geisler to sit down.

Geisler looked around the room. It was elegant but dark and overbearing, with the only light coming from two silver wall sconces. The oak paneling on the walls was dark and gave the effect of the walls closing in on the room.

"I'm impressed, Paul, but this is a little extravagant, isn't it?"

Welte took a sip of his drink and looked over the top of his horn-rimmed glasses.

"Extravagant? Come now, Karl, it isn't every day that one has lunch with the chairman of Union Suisse. I'm honored."

He picked up a gold cigarette case that had a lighter built into it and flicked it open.

"Can I offer you a cigarette? They're Turkish . . . a very interesting blend of Turkish and Indian tobaccos."

Geisler refused.

Welte lit the long, slender cigarette and exhaled the smoke, filling the room with a musky, acrid smell.

He set the gold case down, moving it closer to Geisler, as if to keep his offer open. Then he reached under the table and pressed a button. The door to the left opened, and the maître d' came into the room.

"What will you have to drink, Karl?" Welte held up his empty glass. "I'm afraid I've gotten a head start on you."

Geisler ordered a Dewar's and soda, and the waiter left.

The door closed, and Welte glanced around the empty room as if to check if anyone was still there. Satisfied, he leaned back in his chair with his hands folded over his stomach.

"I don't suppose it's any secret these days that I've been dealing in gold with the Russians."

Geisler shrugged.

"Well, as you know, it's all perfectly legal. More than anything else, I think I'm resented for the fact that I got to them first."

Geisler wanted to tell him that he wasn't resented for doing business with the Russians at all but for the illegality of the transactions. And they *were* illegal, even if Welte refused to believe it. He decided against this, however, and said, "That may be true, but I'm sure it's not what you reserved this expensive room to tell me."

"You're quite right, obviously," Welte replied. Again he glanced around the empty room.

"Karl, what do you think of the Russians?"

The question surprised Geisler. Welte knew the Russians far better than he. What was the gold dealer leading up to? Purposely his answer was somewhat indirect.

"Frankly I haven't had much contact with them, since they're not what you would call international financiers. The ones I've met, however, I find to be dull and uninteresting."

Welte smiled. He leaned closer.

"They may be dull and uninteresting, but they're about to *become* international financiers; and they're going to do it big, bigger than you could possibly imagine."

He took off his glasses to emphasize his next point.

"They want a bank to serve as their entrée into the international financial community, a bank that has investment contacts on an international scale, a bank like yours, Karl, a bank like Union Suisse.''

Before Geisler could react, the door opened behind him. It startled him momentarily, as his mind was still absorbed with what Welte had said. The maître d' had personally brought his drink and was waiting for their orders.

Geisler fumbled with the menu and ordered the simplest thing on it, a Maison salad. Welte patted his stomach and ordered Entrecôte de Boeuf à Poivre with Asparagus Hollandaise and a bottle of Château Simard Emilion. The waiter left.

Welte leaned back, studying the chairman of the largest bank in Switzerland.

Geisler had used the time ordering to regain his composure. After forty years in banking, he thought there was nothing left that would surprise him, but this was totally unexpected. He took a sip of his drink and said calmly, "Obviously this is a surprise to me, Paul. The Russians have been financial isolationists since World War II. Why should they change now?''

Welte smiled and took a long drag on his cigarette.

"Their needs have changed. They've been forced to expand.''

Geisler pressed him further.

"Then why look to a Swiss bank? Why don't they expand their own bank's capabilities?''

"Because," Welte answered, "their system of government will not allow it. But let me go back to the beginning.

"Three days ago I met with my Russian client. He's a gold trader with Baltroff, the government bank in Leningrad, but apparently serving as an emissary for the Russian Politburo. He told me the Politburo decided they had to expand financially into the international market. They found their own banking system too limiting. By not being members of the International Monetary Fund or the Bank for International Settlements, their currency has never been valued—or, for that fact, devalued—against world currency. Also, by not being a part of the world banking community, they have never been privy to the everyday discussions that move world commerce. But now they find their needs have changed. They realize that they need more international communication to trade gold; to buy machinery, technology, and food. They need a financial conduit to the rest of the world."

Welte went on.

"I recommended Union Suisse not only on the basis of the bank's experience in dealing on the world market but on their ability to maintain the anonymity of their clients. The Russian seemed particularly interested in the latter point, and it wasn't until later that I realized why. And this will answer your question, Karl. They can't justify operating within a capitalist system to a people who have been taught it's inferior to their own. They need Swiss banking, where they can remain anonymous behind Swiss secrecy."

Geisler didn't expect an answer to his next question, but he asked it, anyway.

"Did your client indicate what banking services would be required and how sizable the Russian transactions would be?"

Welte considered the question carefully, then answered.

"No, I suspect we would find that out at the next level, if you were interested."

It wasn't important, anyway. What was important to Geisler was that the Russians were now contemplating the use of a major Swiss bank. It was true, of course, that ever since gold was discovered in the Urals in the late 1800s, the Swiss had been involved in trading it on the world market. It was also true that Swiss banks had acted as agents for the Soviets to purchase stock on the New York Stock Exchange; in fact, the Soviets held stock in major U.S. defense industries until laws were passed in the late 1970s prohibiting it. But those were all somewhat clandestine operations. If the Russians were thinking of dealing with a bank his size, they must be ready to deal in large quantities of money. That meant large commissions for the bank, and large commissions translated into power for Karl Geisler.

But he didn't trust Welte.

How much was he making on this deal? Welte had mentioned that "*we* would find out more information at the next level." He suspected that he was acting as a consultant to the Russians for a very large fee.

The luncheon lasted for over two and a half hours. Geisler tried to get more specifics, but Welte had little additional information. Apparently the Russians were using him merely to feel Geisler out.

The meeting ended with the two men agreeing that Geisler would meet with his board of directors for a decision and contact Welte within three days. In the meantime he would press the Russians for answers to his questions.

By the time Geisler left the restaurant, he was exhausted. He called his secretary, had her cancel his afternoon appointments, and had his car delivered to the restaurant. The drive home would give him time to think things through. There was a lot at stake here, and he needed time to sort it out. Also, getting home early would give him time to relax before his guests arrived for a dinner party he was giving that evening.

Traffic was light as he made his way out of the city. In just a few minutes he reached the Autobahn, and now he was cruising along in the inside lane. He didn't notice the white Peugeot behind him.

The more he thought about the lunch, the more the magnitude of the Russian proposal came into focus. If the Russians were thinking of transactions in even the $100 million range, the assets of the bank would increase such that business ventures now jointly financed by the Big Three Swiss Banks could be handled by Union Suisse alone. There wouldn't be a need for the traditional splitting of commissions. Union Suisse would have the power to go it alone. Since he owned forty percent of the bank's stock, he could become one of the most powerful bankers in Europe, if not the world.

He decided he would not involve his board of directors at this point. There were two reasons. One, he didn't as yet know all the specifics. The Russian proposal might not be entirely legal. From what Welte had said, there was an inordinate amount of interest shown in the discretion with which his bank operated. When it came to the board of directors, however, a transaction was either legal or it was not. It was either black or white. Geisler tended to see shades of gray in between.

Secondly—and this was just speculation—the Russians might be thinking of compensation for himself, apart from what the bank might make. Yes, he would keep the whole thing a secret from them, at least for now.

As he drove off the exit to Klöten, the white Peugeot passed him and continued on the Autobahn.

It was only a short drive to the village of Winkel. He stopped at the traffic light in the center of the village and turned onto the country road that led to his estate. Minutes later he passed a utility truck parked on the side of the road about a hundred meters from his driveway. The truck had been there for two days now. He smiled. Those utility workers certainly didn't overwork themselves. He had seen the driver taking a nap in the front seat when he passed by the previous day.

The man inside the truck was not asleep, however. He took careful note of the time the Jaguar passed. Having entered it into a small notebook, he got out of the cab and walked to the rear of the truck. He opened the door and stepped inside, where he sat down at a console and put on a headset. With quick movements he flicked on a series of switches, then expertly adjusted the dials in front of him.

He took personal pride in the electronic surveillance equipment in the truck. He had developed most of it himself. Over the past three days it had worked perfectly, monitoring all of Geisler's telephone conversations. He was equally proud of the small diamond brooch that one of Geisler's guests would be wearing that evening.

The dinner party was relaxing. Over the past two years Geisler had acquired a whole new group of friends. Many of them were in the arts: writers, musicians, film directors. He loved being associated with the young, beautiful people. They looked up to him and respected his high position. At the same time he was inspired by their energy and drive. They made him feel young.

That night there were over thirty guests attending the black-tie affair. After enjoying a six-course dinner, they were having drinks in the huge living room that Geisler had remodeled three months ago.

The previous year he had decided to redo the entire sixteen-room mansion. The interior would be changed to complement his new life-style. Elena had adored the Tudor-style house with its rustic stone and large leaded-glass windows. It provided the perfect setting for the antique furniture she'd acquired from all over Europe. The result was an effect of old-world charm, serene elegance.

His new life was one of excitement, of youthful friends and a modern spirit. The house needed to reflect that outlook.

For three months he searched for a designer who would be able to transform the interior into something new and unique without disturbing the classic exterior of the house. The outside would reflect the power and wealth of his position, while the inside would reflect the youth and excitement of his soul.

He settled on Roberto Orsini, an Italian designer who had been working recently in New York for the young *nouveau riche*. Orsini completely gutted the house and removed a section of ceiling over the living room. This resulted in a cathedral ceiling with balconies on the second-floor bedrooms that overlooked the room below. That was the room they were in now. It completely dominated the whole house.

It had a pool in the center, with a fountain featuring a statue of a man and a woman locked in an embrace. The floor was Italian marble, as were the walls, except for one, which was glass from floor to ceiling.

The furniture was low and sleek. A sectional done in Spanish leather ran in an L-shape along two walls. The opposite wall featured a custom-designed white-enameled unit that contained a quadrophonic sound system and a motorized, thirty-five-millimeter movie screen that could be lowered from the ceiling.

Earlier in the evening, one of his young friends introduced him to a tall, blond woman dressed in an elegant white evening gown. She was stunning and wore a brilliant diamond brooch that was the perfect accent for her satin gown.

He lavished his attention on her, and they spent most of the evening talking together. Her name was Nina Praeger, and she was vacationing in Switzerland between modeling assignments in Germany. They talked about everything from skiing to the German photographers she had worked with. Most of them were more interested in taking her to bed than taking her picture.

She pressed closer to him as the trio he hired for the evening switched from a driving disco beat to a slow waltz.

"I'm glad they're playing something slower," she whispered, moving closer to him.

"I slipped the piano player a little something extra," he said softly.

She laughed. "You paid him extra for that?"

"Of course," he answered. "I consider you the most important part of the whole evening."

He moved his hand down her bare back. She leaned back against it, as if to test his strength. Suddenly he turned with the music and, with one smooth motion, drew her back to him.

She looked at him, a satisfied curl to her smile.

"You waltz very well. Is it your favorite?"

"Yes," he said. "I feel very comfortable with it." He paused and then added, "As I do with you."

She arched her head back and laughed softly.

"Now, the line from all the movies is . . . 'I bet you say that to all the girls.'"

"No," he said very quickly. "As a matter of fact, there are very few women I do feel comfortable with."

"Oh, come now," she said, brushing back a strand of her long blond hair with a sweep of her hand. "A man as wealthy and powerful as you must have women crawling at his feet."

He liked her playfulness. She had a way about her that made everything seem light and fun. Underneath, however, he suspected someone much more calculating. He decided to try to get to that part of her.

"There are women, of course," he answered, "but they only see power as money. None of them have made me feel as powerful as my money."

"I think it would be a most interesting challenge," she said in what was almost a whisper.

"Oh?"

"Well, certainly. To feel that much power would be a thrill that I've never experienced before."

He leaned back a little so he could see her eyes.

"And, of course, you are a woman in pursuit of new experiences."

She looked up at him with a slight grin.

"What do you think?"

Later he unclasped the diamond brooch from her wonderfully arched neck and placed it on the night table. Slowly his lips tasted her perfume, and his hands wandered over her young, firm breasts. Who was she, this child young enough to be his daughter? He knew the answer. She was like the others, infatuated with power, possessed with the desire to hold it in her hands and consume it.

And she did.

He felt passion like he had never known before as her lips moved over his erect penis. His body tingled with anticipation of the climax he knew would come momentarily.

But no, just as he was about to explode, her hands expertly reached around his testicles and squeezed the skin on the upper part of them tight. His body convulsed with pleasure, but there had been no climax.

She moved over him and lowered herself on to his still erect penis. As she slid down over it, she drew herself tightly around it. Again his body tensed, waiting for the climax, but once again he felt the thrill of ejaculation without it actually happening. She arched backward and moaned with pleasure as she climaxed.

He felt like he could satisfy her forever. He was strong and powerful, able to bring this woman more than half his age to the heights of ecstasy.

She relaxed the pressure around him, and again his body cried out for the release of the fire boiling inside him. He heard her cry out again, and the power within him rushed into her. His mind was dulled and blurred with passion, but he heard himself utter the same word over and over again, although it was barely more than a whisper. "Power, power, power."

The man in the utility truck removed his headset and switched off the recording equipment. He had gotten what he wanted.

Three days later Geisler called Welte and told him of the bank's interest in the proposal. Immediately a meeting was scheduled with Welte's contact, a man named Persoff, to take place the following week in Geneva. The meeting, however, turned out to be merely a sparring match, with the Russian

attempting to find out all he could about the discretion of Union
Suisse and Geisler attempting to find out how much investment
capital was involved.

But the following day, while Welte and Geisler were still in
Geneva, the Russian called at their hotel. He told them a
meeting would take place in one week with V. A. Gagarin,
Deputy Minister of Finance and member of the Soviet
Politburo. The meeting was to be held in Prague. The deputy
minister was on a tour of the Soviet bloc countries and would
have two hours to meet with Geisler on June 7.

Welte didn't like it. Geisler was to come alone.

On the morning of the seventh, Geisler flew to Prague and
checked into the Veyden Hotel. After freshening up in the
three-room suite reserved for him, he was picked up at nine-
thirty sharp and brought to the Russian embassy. As he
emerged from the chauffeur-driven limousine, he was met by
two officials who escorted him into the building and led him
down a long, marbled corridor to the main conference room.
They ushered him inside, then turned and left, closing two
large wooden doors behind them.

Geisler looked around the room. By Communist standards
he thought it quite elegant. The walls were solid oak from the
floor to the very high arched ceiling, from which hung a
magnificent crystal chandelier. The long conference table was
a matching oak with heavy, carved wooden chairs. The
cushions, he noted, were appropriately red. At the far end of
the room was a bronze bust of Lenin, which seemed to stare at
him with immense authority.

The large doors opened behind him, and two men came into
the room. Geisler took the older one to be Gagarin. He looked
about his age but was heavier. He barely fit into his outdated
three-piece suit. The younger man looked like a bookkeeper:
horn-rimmed glasses, slicked-down hair, dark blue suit. He
spoke first, in very good English.

"Mr. Geisler, may I welcome you to Prague. My name is
Valery Shrenkov, Chief Translator for the Ministry of Finance."

He extended his hand and Geisler shook it.

"May I introduce you to Comrade Vasily A. Gagarin,

Minister of Finance. Mr. Gagarin speaks no English. Please speak slowly so I may translate accurately."

Geisler had been taken by surprise. He hadn't expected to meet with the minister alone. Gagarin apparently sensed this and gestured to the long line of empty chairs.

Shrenkov translated.

"There will be no one else attending, Mr. Geisler. Due to the importance—and I might add, secrecy—of what I have to say, it is better that we meet alone. No one knows of this meeting except Mr. Shrenkov and members of the Politburo."

"I understand, sir," Geisler heard himself say. He couldn't remember the last time he had called someone "sir."

"Good," Gagarin continued. "I understand both Mr. Welte and Comrade Persoff have informed you of our intentions to seek the services of a Swiss bank. I must tell you that we have done extensive"—he was searching for the right word to be translated—"we have done extensive *research* on both you and your bank and have decided on Union Suisse."

Geisler nodded in appreciation. "Union Suisse is honored, Mr. Gagarin. However, neither Messrs. Welte or Persoff were specific as to why the Soviet Union is seeking our services."

Gagarin sat with his hands folded and replied through the translator. "Because we are businessmen, Mr. Geisler. At home we have expounded Communist ideology to our people for over seventy-five years. But today, that ideology is in direct conflict with the capitalist system of international finance. We need to operate within that system if we are to compete in the world market, but we need to do it secretly."

Geisler smiled at the minister of finance, realizing the contradiction in his remark. Communism wasn't working, but they would never admit it to their people.

"I understand your desire for secrecy, but as you know, the financial community you speak of is a very close fraternity. If you were to enter it, even through our bank, it would be very hard to keep any secrets."

Gagarin listened to the translation and then pointed a finger in the air for emphasis.

"Ah, but we do not intend to enter it directly," he replied.

With that he removed an envelope from his breast pocket and passed it across the table to Geisler. He opened it and found a detailed proposal inside. Quickly he scanned the three-page document. Union Suisse was to establish two holding companies in Switzerland. One was to be in Zurich, the other in Geneva. Under Swiss law these companies would require six Swiss directors and certain qualifying Swiss stockholders. It was suggested that Geisler name six close banking associates as directors of the holding companies.

He knew that getting the directors would not be difficult, as it was not unusual for bankers to hold directorships of corporations that never did a franc's worth of business in Switzerland.

The document went on to say that the holding companies were to purchase two corporations in the United States; the First Savings Bank of Southern California and the Ball Corporation, which owned three gambling casinos, two in Las Vegas, the other in Atlantic City, New Jersey. Union Suisse would act as the bank trading on the world market for both holding companies.

Everything so far was legal under Swiss law. The question now running through Geisler's mind was how much money was involved.

Gagarin was reading his mind. He spoke quickly now, and Shrenkov translated almost simultaneously.

"Initial funding of the two holding companies—one billion American dollars.

"Estimated fees and commissions to Union Suisse—approximately two hundred and forty million dollars the first year."

Before Geisler could react, Gagarin passed a second envelope across the table. This one was marked "Confidential."

Gagarin's pudgy, round face lit up.

"Please open the envelope, Mr. Geisler. Read what it says, but I would prefer if you remain silent. We have to have some secrets from our Mr. Shrenkov, now don't we."

Shrenkov seemed amused with what he had translated and smiled at his superior.

Geisler opened the envelope. In it was a contract drawn up in his name that outlined the compensation he would receive personally for his services. He skipped over the fine print to the typed numbers on the bottom line. For organizing the holding companies and serving as their chief executive officer, he was to receive $2.5 million the first year.

Gagarin rose from his chair. Shrenkov, like Geisler, was surprised at the abruptness with which the meeting was ending. Translation.

"That is all for now, Mr. Geisler. Please study the proposal and remember that what was said here today will remain in this room. We will expect your decision within a week through Mr. Welte. Have a safe trip back to Zurich. Good day."

With that they left the room. Three days later Geisler declined the offer.

There was something wrong.

He had read the proposal three times and each time found the same thing missing: the objective. What was the Russian objective? The setting up of holding companies was not unusual, the buying of companies in the United States perfectly legal. But why such a large initial sum of money? Why American money? It was as if they were trying to put somebody out of business. But who?

Before he could take any steps toward an agreement, he would have to know the answers to these questions. He informed Welte of this, and Welte said he would contact Moscow. In three days the answers came.

It was nine A.M. when the phone rang on Geisler's desk. It was his secretary calling from the outer office.

"Mr. Geisler, there is a man downstairs in the reception room who insists on seeing you. He wouldn't give his name, but he said to tell you he's from Prague."

Geisler flipped the switch on his desk console, and an image flashed on the screen in front of him. Standing in the lobby was Shrenkov, the Russian translator.

He pressed the intercom switch.

"Anna, please send the gentleman up."

Minutes later Shrenkov walked into his office. He was carrying a leather briefcase.

"Mr. Shrenkov, how nice to see you. What brings you to Zurich?"

Geisler gestured toward a chair, but Shrenkov remained standing.

He began to speak in a low voice. The words were hurried, as if he desperately wanted to say what he had to and just leave.

"I have a message for you."

"A message from whom?"

"From Mr. Gagarin."

Shrenkov opened the briefcase and took out a small envelope, which he handed across the desk to Geisler, who opened it. Inside was a U.S. one-hundred-dollar bill.

Geisler held the bill out to the interpreter. "This is a message from Gagarin?"

He nodded. "Mr. Gagarin said to tell you that this will answer all of your questions."

Geisler looked at the bill closely. It was brand-new, right off the press; the kind that stick together when a teller counts them out. He held it up to the light; nothing unusual. Finally he turned to Shrenkov, who was fidgeting with the clasp on his briefcase.

"May I ask what this is supposed to mean?"

Shrenkov answered quickly. "I would suggest that you have your laboratory examine the bill."

"Examine it for what?"

"My instructions are to have you examine the bill in as much detail as you possibly can. I suggest that you do it immediately. We understand that you have a man on your staff who is quite capable."

"That's true, we have a Mr. Krueger, but . . ."

"Have him examine the bill, Mr. Geisler. I'm staying at the Europa Hotel. You can contact me there at any time within the next three days. I must leave now. I have another appointment. Good day."

Satisfied that he had accomplished his mission, he turned and walked out the door.

Geisler stared at the bill. How would a U.S. one-hundred-dollar bill answer all his questions? He suspected the Russians were toying with him, but he would be foolish not to pursue this. He picked up the phone and called Henry Krueger.

Krueger was an expert on forgeries and counterfeiting. Known throughout Europe as the best, other banks often called upon him to identify suspected counterfeit bills. The bank was fortunate to have a man of his reputation on staff. Within five minutes he was in Geisler's office.

A very studious-looking man in his early fifties, Krueger constantly had a pipe in his mouth, most of the time unlit. He sat across from Geisler, trying to light it for the third time.

"Henry," Geisler began, "one of the bank's customers received this bill. For some reason he thinks it's counterfeit. I don't know why, it looks perfectly good to me, but I'd like you to subject it to every test you have, ink, paper, engraving, everything. The man is a very important customer to us, so let's be sure we're absolutely correct in whatever we tell him."

Krueger put on his glasses and took the bill from Geisler. Slowly he rolled it between his thumb and index finger, feeling the paper. Then he walked to the window and held it up to the light. First he looked through one side of the bill, then the other. Satisfied, he wet his thumb and rubbed it over the surface.

Geisler knew that even good counterfeits seldom passed this initial test. Krueger's sensitive fingers could readily detect counterfeit paper.

Finally he put the bill back in the envelope and put it in his breast pocket. Geisler had never seen him look quite so perplexed. Usually he was able to give him a first reaction after examining a bill, but this time he simply said, "It's either genuine or a very good counterfeit. I'll run it through some tests personally and have the results for you by the end of the day."

Five hours later Krueger called.

He had completed all the necessary tests and asked if he could come up with his report. Geisler said he would see him immediately.

Minutes later he held up the bill, which was now in a special plastic envelope. He stared at it as he spoke.

"Well, what your client has here is genuine, all right. Ultraviolet and chemical analysis prove that the inks are U.S. government grade. I've X-rayed the paper, and the fiber is consistent with the government manufacturer's. The entire engraving under a one-hundred-power microscope is sharp and clear. The check letters and the serial numbers are surprinted and definitely are part of a sequence. My tests don't find anything unusual at all except . . ."

"Yes, Krueger, go on," Geisler said, leaning forward across the desk.

". . . except we usually don't find bills this new in Switzerland."

"What do you mean?" Geisler asked, trying to remain calm.

"My tests show that this bill was printed within the last twenty-four hours. Your client must have come from a United States mint to Switzerland in a very fast jet."

Geisler leaned back in his chair. Now he understood. The bill hadn't been printed in the United States; that was impossible. It had been printed in Russia. The Russians had a perfect counterfeit U.S. one-hundred-dollar bill.

Gagarin was right. The bill had answered all his questions. Now he knew who they were trying to put out of business. The Russians were printing American dollars—counterfeit dollars to flood the U.S. economy. They were planning to bring down the economy of the richest nation in the world. The United States would be destroyed.

And they could succeed. Their plot, as he now saw it forming in his mind, was entirely possible. If he allied himself with them, he could achieve power beyond his wildest dreams. Not only would he be the most powerful financier in Europe, he would be the most powerful financier in the world.

That evening he called Shrenkov's hotel and accepted the offer.

Henry Krueger didn't sleep all night.

The one-hundred-dollar bill Geisler had him analyze had kept him tossing and turning. It couldn't have been printed in the United States. He had lied to Geisler. He told him that it was printed within the last twenty-four hours; actually his tests had shown it was as little as twelve.

He wanted to see his superior's reaction to the longer time. It was what he expected. Geisler made up some story about his client working for the government in Washington and arriving in Switzerland the previous morning. According to him, the man could have picked up the newly minted bill in less than twenty-four hours.

Well, that certainly wasn't possible in *twelve hours*. That bill was counterfeit and had been printed somewhere in Europe. It was the best counterfeit he had ever seen. Perfect. Absolutely perfect in every detail.

He looked at the alarm clock on the night table. It was six A.M. There wasn't any sense in trying to sleep anymore; there was too much on his mind. He would have a quick breakfast and start out for work. There was some checking he wanted to do at the office. Recently he had heard reports of the Russians purchasing large amounts of pigment from the Far East. He wanted to check that further. Some discreet phone calls to personal contacts would provide him with answers.

He dressed and gulped down some coffee and toast with jelly. He looked at his watch. Six twenty-five. There was just enough time to make the six-thirty electric trolley at the end of the block. Quickly he bounded down the steps of his apartment building and started down the empty street.

He never saw the white Peugeot pull away from the curb behind him. It accelerated quickly as he hurried along. Suddenly he sensed the presence of the car and turned. It was too late; the car was already up on the sidewalk, bearing down on him. Before he could leap clear to avoid it, the car struck him in the back at forty miles per hour, severing his spine. He died instantly.

3

Washington, May 21, 1990 (UPI)—

IN A SPEECH BEFORE THE AMERICAN BANKING ASSOCIATION, CHAIRMAN JOHN STEVENS, JR., SPOKE AGAINST PROPOSED GOVERNMENT REGULATION OF BANKS HANDLING FOREIGN INVESTING IN THIS COUNTRY. HE CAUTIONED AGAINST THE GOVERNMENT SETTING LIMITS ON WHAT HE TERMED "ECONOMIC OPPORTUNITIES FOR FOREIGN INVESTMENTS THAT NATURALLY OCCUR WITH A RISE IN OUR ECONOMY."

HE SAID, "FOREIGN INVESTMENTS ARE THE LIFEBLOOD OF ANY ECONOMY. OTHER COUNTRIES DO NOT SET LIMITS ON U.S. INVESTMENT, WHY SHOULD WE?"

THE SPEECH WAS A RESPONSE TO RECENT GOVERNMENT ACCUSATIONS THAT U.S. BANKS ARE MAKING LARGE COMMISSIONS ON FOREIGN TRANSACTIONS THAT COULD POTENTIALLY POSE A DANGER TO THE ECONOMY.

New York City
May 21, 1990

BOB TOMPKINS WAS falling through space. His mind was racing back in time as he tumbled down a dark abyss that seemed as endless as time itself. He was reliving his life moment by moment. Years flashed by as he raced back in time. It was like watching a film of his life running backward at high speed. He was forty, his grandson was born; he was thirty on a picnic with Helen; he was twenty-four and it was their wedding day; he was nineteen and in the Army. When would it all end? The images were going by too fast.

But suddenly it stopped. He was at a place fixed in time. He was late for something. Yes, there was somebody he had to meet. It was Helen. They were supposed to meet after school and go for some ice cream. He ran faster, taking in deep breaths that filled his lungs with the fresh spring air. As he came around the corner by the high school, he saw her at the end of the block. She was standing with her back to him, looking in the other direction. He loved the way she looked with her rolled-up jeans and tight-fitting jersey. Her long blond hair flowed over her shoulders, halfway down her back. She turned, and her brown eyes lit up as she saw him running toward her. She smiled mischievously, then whirled around and started to run, waving her arm as an invitation to catch her.

He ran after her. His breath was coming very quickly now, but not fast enough. He couldn't gain any ground. His legs were moving as fast as they could, but he wasn't getting any closer. Desperately he tried to breathe harder, but it was as if someone were holding something tightly over his mouth. Helen was still running with her back to him. He called to her. "Helen, wait for me . . . wait . . ."

Suddenly the pressure was released over his mouth and he was able to breathe easier. Helen was gone. He looked up into a blinding light, and there was a face behind it. It was a man with a stethoscope around his neck, and he was checking his pulse. The man held an oxygen mask that apparently he had just removed from his nose and mouth.

He tried to look around but found he was strapped down. It appeared at first that he was in a hospital, but then he realized they were moving. He was in an ambulance.

There was a dryness in his mouth, and the taste of something medicinal that seemed to make him want to keep swallowing. His head was pounding, and his legs seemed heavy as he tried to move them.

His immediate thought was that he must have suffered a heart attack, but then the events before he lost consciousness slowly came back to him: Helen's empty closet; the man in the darkness; the sharp, piercing pain in his back.

His tongue seemed twice the size of his mouth, and his words came slowly as the man over him removed a blood-pressure cuff from his arm.

"Where am I? What happened to me?"

The man didn't answer but looked off to his left. Tompkins couldn't move his head far enough to see, but he was aware of someone else in the ambulance. He kept his eyes on the man over him. He was in his middle fifties, gray hair, glasses, sharp nose; too dignified, he thought, to be an ambulance attendant. Again the man looked to his left, nodded once, and put his hand reassuringly on Tompkins's shoulder.

"Mr. Tompkins, you're going to be all right. We're just minutes from where we'll be able to take good care of you."

"What happened to me?"

"You're going to be fine. Just try to relax."

Tompkins leaned back. He didn't have the strength to say anything else. Besides, there was nothing more he could do until they got to the hospital.

He never got there.

The inside of the van he was in was a fully equipped ambulance, but the outside had lettering on the doors that read, "Mid City Printing, 147 West 23rd Street, N.Y.C." Within minutes it pulled up to a five-story brick building bearing the same name. Large overhead doors opened, and the van drove inside. It came to a stop. The rear door opened, and two men removed the stretcher on which Tompkins was strapped. Before he could say anything, the stretcher was placed on a wooden table and the straps removed. Slowly the attendant from the ambulance reached under his arms and raised him to a sitting position. He looked around. He was in a warehouse. There were reams of paper stacked on skids everywhere. Long fluorescent lights stretched across the ceiling, but only the one directly above him was lit. In the shadows he saw four men staring at him. The tallest of them stepped forward and addressed the ambulance attendant.

"How is he?"

The attendant referred to handwritten notes attached to a clipboard.

"He's fine. His blood pressure is one-twenty over eighty, and the pulse is near normal. The drug is wearing off."

Tompkins's senses were dulled, but he heard the words clearly. He struggled to speak, and when he finally did, his words were slurred.

"What . . . what drug? Who . . . who are you and what have you done with Helen?"

The man who seemed to be the leader moved closer and extended his hand in a gesture of reassurance, but Tompkins moved away from him. The man quickly withdrew his hand and took a step backward. He spoke slowly in a low voice.

"Mr. Tompkins, my name is Anthony Cutrone. First of all, let me assure you that you have not suffered a heart attack or a stroke. You're not seriously ill. You've been drugged. The effects will completely disappear by morning, and you'll be as good as ever. We've taken elaborate measures to assure that."

Tompkins's dulled mind was forming questions, but he found it very difficult to speak. Before he could, Cutrone went on.

"You're being held hostage because of your skill as an engraver. It's a skill we're in need of. Let me just say for now that we're part of a group whose job it is to produce counterfeit money for some very important clients. During the next few months, instead of making engravings for the government, you'll be making them for us."

He paused, waiting for Tompkins to speak. When he didn't, he went on.

"As for your wife, she was taken from your home before your arrival earlier today and is on her way to a climate suitable for her arthritic condition. She'll receive the best of care, far better than she was getting in Hartford." He looked at Tompkins carefully. "Do you understand everything I've said?"

Tompkins nodded.

"The pain you felt in your back earlier was just an injection of a drug administered by our doctor here. The discomfort you're feeling now is the aftereffect of it. You'll be taken now to a room we've prepared, and there you'll be given a mild sedative that will make you sleep. In the morning, when your mind is clear, we'll talk further about what's expected of you."

Cutrone motioned to the doctor, and he gently pulled Tompkins down onto a movable stretcher. Two men then pushed it toward a freight elevator. Tompkins was glad to lie back. He was exhausted. His eyes had difficulty focusing as he watched the darkened ceiling of the warehouse pass over him.

Suddenly he was in a brightly lit elevator. It went up three floors, and then he was wheeled down a dark corridor. A door opened and he was pushed into a small room.

The stretcher was lowered, and his body was rolled onto a twin bed. His shoes were removed and the doctor went over to a basin and filled a paper cup with water. He was so thirsty. His tongue passed over his lips in anticipation of the liquid. The doctor placed two tablets on his tongue, which he accepted as a prerequisite to getting the drink. He gulped at the water, and the pills slid down his throat. Within minutes he heard the door close, the lock being secured. Then sleep came. He welcomed it. God knows what awaited him the next day.

The man who had introduced himself as Anthony Cutrone sat in a room directly below Tompkins. He was a tall, athletic-looking man who appeared to be about thirty-five but was probably older. His tight-fitting sweater and jeans emphasized his well-developed arms and upper torso, the result of working out with heavy weights three times a week. His hair was wavy and jet-black. It framed a face with hardened features that revealed a past lived fast and dangerously. Piercing hazel eyes constantly shifted about, seeking out new information to be stored and filed for further use. He was clicking a ballpoint pen open and closed, studying its mechanical design.

With him was an older man who was taking some cans of beer from a small refrigerator. He opened the cans and poured them into two glasses, one of which he put in front of his superior.

"For a man who's just completed the most important part of our assignment, you don't seem very happy, Yuri."

Yuri Vladislav, KGB agent in charge of one of the most important operations ever launched by the Soviet Union, looked up at his friend.

"It did go well, didn't it, Mikhail."

"As they say in Brooklyn, like a dream, man, like a dream. And please, the name is Sal . . . Sal Barbieri."

Vladislav put the pen down and took a sip of beer.

"I know, tomorrow we all begin playacting at being real New Yorkers."

Mikhail leaned back in his chair and smiled. "Well,

tomorrow is tomorrow, but tonight we're a success, so drink up, old friend."

Vladislav sipped the cold beer. It was one of the things he had grown to enjoy about America. Ice-cold Schaeffer was hard to find in Kiev. He looked at his friend of over fifteen years. Mikhail was gulping the beer from the can, foam flowing down his chin. Lately he was beginning to show the effects of his beer drinking. He was forty-four, and his waist size was quickly catching up to his age. Already the short five-foot-nine frame was having difficulty carrying the excess weight. But like many plump people, he had a round, cherubic face with reddened cheeks. His hair was turning gray and constantly had a cowlick in the back, even when it was neatly combed. The total effect was disarming. He looked like an ordinary guy from Brooklyn you'd meet in a bar, which is why Vladislav had chosen him to be his second in command.

Vladislav lit a cigarette. Marlboros were also a fringe benefit of this assignment.

"Tell me about the whole day, Mikhail. I want to know every detail."

His friend put his feet up on the small wooden table and leaned back so that his chair was propped up on two legs.

"Details, Yuri, you're always worried about details. The kidnapping was a success. Tompkins is here to prove it."

The smile disappeared from Vladislav's face.

"You know better than that. Attention to detail is a talent that we were chosen for, and a talent that will keep us alive."

His eyes shifted to the typewriter in the corner of the neatly kept room.

"Besides, I need the information for a report to send on to Moscow."

Mikhail continued to lean back in his chair but reached into his shirt pocket and took out a small pad, which he propped up on his knee.

"The *details*," he said, emphasizing the word, "are all here, but believe me, everything went according to plan."

"I'd like to hear it all."

Mikhail scanned the first page of notes and shrugged his shoulders.

"He really was easy to monitor, because he followed a very

tight schedule. Shopping every Tuesday, which included
getting gas, going to the cleaners, and buying groceries.
Wednesday, he took Helen to the doctor. Thursday was spent
shopping for odds and ends, and on Saturday they went to an
evening movie. Sunday, they went to Mass at eleven o'clock,
and then the week started all over again. With her arthritis they
were practically recluses."

Vladislav tapped his fingers on the table nervously.

"I know most of that. Bring me up-to-date on today."

Mikhail flipped over some pages, then read from them
directly.

"Eleven thirty-five A.M. . . . Tompkins left his home to
begin Tuesday shopping routine . . . expected home six-
thirty P.M. . . . using Mercedes we have house under surveillance every thirty minutes . . . one-thirty P.M., we enter
house . . . Helen sleeping upstairs . . . she offers little
resistance . . . inject her with four hundred fifty cc's Pentothal . . . taken to Cessna 450 in Wallingford, which de-
parted at twelve-ten P.M. . . . six-oh-five P.M., make contact
with Tompkins at Knollwood Shopping Center . . . proceed
home ahead of him and inject five hundred fifty cc's Pentothal
in the bedroom . . . he's taken to garage on Albany Avenue
and transferred to ambulance van . . . depart 7:28 P.M. for
New York . . . arrival 11:31 P.M."

Vladislav finished the last of his beer. He turned and took a
ledger from the shelf behind him. He opened it and made some
notes on the first page.

"Question: Where is the Mercedes?"

"Driven inside the trailer truck that delivered the ambulance
to Hartford. It'll be arriving here shortly."

"Good. I want it stripped and the body banged up, then
leave it sitting somewhere in the Bronx to be picked clean by
tomorrow evening. What about the trailer truck?"

"It goes back to Ryder rental tomorrow."

"Did anyone see you getting Helen into the car?"

"No one. Both neighbors on either side work during the day,
and the children are in school. There's an old lady across the
street, but she and Helen are also on a regular routine. She
comes over every Tuesday and Thursday for lunch. She leaves
by one-fifteen. We got there right after she left."

"Is everything ready in Florida?"

"Everything."

"Good, we'll get Tompkins to write a letter tomorrow to his son and some of their friends. Then we'll have the Florida agents mail them on to Hartford. What about the relay telephone?"

"It's in place. When we feel Tompkins is ready, we'll relay a select call up."

Vladislav leaned back in his chair and seemed to relax. He closed his eyes and massaged them with the tips of his fingers.

Mikhail looked at his friend. He knew what he was going through. The pressure put on him by the Kremlin had been tough, but over the past four months it had been impossible.

Three months ago Helmut Schmidt, the eighty-two-year-old German engraver working on the plates for them, died of a heart attack. At that time Schmidt had completed work on updating the plates for the hundred-dollar bill that he had begun forty years ago for the Nazis. A week after that, another setback had occurred. President Turner installed a new Secretary of the Treasury, making it necessary for a new signature to be engraved. Also, modifications were made to the illustration of Independence Hall on the back of the bill.

Schmidt had only completed seventy-five percent of the work on the plate for the twenty-dollar bill before he died. That twenty was absolutely necessary for the plan to succeed. Hundreds alone would be too difficult to pass. Vladislav had gotten all the equipment in place for Schmidt. Everything had been ready, but then Schmidt died. Suddenly a new engraver had to be found, one who could complete his extraordinary work. After nearly a month of searching, their intelligence agents found there was only one man who could possibly do it. Now they had him upstairs, safely tucked away.

Mikhail took two more cans of beer from the refrigerator and pushed one of them in front of Vladislav. It was time to lighten his friend's mood.

"Yuri, do you know what we're going to do once we start printing those perfect hundreds and twenties?"

Vladislav opened his eyes and rested his chin in his hands.

"What?"

"We're going to take a few samples off the presses, get us two of the most beautiful women in New York, put them in a suite in the Plaza, and stuff the place with a hundred cases of beer."

Vladislav smiled.

"Then what?"

"Then, in true Communist fashion, we're going to share it all."

"Oh?"

"Yeah, I'm going to have the women and you're going to have the beer."

Vladislav laughed and opened the can.

"You couldn't stand to watch me drink the beer. I'd have the women after the first one."

Mikhail watched him take a few sips, then answered, "You're probably right. When it comes to beer, I have very little willpower."

"Well, you'd better find some, because the next three months will be a test of willpower and concentration," Vladislav replied, returning to the subject at hand. "Remember, Tompkins mustn't know we're Russian. He's got to be absolutely convinced that we're just a small counterfeiting operation producing money for some underground group, probably the Mafia. That's what he'll be told tomorrow when we begin our little charade."

Mikhail studied his friend carefully.

"Is all this really necessary, Yuri? Why don't we just tell him who we are? He doesn't have any choice but to work for us anyway, if he wants to see his wife again. Okay, so we've all been picked for our ability to speak perfect English and to be convincing New Yorkers, but why bother if we don't have to?"

Vladislav became visibly angered. They were too far into the assignment for these questions to be raised.

"Because . . ." he began, his eyes narrowing, "it's a question of motivation as far as Tompkins is concerned. His motivation to cooperate with us will be to save his wife. Even so, that will be in conflict with using his skills to help counterfeiters. But if he finds out who we are, he'll be betraying his country. He may not be able to justify that even if his wife's life is threatened. Making plates for counterfeiters is one thing, but making them for the enemy is another."

He pointed his finger at Mikhail.

"Remember, we don't have Helmut Schmidt working for us now. Schmidt was not only a skilled craftsman, but a man inspired. After his family was killed by American bombing, his hatred caused him to work for Hitler to develop paper and the plates. When Hitler failed and he saw that we could potentially destroy the United States, he *willingly* worked for us. *Willingly*, Mikhail—that's very important."

"I understand, Yuri, but—"

"I hope you understand," Vladislav shot back. "And I hope the men understand, because one small mistake and the whole assignment can fail."

He lowered his voice and spoke very slowly, as if he were afraid that one of his words would not be heard.

"Failure of this assignment because of a breach in security, which this would be, will not be acceptable. Not when the Premier himself has told us personally of its importance. Over ten years have gone into this since Schmidt came to us. Ten years of technical development and training by this group to enable us to pass for native Americans to work in this country. One small mistake and it all will have been for nothing.

"So we'd better be convincing to our Mr. Tompkins upstairs. Tonight was easy. He was drugged and barely aware of where he was. Tomorrow his senses will be very alert. We've got to play our parts well, or we're not going to succeed."

Mikhail twisted the beer can into a ball and put it down on the table. He had that innocent look on his face that Vladislav had seen many times. It was always there when he was trying to get out of a situation gracefully.

"All right, all right," he began. "I was only questioning whether my tremendous acting ability was necessary or not. You know I'm always prepared to give a performance."

Vladislav looked at him pensively.

"That's for sure."

Mikhail cocked his head to the side as he slouched down in the chair. Suddenly he looked more casual, more easy going, more American.

"Wanna check me out, Mac?" he said in a heavy Brooklyn accent.

"I'm a real American."

Vladislav lit another cigarette and blew the smoke up toward the hooded light that hung over the table.

"What's your name?"

"Sal . . . Sal Barbieri."

"Where were you born, Sal?"

"Brooklyn. DeKalb and Clinton, 1937."

"Where'd you go to school?"

"P.S. 38 and the High School of Music and Art in Manhattan."

"Dodger fan?"

"Whaddaya kiddin'? Of course."

"Ever see them in a World Series?"

"Yeah, against the Yankees."

"What year?"

" 'Fifty-two. They got beat four games to three."

"Who was playing third base?"

"Billy Cox. But who played in the last game?"

Vladislav thought for a minute.

"Billy Cox."

"Bullshit." Mikhail pointed a finger at him. "Cox was hurt, and Sammy Foster played third. You son of a bitch, you're probably a fuckin' Russian agent."

The next morning Tompkins awoke to the sound of a key turning in the lock. He sat up in bed, realizing that he was still fully clothed except for his shoes. His body retreated back against the headboard as the door opened. A short, slight man wearing glasses came into the room carrying a bundle of clothes and a shaving kit, which he put on the dresser. A second man stood in the doorway watching.

The shorter one gestured toward the items on the dresser and said, "There's clean clothes for you to change into and some shaving gear." He walked over to the door near the bed and opened it, revealing a small bathroom. "Get yourself cleaned up right away. We'll be back in thirty minutes." He turned and left, the bolt clicking in the lock behind him.

Tompkins rubbed his eyes, trying to get his head cleared. He

vaguely remembered arriving at a warehouse the night before.
There were men standing under a single light, a doctor,
anesthesia, Helen. Where was Helen? They had kidnapped her
too. He bolted from the bed and ran to the locked door, about
to pound on it and cry out for her. His hand almost smashed
against it but he stopped it in midair. More of last night was
coming back to him. A man was saying, "We need you for
your engraving talents." Also, there was something about
counterfeiting. So . . . they needed something from him. He
had cards to play if he stayed rational; or at least appeared
rational.

He had to try to get control of himself, but his whole body
was trembling. The pressure was starting in his chest like it
always did when he got in a tense situation. He took some deep
breaths and after a few moments seemed to calm down.

He turned and looked around the room. It was very small but
appeared neat and clean. The furniture consisted of a twin bed,
an old wooden dresser painted black with an oval mirror, one
metal folding chair, and a night table with a goosenecked
reading lamp. The walls were painted a soft beige, and the
floor was worn, planked wood. There were no windows.

The door on the far wall had two coat hooks on it, which was
the only place he could see to hang clothes. He went into the
small bathroom. It had a toilet with an overhead tank and pull
chain, a small sink with a medicine chest over it, and a metal
stall shower. Water dripped from the shower head down to the
rusted drain on the floor. Again, the walls were painted drab
beige.

Standing in front of the sink, he looked at himself in the
cracked mirror of the medicine chest. His hair was disheveled,
and his beard was a white stubble. He took off his glasses and
rubbed the fleshy skin under his eyes. Why was this all
happening? he thought. What have they done with Helen? His
fingers trembled as he undid the buttons of his shirt. There was
a queasy feeling in his stomach, and for a moment he thought
he might vomit, but the feeling passed.

Having undressed, he stepped into the small metal shower.
The water sputtered for a minute through the rusted shower
head before it came out in uneven spurts that splashed over his
body. Over the years it had been in the shower where he'd

observed the deterioration of his body. Gone were the straight, muscular shoulders, tight chest, flat stomach, and sturdy legs. It seemed as if the water had washed them away, having slowly eroded his body as waves erode a rocky shore, turning it to sand. What remained was a sagging chest covered with hair turned gray, a paunchy stomach, and legs filled with veins that formed a blue network of lines running from his thighs to his ankles.

He wondered if he could cope with this situation mentally. Would he be able to handle it physically? Was his aging body up to the stress and anxiety that was already upon him? He would soon find out.

After the shower he shaved quickly and changed into the gray shirt and work trousers that had been left for him. He was sitting on the bed putting on his·shoes when again he heard the key turning in the lock. The same short man came into the room. He was alone.

"Follow me," he said in a terse voice.

Tompkins followed him down a hallway in which there were several tinted-glass doors. At the end of the hallway the man opened a door and gestured for him to go inside. Seated at a kitchen table were three men. He recognized one of them as the man who had spoken to him the previous night. He forgot his name, but he remembered the face: dark, stern, dangerous. The man next to him was heavyset, with a friendly face. By contrast, the third man was thin, with a long, angular face and a sharp nose, underlined by a pencil-thin mustache.

They studied him as he nervously looked around the room. It was a small dining room. There were three tables with chairs of varying sizes and shapes. The wall to his right had two windows, but he couldn't see outside. The insides had been painted black. To his left was a serving area through which he could see a small kitchen. The short man who had brought him into the room was back there making coffee.

The man who seemed to be the leader spoke first.

"Please sit down, Mr. Tompkins. Can we get you some coffee and a little breakfast?"

Tompkins's nervousness disappeared, and anger replaced it as he heard the question. Here were men who had kidnapped him and Helen, yet they sat there in a very civil manner, inviting him to breakfast.

He spoke slowly, but he could hear his anger coming through every syllable.

"No, I don't want any breakfast. I want to know why you've taken me from my home and where my wife is."

The heavier man with the friendly face put down his coffee and shrugged his shoulders in a carefree manner.

"Look, why don't you sit down and have a little something to eat. Frank's back there making eggs and toast. If you don't eat, I'll have to eat your share." He patted his stomach. "And I really don't need that."

Tompkins didn't move. He stood in silence, his eyes moving from one man to another. Suddenly the man he remembered from the night before stood up. His eyes narrowed, and his face tightened as if he were about to shout. But his words came out very controlled, almost in a whisper.

"Sit down."

The words went through him like an electrical current. Slowly he sank into the chair behind him. The man sat back down across from him. He folded his hands on the table.

"Let me begin by introducing myself again. I don't think you were in any condition last night to remember much. My name is Anthony Cutrone." He gestured to the men next to him. "Sal Barbieri and Paul Fields."

The two men nodded.

"We're in the counterfeiting business, Mr. Tompkins, and that's why you're here. We need your help." He paused, looking for a reaction. Finding none, he went on. "We've been contracted, shall we say, by certain clients to produce one hundred and fifty million dollars of counterfeit bills. It's to be made up of perfect hundreds and twenties." He emphasized the word *perfect*. "We already have plates for the hundred, but they need minor alterations. We need even more help with the twenty."

The man called Frank came out of the kitchen with a breakfast tray and set it on the table. He served everyone scrambled eggs, toast, and coffee, including Tompkins, then left the room. Cutrone went on, ignoring the food, as did the others.

"We have three months to deliver the money. It has to be money that can't be detected as counterfeit by anyone, even government experts. When the job is completed, you'll be paid three hundred thousand dollars in genuine currency and be reunited with your wife. Right now she's staying in a villa outside the country."

Having finished what he had to say, Cutrone buttered some toast and began eating. The others followed his lead. The man with the friendly face looked up occasionally and gestured for Tompkins to join them. He hadn't eaten in over eighteen hours, and the food was very inviting. Finally his stomach overruled his mind, which told him to resist, and he began eating.

Cutrone took it as the first sign of cooperation and said, "We'll begin by showing you the plates we've developed so far, and the equipment we have. Then you'll meet the rest of our group of eight master craftsmen."

Tompkins's fear again turned to anger. This arrogant bastard was just assuming that he would cooperate to make illegal plates. He looked up from his food at Cutrone.

"What makes you think you can make perfect plates when nobody in over two hundred years has been able to? You need inks that only the government can purchase, you need special paper made by only one manufacturer in the world exclusively for them. You need presses that aren't made commercially, and you need high-quality engravings. I don't know who's paying you to do this, but it's impossible."

He stopped. Cutrone wasn't even looking at him. He was busily involved stirring his coffee. Tompkins's anger rose even further, to a point where he was surprised to hear himself say, "Besides, even if it could be done, I'll be goddamned if I'll become a part of it."

He didn't even see the hand that dealt a blow to his face from the other side of the table, but it knocked him backward out of his chair to the floor. A trickle of blood ran down his chin from his lip. He wiped it with his hand and slowly sat up. Cutrone was standing over him.

"You're an old man, Tompkins, and we don't want to hurt you; but you will work on the plates." He reached down with one hand and lifted him by the elbow to a standing position. He held on to his arm firmly and led him out into the hallway. On the wall was a pay phone. His voice was still calm.

"One call on this phone and your wife will wish she were dead. The movement of her arms and legs are limited, aren't they?" With a quick motion he pulled Tompkins's arm behind his back. He felt the pain in his shoulder begin to mount as Cutrone applied more pressure.

"Your wife's arm couldn't be brought halfway behind her back without causing severe pain, could it? Forced into this position, she would already be unconscious from the pain. Don't make me use that phone, because if I do, you'll be forced to hear her suffering, and I don't think you'll be able to stand it."

Cutrone released his arm and Tompkins turned to face him.

"You really are an animal, aren't you?"

Cutrone looked down at the floor, avoiding his stare.

"No, I'm a businessman. I have a job to do, and I'm going to do it."

"You have an impossible job, because even if I did cooperate, there's no way it can be done."

Cutrone smiled.

"Oh, but there is."

He called back into the room for the other men.

"Sal, Paul. Let's give Mr. Tompkins a tour of the plant."

What Tompkins saw in the next hour amazed him. The printing plant consisted of five floors. Rooms for the men, the cafeteria, and his room were on the third floor. On the fifth floor there was a large recreation room that contained a pool table and a television set plus a supply room. The fourth floor had an engraving room with some of the newest equipment he had ever seen. There were the typical awls and punches that were standard engraving hardware, but the magnifying glasses were the latest state-of-the-art optics manufactured in Switzerland. The government didn't even go to this expense.

Next to the engraving room was the camera room. It housed a xenon light-separation camera, which the man called Sal demonstrated for Tompkins. Sal knew the camera inside and out. Despite his humorous attitude, Tompkins had the feeling that this was a craftsman who took tremendous pride in his work.

From there he was taken down in the elevator to the second floor. There, two Miehle four-color presses were printing some outdoor twenty-four-sheet posters. Ironically they were recruiting posters for the U.S. Air Force. JOIN OUR FIGHTING TEAM IN THE AIR, the headline shouted. Apparently the U.S. government was helping them maintain a front without knowing it.

They briefly passed through the first floor. It was the warehouse he had been in the night before and was used to store reams of paper and other equipment.

He was then brought back up to the second floor. Just off the elevator were two wooden crates, piled one on top of the other, that almost reached the ceiling. Together they covered most of the wall space visible from the elevator. They looked like crates that heavy press sections might have been shipped in. Cutrone walked around the side of the bottom one and pulled at a piece of lath. Part of the crate swung open, revealing a door that went into another room. They walked through the crate into what was another press room, concealed behind the packing crates. Tompkins was amazed at what he saw.

In the center of the room was a two-plate two-color intaglio press, an exact copy of the type used by the Bureau of Engraving to print small runs of currency. The press was capable of printing a single impression up to two colors from a single steel-plate engraving. It had a stacker on one end, which held five thousand sheets of paper, each sheet large enough to eventually become sixty one-hundred-dollar bills. The press was being operated by three pressmen and was running at full speed. The large sheets were being picked up one at a time, fed on to an impression cylinder, and held by grippers until the impression was received from the inked plate on the plate cylinder. The sheet was then transferred to chain-supported gripper bars, given a blast of air, and deposited on the delivery pile. Sixty brand-new one-hundred-dollar bills appeared every five seconds.

"You seem surprised at our equipment," Cutrone said as he gestured toward the press. "You thought the government had an exclusive on it, I suppose."

Tompkins walked along the side of the machine, examining it closely. A few modifications had been made with the gripper placement, but essentially it was the same press used by the Bureau of Engraving; only the Bureau's were much older. Even though it was soiled from use, he could see that it had been built recently. He couldn't find any manufacturer's nameplate.

He turned to Cutrone, who was standing with his hands folded across his chest, obviously proud of what was in front of him.

"Where did you get it?" he asked, having to raise his voice over the roar of the machine.

Cutrone leaned forward so he could hear him.

"We didn't get it from anywhere. We built it."

He turned to the man with the pencil mustache who was standing beside him.

"I shouldn't say 'we,' really. Paul is the one who built it . . . from scratch."

"Where did you get the plans?"

Paul answered in a sardonic tone, "Your Bureau of Engraving isn't as security-tight as you would like it to be. We were able to buy the plans. It cost us a little money, but one hundred and fifty thousand dollars is a lot of money for a poorly paid government employee . . . as you well know."

Tompkins looked back at the press. Just then, Cutrone signaled to one of the pressmen. The man reached for one of the control buttons and the machine ground to a halt.

Cutrone took the top sheet from the stacker and laid it on a large table. From where Tompkins was standing, he could already see that the bills were of good quality. These men may be criminals, but they were also professionals.

Paul handed Cutrone a mat knife and a large metal ruler. With a few quick strokes of the knife along the blade, he cut four hundred-dollar bills from the sheet. He gave them to Tompkins. "Take a look and tell me what you think," he said confidently.

As soon as Tompkins's fingers touched the paper, he knew it was very high quality. The texture of the paper manufactured by the Crane Company in Massachusetts had a distinct feel when it was new, and even when it got old. Bank tellers know the feel, tellers at racetracks know it, anybody who handles money every day knows it. If what he had in his hand hadn't been manufactured by Crane, it might as well have been.

Cutrone saw his reaction to the paper quality but didn't say anything. Actually the paper was the key to the whole plan. No matter how good Tompkins's engravings were, the paper had to be flawless. And it was. In 1944, Schmidt had developed formulas that duplicated Crane's perfectly. Even today the basic formula was used with few modifications. On rare occasions, when changes were made in the specifications, they were alerted by an informant inside Crane. The information was passed on to their supplier in Argentina, who shipped two hundred and fifty thousand sheets a month, topped off with specialty paper used for the legitimate work of the plant. The plan worked perfectly.

Tompkins studied the picture of Franklin on the front face of the bill. A counterfeit portrait usually filled with ink, leaving it looking very heavy without much detail. This was the result of counterfeiters using second- and third-generation copies of the original and losing detail along the way. This portrait was crisp and clean, indicating the use of a very good engraving.

The back of the bill was equally good, although he noticed that part of the illustration of Independence Hall was missing, as were parts of the scrollwork along the side. This was probably "the minor modifications needed" that Cutrone had mentioned.

He handed the bill back and Cutrone put it in a plain white envelope along with the others. The men in the room stared at Tompkins, waiting for a reaction. Finally Cutrone broke the silence.

"Well, what do you think?"

"I think it's very good."

"It's better than very good, it's perfect. At least it will be, once you make the alterations to the plates."

"How do you know I can do work as good as what's been done?"

Cutrone's eyes narrowed as he looked directly at Tompkins.

"I'm betting that you can, and so is your wife."

He took Tompkins by the arm and led him out of the room to the elevator. They went back up to the dining room on the third floor, accompanied by Sal.

Frank had cleared the plates away and put an overhead projector on the table. A portable screen stood against the blackened window. Cutrone took the bill out of the envelope and put it under the lens. He looked up and said, "I want to show you the quality you'll be working with. I think you'll agree it's quite extraordinary."

Sal turned off the lights, and the image of the bill flashed on the screen. Cutrone was adjusting the lens so that the image was getting bigger and bigger. Tompkins watched the portrait of Franklin fill the screen, then just the face, then a part of the face, then just an eye. The eye blurred, then became perfectly sharp as Cutrone manipulated the focusing knob.

The eye stared at them, sharp and clear. There were no broken or ragged lines in the steel-etched portrait. There was no clogging of the dark areas. The engraving was as good as anything the government was using now. In many cases it was better because these plates hadn't been subjected to printing the sums of money the Bureau prints every day.

Cutrone's voice showed a respect for the craftsmanship that was projected on the screen.

"Look at the detail of the line work here. Each line is precise and unbroken. Perfect detail."

Slowly the eye slid off the screen as he moved the bill under the lens. An area just to the right of the portrait appeared near the Department of Treasury seal. The printing in this area was minimal, so the texture of the paper was apparent. Tompkins could begin to see the fiber.

Cutrone wasn't satisfied. He turned the projector off and the room lights came on. He took a small case from his pocket and opened it. Inside was a loupe, a small magnifying glass used by engravers to examine detail. He looked at the bill under the loupe for a moment, then handed it to Tompkins.

"Look at the fiber and tell me what you see."

Tompkins put the glass against his eye and brought the bill up to it. Slowly he moved across the portrait to the Treasury seal. The fiber was very visible. Most counterfeiters attempted to print the texture onto poor-quality paper; this fiber was the real thing. He looked at Cutrone, who had a smile of satisfaction on his face.

"Where did you get the paper?"

Cutrone looked at Sal, who was grinning.

"From the same place the government gets theirs."

"That's impossible."

"Not really, when you have a source inside. Whenever a change is made in the fiber, we get a small sample. We forward that to our supplier outside the country, who copies it exactly. Did you notice the metallic fiber in the weave?"

Tompkins put the bill under the loupe again. There it was, very fine strands of red metallic fiber. As he studied it he could hear Cutrone saying, "They recently changed the frequency the fiber emits when it's put under a frequency monitor. We knew it as soon as it happened."

Tompkins stood up and gestured to the bill in his outstretched hand.

"I don't know why you need me to finish this work. Where's the guy who did all this for you? He's a genius, have him do it."

Sal snuffed out the cigarette he was smoking by dropping it into his empty coffee cup.

"He's dead. He died three months ago. And, you're right, he was a genius."

"Well, I can't do this kind of work. There's too much detail. I could never duplicate the quality. Maybe fifteen years ago . . . maybe, but not now. You're asking too much."

Cutrone came over and snatched the bill from his hand. He turned and walked to the door and opened it so it swung out into the hallway, revealing the wall phone. With his back still to Tompkins, he said, "You have the skill. We know that because we checked you out very carefully. The question now is simply whether or not you'll use it."

Tompkins's heart was pounding as he saw the phone over Cutrone's shoulder. He could feel the beads of perspiration forming on his forehead.

"I can't do it, I tell you." His voice was rising as he felt himself beginning to lose control.

Cutrone took two steps into the hallway and stood in front of the phone. He reached into his pocket for some change. As he put it into the coin slot and began dialing, Tompkins bolted out of his chair for the door. Before he could get there, Sal grabbed him around the chest from behind. He felt the pressman's arms tighten around his chest. Cutrone was dialing the last few digits.

"All right, all right," he said in almost a whisper. "I'll do it. I'll do what I can."

Cutrone held the receiver in his hand. A voice could be heard on the other end of the line.

"Hello . . . hello . . . is that you, Tony?"

It seemed like an eternity before he placed the receiver back on the hook. He turned to Tompkins but said nothing. Then he walked away.

Work began on the twenty. Vladislav had decided to complete that first, because the lower denomination was easier to circulate initially. Once they gained confidence that the bill could be passed undetected, then the hundred would quickly follow.

Modifications needed on the front side of the bill were minimal. Two signatures needed to be changed, those of the Treasurer of the United States and the Secretary of the Treasury. Also, some new scrollwork had to be added to the base of the Jackson portraits.

On the back side, the flag on top of the White House was to be made more prominent, along with the sky over the building. A tree to the left of the portico also had to be made smaller to reveal more of the building. Scrollwork around the numerals at the base of the bill had not been completed by Schmidt. Neither were the numerals.

Tompkins began his day as he would for the next four months. He was awakened at six-thirty in the morning, given time to shower and shave, and by seven-fifteen was eating breakfast. At precisely eight o'clock he was taken down to the second floor by Frank. Cutrone and Sal were waiting for him in the small engraver's room that had been set up for him.

The room had a heavy desk with a slate top. A swivel lamp and magnifying glass hung over it. Some cabinets had been built against the wall to hold tools. Although the walls were open to the ceiling, an eight-foot wall provided privacy from the two other engravers who were involved in making copper offset plates for the legitimate business of the plant.

Tompkins stood in the doorway, taking in the sounds and smells of the room. The pungent aroma of ink and etching acid brought back thirty years of being in a room like this. The steady hum of a proofing press outside the doorway was accentuated by the hissing sound of compressed air as it lifted sheets of paper onto the grippers. The pinup calendar someone had left on the outside wall was also familiar. One thing was not, though. The only window in the room was again painted black from the inside. A mesh screen was in front to protect it. He was not going to see outside. They were not going to let him know where he was.

Cutrone stood up and turned the metal swivel chair toward him.

"Good morning," he said with the half smile that was to become familiar to Tompkins. It was as if he wanted to be friendly but something inside him prevented it.

"We have a surprise for you."

Sal bent down and opened up the bottom drawer of the heavy desk. He took out a wooden box with a leather handle that Tompkins recognized instantly.

"We thought you might be needing this, so we brought it with us."

He put it on the desk in front of him.

Tompkins clicked open the small latch and looked at the engraver's tools he hadn't used in ten years. Neatly arranged in two rows were razor-sharp metal cutting shafts with wooden ball handles. He ran his hand over them, feeling the sharp edges. They were all there, the single tool with a squared bottom, used to cut into detail areas of a steel plate. The grouper, with a rounded bottom for larger areas. There was even a custom tool he had made himself from a three-quarter-inch file. It enabled him to create hairline detail in the steel.

He lifted the tray out of the box. Underneath was the Indian stone used to sharpen cutting edges, and emery paper to smooth off metal burrs. There were even some tools that went back to his halftone copper engraving days, punch-up tools, a small hammer, a burnisher, a linen glass, and a plastic one-hundred-twenty-line dot screen.

He looked up at Sal.

"Where did you get these?"

"They were in your bedroom closet up on the shelf behind an old top hat. You must have been quite a strutter in your day."

Tompkins remembered the hat. He had gotten it for his son Bill when he was a freshman in high school. The thespian club had put on a musical comedy, and Bill had done a soft-shoe routine. It brought down the house.

Cutrone said, "We thought you'd be more comfortable with your own tools."

Tompkins picked up the grouper and slid his fingers along the sharply honed edge.

"Thanks," he said. "That was real considerate of you."

Frank came into the room carrying a small wooden box, which he put on the table. Cutrone lifted the top off, reached in, and carefully removed a steel plate. It was the plate for the twenty-dollar bill that Schmidt had not completed. Cutrone then took a rolled-up press sheet that was leaning against the wall and tacked it up in front of Tompkins. It was a blowup of an impression made from the engraving.

Cutrone traced the edges of the bill with his index finger.

"We blew this up so you can get a good look at Schmidt's work. As you can see, it's very good."

Tompkins looked at the blowup. Cutrone was right. It was good. Maybe too good for him to duplicate.

Sal reached into one of the cabinets and took out ten pieces of steel. He put them on the table beside the twenty-dollar plates.

"Okay, it's practice time," he said, picking up one of the engraving tools. "In a few weeks you'll make Schmidt look like a two-bit counterfeiter."

The steel pieces had the parts of the bill that needed to be completed projected on them. They were to be used as practice before he attempted any engraving on Schmidt's work.

"We'll leave you now," Cutrone said as he walked toward the door. "Frank will stay with you to get anything you want. If you need more practice plates, let us know and we'll make the projections on them."

They left the room. Frank took a rolled-up *Playboy* magazine from his pocket and began reading it.

Tompkins stared at the blowup of Schmidt's work that hung in front of him. It was extraordinary. There were very few government engravers who could do as well. Every engraver had a style. That style caused differences from bill to bill under magnification. They were always very slight; an extra line in the shadow area of a letter, an extra-heavy line in an eyebrow; little discrepancies existed from engraver to engraver. He not only would have to get his own technique back, but also he would have to emulate Schmidt. In a way it was like learning somebody else's signature.

He moved one of the practice plates in front of him. The feel of the steel in his hand felt good. The clean, polished surface had always reminded him of a clean, coated piece of paper waiting for the artist's first few brush strokes.

Slowly he picked up a grouper tool and rubbed it across the Indian stone in smooth, even strokes. He could feel the honed shaft sharpening under his fingers.

He swung the magnifying glass over the practice plate. Immediately the images were twelve times bigger. It was like looking into a different world, a world of curved lines and shapes. A triangular area of black with five progressively shorter lines under it filled the glass. It was the shadow area of the letter *T* in the word *twenty*. Under the glass it was like a complete painting that had to be matched.

The point of the tool cut into the metal as he applied pressure to it. He made the first line; too long, too deep. He tried a second line. Again he cut into the steel and moved the point of the grouper. That was better . . . a little too deep but better. The third line. It had a slight curve at the end. He felt the tool break the metal, and he moved it sideways in a straight line. Now for the curve. He felt his fingers respond, but not quick enough. The curve was too wide and came too late. He would try again.

By five o'clock he had gone through eighteen practice plates, having asked for more after lunch. He was about to start on another when he heard a key in the lock. Frank, who was sleeping, jumped up and opened it. It was Sal.

"Hey, Bob. What ya say we knock off now, huh? You've done enough for one day."

Tompkins swung the magnifying glass aside and looked up.

"I'd like a little more time to work."

"You're kiddin'. How much?"

"Maybe another hour or so."

Frank looked at his watch and shook his head, irritated at the idea of staying in the small room any longer.

Sal took a few steps into the room and looked at the plates on the table.

"We can't afford any overtime, you know," he said with what Tompkins knew to be a phony smile.

"I need a little more time."

"Suit yourself. I'll save you some dinner and a beer."

He left. Tompkins heard the lock click. Frank went back to sleep.

It was seven o'clock before he finished and Frank brought him upstairs. He had accomplished what he'd wanted for the first day.

Six nights later Vladislav opened the door to the room Tompkins had been working in. He turned on the adjustable lamp over the desk and sat down. Practice plates were neatly stacked in front of him. Schmidt's original lay in the box.

He arranged the plates in four rows of five each and began to examine each one with the loupe. He bent over them, moving the glass from plate to plate, and what he saw was a man attempting to regain an art he hadn't practiced for over ten years. The lines on the first plate were unsteady, unsure, but each progressive plate showed improvement. There was confidence in the lines. Each stroke began to show a commitment, not hesitation. There was a sign of confidence, a belief in one's ability. Vladislav saw more and more of it in each plate he looked at. By the time he got to the last one, he was not only able to see Tompkins's style return but also a style imitating Schmidt's.

He set the plates aside.

As he was about to turn out the light, something about the Schmidt engraving lying in the box caught his attention. Some freshly engraved lines near the White House illustration were reflecting light from the lamp. Slowly he raised the plate out of the box and put it in front of him. A small, unfinished area of the White House had been worked on. He put the loupe over it.

What he saw was amazing. It was as if Schmidt had returned from the grave to complete his work. If it weren't for the difference in color of the newly engraved lines, it would have been impossible to determine where Schmidt had left off and Tompkins began. Every nuance that was in the German engraver's work had been carried out. The lines were the same quality, the drawing style flawless.

Vladislav put the engraving back into the box and turned off the light. Three months ago KGB agents in Washington had assured him that they had found the only man in the world who could do this job. They were right.

4

Moscow, July 8, 1990 (TASS)—

SOVIET PREMIER VALENKOV SAID TODAY THAT RUSSIA WOULD REDUCE ITS MILITARY BUDGET FOR 1991 TO SOME TWENTY BILLION AMERICAN DOLLARS. THIS IS THE FIRST REDUCTION IN ARMS SPENDING BY THE SOVIET UNION SINCE THE END OF WORLD WAR II. THE PREMIER CALLED UPON THE UNITED STATES TO FOLLOW THE RUSSIAN LEAD. HE SAID PRESIDENT TURNER'S PLANS FOR INCREASED U.S. MILITARY SPENDING WERE "DANGEROUS AND COUNTERPRODUCTIVE TOWARD LESSENING THE TENSIONS THAT EXIST BETWEEN OUR TWO COUNTRIES."

New York
July 8, 1990

FOR THE NEXT five weeks the routine was the same. Every day Tompkins was awakened at six A.M., had breakfast, and then was brought to a small room where he put in at least eight hours working on the plates. The only break came every week or so when he spent a morning writing letters and postcards to be mailed in Florida. Besides the letters, one call was made to his son, and another relayed up to him from Florida.

He was terrified of the calls. One slip and Cutrone would threaten harm to Helen. It was amazing how much his fear could cause him to act naturally, almost sound happy. He was sure, though, that his son knew something was wrong, but oddly enough, Cutrone assured him that he was convincing.

The walls of his tiny engraving room were now covered with proofs that had been run off every few days as he progressed with the work. The twenty was nearly completed, but what remained was tedious work. Alterations to the White House on the back would take another week or so. Work on the hundred was coming along also, but more time was still needed to complete complex scrolls and numerals.

The routine was wearing him down. Frank was his constant guard for twelve hours a day. As he worked, the slightly built man would drink coffee and read girlie magazines. He seldom spoke, except to answer direct questions. Tompkins suspected, though, that he knew more about engraving than he let on. A number of times he would ask him to get a tool from the cabinet, and Frank always knew which one it was.

Sal was the only one who made an attempt at being friendly. Like Tompkins, he was a baseball fan and continually wanted to talk about the game. Each day he brought him the scores, which he ripped out of a newspaper. Occasionally he brought a sports magazine. That was the only contact Tompkins had with the outside world. For two weeks he hadn't been allowed to watch television, read newspapers, or see anything outside of the plant.

During the day, when he ate lunch in his room, he would stare at the blackened window and try to imagine what was on the other side. The sounds were of a city; buses, traffic, police sirens at night. He wondered what city. Was it New York? Boston? Philadelphia? For all he knew, it could still be Hartford. He listened in on conversations he could hear on the other side of the wall, but everything the men said was guarded. They never seemed to forget that he was in the room behind them.

In the evening he ate in the dining room with Frank, who sat at the other end of the long table and said nothing. By eight o'clock, he was back in his room where he would read one of the sports magazines and then get ready for bed. Lately he had started to do exercises before retiring. The constant bending over the plates had stiffened his back and legs. He found the exercises helped loosen them.

Before he fell asleep, he would write a letter to Helen. So far he had only received one short note from her. It said simply, "I'm all right. Love, Helen." He had been given it on the fourth day of his captivity. It was meant simply to serve as proof that Cutrone's men were holding her. Each night he would look at her letter before he wrote. Soon he began to realize that those five words written on a piece of notepaper were all that was sustaining him. They were his strength to face another day.

The alarm clock went off next to him. Six-thirty. He got up and went into the bathroom where he showered and shaved. As he was putting on his trousers, there was a knock at the door. He looked at the clock; Frank was early. There was another knock. "All right, I'm coming," he said as he went to the door and opened it. He was surprised to find Cutrone. He was holding a manila envelope in his hand.

"May I come in?"

Tompkins moved aside.

Cutrone came into the room and looked around. The bed hadn't been made yet, a sports magazine was lying on the floor. Cutrone bent down and picked it up, then sat on the bed. He looked at Tompkins, who was still standing in the open doorway.

"Please close the door. I'd like to talk to you."

Tompkins closed it and sat down in the metal chair. He looked at Cutrone. The man didn't frighten him the way he did the first few days. Tompkins sensed that he had grown to respect his work. He probably realized now how much he needed his skill.

"What do we have to talk about? Aren't you happy with the work?"

Cutrone put down the magazine.

"On the contrary. The work is excellent, and you're making good progress."

"Well, then . . ."

Cutrone held up the manila envelope.

"We've decided to change our plans. We weren't going to give you any letters from your wife until the plates were complete, but we've decided against that."

Tompkins felt his heart beat quicken as Cutrone took two letter-size envelopes from the larger one.

"Your wife has been writing just about every day, and we have over thirty letters. We've decided to give you two of them every day as long as the work continues to our satisfaction."

He handed him the letters.

Tompkins's first instinct was to rip them open and read them, but he resisted the temptation. He was ecstatic over getting the letters, but now Cutrone had another way to use Helen. She had been his incentive to do excellent work; now he was using her letters to assure the speed of that work. Cutrone was trying to show some humanity in giving them to him, but his underlying motive was insidious.

He knew Cutrone wanted the display of emotion that he was holding back. He wanted an outpouring of appreciation for the letters. Well, that's exactly what he felt inside, but he'd be damned if he would show it.

He stood up.

"Thanks for the letters. I'd like to read them alone if you don't mind."

Cutrone was watching him closely. His training had taught him to look for little things. Although Tompkins was maintaining a facade of coolness, the sensitive fingers that etched smooth, clean lines into steel were trembling as they held the envelopes. The engraver had only spoken a few words, but the determined voice was on the verge of cracking.

"I think when you read the letters, you'll find that your wife is being treated well. We're trying to make her as comfortable as possible. We'll continue to do so as long as you're cooperating."

Tompkins simply stared at the letters.

"I want you to know that your work has been excellent so far. As long as it stays that way, you and your wife will be safe."

Cutrone got up and walked toward the door. As he opened it, he turned back to Tompkins. His voice was soft, almost apologetic.

"We have our motives, of course. I realize that. But on the other hand, we're human beings. We don't take pleasure in doing this to you."

Tompkins said nothing. Cutrone closed the door lightly behind him.

Quickly he tore open one of the envelopes and unfolded the letter. It was dated May 24, three days after they had been kidnapped. The letter was only about five lines long, and the handwriting was barely legible. Helen's arthritic fingers didn't have very much control, and it was painful for her to write anything at all. He put on his glasses and started to read.

May 24, 1990

My dearest Bob,

I want you to know I'm fine and being well taken care of. I'm counting the days until you're with me.

Love,
Helen

He opened the second letter. At first he couldn't believe she had written it. The handwriting was smooth and even. The letters were formed much better and were easier to read. It was as if the arthritis had completely disappeared. He looked at the date, June 28, nine days ago.

My dearest Bob,

I love you and miss you. I'm feeling better every day because the climate is warm and dry. Also, I'm getting treatments from a therapist that are helping me a great deal. I have better use of my fingers now, as you can probably see from the neater handwriting. The muscles in my back and legs seem looser too.

I received another letter yesterday. Parts of it were blacked out as usual, but it was good to hear from you. It reminded me of when we were writing to each other in college. You know, I never told you that I still have all those letters at home, hidden in the attic. There must be close to five hundred of them. Remember how we wrote every day? My roommate, Barbara, thought it was silly, and I'm sure your friends did, too, but I think we did it because our love was something special. Even though we often didn't have anything interesting to say, it was a time during the day when we sat and thought about each other. And I always thought wonderful thoughts. I still do.

I keep asking, but they won't tell me where you are or why they're holding us prisoners. All they'll say is that I'll find out in good time and that I'm not to speculate in any of my letters. Anyway, I don't care as long as you are safe. No matter what they're forcing you to do, everything will be all right once we're back together again.

My darling, being apart from you has made me realize more than ever how much I love you. I've always known it, but never how much until now. I pray every night that you're well and will return to me soon.

Your loving wife,
Helen

He stared at the letters and tried to hold back the tears that he knew would come, anyway. Every night he had lain in bed thinking about her, but now he felt the full impact of his loneliness. The letters were a part of her. She had touched them, held them in her hand. It was as if part of her were in the room. He pressed them to his lips and felt the tears run down his face. Then he let himself go and released all the pain and anguish that had been inside him for far too long.

That day he worked harder than ever. The need to be back with Helen overwhelmed him. She was safe; in fact, her arthritis was better than it had been in years. The letters were proof of that. Something good had come out of this terrible ordeal, after all.

Frank was surprised to hear him say what a nice day it must be outside. When the sun was shining brightly, it poured so much light on the blackened window that every brush stroke in the paint showed.

Sal came by in the middle of the afternoon to give him the previous day's baseball scores and found him smiling for the first time in five weeks. As soon as he came into the room, Tompkins stopped what he was doing.

"What did the Yanks do against Boston?"

Sal looked at the clipping in his hand.

"They didn't do anything. They got shut out, 4–0."

Tompkins shook his head.

"Well, they're gonna win tomorrow."

"Wanna bet?"

"Yeah, a hundred bucks," he answered as he slapped a

hundred-dollar bill from the previous day's proofs into Sal's hand. Sal looked at the bill, pretending to be surprised.

"Is this any good, Mac?"

"No, it's not. A government agent on the ball would know in a minute that it was counterfeit."

He picked up the plates in front of him.

"But tomorrow, when they run proofs from these . . . yeah, the bills will be perfect."

Sal laid the newspaper clipping on the desk.

"So tomorrow's the day."

Tompkins turned and gestured toward Frank.

"Tomorrow's got to be the day. He's read all the *Playboys*."

Later that night Tompkins sat in bed rereading Helen's letters. The men were in the next room playing poker, as they usually did two or three times a week. Sometimes he would half listen to their conversations, but they were very careful and only talked about sports or work being done in the plant.

He reread Helen's second letter. She had said that the climate was warm and dry. He wondered where she could be. Maybe it was Florida. That's where Bill's call had come from. Or maybe it was the Caribbean. If it was, it would be ironic. She had always wanted to visit one of the islands.

He read through the letter again and focused on one line. "No matter what they're forcing you to do, everything will be all right once we're back together again." Lately he didn't think much about what he was being forced to do. In the beginning he had, but then he became engrossed in working on the plates. He had done some speculating on what the money would be used for. His thoughts had ranged all the way from the Mafia using it to buy real estate in a foreign country, to Israel using it to purchase American military equipment. Who knew? It really didn't matter. What he had to do was supply plates that would get him to Helen. He pressed the letters to his lips, put them on the night table, and turned out the light.

He must have been asleep about two hours when he was awakened by loud conversation in the next room. There was a violent argument going on. Sal was yelling at the top of his voice at a pressman named Steve, who he had seen only once before. From what he could hear, Steve was complaining about not having any time off to spend his winnings.

"What good is the money if you don't have any fuckin' time off to spend it, anyway," he was yelling. "I'm sick of this goddamn place. I'm sick of being in here every hour of every day, cooped up and printing your lousy money. I don't give a shit what you say. I'm going out tomorrow night and I'm going to have some fun. Fun!" he shouted. "Do you understand the word, or was it left out of your English classes?"

A chair crashed to the floor. The sound of footsteps was heard as Sal ran around to the other side of the table.

"You'll do what we tell you, or you'll be on the first plane out of here in the morning. And you know what will happen to you when you get home."

Steve shouted back.

"Well, I'm not waiting for morning. I'm going out right now."

There was the sound of a scuffle. And then, *"Ty ne ostanovish menya. Daje ne pytaysya."*

"Stop it. Are you mad?" someone shouted.

It was Cutrone. He must have come into the room. There was complete silence, then some low conversation that Tompkins couldn't make out. He heard the door of the other room open, then footsteps in the hallway, coming toward him. He rolled over in the bed so his back was to the door. The key clicked in the lock and the door opened, letting a sliver of light into the room. He felt Cutrone's eyes watching every movement of his body. His breathing was slow and easy as he tried to simulate a deep sleep. Cutrone took a few steps into the room. Now there was complete silence except for his breathing. Cutrone stood there for what seemed an eternity waiting for the slightest false move. Finally he turned and left quietly, closing the door carefully behind him. The lock clicked.

Tompkins lay still, afraid to move. His mind was racing madly. The words he had heard were like a bomb going off, exploding thousands of pieces that were now falling into place. Questions that he had asked himself during the past six weeks now had answers. He wasn't making plates for some underground Mafia operation. He was making plates for the Russians.

The next morning he hurried Frank through breakfast and was in his engraving room a half hour earlier than usual.

Nobody was at work yet in the plant. He took the plate for the hundred-dollar bill out of the drawer and put it under the magnifying glass. Using the grouper tool, he etched into the scrollwork on the back side of the bill. In less than a few seconds he had set back work on the plate more than two weeks.

He looked at Frank. He was reading one of the sports magazines Sal had left. Setting the hundred aside, he examined the twenty next. First he looked at the portrait under the glass, then checked the back side. By moving the plate, he positioned the top part of the White House under the glass. There was an area of sky that needed to be completed at the top of the cupola. Also, the flag needed to be finished. He decided that he would not have to mar the plate. It was sufficiently incomplete to offer him the time to do what he planned.

A key turned in the lock. Frank reached over and opened the door. It was Sal and Cutrone. Cutrone seemed unusually happy.

"I see you're getting an early start this morning. You must have gotten a good sleep last night."

Tompkins's heart beat faster. Did Cutrone suspect he knew they were Russian? He smiled nervously.

"Yes, I slept well, so I got here a little earlier this morning."

"Well, Sal tells me you've got the hundred completed. That's great news."

He took three letters from his pocket and held them up.

"We'll just take the plate and run off some proofs and you'll have these letters read before noon."

Sal went to reach for the engraving but Tompkins held his hand over it.

"It's not finished," he said calmly.

"Come on, Bob, you said you'd have it today," Sal said, putting his hand on Tompkins's shoulder.

"Well, it isn't ready," he said, standing up and ridding himself of Sal's hand. "I made some errors in the foliage on the back side. It'll take two weeks to fix."

"It'll take what?" Cutrone said, as if he couldn't believe what he had just heard.

"Two weeks," Tompkins repeated.

Cutrone sank into the chair. The plate was on the table in front of him. Tompkins saw fear in those narrow eyes for the first time as he stared at it. He expected him to shout furiously, but he simply swung the magnifying glass over the engraving and said, "I don't have two weeks. Where is the error?"

Tompkins leaned over and positioned the glass over the top of Independence Hall. He used the grouper to point to the flaws.

"There," he said. "I cut a little too far to the outside of the peak in the roof. I don't know why, but it happened."

Cutrone swung the glass aside.

"I don't have the two weeks. I've got to have it before then."

Tompkins studied him from the back. He wasn't moving a muscle, but there was rage building inside him.

I know you don't have the time, you Russian bastard, Tompkins thought to himself. *You're probably weeks behind the schedule Moscow gave you, and your ass is on the line.*

"It'll take two weeks. It can't be done in less," he said. "The only alternative is to use the plate the way it is. The flaw is very small and probably won't be noticed by anybody."

Cutrone stood up. He was losing control.

"The plate has to be perfect," he said, his voice rising. "I told you that weeks ago. I won't accept it unless it's flawless. Ten days, that's all you have, not just for the hundred but for the twenty also." He pointed a finger at Tompkins. "I warn you, there can't be any more mistakes. If they're not finished in ten days, your wife's cure will have been for nothing. I'm sure you've noticed how she's progressed from reading her letters. Well, that will all be for nothing if you fail. I guarantee you, she'll be far worse off than she's ever been."

Tompkins answered quickly. The next few moments were crucial.

"I can have them ready on one condition."

"What's that?"

"I have to work alone."

"Why?"

"Having someone else in the room is ruining my concentration. I've got to work without being disturbed. That's the only way I'll get them done on time."

Cutrone turned to Sal, who simply shrugged. Frank seemed anxious at the idea of being freed from his boring responsibility.

"All right," he said finally. "You'll work alone, but at the end of every day I'm going to check the work personally. If I see any more mistakes or falling behind schedule, your wife will pay for it."

Without saying anything more, he walked out, Sal following behind him. Frank gathered up his magazines and shut the door.

Tompkins was alone. He looked down at the plates in front of him. In ten days they would be perfect. At least, they would appear to be.

For the next week Tompkins put in at least twelve hours a day with time out only for a light lunch and a short dinner break. Each night Vladislav checked the work and found his progress to be on schedule and done expertly. It was strange that an engraver of Tompkins's ability had made the mistake he did, but Vladislav accepted it as a human error, that could happen to the best. In retrospect, having Frank guard him might have contributed to his losing his concentration. If that was true, it had been a costly mistake.

Moscow had been pressing him for the completion of the plates for over a month now. When they weren't ready on schedule, Gagarin had gone ahead, anyway, and purchased the casinos and the California bank through Geisler's holding companies. That meant that over $200 million had been spent in the hope of his delivering perfect plates. The pressure on him was unbelievable. The success of the whole operation rested in his hands.

Finally, on the evening of the ninth day, Tompkins told him the plates were finished. The following morning Vladislav and Sal supervised the running of the first proofs. Photographic enlargements, ten times up, were made from them and examined carefully. Both plates were perfect, right down to the smallest detail.

For the first time in six weeks Tompkins was allowed to leave his engraving room and go down to the pressroom on the second floor. As Frank brought him in, he saw the sheets of hundreds coming off the press. He guessed that over five hundred sheets had been printed already. Off to the side, tacked on the wall, were the blowups of both bills. Cutrone and Sal were comparing some of the printed ones to the blowups under a magnifying glass. Tompkins noticed something else: The windows of the room had recently been blackened.

"Hey, Bob, you've produced a masterpiece here," Sal said in his usual patronizing manner. "The bills are perfect. Couldn't be any better."

He stepped aside, allowing him to move closer to the table. Cutrone was looking through a glass at the twenty. He looked up.

"We can't find any flaws in the bills, and Sal says the plates are printing beautifully. You've done a good job."

That was one of the few compliments he had gotten from Cutrone since he'd started the engravings. He decided to take advantage of it and press him further.

"Now that you've got the plates, when can I expect to see my wife?"

Cutrone hesitated and then said, "You won't see her right away."

"Why not? I've completed my end of the bargain."

"Not quite. We need you a little longer."

"For what?"

"If the plates break down, we'll need you to repair them immediately."

Tompkins could feel himself beginning to tremble. He had worked long and hard to complete the work. Every day had been one day closer to being with Helen again. Now they were going to delay it.

"The plates can't break down," he said desperately. "You only have to produce a hundred and fifty million dollars. This press can run that off in less than a week."

Cutrone turned away from him and went on examining the bills through the magnifying glass. Without looking up, he said, "We've decided to print more than that."

5

Las Vegas, Nevada, August 2, 1990
(*The New York Times*)—

THE THUNDERBIRD CASINO ANNOUNCED IT WOULD REOPEN
TOMORROW AFTER BEING CLOSED FOR SIX WEEKS. THE
CASINO UNDERWENT EXTENSIVE RENOVATION WHEN IT WAS
PURCHASED IN SEPTEMBER BY THE ROYCE CORPORATION OF
CHICAGO. ROYCE IS OWNED BY BETSEN & CO., A HOLDING
COMPANY IN ZURICH, SWITZERLAND. THE CASINO WAS
PURCHASED BY ROYCE FROM ENTERTAINMENT INTERNATION-
AL FOR AN ESTIMATED 20 MILLION DOLLARS. SPOKESMEN
FOR ROYCE SAID OVER THREE MILLION DOLLARS WENT INTO
THE RENOVATION.

Las Vegas, Nevada
August 2, 1990

FOR THE PAST six weeks there had been a dark spot in the
middle of the glittering Las Vegas strip. The Thunderbird
Casino had been closed for renovations and left a gaping hole
in the four-mile stretch of flashing light. But tonight the lights
were back on. Las Vegas's largest casino had reopened and the
crowd poured into the newly refurbished main room.

It was the height of elegance. Giant crystal chandeliers hung
from the tinted glass ceiling over a velvetlike carpet. The
gaming tables were chrome with crimson pads instead of the
traditional green. Croupiers in black tuxedoes wearing white
gloves manned the dice tables while young ladies in satin
gowns carried silver trays with drinks for the players.

But all the renovations were not apparent to the crowd that

filled the room. During the renovation, interior walls had been ripped away so electrical wiring could be run to new computer cashier machines. Unlike other casinos on the strip, the Thunderbird's automated system would offer the convenience of both buying and cashing in chips at each table.

At least that's what the advertisements for the grand opening said. The KGB agents who installed the system knew otherwise.

Their work had been difficult, for it was done apart from the normal decorating of the interior and mostly at night. But it had been done well. Besides the electrical work, additional shafts had been added to the air-conditioning system. They ran from the main floor into the basement. Their use was not intended to bring air up to the main floor, however, but to carry money down.

Elena Pryde was one of five agents who had been specially trained in Kiev to operate a highly sophisticated computer that was the key to a system that would pass over three hundred thousand dollars of counterfeit money a day. Seventy other dealers throughout the casino had been taught by these five but were totally unaware that they were passing counterfeit currency.

The machine itself was very small and was built into the table so it didn't interfere with her handling of the cards. Only a small keyboard was exposed on her right. A special revolving drawer opened out below table level. The drawer was activated if a customer purchased his chips with either a twenty- or a hundred-dollar bill. When the bill was placed under a pressure-sensitive roller, the computer recorded the deposit. In less time than it took the shutter of a camera to click, the drawer revolved a full three hundred and sixty degrees, dropping the genuine bill down a chute and replacing it with a counterfeit one. The counterfeit was then paid out to another customer cashing in chips. The computer kept the money in the drawer in perfect balance with the chips outstanding all under the watchful eyes of the Nevada Gambling Commission.

Elena pressed the release button on the computer keyboard. The drawer opened. She removed two hundred-dollar bills and then placed them back under the rollers. As she closed the drawer there was a click that was barely audible. The drawer had flipped over and was ready for the first transaction.

The casino filled almost immediately. People were anxious to see what it looked like inside and to try their luck in the new room. All seven seats at Elena's blackjack table were now occupied.

She scanned the players, three women and four men. Five of them looked like normal tourist types, one was probably a heavy hitter. The player in the end seat to her left she recognized immediately. It was the man she had trained under in Kiev, the man who had devised the system she was working with now, Yuri Vladislav.

Money to purchase chips came on the table. This would be the most crucial test of the new computer system. Every player would be buying chips at once. Vladislav was watching her closely. Twenty, twenty, ten, five, one hundred dollars from the heavy hitter and another one from Vladislav. Click, click, click; the closed drawer rotated at one-hundredth of a second. Chips were automatically dispensed as counterfeit replaced real money at blinding speed inside the drawer. The system was working perfectly.

Vladislav looked at her over his cards. A slight nod of his head acknowledged his recognition of her and the perfect execution of the machine.

Cards were dealt, and hands were played, some of the players winning but most of them losing. The games were played smoothly at a fast pace. There had been concern that the machine would slow down the tempo. It didn't.

In twenty minutes the five tourists were gone, leaving Vladislav and the heavy hitter next to him with a new group of players. The man was a tall, overweight Texan who had appeared intoxicated when he started playing and had since accepted two more drinks from the cocktail waitress. Despite his drunkedness, he managed to win one hand after another. Vladislav was losing.

"Y'all havin' a bad run there," he said, turning to Vladislav. "This li'l dealer here's been Lady Luck to me. Yuh hang in there, though, and yours is bound to change sure's a bear'll lead you to honey."

Vladislav turned over his cards.

"Thanks for the encouragement but I think I'll cash in while I still have money to get back to New York."

"New Yorker, eh," he answered, leaning back in his chair. "You big-city folks are outa yer element here. Too conservative. Too afraid to take a chance. Ya bet too conservative and yer gonna lose every time."

The game ended and the Texan showed his cards. Five, three, jack, deuce. Elena had eighteen. He let out a yell and drained the glass in front of him.

Vladislav pushed his remaining chips toward Elena. She dropped them down a slot. The computer tabulated their value and paid out a counterfeit twenty-dollar bill.

"Well, maybe I'll cash in these little babies too," the Texan said as he moved his chips across the table. "Maybe try my luck on the craps table over there."

The computer dispensed eight counterfeit hundred-dollar bills. Vladislav watched as he carefully counted the crisp new bills. Tompkins's engraving, the paper, the inks, and all the hard work was now paying off.

"Listen here, friend," he said, waving the bills in the air. "Why don't I buy us a real drink at the bar instead of this watered-down stuff they give ya here."

He pointed a finger at Vladislav. On it was a large diamond-studded ring.

"Then we'll come back here and I'll show ya how to play this here game. Like I said, ya gotta play it aggressively to be a winner."

He leaned closer to the KGB agent. Vladislav moved away slightly to avoid the strong Scotch odor.

"Actually I can play that way because I don't give a shit whether I lose or not," he said in a slurred voice. "I got forty thousand acres back home in south Texas with vegetables on 'em. Green gold, baby. It's like growin' these bills. Got cheap illegal labor pickin' the stuff. They're losers, man. Know what my profit margin is? Sixty percent. Ya hear that? Six-oh percent. That makes me a winner before I even get here. And when I win on top of that"—he waved the counterfeit bills in the air—"well, I just feel like sharin' it. What d'ya say, how 'bout a drink?"

"No thank you," Vladislav answered quietly. The Texan

thoroughly disgusted him, but at the same time Vladislav felt a tremendous sense of pleasure. Here was a perfect example of the system his country would defeat; a system that perpetuated vast inequities in its distribution of wealth. While some of its citizens barely had enough money to live on, others had money to squander on pleasures that never would be satisfied.

He knew this drunken Texan was the extreme, but as he looked around the casino there were many others like him. They were people who had made vast sums of money on other people's inadequacies. Uneducated minorities supplied the menial labor while the privileged class lived in luxury. He had seen it both here and in New York. There it constantly amazed him that in the distance of a few short blocks one could walk from the town houses of Park Avenue into the ghetto of Harlem.

His country's system was the one that would prevail. Socialism, as proposed by Lenin, would bring equality of wealth with a guarantee of care and well-being for all its citizens. No, this man wasn't a winner. Already he was a victim of a silent attack by his country that would result in the downfall of capitalism. He was now carrying over eight hundred dollars in counterfeit money, which was just the beginning of a wave of currency that would flood the economy.

His visit here was a success. The machines were passing money undetected. By the end of the evening, over seven hundred thousand dollars of counterfeit would be passed.

In another two weeks the two casinos in Atlantic City would also begin passing counterfeit bills, followed a week later by the California bank. By the end of February, over $300 million a month would find its way into the economy.

In twenty months there would be an increase from $46 billion in U.S. currency to $54 billion, with better than eighty percent of it counterfeit. Federal Reserve audits would detect the increase, but there would be no way of stopping it.

Once word leaked that a large percentage of the currency was counterfeit, the repercussions to the economy would be devastating. The value of the dollar would plummet to a new low and would put the economy in a state of irreparable collapse.

A smile crossed Vladislav's face as he shook hands with the Texan.

"I'll pass on the drink if you don't mind," he said. And then, pointing to the counterfeits in the Texan's hand, he added, "Don't spend that all in one place."

Three nights later a garbage truck made its way down the service entrance of the Thunderbird Casino. It drove around to the rear of the building and backed up to the loading dock. The driver gave two blasts of the air horn, and a large overhead door opened. He got out and jumped onto the loading platform. After speaking briefly with the man on the platform, they walked over to sixteen plastic trash bags lying under the air-conditioning vent. Carefully they loaded them one by one into the truck. The driver then started the auxiliary motor, and the bags were swept up into the huge dump of the vehicle. The loading-dock door came back down, the driver got in, and the truck drove away.

Within ten minutes it pulled into the carting company warehouse where $6 million of genuine twenty and hundred-dollar bills were transferred to an armored truck. In three days the casino had passed $6 million of counterfeit money, and now the Russians were about to put the equivalent amount of genuine bills back into the economy.

That same evening the armored truck left for another acquisition of the Swiss holding company, the First Savings Bank of Southern California. Three days later the bank transferred the funds to Switzerland into a numbered account at Union Suisse. By the end of the week, all the cash was reinvested back into the United States by the two Swiss holding companies, and the currency put back into circulation.

The collapse of the U.S. economy had begun.

6

Boston, Mass., September 12, 1990 (AP)—

THE DOW JONES AVERAGE OF THIRTY INDUSTRIALS FELL 15.4 TO 850.68 TODAY, AMID GOVERNMENT ECONOMISTS' REPORTS PREDICTING A CONTINUING FALL IN THE ECONOMY. HARVARD BUSINESS SCHOOL PROFESSOR OF ECONOMICS HOWARD ROSEN POINTED OUT THE VULNERABILITY OF THE U.S. ECONOMY TO FOREIGN MANIPULATION IN ITS PRESENT WEAKENED STATE. "UNLESS COOPERATION FROM OUR ALLIES IS REALIZED," HE SAID, "THE TENUOUS U.S. MARKET CAN BE SEVERELY DAMAGED." HE URGED SUPPORT FROM THE LARGE INVESTING NATIONS SUCH AS WEST GERMANY AND THE ARAB STATES TO KEEP THEIR PRESENT DOLLAR HOLDINGS INTACT AND NOT TO SHIFT TO OTHER CURRENCIES.

September 12, 1990
Lucerne, Switzerland

KARL GEISLER STOOD on the porch of his new twenty-room house overlooking beautiful Lake Lucerne. The home was in the tiny village of Seeburg, which looked directly across the lake at Lucerne.

Towering above the quaint city was Mt. Pilatus, whose snow-white image reflected into the deep blue lake. At this time of year it was sharper than ever, for the air was crisp and clean. It shined like a diamond in the ice-cold water.

Geisler took in a deep breath of the fresh, clean air. This was his favorite place in the world. He had never quite known why, but now the reason became clear. It was the mountain.

It dominated the city below. In winter, just a slight

movement of its upper peaks could send an avalanche of snow crashing down. In the summer it threatened to flood the lake, causing it to overflow the piers in the downtown area. In the fall it showed its power when severe thunderstorms came over the city. The crashing thunder and lightning echoed off the walls of the mountain as if it were shouting its defiance to the gods.

There was power in that mountain. It dominated the lives of the city's one hundred thousand inhabitants. On a whim it could snuff them out. It was power he could relate to.

He thought ahead to next summer. Then the lake would be warm and calm. The fifty-foot yacht that was being built for him in Marseilles would be completed, and he would sail around Pilatus. By then the Americans would be begging him to save their economy from the Russians. Like the mountain, at a whim, he would be able to send an avalanche of money down on their economy in a single stroke.

The air was beginning to get chilly and he went inside. Alain, his steward and chauffeur, took his down jacket and hung it in the hall closet. Geisler walked over to the fireplace and warmed himself. Within minutes Alain was there with a brandy.

"Is everything ready for this afternoon?" he asked.

"Everything is ready, sir. The launch has been sent for your guests, and they should be arriving within the hour. The dinner for ten is being prepared and will be served at seven o'clock. Is there anything else?"

"Yes," he answered. "Where is Miss Praeger?"

"She's in the sauna but said she will be down shortly."

Satisfied that everything was in order, Alain left the room. Geisler stared out at the lake through the picture window in the living room. This afternoon another step would be taken toward the completion of his agreement with the Russians.

So far everything had been going well. The first of the monies acquired through the exchange of counterfeit currency by the U.S. casinos and the California bank was scheduled to arrive in Switzerland within the next week. It would be deposited into numbered accounts at his bank for reinvestment back into U.S. banks. Everything was going according to schedule on his end, and Moscow was happy.

However, it had reached a point where he could no longer conceal the plan from his board of directors. The reinvesting of the funds would require him to draw upon various resources of the bank, which would make his involvement with the Russians impossible to hide. For that reason he had invited the eight-man board to come down from Zurich for a meeting at his home. He felt that the change of scenery would be conducive to his success. Although two members complained of traveling in the cold winter weather, finally everyone accepted.

The plan was to tell them as little as possible. He would explain that the Russians had selected Union Suisse to represent their interests in the international financial community and what that might mean in terms of compensation for the bank. Any reference to the Russian plan of financial domination over the United States and, of course, his personal compensation would be carefully avoided.

He didn't expect any opposition to the plan except from one, or possibly two, members of the board. The board members hadn't changed in over six years now, and they had basically approved everything he'd proposed during that period. When you owned as much of the pie as he did, there were few people that would oppose you.

Nina had come into the room. He knew it without turning around. She had found a perfume in Paris that thoroughly excited him.

"Do you like my dress?" she said as she did a pirouette. It was a bright red silk creation she had recently ordered. He couldn't remember the French designer's name.

"Elegant, absolutely elegant," he said.

She came over and kissed him on the cheek, then took the brandy that Alain had thoughtfully left for her.

"Do you think your guests will approve?"

He looked at the low-cut bodice and the way the silk clung to her slender hips.

"They're eight old men, my dear, but when they see you in that, they'll feel twenty-one all over again."

"Is that how you feel?" she said as she adjusted the front of his white cardigan sweater.

"You know the answer to that. I'm feeling younger every day."

He picked her up and spun her around the room. She laughed as she held him tightly.

"Put me down, you'll hurt your back."

He stopped turning but still held her a few inches from the floor.

"Never. I'm going to attach you to me forever."

"You're saying that now, but you're a very wealthy, good-looking man, Karl. You can have any woman you want."

He lowered her to the floor, then took her hands and held them in his.

"I don't want any other woman," he said in a voice that surprised her with its sudden seriousness. "Do you realize what my life was before I met you? I had just about anything money could buy, but I didn't have anybody to enjoy it with. There were women, but they were looking for a piece of the power I had, nothing else. In you I found something more."

She smiled but said nothing, preferring to let him go on.

"I found you wanted me not just for what I had. And that, my dear, is the most thrilling thing that has ever happened to me. I feel young again, younger than ever, and I want to give you the world. I want to lay it at your feet."

She laughed but then took his hands and put them against her lips.

"I mean it, Nina," he said, drawing her close to him. "I have the means to do just that."

Then he kissed her on the neck, just above the diamond brooch she had worn the first time they met.

The board of directors arrived on the launch thirty minutes later. Cocktails and hors d'oeuvres were served in the second-floor sun room, which afforded a beautiful view of the lake. The group filled each other in on the latest financial events, some of them not having been together for several weeks. Nina mixed into the conversation easily, and Geisler could see the normally stuffy bankers begin to relax.

One, however, was far from stuffy. His name was Walter Schein. Geisler suspected that if there was any opposition to his plan, it would come from Schein. He owned the largest watch company in Switzerland and had served on the bank's board for the past twelve years. At seventy-eight, he was known throughout the country as a tough, hard-nosed executive who had built his company from scratch. Now it had sales of over $600 million a year in thirty countries. Nina had him laughing over something she had said. Geisler moved over to join them.

"Your young lady and I find we have a lot in common, Karl. We're both from Bavaria. In fact, we were born in the same town, Munich."

"Oh, that is a coincidence," Geisler said matter-of-factly.

"But," Schein went on, pointing his finger in the air, "the coincidence doesn't end there. When Nina goes back to visit Munich, she stays in a small hotel on Wilhelmstrasse."

"Ah," Geisler said. Nina turned her head toward him and winked.

"And it seems that the same hotel was once an apartment house where I lived on the third floor as a young man." He turned to Nina. "Tell him where your room is."

"Three-A. Right at the top of the staircase."

"That's my room, Karl. This woman has been sleeping in my bed."

Nina put her hand on the old man's shoulder and whispered loud enough for Karl to hear.

"I was there six months ago, where were you?"

Schein laughed heartily.

"I was there sixty years ago, where were you?"

Alain appeared in the doorway and announced that dinner was being served in the main dining room. Everyone followed him downstairs to the large room on the first floor. The dinner was prepared by Geisler's new French chef. He had lured him away from the five-star Hotel Ballances in Lucerne a month ago. As always, the five-course dinner was superb.

The conversation during the meal was animated and lively. Geisler and Paul Meyer, Union Suisse's executive vice-president, recounted stories about the early days of the bank. Walter Schein had managed to sit next to Nina, and they were thoroughly enjoying each other. The wine flowed freely from bottles poured by waiters who refilled glasses as soon as they were emptied. For what was to follow, the mood of the group was exactly as Geisler wanted it.

When dinner was over, they retired to the drawing room where the business meeting was to be held. Brandy was served. Two waiters brought an easel and set it up in the corner of the room. Geisler opened a carrying case and removed charts that had been prepared earlier. He put them on the easel, then turned to the board.

"Gentlemen, if I may, I'd like to begin our meeting. Since this is a meeting of the board, we'll not be able to enjoy the company of our lovely hostess. I'm sure you all have taken pleasure in the beauty and grace she's added to the evening as much as I have." He kissed her hand. "Nina, if you'll excuse us."

She smiled at him, then said to the group, "I suppose it follows that if nonmembers of the board aren't allowed to stay, members won't be allowed to leave."

She went over to Walter Schein, who got up from his chair.

"That's unfortunate, because Mr. Schein and I were going to slip away somewhere."

Everyone laughed including Schein. Then each man came to her and kissed her hand. A waiter opened the door for her and she left. Geisler had seen grand entrances in his day, but *this* was a grand exit. She had handled herself well; he was proud of her.

Everyone directed their attention to him now as he stepped to the easel.

"Gentlemen, I have some news that should surprise all of you. Since our last meeting a very interesting development has taken place. We have, shall I say, a major investor who is interested in our bank's services."

Emil Klug, a pudgy investment consultant from Geneva, held up his glass and said, "Let me guess, Karl. It's the U.S. Treasury. They're closing down Fort Knox and they want to rent a safe-deposit box."

Everyone laughed. Geisler smiled at the consultant's little joke.

"It's funny you should mention a safe-deposit box, Emil, because that's essentially what this client wants, only it's not the United States, it's the Russians."

There was silence.

Geisler watched the reaction of the group to what he had

said. Some were more surprised than others. Meyer, the bank's executive vice-president, and Kurt Furst, the controller, weren't surprised at all.

Two months ago Geisler had appointed them directors of the holding companies he had organized for the purpose of investing in the United States. The client then was unnamed. Now they knew who it was.

Judging from the initial reactions, he now felt he could expect some problems from three people: Emil Klug; Henry Brandt, an old-line banker; and, most of all, Walter Schein. The problem, however, would not be insurmountable; he did own forty percent of the bank.

Schein was the first to speak.

"I think you'd better explain your analogy, Karl. Just what do the Russians want?"

"They want essentially what I said," Geisler answered. "A safe, discreet place to deposit their money for investment into the international market. What they want mostly, though, is secrecy. That's why they've come to us."

"I usually find the word *secret* to be somewhat synonymous with illegal, my friend. What do they want with us that their own banks can't give them?"

"I asked them the same question, Walter, and believe me, there is nothing illegal about what they want. They have a real need that their banks can't provide, a need to expand out into international finance."

"So," Schein answered, "let their banks become international banks."

"Ah, but that becomes capitalism, doesn't it?" Geisler shot back quickly. "They can't afford to let people who have been taught that Communism is the ultimate system know that the government has turned to capitalism in order to progress."

"After a hundred years, what's finally bringing them to that conclusion?" Klug asked.

"They're being very pragmatic, Emil. It just isn't working for them. But it doesn't matter; their people will never know, anyway. Operating discreetly behind Union Suisse, they'll become a part of the world financial community. We'll act on their behalf, as we would any international client."

Kurt Furst, the controller, was obviously trying to turn the discussion in a positive direction when he asked what services the bank was to provide and what the compensation would be. Geisler used charts prepared from Gagarin's estimates, and those of his own experts, to answer the question. The board was impressed. They realized, as Geisler had when he first saw the figures, that Union Suisse would become the largest bank in the world within a year.

Questions continued for another hour. Schein continued to oppose the bank's involvement with the Russians. He vehemently argued that a bank representing a nation put it in a dangerous political situation and that there wasn't any precedent for anything on this scale. Geisler argued that Worldbank in New York had managed funds of over $1.7 billion for the government of Kuwait during the 1970s. Other banks had represented the Japanese and invested funds into the U.S. economy during 1974, totaling over $34 billion. There wasn't any reason why Union Suisse shouldn't take advantage of this opportunity to become one of the most powerful banks in the world.

The meeting had reached a point where Geisler thought it appropriate to take a vote. There wasn't any reason for a secret ballot, so he suggested an oral vote. To his surprise, the count was eight in favor and only one against. Apparently the large bank commission figures had convinced Furst to vote in favor. Only Schein was opposed.

"I will not be a party to serving the Russians in any way," he said, upon seeing he was the only dissenter. He stood up and paced around the room.

"All we seem to think about lately is how much money we're going to make. Lord knows every one of us has enough to live three lifetimes, but still it seems to be the prime consideration. What about moral values? Are they completely passé in this so-called modern world of ours? It seems so. Here we are, willing to serve a government that's trying to take over the world and enslave mankind. Well, I'll tell you this, I'll have no part of it."

Geisler walked over to the picture window and stood behind him.

"Aren't you being a little extreme, Walter?" he said, trying to calm the older man down. "We aren't talking about financing the building of a neutron bomb, we're talking about the business of banking. If the Russians intend to participate in the international market, that could very well be positive. I'm sure they want to do business with the Common Market, with West Germany, possibly even Israel and the United States. They can't do that openly. It has to be done through a very discreet third party. That's why they need us."

Schein turned and faced him. The others were listening intently.

"I don't trust them. I never have and I never will. They're sneaky bastards—they're crude and they're devious. I won't have any part of them. And if I were you, I'd be damn careful as to how I place their money. They very well could be using the bank as a front to put big money into a country to take it over."

Geisler looked at the others quickly, to see how they had reacted to Schein's last words. One or two were beginning to consider it. He acted quickly.

"We've taken a vote, Walter, and you're the only one who has voted against the proposal. Because discretion would be required to handle the account, I would prefer a unanimous vote."

Schein folded his hands behind his back and stared at the rest of the board.

"You won't get it from me."

"Very well," Geisler replied. "As a member of the board, though, you will be required to maintain absolute secrecy in this matter. Nothing must be said outside the room by anyone."

"You have my word on that," he said. "But"—there was a long pause as he selected his words carefully—"I am going to look into this whole situation more carefully on my own. I don't know what they're up to, and I don't think you do, either. But I know some people who might."

Geisler answered him immediately.

"I would ask that you do it only if it doesn't jeopardize our position with the Russians. You must realize, this is a very big piece of business for us."

Schein lit up a cigar and blew smoke into the air.

"Don't worry about that. I'm a very old man, and I've got some very old, trustworthy friends."

It was eleven-thirty when they decided to end the meeting and retire for the evening. Geisler had arranged for an early breakfast the following morning, and then the launch would take them back to Lucerne. Most of the group had to be back at their desks before noon.

As they left the room, Geisler stayed behind to turn off the lights. He walked over to the lamp near the fireplace. Something sparkled behind an ashtray on the grand piano. It caught his eye momentarily. He went over and was surprised to see a piece of jewelry. It was a necklace, and the clasp had broken loose from the delicate gold chain. He held it up to the light to examine the piece more closely. Then he recognized it.

It was Nina's diamond brooch.

Two days later Geisler and Nina were sunbathing in the solarium. Lying side by side, their nude bodies glistened as beads of perspiration formed on their skin. Just a few hours each day under the specially designed glass roof had turned their bodies a golden brown. Now both of them were floating on that thin edge that separates total relaxation from sleep.

Their eyes were closed. Nina's hand reached out and touched his. Normally the sensation would have aroused him immediately, but both of them were suspended in a feeling of pleasure that transcended sex. It was a feeling of warmth, of nourishment for the body, and most of all, a knowledge that the outside world was fighting the cold and the wind.

The telephone rang.

Geisler had told Alain to screen all the calls. Only something extremely important was to be put through. He reached for the receiver and brought it to his ear. Alain's voice was soft, realizing that he had probably awakened his employer.

"Sir, you have a long-distance call from Zurich. It is Mr. Schein's secretary. She says it's urgent that she speak with you."

Geisler reached for the terry-cloth towel next to him and wiped his brow.

"Very well, put her on."

"Mr. Geisler?" the high-pitched voice on the other end of the line asked.

"Yes, what can I do for you, Hilda?"

"Mr. Geisler, something terrible has happened. Mr. Schein, he's . . . he's dead."

"He's what?" Geisler said. He got up from the lounge chair and was standing there naked, holding the phone in his hand. "What happened?" he whispered. Nina was dozing.

Schein's secretary was sobbing uncontrollably. It was a few moments before she could continue.

"He was shot this morning outside the house as he was leaving for church. His car was waiting to take him there. When he came down the sidewalk, another car came by and he was shot. He died before we could get him to the hospital."

The words cut through his brain like a knife. His mind was assimilating the information and beginning to draw conclu- sions. And the conclusions were frightening.

"I'm very sorry, Hilda," he said softly. "Mr. Schein was a dear friend of mine for many years. If there's anything I can do, please don't hesitate to ask."

"No, there's nothing," she said. "Everything is being taken care of. I wanted you to know because Mr. Schein had just come from your meeting and said that he was leaving for Zurich next week to check on something for you. I don't know if it was important or not."

"No," he answered. "I'll take care of it myself. Don't you worry about it, and please express my sympathy to Mrs. Schein. And again, if I can do anything at all, please let me know."

"Thank you, Mr. Geisler. You're very kind."

She hung up.

He stood there holding the phone. The Russians. They had found out about Schein objecting to the bank's involvement with them and had killed him. It was terrible and he abhorred it, but what terrified him was how they had found out. He had reported nothing to them. The board was sworn to secrecy. He knew all of them well. Who was the informer? What were they paying him? Was his assignment to keep a watchful eye on

him, to keep his power in check? Was it Furst? Or Meyer?
They knew the most about the involvement with the Russians.
Who was it?

He lay back on the lounge and tried to sort it out. There had
to be a way to find out who was watching him. If he was to
gain the power he imagined for himself, he would have to be
free to operate in his own way.

Nina removed the plastic caps that were shielding her eyes
from the sun and turned to him.

"Who was that, darling?" she murmured.

"It was Walter Schein's secretary," he said. "I'm afraid it's
terrible news. He died early this morning."

"Oh, I'm sorry, dear. He was such a nice man."

Then she turned over on the lounge to sun her back.

7

New York, September 19, 1990 (AP)—

TODAY THE FED M1-A REPORT SHOWED A $3.4 BILLION
DECLINE IN THE NATION'S MONEY SUPPLY FOR THE WEEK
ENDED NOVEMBER 2. THE M1-A IS A WEEKLY SUMMARY OF
THE BASIC MONEY SUPPLY, INCLUDING CASH IN CIRCULATION
AND COMMERCIAL BANK DEPOSITS.

THIS INDICATED A DECREASE IN THE PUBLIC'S NEED FOR
CURRENCY. APPARENTLY THERE IS MORE CASH IN THE HANDS
OF THE AMERICAN PUBLIC THAN GOVERNMENT FIGURES HAD
PREVIOUSLY INDICATED. IN THE PAST THREE WEEKS BANKS
HAVE REPORTED INCREASES IN "VAULT CURRENCY," WHICH IS
CASH DEPOSITED BY CUSTOMERS.

New York
September 19, 1990

BOB TOMPKINS COULD tell when the presses printing the
counterfeit were running. The steam radiator next to his bed
vibrated. For six weeks now he had kept a tally of the running
time. He estimated about two hundred and fifty thousand
sheets a week. Assuming they were printing an equal amount
of twenties and hundreds, as much as eighty-five billion dollars
had been printed. Yesterday, when he had asked Cutrone how
much longer he could expect to be there, he told him they had
only printed sixty-five of the eighty million needed.

Since he'd finished the plates his days were filled with
boredom. Most of the time was spent in his room reading,
except for the three meals he ate a day in the dining room.
Cutrone seldom spoke to him, and Sal stopped coming by to

visit. There wasn't any reason to be overly friendly. They had gotten most of what they wanted from him.

Only one small repair had been needed on the plates during the eight weeks, and that had taken just two days. At least it was a break in his boring routine. With nothing to do but read week after week, he'd become worn down mentally. Even the letters from Helen, which came every two or three days now, weren't enough to sustain him. Her life, like his, was a monotonous routine. The letters continued to be optimistic, but there was a feeling of hopelessness between the lines.

He had written three letters to his son and one to Mrs. Gilroy, all dictated by Cutrone. They spoke of the warm Florida climate and how it was helping Helen's condition. They supposedly owned a condominium, which was two blocks from the beach. Every day was filled with activities that they enjoyed with their many friends. Life was wonderful.

Besides the phone call, his son had also written to the Florida address. The family was planning a ten-day Thanksgiving vacation to Colorado where they were going to go skiing. He had the feeling that if he and Helen were really living in Florida, they would have spent there Thanksgiving alone anyway.

In an attempt to keep up his morale, he had taken to playing mind games. He'd read somewhere that prisoners incarcerated for long periods of time handled their situations better if they found a way to escape mentally. His game was to take one of the magazines that Sal had given him and arbitrarily open to a page. He would look at a picture and associate it with something he had done in the past. He opened the magazine to a page in the middle. There was a picture of a hockey player making a quick turn on the ice to avoid a defense man. His body leaned at a sharp angle, and ice sprayed off the blades of his skates. Ice . . . skating . . . that was easy. Before Helen had gotten arthritis, they had gone skating at an indoor rink near their home every Friday night. They had both skated since they were kids, and loved the sport. He closed his eyes. In his mind he saw the two of them coming out on the ice. As usual, the rink was filled with teenagers. Most of them chased after each other, bobbing and weaving through the crowd, occasionally falling when they turned too sharply. Parents with young children tried to stay away from them as they taught their young ones to skate. There were a few older people on the ice, but he and Helen seemed to be the oldest.

What they liked about the rink was the organ music. It was perfect to skate to. Most of the selections were waltzes where you could glide to the rhythm in long, easy strides. Tonight the rink was too crowded to skate together, so he moved through the skaters alone, occasionally passing Helen and waving to her. She waved back and smiled. He skated for about twenty minutes, and then the music stopped.

An announcement came over the PA system.

"Ladies and gentlemen, tonight we have something special. The next selection will be for couples only. Let's have couples only. Find yourself a partner. All couples on the ice."

Helen came up behind him and took his hand.

"Aren't you going to ask me to dance?"

"Sure. Let's go." He pushed off and stopped at the center of the rink. Helen slid in behind him, gracefully turning on her skates to come to a quick stop. He took her hand and put his arm around her waist. They stood together, waiting for the music to begin. It was a waltz. They started forward, their bodies alert to the feel of the music as they found the rhythm. He felt her body movement begin to blend perfectly with his. A stride, a shift in weight, a glide, a movement left, then right, they were in perfect harmony. They danced in slow, winding arcs around the other couples; two bodies that had become one with the music.

Helen leaned back in his arms and smiled up at him. How beautiful you are, he thought. At sixty, she was still an attractive woman. Her figure was remarkably the same as it had been twenty years ago. If it weren't for the fluff of silver hair showing from under her wool hat, she could have been mistaken for a much younger woman.

Her face had aged gracefully. The lines in her skin that had come with age had done little to mar the beauty that had always been there. Her large brown eyes now looked out under gray brows, but they still sparkled with the same intensity.

They did a turn to the left. He felt her body begin to pull away in the opposite direction. Instinctively he let her move away to give her room to regain her balance. But she wasn't falling, she was turning. He still held her with one hand. In perfect step with the music, she turned once, then twice, then spun back against him. They were in a flow of movement now that took them first to the right, then to the left. Out of the corner of his eye he saw one couple leave the ice to watch them from the side. Another couple left, then another. Now they were skating alone; the whole rink was theirs. Their turns widened, and they could glide in long, sweeping arcs. They had skated together hundreds of times before, but now, with the rink empty and an audience watching, they were outdoing themselves.

The waltz was ending. They went into another wide, sweeping turn. Helen spun out in front of him. She pirouetted under his arm, and then, with a spray of ice from under their skates, they came to a perfect stop. The crowd along the edge of the rink applauded enthusiastically. They took a little bow and skated off.

As they came to the side, the crowd opened up and let them through. It felt wonderful. People were smiling and still applauding. He helped Helen over to the wooden bleachers where they sat down to catch their breath.

"You looked like a young Dorothy Hamill out there," he said as he leaned back against the bleacher step.

"Surprised you, didn't I," she said.

"Yeah, I didn't know you could still do those fancy turns."

"Oh, I knew I could," she said, her brown eyes sparkling. "I was just waiting for an audience."

"Show-off."

"Me?"

"Yeah, you."

"I didn't see you holding back out there, Mr. Dick Button."

"Dick Button? There's no comparison."

"I suppose you've got more Olympic medals."

"No," he said, taking off his woolen cap, "more hair."

She looked at him out of the corner of her eye. He had learned over the years that the look meant he wasn't being very funny. Before he could say anything more, her hand shot out and she mussed up his hair.

"Now that we've given our evening performance, can we go home?"

He looked out on the rink. It was a little less crowded than before.

"I thought we'd rest up for a while and then go back out."

She reached down and massaged her legs around the knees.

"I really can't. My legs and arms are stiffening up."

"That's just from the skating. We haven't been in a while."

She looked up at him, the pain showing in her face.

"I don't think so. We'd better go home."

He found out later that she had experienced the stiffness off and on for weeks but hadn't told him. It was the last time she would ever skate. Within a month she was barely able to walk.

He opened his eyes. There were footsteps outside in the hall. A glance at his watch told him he had fallen asleep for over an hour. The sports magazine was lying in his lap. He put it aside as the key turned in the lock. It would be Frank coming to take him down to lunch.

The door opened. Frank came into the room. Tompkins was surprised to see him carrying two suitcases, which he put on the bed. Tompkins turned. Cutrone was standing in the doorway.

"You're going on a little trip tonight, so we brought you some clothes. Open the suitcases."

He got up and went over to the bed. The first suitcase opened with a click. Inside were neatly folded clothes. They were summer clothes: shorts, polo shirts, two bathing suits, summer slacks, socks, underwear. He looked at Cutrone, who was leaning against the doorway, his arms folded across his chest.

"Open the other one."

The second suitcase contained a blazer, more shorts, shirts, sandals, and a V-neck sweater. He was going to see Helen. It had to be; she was in a warm climate. He turned to Cutrone.

"So at last you're letting me go."

Cutrone lit a cigarette.

"No, we're not letting you go. We're taking you to your wife."

"I thought my end of the bargain was over. I made the plates to your satisfaction, you've kept me here while you printed more money than you originally said. What more do you want?"

"We want you available."

"For what?"

"We're going to continue to print more money."

"How much?"

"That's none of your concern. Our client needs much more than we planned, so we need you available should anything break down. However, we're not going to hold you here any longer. You'll be with your wife."

"So we're still prisoners."

"For a while, yes."

Of course they still needed him. God knows how much money Moscow had ordered this Cutrone to print. Tompkins wouldn't ask any more questions; it might jeopardize what was being given him.

"So," Cutrone continued, "you should be happy. You're going to see Helen."

"When do I leave?" he said, taking a shirt from the suitcase.

"Tonight. We want you to try on all these clothes before then. If anything doesn't fit, Frank will replace it this afternoon. You'll leave right after dinner."

"When will I see Helen?"

"Before midnight."

Cutrone was about to leave the room, but he turned back.

"You did excellent work for us. That's why you're going. We could have held you here until we finished the printing."

Tompkins nodded.

"I realize that."

"Then enjoy it. You'll be with Helen in a warm climate with everything you could possibly want. You should be happy."

It seemed as if Cutrone wanted this reunion with Helen to justify the four months he had held them prisoner. But how do you justify taking away four months of someone's freedom and then rewarding them with what they should have had all along? Oddly enough, the man did have a heart. He had seen glimpses of concern for him as another human being, but it was clear that duty would override that concern when necessary. Maybe the man was just in the wrong business.

He looked away from him and said, "Maybe it's hard being happy when you haven't been for so long."

Cutrone came over and reached into one of the suitcases.

Underneath some clothing was an envelope. He took it out and held it in front of him.

"This is the three hundred thousand dollars we promised you when you started the work. You'll be free to buy anything with it when you get to where you're going."

Tompkins took the envelope.

"Anything?"

"Yes, anything," Cutrone replied.

Tompkins looked away and said, "Anything but freedom."

That evening, Frank and Sal came to his room. They found him sitting on the bed dressed in white slacks and a print shirt under a blue blazer. His bags were beside him.

"Well," Sal said as he came into the room, "you look like a new man. Ready to go?"

Tompkins got up off the bed and said, "I've been ready for four months!"

"You're gonna love it where you're going. You'll relax, be with your wife, and have plenty of money. It's going to be okay."

He reached into his back pocket and took out two rolled-up sports magazines.

"Here's something for you to read on the plane."

"Airplane?" Tompkins asked. He couldn't imagine them putting him on a commercial flight.

"Oh, yeah, my friend, this is no car ride. You're going a long way."

Sal picked up a suitcase and Frank took the other. As they left the room, he stopped to look back for a moment. The room had been a prison cell for over four months. He had been alone and forced to go through a terrible ordeal, but he had made it. Even at this stage of his life, when he thought all the fight would have left him, he had overcome fear and survived. He was proud of himself for that.

They took him down in the elevator to the first floor. The door opened, and they stepped out into the warehouse, which was dark except for the light coming from one small lamp. Next to it were a pair of dark glasses, surgical gauze, and tape. A white cane was leaning against the wall.

Sal said, "We're going to have to turn you into a blind man

for the trip. At least until we have you on the plane. Sorry, but it has to be done."

Tompkins took off his glasses and put them in his breast pocket.

Frank put the gauze over each eye, taped it, then put dark glasses on him. He felt the cane being put into his hand, and Sal took his arm. Then the door opened and the cool night air came into the room. It felt good. It was the first fresh air he had breathed in months.

They guided him down the steps of the building and into the backseat of a car. Sal sat beside him while Frank drove.

This was the time to stay alert. For months he had tried to find out where they were holding him. He didn't know how the information could be of use to him, but ever since he had become a prisoner, he'd been tormented by not knowing where he was. Also, they had gone to great lengths to conceal his location. Blackened windows, mailing labels removed from magazines, carefully edited conversations. It had become a challenge, a game to catch them at a mistake. So far they hadn't made any.

He listened for sounds. Like a blind man, his ears were replacing his eyes. It was about six o'clock, so unfortunately everything was quiet. He heard a bus, a siren, and music from a portable radio in the street. The car stopped for traffic lights every five or six blocks, but then they went up a ramp and were on a highway. There was the smell of water, maybe a river. They stopped for a toll booth. He heard the fare register in the machine and the car start up again. It picked up speed; they were on a major highway now. There were large trucks and cars passing them. After about twenty minutes they came down another ramp and slowed down. The car made some turns through side streets. A prop plane passed low overhead, probably landing. He didn't hear any jets. It must be a small airport. The car stopped.

It wasn't until Sal spoke that he realized no one had said a word since they'd left the printing plant.

"We're here. This is where we part company, Bob. Let me just say that I wish we could've met under different circumstances. I know Tony feels the same way."

"Don't we all," Tompkins said quietly.

Sal said nothing for a moment. Tompkins could feel him wanting to say something where he could relate to him as a man instead of a prisoner, but he wasn't able to.

Finally he said, "The plane is about a hundred feet away. We'll guide you over to it. Keep the cane in front of you and move along quickly. When we reach the plane, you'll go up some metal steps. A man inside will help you up. His name is Tom."

They got out of the car and he heard the low whine of a small jet. The wind blew across his face as he walked between Sal and Frank. He kept the cane ahead of him. It struck a metal step. He felt a hand directly above him take his left arm and guide him up the steps. Once inside the plane, a second person helped him to his seat.

He felt his glasses being removed and fingers gently pulling off the tape over his eyes. Then the gauze was taken off. He blinked his eyes for a minute, then looked up. There was a man standing over him, and another in the seat across the narrow aisle. The one standing over him was young, maybe twenty-three or so. He was dressed in a turtleneck sweater, jeans, and sneakers.

"I'm Tom," he said in a friendly voice, "and this is Rudy." Rudy was heavyset, thirtyish, with dark hair, dark glasses, and a paunchy middle.

Tompkins turned away and started to lift the plastic shade over the window.

"Please don't touch the shade, Mr. Tompkins," Tom said as he reached over the seat to grab his arm. "It's to stay down the entire flight."

"Where are we going?" Tompkins asked, directing his question at Tom, who seemed to be the friendlier of the two.

"I can't tell you that either, except we're taking you to your wife. The flight will be about three and a half hours."

"I guess if I don't know where I'm coming from, there's no point in knowing where I'm going, either," he said cynically.

"You'll know when it's time for you to know," Rudy answered as he took a paperback from the seat pocket in front of him.

Tom looked disapprovingly at him, then turned to Tompkins.

"Is there anything I can get you to drink after we take off? We've got a full stock of liquor up front."

Tompkins realized that this young man was probably a Russian agent, so he behaved cautiously. At the same time his kindness deserved some sort of acknowledgment.

"Thank you but I'm fine. I appreciate the offer."

"That's okay," he replied. "Listen, I have to go up front now. I'm the copilot. Rudy will be here with you. If there's anything you need, let him know."

He patted Tompkins on the shoulder, then went through a door to the cockpit.

Rudy glanced over at him, then returned to his book. Tompkins looked around the interior of the plane. It was a ten-seater, probably a Learjet. There was thick carpeting on the floor. The bucket seats were done in gray suede. It looked like one of those company Learjets he had seen pictures of.

He felt the plane begin to taxi out to the main runway. Without stopping, it turned and suddenly picked up speed. He had never been in a jet this small before, and was surprised how fast it accelerated during takeoff. It was only a few seconds before he felt the wheels come up and the plane shoot into the air.

He took the sports magazine Sal had given him out of his coat pocket and began to read. Within minutes he started to doze. The magazine fell from his hands to the floor and he was asleep.

Two and a half hours later, the plane slowed to begin its descent. The change in the sound of the engine woke him out of a sound sleep. He looked across at Rudy, who was sipping a drink and still reading his book. Noticing that he was awake, he said, "We're just about there. Make sure your seat belt is on."

The belt was at his side. He must have taken it off after the plane was in the air. He clicked it shut.

The plane descended quickly, and he felt the wheels squeal against the runway. With a roar, the engines reversed and his weight shifted in the seat in response to the tremendous braking power of the plane. Slowly the pressure against his body was released as the jet braked onto the service runway. In a few minutes it came to a complete stop.

Rudy got out of his seat and sat down next to him. He reached into his pocket and took out gauze and a roll of tape.

"This has got to go back on again," he said. "We're going to have to take you through the terminal building out to a car in the parking lot. Tom and I will be on either side of you all the way. Just act like you did when you got on the plane. Keep the cane out in front of you and use it to feel your way. Got that?"

"Yes, I've got it."

"Good, now let me get this on you."

Everything was dark again. Rudy helped him to a standing position, then he felt somebody take his other arm.

"It's me, Mr. Tompkins," Tom said. "Careful now, the door is on your left just ahead of you."

He felt the warm night air coming into the plane. It had a salty taste to it. They must be near the water. Slowly he came down the steps and onto the tarmac, guided by the two KGB agents. They moved beside him and walked briskly to the terminal.

Inside, he sensed that the building was relatively quiet. They had picked a perfect time to bring him in.

He heard a new voice. Somebody was meeting them. Although he listened hard, he couldn't hear what was being said. After a few minutes they started walking again. Tom spoke.

"We're coming out of the building now and into the parking lot. Just another minute or so and we'll be in the car. Keep the cane out ahead of you."

He heard electric doors open ahead of him, and they walked through. To his surprise he felt hard-packed ground and small stones under his feet. It had taken very little time to walk through the terminal.

"The car is just ahead, a few more feet," Tom said.

They stopped. He heard the door open and he was helped inside. Both front doors shut and the car started. He felt Tom beside him; Rudy and the new man were in the front. As the car turned onto a paved road, the new man spoke.

"That went off perfect. How did it go on the other end?"

"No problem," Rudy answered. "A blind man got on a private plane."

"Good. We were a little concerned."

"You worry too much, Bruce."

Tompkins felt the car climbing up one hill after another. It was winding around curves, which caused him to sway from side to side between the two men. He was trying to draw a mental picture of the terrain, based on the movement of the car. It must be an island. He had smelled the salt water, and initially the car had traveled over a flat stretch of land. Then it had climbed and now it was descending. Once he had seen slides of Bill and Elaine's vacation trip to Guadeloupe. The island was flat around the beach perimeter, but like most of the Caribbean islands, it was mountainous in the center. The flight time had been a little over three hours. It had to be one of the islands.

They drove for about fifteen minutes, then the car slowed down.

"Well, here we are," Tom said as they turned off the road. Tompkins felt the car brake as it slowly went down a steep incline. It went another hundred feet or so and then stopped.

He felt his heart begin to race. Helen was here. He would see her in another few minutes. It was as if he hadn't seen her in years. The past four months had been so frightening that it seemed much longer.

The others got out of the car, and Tompkins felt Tom's hand reach back to help him. He slid across the seat and got out.

"We can take off his blindfold now," the man called Bruce said.

Tom took off the dark glasses, the tape, and the gauze. Tompkins reached into his pocket for his glasses. When he put them on, he saw that he was standing in a driveway overlooking a large body of water. The moon was shining brightly, illuminating a small complex of three stucco buildings with tile roofs. Between them and a sandy stretch of beach were neatly kept grounds with lights along the walks. A cool breeze was blowing across the water.

Tom took the bags out of the trunk, and they walked toward the building closest to the water. There were lights on inside. They came around the front and went up to the door. Bruce opened it and they went inside. Tom put the bags down in a spacious living room.

"Your wife is over in the next house. We'll bring her here in a few minutes," Bruce said. "But let me introduce myself. I'm

Bruce Rizzo, and I'm in charge of the group here. You've already met Rudy Pollack and Tom Travis. All together there are nine of us here to make sure you don't try to escape and swim back to New York."

He gestured for him to sit down on the sofa. Rudy produced a crudely drawn map of the compound and the surrounding property.

"This is where we are now, in this building. The beach is in front of us. Along both sides of the property is a ten-foot chain-link fence that runs around to a gate in the front. The gate is manned by one of our men twenty-four hours a day. I'm telling you this for your own safety. Don't try to go outside those boundaries.

"Your wife knows our daily routine. She'll explain it to you. It's leisurely and can be very enjoyable if you follow a few simple rules. Any questions?"

"Yes. How long are we going to be here?"

"That depends," he said hesitantly. "It's up to Tony Cutrone."

"I figured that," he said. "But you must have some idea how long you and your men are expected to be here."

"We'll be here until enough money has been printed to satisfy our client. I would say a month or so."

"And then?" he asked.

"Then we'll leave this place and it'll be yours. But don't worry about that now. Just enjoy it."

He got up to leave.

"The reason you're here is strictly insurance against the plates breaking and needing repair. I think the hardest part of all this is over for you."

He hoped that was true, but he doubted it.

When Helen walked through the door, he couldn't believe it was her. Her skin was a golden brown and was accentuated by her white shorts and sleeveless shirt. Her hair was shorter than usual, and it made her look younger. She looked wonderful.

They stood motionlessly looking at each other from across the room, neither of them knowing what to say. It seemed that for months he had been dreaming of this moment, but now the words just wouldn't come. Then she came to him. The four or five steps she took amazed him. She was hardly limping, and her arms moved freely as they came around his neck and drew him close to her.

"Thank God you're here," she whispered. "I didn't think I would ever see you again."

"I wasn't sure, either," he said.

"I love you," she whispered.

"I love you too," he answered softly.

She began to cry. He took out his handkerchief and wiped her eyes.

"I know," she said sobbing, "but it was so long. They gave me so many false hopes that I would see you. I'd start counting the days and then the day would come, only to find you not here. Then the counting would start all over again."

"They did the same to me," he said, holding her close. "It would have been better if they had said from the beginning that it would be four months."

She looked up at him, the tears rolling down her cheeks. "Who are they? What do they want?"

He took her hand and led her over to the sofa. They sat close to each other, still holding hands.

"I think they're Mafia," he said slowly. This was probably the first time he had lied to her in over forty years, but he couldn't tell her the truth. It would be too much for her to bear.

"Mafia!" she said. "What would the Mafia want from us?"

"From me," he answered, looking into her eyes. "They wanted me to make plates for them."

"What kind of plates?" she said haltingly, as if she were afraid of the answer.

"Counterfeit plates." He spat out the words quickly, as if he hoped she wouldn't hear them.

"Oh, no," she said with a sigh. "I knew it had to be that. I tried to tell myself that it might be something else, but in the end I knew that's what it would be."

"I had no choice, Helen, you know that."

"I know." She turned away. "You didn't have a choice because of me."

He drew her back to him and said softly, "You mustn't blame yourself for anything I did. There was no resisting them.

They would have killed me if I hadn't done what they wanted."

She shook her head.

"No, they wouldn't have. You're the only who could *do* what they wanted. You had to do it because of me. They threatened to kill me, didn't they?"

"It doesn't matter now," he said, lifting her chin with his hand. "Helen, they're nothing but small-time counterfeiters. They said they were working for some client. The money is probably going to be used to finance some drug trafficking and God knows what else."

He looked around the room and wondered if the Russians had bugged it or not. With all the security precautions they had taken so far, he wouldn't be surprised if they had microphones everywhere. He would have to be careful what he said just in case.

"Besides," he went on, "they're just going to get caught, anyway. The paper they were using was pure crap, and their printing equipment was straight out of the dark ages. The first bank teller that gets his hands on that money will know it's phony."

"You really think they're Mafia," she said.

"I know they are. And if they're not, they're working for them."

"You're probably right. Who else could afford all this?"

She tried to smile, but he could see the fear in her eyes. It was fear that had been stirring inside her for months and could no longer be contained. She put her arms around him and he could feel her shaking. He held her close.

"What's going to happen to us?" she said, sobbing.

"Nothing," he whispered, "nothing."

"I'm afraid that now that they don't need you anymore, they'll kill us."

"You're wrong. They still need me."

"Why?"

"To repair the plates if anything goes wrong. They're still printing money."

"How much longer will they be printing?"

"Weeks, maybe months. But by then they'll get caught and we'll be free."

"I'm so afraid."

"I know," he said, "but as long as they still need me, everything will be all right." He smiled at her. "Now let me get a look at you." She got up and stood facing him, a shy smile on her face.

"Your tan looks terrific," he said. "You look like a sophisticated lady who's just returned from Palm Springs."

"Well, thank you, sir," she said. "But that's not the best part. Look at this."

She held her arms straight out. Then, with quick movements, she bent her elbows and touched her hands to her head.

"And how about this," she said proudly.

With her feet together she raised both arms over her head and bent forward to touch her toes. She didn't reach the floor, but she got a good three quarters of the way down.

"Hey, take it easy," he said. "Don't overdo it. You'll hurt yourself."

"Nonsense," she said, taking both his hands and holding them in hers. "I do this every day, along with a whole bunch of other exercises. Did you meet Tom? He's the physical therapist and he's done wonders for me."

"He was the copilot on the plane. Quite a versatile guy."

"He's the nicest of them all," she said. "He planned all the exercises and gives me my medication."

"Medication? What kind of medication?"

"I don't really know. All he would say was that it was a form of cortisone. I get two injections every day."

"I never heard of anything like that," he said. "The doctors in Boston didn't even mention it."

"Oh, yes, they did, dear. Don't you remember they said that the Russians were working on something using cortisone?"

He tried not to react. Instead, he got up and went over to her. He took both her hands and drew her close to him. How he loved her. If being away for four months had told him anything, it was that he loved this woman more than life itself. Other women would have cracked months ago, but her love was strong enough to bear it. And so was his. Without her letters he never would have made it. But now she needed hope. She needed encouragement that they would be free, even if it was false hope.

He held her close and, thinking of the microphone that might be in the room, whispered, "There's nothing to worry about now that we're together and they still need me. Besides, we're going to walk away from this place free. A lot of people have to be looking for us by now. They'll find us sooner or later. We're going to get out of here, Helen, I promise you that."

Later they lay next to each other in bed. It was good just to be close to her again. He held her hand. Ever since she had gotten the arthritis, they hadn't enjoyed sex. It was too painful for her. They contented themselves with just being near and holding each other.

She turned toward him and squeezed his hand.

"There's one exercise that I haven't shown you yet," she whispered.

"What's that?"

"Come here and I'll show you."

In the moments that followed, all the pain and anxiety that was within them was replaced by love and affection. Their union produced a strength that would carry them through the pain and suffering that they both knew was ahead.

8

Omaha, March 3, 1991 (AP)—

TODAY THE FIRST FEDERAL BANK OF OMAHA REPORTED THE
HIGHEST VOLUME OF CURRENCY IN THEIR VAULTS SINCE
1946. BANK PRESIDENT HAROLD E. BURNS SAID HE PLANNED
TO NOTIFY THE FEDERAL RESERVE IN WASHINGTON OF WHAT
HE SAID WAS "A DRAMATIC INCREASE IN BANK CASH
DEPOSITS OVER THE LAST THREE MONTHS."

Washington, March 3, 1991 (UPI)—

THE FEDERAL RESERVE BEGAN CAREFULLY MONITORING M1-A
AS IT CONTINUED TO FALL FOR THE FIFTH WEEK IN A ROW.
WHEN QUESTIONED AS TO THE REASON FOR THE DECLINE,
SECRETARY OF THE TREASURY DILLON AVOIDED COMMENT.

New York
March 3, 1991

HENRY DAVIDSON STOOD in his office in New York's Pan Am
Building looking down on Park Avenue, fifty floors below. He
sipped coffee from a paper cup and watched the snarled traffic
in front of the Waldorf. This morning's *Times* had run an article
saying that the Soviet Foreign Minister, Andrei Sarandov, was
meeting with Secretary of State Fred Patterson in the hotel. As
usual, the New York Police Department wasn't taking any
chances with security. There was a small army of blue on either
side of the avenue.

He was glad he wasn't concerned with security anymore.
When he joined the Secret Service twenty years ago, his first

assignment was the presidential detail. The job had been impossible. With President Johnson wanting to shake every hand thrust at him, there was the constant worry of the President being shot or, worse yet, being shot himself. At twenty-six he'd been able to handle it, but at forty-six he doubted if he could. Now he had all he could do to track down counterfeiters for the Treasury Department. With just twenty men to cover the eastern half of the country, it was often a ten-hour-a-day job.

He turned and looked at his cluttered desk. Right now he had three assignments going at the same time. Two of them involved the counterfeiting of bank notes, which over the last five or six years had become a bigger problem than counterfeit currency. The notes were easier to duplicate and were actually more profitable to pass. The Mafia had learned quickly and were now heavily into it.

The third case involved a counterfeit stamp operation that they were close to shutting down in New Jersey. A small gang was printing sheets of twenty-two cent stamps and selling them to small businessmen. With the high cost of mailing and the poor service from the Postal Service, he doubted that the businessmen even considered it unethical.

He sat down and moved the files aside. Before he started the day, he liked to finish reading the paper he never got through on the train. The twenty-five-minute ride from his suburban Westchester home was never time enough. There were some articles in the business section that he wanted to look through. It seemed that Washington was concerned with the recent surge of cash flowing into banks. The article pointed out the dangers to the economy. Apparently the stock market was concerned, too; it had dropped another ten points the previous day. He was about to call his broker when the phone buzzed. It was his secretary.

"Washington's on the line, Dave."

Eileen called him Dave, as did the rest of the staff. He disliked formality in the office. It would have meant his being called Mr. Davidson or, worse yet, Henry, which he despised.

"Which bureaucrat is making calls this early?" he said as he tore one of the articles out of the paper.

"A high-level one," she answered. "It's John Cristaldi."

"Cristaldi? He hasn't called in two weeks. Probably wants tickets to another Ranger game."

"I don't think so. He sounds serious."

"Okay, put him on."

The telephone clicked, and she put the Undersecretary for Monetary Affairs through. Davidson automatically held the receiver away from his ear in anticipation of Cristaldi's loud voice.

"Dave," he shouted. "How's things in the big city?"

"Hectic as usual. Too many people in too little space."

"Well, here's your chance to get out of there for a day. We need you in Washington for a meeting tomorrow. Nine A.M. sharp. Treasury Building. Can you make it?"

Davidson looked at his calendar. Nothing was penciled in for tomorrow.

"I suppose so. What's up?"

"It's high-level. Has to do with some recent bank audits. I don't want to go into it on the phone, but let's say that it's important enough for Patterson and Nietsche to be there."

Davidson turned and looked down at the scene in front of the Waldorf.

"I thought Patterson was here in New York."

"He is," Cristaldi answered, "but he'll be returning here tomorrow, specially for this morning."

"That does sound important."

"It is."

"What do I need to bring?"

"Bring Fuller, he may be helpful."

"Okay, we'll be there. Can you tell me anything more?"

"Nothing. See you tomorrow."

He hung up.

Davidson got up and walked over to the window again. There were two limousines parked in front of the Waldorf now. One had American flags on the front fenders; the other was unmarked. The two men were already meeting inside the hotel. He wondered what was being said, but as he looked down on the two cars, somehow he knew it would have an effect on the following day's meeting.

He picked up the phone and asked Eileen to send Hal Fuller in.

Hal had been working with him for five years now as a special assistant. At twenty-six he was the youngest man in Davidson's group, but probably one of the most brilliant. After attending Rensselaer Polytechnic Institute, he had worked on photoengraving for two years, then had gone on to Switzerland to study papermaking and printing. Returning to the States, he trained in Maryland and became a Treasury agent assigned to Davidson's group.

His knowledge of engraving and paper was invaluable. At least two counterfeiting operations had been broken recently because of his knowledge of counterfeiting techniques. What was even more valuable, though, was his enthusiasm. Where he would tend to be bored with the routine, Hal was eager and enthused with each new assignment. Having him at his side was like a shot of adrenaline. At this stage of his career he needed that.

Fuller came into the office and sat down in the chair on the other side of his desk. When he was seated was the only time he got to speak with him at eye level. Standing, Davidson towered over him. They were referred to around the office as Mutt and Jeff. Davidson, a heavyset man standing at six-foot-three, was an overweight two hundred and thirty pounds. His features were flabby. The full cheeks and pinched nose made him feel like his face was an overblown balloon. Friends called it friendly-looking; he called it flab. Hal Fuller, on the other hand, was a wiry five-foot-six and was lucky if he weighed one hundred and fifty soaking wet. But his looks were deceptive. The boyish face and the sandy hair give him an innocent-little-boy look. That had cost Davidson when they'd first met. Hal had taken a good portion of his lunch money over the first two weeks by beating him at arm wrestling. Everybody at Kelly's Bar on Third Avenue now knew how strong he was.

He put a manila envelope on the desk and opened it.

"How ya doin', Dave?"

That was his opening line every morning. Davidson knew he really didn't care how he was doing. He didn't care that the damn 8:14 train had come at 8:45, and he'd stood all the way; or that three of his five kids were home sick with colds and Elaine was climbing the walls. It was "How ya doin', Dave?" every morning, and then how he was going to crack every counterfeiting operation in the country. He wished he were twenty-six again and had all that energy. On second thought, maybe he didn't.

"Dave, I've got film on two more businessmen going into that printing plant in Newark to pick up counterfeit stamps. That makes seven. All we have to do now is show them the film and they'll finger the guys inside in a minute. We should be able to raid the place in a few days."

"It's probably going to have to wait, Hal," Davidson said, lighting his pipe.

"Wait? We've got to go while this is hot. If they get wind that we're on to them, they'll cover up like clams."

"It'll have to wait. Cristaldi called a while ago and we have a heavy meeting in Washington tomorrow. That means something bigger than counterfeit stamps is brewing."

He could see Fuller's eyes light up as he closed his folder.

"What kind of heavy meeting?" he said excitedly.

"I don't know yet," Davidson said, puffing on his pipe, "but it sounds interesting. Maybe it's a coincidence, but today we've got the Secretary of State a few blocks away meeting with the Soviet Foreign Minister and making a special effort to be at this meeting tomorrow. We've also got Eric Nietsche, the President's economic adviser there. So far that equals Russians and money, right? Then we've got me and a special request for you to attend. That means counterfeit money. How it all fits together, or if it fits together at all, will be interesting."

Fuller laughed.

"Hey, look who's doing all the speculating now. I thought I was the one who blew these things all out of proportion."

Davidson turned his chair and looked out on Park Avenue.

"I know, Hal, but I've got a funny feeling about this one."

At nine A.M. the next morning, Davidson and Fuller walked into the main conference room of the Treasury Building. They were the last to arrive. Davidson was surprised to see that in addition to the people Cristaldi mentioned the previous day, two members of the Senate Banking Committee and his boss, Secretary of the Treasury Allen Dillon, were there. He thought it odd that Dillon hadn't called him prior to a meeting of this level.

Nothing had started yet, and everyone was having coffee and Danish, which was being served by two aides. Cristaldi came over to greet them.

"Good morning, Dave, Hal. Sorry to have called you on such short notice, but it was absolutely necessary."

Davidson looked around the room.

"I'm sure it was. You've got an impressive group here, John."

Cristaldi was about to answer when the Secretary of State, Fred Patterson, moved to the head of the table. He tapped his saucer with a spoon. The room became quiet.

"Gentlemen, I'd like to bring the meeting to order. Please find a seat at the table and let's get started. We've got a lot of items on the agenda."

Davidson and Fuller sat next to each other at the far end of the table. Their superior, Secretary of the Treasury Dillon, nodded to them in recognition.

Patterson opened a folder, took a page of notes from it, and placed it in front of him. Davidson noticed the meticulous manner in which he arranged the sheets of paper on the table. Everything was in perfect order, as was everything else about the distinguished Secretary of State. His gray hair was combed with every strand in place, framing a perfectly sculptured, handsome face. His blue-striped suit looked like it had come directly from the tailor to this meeting. Davidson felt sloppy.

Patterson continued.

"We've gotten you all together this morning because of two developments that have occurred within the last five days. Developments that could seriously endanger the economy of the country. You're each here because of your expertise in the areas involved, so please feel free to ask any questions you may have as we go along."

Cristaldi put some charts on the easel next to him.

"We're dealing with two serious problems. The first came to light as a result of recent bank audits that the Treasury Department undertook, the second from confidential reports that the Securities and Exchange Commission handed us two days ago.

"It seems that we again have come to a situation similar to what the economy experienced in 1976, when foreign currency investments reached dangerous proportions. If you remember, they totaled $174.3 billion. Most of it turned out to be OPEC oil dollars that were pouring into the country.

"Our situation now is much worse. The SEC reports that during the last three months we've had a dramatic—and, gentlemen, I emphasize the word *dramatic*—increase in foreign currency investment. Figures show an increase of over nine billion dollars in the last seventy days, and it's now continuing at an even higher rate. John and Treasury Secretary Dillon will take you through charts that break down where the currency is being invested."

Davidson looked around the table. From the reactions he saw, it seemed everyone was equally surprised by what the Secretary of State was saying, except Dillon. He'd probably received the report from the SEC and had judged it important enough to pass up to the highest level.

Patterson continued.

"The money came out of a numbered Swiss account and was invested by just two Swiss holding companies. We, of course, inquired as to who the investors are and have received a polite refusal to reveal their identities. As you know, Swiss law doesn't require banks or holding companies to reveal the identities of their depositors.

"What is alarming is the fact that a substantial amount of this money is in highly volatile short-term deposits payable in thirty days. This puts these investors in a very liquid position, and if it continues at this rate, it will become an extremely dangerous situation."

He took a chart and put it up on the easel.

"As I said, John will break this down for you, but you can see that by the end of the month this Swiss money will total over $180 billion. We know right now that two New York banks are receiving overnight deposits in excess of a billion dollars.

"In 1976, we considered the OPEC situation dangerous, but if this influx continues, it will put the economy in an even more unstable position. Should these short-term notes be called all at once in sums of this size, the dollar would plummet on the international market, causing a collapse of the economy in a matter of days."

Patterson paused for a moment to let the information sink in. He looked around the table for reactions or questions. Davidson had one.

"Mr. Secretary, this may seem naïve, but the obvious questions are: Do we know who these banks are? Who is taking in all this foreign money and can they be stopped?"

Patterson gestured to the younger man beside him.

"Rather than answer that myself, let me defer to Senator Hartley."

Hartley looked over his bifocal glasses and said, "Yes, we do know who they are, Mr. Davidson. They're the same banks that held billions of OPEC money in the seventies . . . the same banks that ran up a total of $125 billion of oil money in 1976. Can we stop them? No, not legally. Why do they do it? For money, for commissions . . ." He hesitated, then added, "For greed."

"But surely, Senator, the government can put pressure on these banks if it's in the interest of national security," Davidson said.

Hartley took a sheet of paper from a folder and held it up.

"Let me read some figures to you, Mr. Davidson, of what the Big Six banks in this country allowed to happen in the past without our being able to stop them. These are just a few. In 1974, foreign assets held by them totaled over $150 billion. By 1976, it had gone over $200 billion. In a short period of two years, Arab investments went from $518 million in portfolio stock holdings to $3.8 billion, a 750 percent increase. They bought a brokerage house and a major U.S. aluminum company without our being able to do anything about it. We're talking about international finance in the private sector that is so strong, even we can't control it."

"So, Senator, it's a case of big banking being able to control government." Davidson knew this was a sore point with most of the Banking Committee, and Hartley was no exception.

"You're right, Davidson," Hartley replied. "They feel that they know what's better for the country than we do. Until these figures escalate even higher, any protest we make will simply be met with the feeling that we're overreacting. I can assure you that they'll say we got out of the Arab situation unscathed, and that this is no problem, either. They'll just say the Swiss are representing a client who is making prudent investments."

"All right," Davidson said, "if we can't pressure the banks, isn't there some way we can put pressure on the Swiss to find out who the investors are?"

Nietsche answered. "We've already done that, I'm afraid. Their answer, of course, was simply that they don't have to disclose their clients. When we tried to get in touch with them, they reluctantly told us that if they revealed the client's identity, he would immediately withdraw all the funds out of the country. That's just what Secretary Patterson explained can't happen. Already the figures are high enough to cause serious repercussions to the economy. All we can do right now is try to find out who they are."

Patterson turned to John Phelps, Director of the CIA.

"John, why don't you tell us what's been done so far from your end."

Phelps was a mild-mannered ex–Rand Corporation executive who had been appointed by President Turner eight months ago. Although new in the job, he already had proven himself as a tough director.

"Our people in Switzerland have been working on it for over three weeks now, and so far have come up dry. As you may know, Swiss banking is a very tight group. Even though the banks interact every day, they're very discreet about maintaining the anonymity of their clients. As a result, it's been tough to learn anything. In the past few days we've turned our attention outside of Switzerland to determine who could afford to direct massive amounts of currency into this country. We've gone to the World Bank for assistance, as well as to the Bank for International Settlements. So far they haven't been much help. Now we're starting to talk to people inside countries we might suspect for one reason or another. Certain Middle East countries, Libya, African countries, etc."

Patterson took the chart down from the easel and turned to his notes.

"The question of who could afford it isn't as important as what Secretary Dillon has learned in the past few days. This, I'm afraid, is a very serious situation and potentially a real threat to our economy."

Everyone turned to Treasury Secretary Dillon, who was putting on his bifocals to read a new chart that Cristaldi was putting on the easel. The chart wasn't even in place when he dropped a bombshell.

"Gentlemen," he began, "before I even begin to explain this chart, let me simply say that we are in the midst of the most serious financial crisis this country has ever faced. The influx of investments the Secretary referred to is bad enough, but we have reason to believe the investments have been made with counterfeit money."

The group was stunned. No one moved or spoke. Counterfeit money had been found in the system before, but never on a scale this large. There wasn't a sound as Dillon continued. His voice seemed louder in the stillness of the room.

"As of the last three months, we've got more currency in circulation than the Bureau of Engraving has printed. Bank-vault currency, that's customer money being held in bank vaults around the country, has grown to dramatic proportions. In the last three weeks alone it's grown over three billion dollars. During that same period of time, the Bureau of Engraving has printed only a little over five hundred million dollars. That leads me to one simple conclusion: Somebody else is printing money besides us. Counterfeit money."

He paused to see if there were any questions and found everyone simply staring at him, in a total state of disbelief.

He continued. "The nation's fourteen thousand banks were audited last month by computer. Vault currency on hand: Seventy-three billion. I won't bother to break down the denominations because the total figure is what we're interested in. Seventy-three billion is impossible when the Bureau of Engraving figures only show forty-two billion in circulation.

"Now that means an awful lot of people are suddenly coming up with cash to put in the bank. In fact, more cash than is in circulation. One theory is that it comes from the so-called underground economy. That's unreported income from people like waiters, small cash businesses, etc. Money that isn't reported to the IRS. It's said to run into the billions. Some of that could have surfaced, but it's unlikely. We're talking about large quantities of money. Why would anybody in the underground economy take money he's avoided paying taxes on and bring it out into the open unless interest rates were very high? No, the money is counterfeit. It has to be. And the hell of it, gentlemen, is that it's *perfect* counterfeit. So perfect that if it wasn't for our figures not jiving, we never would have found it."

Everyone directed their attention to Davidson and Fuller. Davidson's mind was spinning, trying to absorb all the information. Dillon hadn't even hinted beforehand that this situation existed. He hadn't heard of any counterfeiting on this scale. They were talking about billions of dollars. You don't put that much counterfeit into circulation without getting caught. Bogus bills were never perfect. There's no way bank tellers and people who handle money every day aren't going to detect them when they're passed in sufficient quantity. The money couldn't be counterfeit.

"Do we know for sure that the money is counterfeit? Has any counterfeit actually been found?" he finally asked.

Dillon answered quickly. He knew the same question was in other people's minds.

"No, that's the hell of it. We haven't found a single one yet."

"Then how can you be sure that they're counterfeit?"

"Because of this audit. It's not totally accurate by any means, but we're talking about billions of dollars over the Bureau's figures. It's got to be counterfeit. There's no other answer."

Davidson was surprised to hear Fuller ask the next question.

"Who's been analyzing the bills, Mr. Secretary?"

"Our Dallas office. We've taken samples from over three hundred banks and didn't find anything."

Fuller went on to say what Davidson had been thinking.

"Gentlemen, you realize that it is next to impossible to print the quantities you're suggesting without being detected. Even if you were able to get perfect plates, which is highly unlikely, you would need perfect paper and inks. No one has ever been able to duplicate what the government uses. If some of the bills were counterfeit, chemical analysis and microscopic observation would have revealed it."

Dillon was becoming visibly irritated about being challenged by his subordinate.

"I realize all that, Fuller," he said as he pointed to the charts, "but those figures don't lie. We're talking about a thirty-one-billion-dollar difference. Now, the numbers could be off—there are many inaccuracies in an audit of this sort, I'll grant you that—but even fifty percent of what we're talking about is serious enough to damage the economy if word gets out." He turned to Phelps. "I assume that all security precautions have been taken."

"They have, Senator, and I would remind everyone here that what we have is top security and is to remain in this room."

There was a long silence. Everyone seemed to be absorbing what had been said and trying to come up with some suggestions. Patterson broke the silence.

"I think it's fairly obvious what has to be done. The Treasury Department has to uncover where the counterfeit bills are being printed. That's difficult, since we don't have a single one to point to. However, as Senator Hartley said, those figures don't lie, and if anyone needs to be convinced further that they're counterfeit, we'll be happy to give them all the numbers we have. The influx of these bills has to be stopped. Unfortunately we can't begin a widespread investigation because it would surely breach security, so Mr. Davidson and Mr. Fuller will be the only people investigating. Gentlemen, I don't need to stress the importance of this assignment."

He turned to Director Phelps.

"Your job is somewhat easier, John. I know your people have been working hard making inquiries in Switzerland and in other European countries, but that will no longer be necessary. You see, I learned yesterday who is responsible for flooding the economy with this currency. But I didn't know how they were doing it until this meeting. But I know who, gentlemen, and I've been told directly by the individuals involved that they intend to defeat this country, not by military means but through our own financial system. Apparently they have already begun."

Davidson thought back to the previous day and the two Cadillac limousines in front of the Waldorf. He knew who Patterson was talking about. It was the Russians.

9

Washington, March 3, 1991 (AP)—

REPORTS OF A SECRET MEETING BETWEEN TREASURY OFFI-
CIALS AND MEMBERS OF THE SENATE BANKING COMMITTEE
CIRCULATED AROUND WASHINGTON TODAY. THE SENIOR
MEMBER OF THE COMMITTEE, SENATOR ROBERT PETERSON,
HAD NO COMMENT WHEN ASKED THE PURPOSE OF THE
MEETING. IT IS KNOWN THAT A LARGE NUMBER OF BANKS
WERE AUDITED RECENTLY BY THE TREASURY DEPARTMENT
AND THE FEDERAL RESERVE. PETERSON ALSO HAD NO
COMMENT ON THE AUDITS.

Zurich, Switzerland, March 3, 1991 (Reuters)—
IN A SPEECH BEFORE MEMBERS OF THE BANK FOR INTERNA-
TIONAL SETTLEMENTS, CHAIRMAN KARL GEISLER EXPRESSED
CONCERN OVER WHAT HE TERMED "UNDERGROUND DOL-
LARS." THESE ARE DOLLARS CIRCULATING IN THE U.S.
ECONOMY THAT ARE NOT REPORTED INCOME ON THE BOOKS
OF AMERICAN COMPANIES OR THEIR INCOME-TAX RETURNS.
GEISLER SAID THAT IF THE TRUE AMOUNT OF THIS CURRENCY
WAS KNOWN, THE DOLLAR VALUE AGAINST THE SWISS FRANC
WOULD BE CUT BY AS MUCH AS 25%. HE CAUTIONED
INTERNATIONAL FINANCIERS AGAINST INVESTING IN WHAT HE
TERMED "AN AMERICAN UNDERGROUND ECONOMY."

HEALEY'S WAS A small pub at the end of a tree-lined street in
Georgetown where Davidson and Fuller went when they had a
problem. And most of the time when they were in Washington,
they had problems. This one, however, was something else.
Davidson's reaction to the meeting was that the Russians

were pulling off something brilliant. He wondered why they hadn't thought of it sooner. Somebody high up in the Kremlin must have sat down one day and thought: Why the hell are we spending billions of rubles every year on weapons to fight the United States when we can beat them without firing a shot? Why not use their own money to defeat them instead of ours? Why not flood their economy with it, bringing down the value of the dollar until it's worthless? Then when their economy collapses, and they're financially defenseless, we'll move in without firing a shot.

In fact, it made so much sense and was so foolproof that the Soviet ambassador wasn't even keeping it a secret. The arrogant son of a bitch was bragging to Patterson that they had the U.S. by the balls already. He and Fuller had to find out where they were printing that counterfeit, and they had to find out fast.

They had taken a booth at the back of the restaurant, which was nearly empty. It was one-thirty and the lunch crowd was leaving to get back to work. Both of them ordered hamburgers and beer, which the waiter brought along with a salad and French fries.

"Well, what do you think?" Fuller said, sipping his beer.

"I think we got ourselves one hell of an assignment. The fact that the Russians would come right out and admit they're attacking the economy means those counterfeits are damn good. They know we haven't found any yet, so we can't prove a thing. And they're so sure of it that they're rubbing it right in Patterson's face."

He took a bite of his hamburger and continued.

"But I'm telling you, I gotta hand it to them. The idea of beating us with our own money is ingenious. Not only that, but we have no defense. We can't accuse them of anything because we haven't found any counterfeits. And if we don't find any pretty soon, there'll be no stopping them."

Fuller poured some more beer into his glass.

"The only thing I see going for us is maintaining secrecy. Patterson is right. As long as the figures for vault cash are kept secret, they can pump in as much money as they want. It's not until word gets out and the dollar starts to be devalued that we're in trouble."

"Well, that's true, Hal, but only up to a point. As the banks acquire vault cash, their demand for currency will decrease sharply and bring M1-A figures down. Those figures have to be published. And when they show a severe drop, it will alert the financial people that something's wrong. But you're right, it's got to be kept secret as long as possible."

"The whole thing is really hard to imagine," Fuller said. "How much counterfeit did they say is out there?"

Davidson took a folded piece of paper from his pocket.

"About thirty billion so far, but there's an additional two hundred million a day coming into the country."

"You say coming into the country. Do you think the Russians are printing it somewhere else?"

"Who knows," Davidson answered. "We can't assume anything yet. It could be anywhere."

Fuller poured himself more beer and stared at the foam as it rose to the top of the glass.

"You know, there's a million questions you gotta ask yourself about this. Like, how do you pass that much counterfeit? How do you get all those billions into the economy? They've got to have some kind of distribution system. The money has got to get from wherever they're printing it to that bank in Switzerland and back into the country again. How the hell are they doing that?"

Davidson looked at his partner. He hadn't thought about how they were passing it yet. But Hal was right; there had to be an elaborate scheme set up to route the counterfeit to that Swiss numbered account. The little he knew about international finance told him that most transactions were wire ones. You simply transferred funds electronically from one account to another. But somewhere there had to be cash to back it up, and apparently it was in that Swiss account or, more accurately, passing through the account.

"I don't know," he answered. "Anyway, it's putting the cart before the horse because our job is to solve the first link to the puzzle: Where are they printing it? Let Phelps and his gang prove Swiss involvement with the Russians, or at least identify the holder of that account. Our job is to find the printing plant."

Fuller leaned back in the booth and stared at his food.

Davidson could see that the enormity of the assignment had taken some of the fire out of his normally aggressive assistant. He knew the symptoms of this kind of behavior. It came from the helplessness of not knowing where to start. He didn't quite know, either, but some ideas were forming in his head. First he had to calm Hal down.

"You know, buddy, this is going to be a long, tough haul, but I gotta tell you, these Russians aren't all that smart. Their KGB has made mistakes before, and we've been able to get the jump on them. So don't let the bigness of this job get you discouraged before we begin. We'll find that plant eventually and nail these guys."

Hal looked at him over the rim of his glass.

"This a pep talk, Dave?"

"Bet your ass it is. We're better than they are, and don't you forget it. If we go at this thing methodically and take it step by step without panicking, we'll beat them."

"Okay, okay, but we need a beginning. Where do we start? How do you find a printing plant printing counterfeit? There must be hundreds of thousands of them that could be printing the stuff."

"Hal, I think what we have to do is begin with the ingredients that they would need to print perfect bills. I can think of four of them: paper, ink, plates, and press equipment. What's the most difficult to get of the four?"

"The paper, obviously."

"Obviously. Only that's going to be the hardest for us to check."

"Why? We can start with Crane."

The Crane Company, located in Fall River, Massachusetts, was the exclusive government supplier of paper. For over fifty years they had provided all the paper used in United States currency, as well as Treasury bonds.

Davidson added some salt to his hamburger and said, "What are you going to tell Crane, that counterfeit currency is flooding the economy? How do you know that they'll ask? You can't tell them the answer, can you? Do you have a counterfeit bill to show them? No, you haven't found one. So what can they compare the counterfeit paper to?"

"You're saying they can't be much help," Fuller said sarcastically.

"Well, not necessarily. I think they can be if it's handled right. What we have to find out is if anybody in a key position has left the company recently, somebody who would know the complete manufacturing process, a plant foreman or a quality-control person. Somebody who might lead us to somebody else. Also, pilferage—paper that may have been stolen at various stages where their process could be studied. All that could be helpful."

"Under what pretext do I make this sweeping investigation?" Fuller said, chiding.

"Tell them it's a Treasury Department check on their security. It's all you can do. I think you'd better get up there tomorrow. Call them this afternoon and tell them you're coming.

"What I'm going to do is check on the other three items. I'll call some contacts in Hong Kong and see if anybody's been buying ink pigment in large quantities. What we're talking about would have taken an awful lot of ink.

"The third item is equipment. Again, I'll check the big press manufacturers—Miehle, Harris, Smith-Rowen—and see if anybody's bought any large amounts of letterpress equipment recently. That might lead us on some wild-goose chases, but it'll have to be checked out."

"What about the plates?" Fuller asked.

"The plates are going to be the toughest of all. Where the hell they got plates good enough so they couldn't be detected is beyond me. Good photographic offset plates wouldn't have been good enough. They've got something better. The only thing we can do is check some of our sources."

"New Jersey Mafia connections?"

"Yeah, among others."

"This is going to take some time, you know," Fuller said, finishing his beer. "How much do we have?"

"Dillon told me when we left the meeting that if we don't nail this thing in four weeks, the economy will be in serious trouble. I mean, *very* serious. He said the President has already been notified of the situation. I'm supposed to report to Dillon daily on our progress. The CIA will be coordinating with us to help their investigation outside the country. The Russians may be printing this stuff anywhere, even inside Russia. Somehow I doubt it, though. I think it's being done right here."

"Why do you say that?"

Davidson swallowed the last of his beer.

"I don't know. It's just a hunch."

The following day at four o'clock, Fuller called him from Falls River. The trip had been a waste of time. Security at Crane was as tight as a drum, and there had been no pilferage that they knew of. Some of the key people had either quit or retired over the past year, but nobody knowledgeable enough to duplicate the paper. Crane was very careful. One individual never knew the entire process, only parts of it.

Davidson hadn't had much luck, either. Checks in Hong Kong and New Delhi, two large pigment-producing areas, showed no new clients buying large quantities, and established customers purchasing only normal-size orders.

Checks on informants who might know of work being done on plates led to nothing. One lead that was promising was a large order of letterpress equipment that had been ordered from the Harris Company in Philadelphia three months ago. Oddly enough, another large order also had been placed about the same time from Miehle by a customer in Stamford, Connecticut. Hal was going to check that one out on his way back from Falls River, then he would check the other.

The following day, both leads turned out to be a dead end. The company in Philadelphia had recently acquired a woman's magazine and needed the letterpress equipment to print it. Further investigation showed them to be an old, reputable firm that went back to the early days of the printing trade in Philadelphia. Hal's company was using their new equipment to print game cards for a large fast-food chain. Both companies were clean.

Davidson was going back to Washington to report to Dillon. Fuller was to meet another informant in New York that evening, and join him the following day. So far they had nothing.

Davidson traveled to Washington, had dinner in a Marriott outside of the city, called his wife, and went straight to bed. He lay there thinking that the next day the pressure would start mounting. Dillon would expect some answers, something that would give them a starting point. He didn't have anything, and he doubted that Fuller would have, either. His mind wandered to the conversation he had had with his wife just a few minutes earlier. He told her that he was on a routine security check of a congressional appointee. Although it was outside his area, he was often asked to check on candidates being considered for high positions who lived in the New York area. Maybe that's what he really should be doing, not checking on inks and equipment but checking on the man.

The phone rang.

"Dave? It's Hal."

The voice sounded discouraged.

"What did you find out from the informant?"

"Nothing. The guy told me about the stamp operation we're about to hit in Jersey."

Davidson laughed. He cradled the receiver against his ear while he rolled over to turn on the light.

"Terrific, that operation will close down by itself now. The whole world must know about it."

"Yeah," Fuller answered. "Six weeks blown for nothing. In trying to solve one thing, we've lost another."

"We're doing the right things, only they haven't panned out yet," Davidson said. "We could go on checking equipment, paper, and inks, but it's going to take too long. Besides, if there was anything blatantly wrong, we would know about it already. I've got another idea. It may be that we should stop trying to find the equipment and start finding the man."

"The engraver?"

"Right, the guy who made the plates. They've got to be original steel engravings if they're perfect bills. That means an engraver who's worked on currency before."

"A government engraver."

"I think so. Who else could it be?"

"Yeah, okay, Dave, the guy might be a terrific engraver, but what about the paper and the inks? Where would he get them?"

"I don't know. Forget that, it's been a dead end for us. Let's find out who's doing the work."

"Okay. What do you want me to do?"

Davidson opened the drawer of the night table and took out the Washington directory. He looked up the number of the Bureau of Engraving and gave it to Hal.

"Find out who has the Bureau of Engraving's personnel files and leave the address with Dillon's office. I'll meet you there as soon as I get out of the meeting."

"Right, see you tomorrow. I hope it tells us something."

"Who knows, at least it's another door opened up. See you there."

He hung up and turned off the light.

Davidson's meeting with Dillon had gone as expected. The Secretary of the Treasury pressed him to find out where the money was being printed within the next two weeks. When he reminded him that just two days had passed since their last meeting, Dillon told him he was very aware of the date, and so was the President. Apparently President Turner was on the telephone with him daily now.

As soon as he came out of the meeting, he received a message from Hal to meet him at the Bureau of Personnel Records on Connecticut Avenue. He would be there at noon.

Davidson hailed a cab outside the Treasury Building and was at the Bureau of Records in ten minutes. A very efficient secretary at the information desk directed him to the second basement level after checking his identification. A guard then took him to the elevator. They descended two floors and went through a series of electrically controlled doors until the guard finally left him in a small area that looked like a library reading room. Fuller was seated at a metal table, surrounded by half a dozen thick record books. He picked some up to make room for him. Davidson had barely sat down when Fuller said, "I've been through all the records of engravers who've left the Bureau since 1979. They keep very good tabs on these guys. They're updated every six months as to where they're living, any trips they've taken abroad, or anything else unusual."

Dave put on his glasses.

"That's good. It'll make our job a lot easier."

"Well, it's not all that easy," Fuller said as he ruffled through some pages. "There's over a hundred guys who've retired in the past fourteen years."

"Yeah, okay, but they all couldn't have been capable of making perfect engravings."

Fuller held up a piece of memo paper that had a handwritten list of names on it. "That's true, but these twelve could have. They are the master engravers who could do the job. All of them were very experienced when they left, and all had done hand engraving on plates. I was just checking them out individually when you came in. Here, take the last three names. You'll find their records in these two books."

Davidson looked at the list. Of the twelve names on it, Fuller had already crossed out six.

"What about the guys you've crossed out?" he asked.

Fuller looked up from the book he was leafing through.

"Either dead, arthritic, hospitalized, or, in one case, legally blind."

Dave looked at the last three names: Underwood, Henry S.; Weinstein, Aaron E.; and Yarborough, Richard A. Hal had them in alphabetical order. He smiled. The guy's efficiency was maddening, but he loved it.

It took him about twenty minutes to find out that Underwood had died in a car accident in 1979. Weinstein had died in 1982, while traveling in Israel. Yarborough was still alive and living in Los Angeles.

He read down the record.

Yarborough had retired in 1978, after twenty-four years of service, and had moved to Los Angeles. There he had joined a number of associations, the Rotary Club, a retired people's organization, and the local YMCA. He and his wife had visited Hawaii in 1981. Davidson was almost at the end of the page when he saw a notation that had been entered recently: "August 31, 1981, suffered stroke . . . paralyzed right side . . . confined to wheelchair . . . under care of . . ."

Davidson was about to close the book when Hal said, "I've got two."

He moved one of the books over so Davidson could see it. On the top of the right-hand page was the picture of a balding, gray-haired man with a white mustache. Hal pointed to the picture with the tip of a pencil.

"Albert Snyder. He's living in Buffalo, New York. The guy was a master engraver who retired a year ago. Looks like a big spender too. Was in Europe last year, the Caribbean during the winter, and lives in a classy neighborhood in the Buffalo suburbs. He's worth checking.''

Fuller put a marker in the page and turned to the back of the same book.

"This one looks like an even better prospect.''

Davidson studied the identification photograph of the second man. He had a friendly face. For a sixty-three-year-old man he had a full head of hair that was neatly combed. He wore thin wire glasses that Davidson thought made him look older than he really was. He looked at the information below the photograph.

"Robert L. Tompkins . . . age sixty-three . . . retired July 16, 1979 . . . present address, 404 Walnut Street, Hartford, Connecticut.''

"Look at this, Dave,'' Fuller said, pointing to the paragraph below the address. "He was forced into early retirement because of new equipment brought in by the Bureau. Because of that, he's not getting a full pension. Also, his wife is arthritic and has been under the care of a Boston specialist. That could be running him a bundle, even if he has good medical insurance. Also, he hasn't been updated since last May. That's nine months since they last talked to him.''

Davidson looked at his energetic assistant.

"Don't start drawing conclusions yet, Hal. I agree they're two good prospects, but that's all they are right now . . . prospects.''

"Well, they're all we've got. Out of a hundred and nineteen names, these two are the only ones that make any sense at all.''

"You're sure.''

"I'm sure.''

"Okay, which one do you want?''

"I'll take the guy in Hartford.''

"I figured you would. They just got a foot of snow in Buffalo last night.''

"I know,'' Fuller said as he handed him the folder.

Fuller began calling the Tompkins house that evening. He tried four times before midnight, getting no answer. The following morning he began again at seven and made two more calls before he decided to start out for Hartford, anyway. He caught an eleven o'clock flight out of Dulles and landed at Bradley Field just before noon. After getting a quick lunch at the airport, he rented an Avis car and drove the eight miles into Hartford.

Walnut Street was a one-way off Albany Avenue. It was lined with private homes, probably built in the thirties. Most were two stories on very narrow lots with just a few feet between them. They were neatly kept, but there certainly wasn't anything ostentatious here. Fuller drove slowly down the street looking for 404.

It turned out to be a white two-story with aluminum siding and a carport off to the side. The first thing he noticed was that it was the only house on the street that had leaves in the small front yard. Apparently they hadn't been raked since last fall.

He parked the car in front and got out. The street was quiet, except for some children playing in the yard next door. He walked up to the front door and rang the bell. There was a screen in the storm door. He heard the bell ringing inside the house, but there wasn't any answer.

"You won't find anybody home, mister."

Fuller turned around. A young woman had come out of the house next door and was pushing a baby carriage.

"Is this the Tompkins house?" he asked.

"Yes," she said, "but they've been in Florida for months now."

She was about to keep walking, but Fuller said, "I'm from their real-estate agency and I have a buyer who may be interested in the house. Can you tell me where I can reach them?"

The woman eyed him carefully.

"No, I'm afraid I can't."

"Is there anyone who can?"

"They have a son who lives out of town somewhere. I think his name is Bill."

"Do you know where? This family is really interested in the house, and it could mean a nice commission for me."

She thought for a moment, responding to Fuller's pleading look for help.

"He lives somewhere along the shore, Bridgeport, New

Haven—no, wait a minute, it *was* New Haven. He doesn't come around much, you know, but I remember he told my husband once that he lived near Yale. That's in New Haven, right?"

"Right. Can you tell me anything else about him?"

She shook her head. "No, that's it."

Hal smiled politely. "Listen, you've been a big help. Thanks." He started toward his car.

She called after him. "Hope the people you have are friendly. The Tompkinses kept pretty much to themselves."

"They seem pretty outgoing," he answered as he opened the door and slid into the driver's seat.

For a minute he thought of checking the neighbors while he was there but decided against it. If he could get to Tompkins's son, it would be a better first source of information. What he needed now was a New Haven phone book. He pulled out onto Walnut Street and headed for downtown Hartford.

Fifteen minutes later he was in the office of the Southern New England Telephone Company. Having identified himself, he was given a small office off the lobby. Along with the latest New Haven directory, he got a computer printout listing the date of phone installations for every Tompkins in the area.

There were five William Tompkinses listed. Three had local phones for over thirty years. One lived in the suburb of Branford; the other lived on Ashley Place, four blocks from Yale. He dialed the number. After two rings a woman answered.

"Hello?"

"Is Mr. Tompkins at home?"

"He's at work now," she said hesitantly.

"My name is Fuller and I'm a business associate of his. Can you give me his office number?"

"What did you say your name was?"

"Fuller. Hal Fuller."

"Oh . . ." She hesitated again. "Well, it's 555–5000. What is this in reference to?"

He hung up.

A computer check revealed that the number belonged to Parker & Shea, an architectural firm in West Haven. When he telephoned, he was told that Mr. Tompkins was in a meeting for the remainder of the afternoon. West Haven was about an hour and a half away. There was a chance he could be there before Tompkins left for the day.

By four-thirty he was in the lobby of a modern five-story building checking the directory for Parker & Shea. William Tompkins was listed as a senior vice-president on the third floor. He was lucky. The receptionist informed him that Tompkins had just come out of his meeting and had returned to his office. She asked what the visit was in reference to. Fuller told her he was a builder in New York who was contemplating construction in the area. A few minutes later a secretary came out and ushered him into Bill Tompkins's office.

Bob Tompkins's son was a good-looking man, tall, a little overweight, with a friendly round face that Fuller thought resembled his father's. He looked a little older than himself, probably in his early thirties. He came out from behind his white Formica desk and extended his hand.

"Pleased to meet you, Mr. Fuller. Won't you sit down."

Fuller accepted the plush, suede swivel chair offered him.

"Thank you for seeing me on such short notice," he said, settling onto the soft cushion.

"Well, we always like to meet new developers coming into the area. We architects like to get in on the ground floor, so to speak."

Fuller acknowledged the bad pun with an obligatory smile while reaching into his pocket for his identification. He decided to come right to the point. It was important to establish an honest relationship early if he expected to get Tompkins's full cooperation.

"Actually I must apologize, Mr. Tompkins, but I'm not in construction. My name is Hal Fuller, and I'm with the Federal Bureau of Investigation in New York." He kept on talking, knowing full well the shock most people got from that pronouncement. "I'm sorry I had to use the construction ploy to see you, but I need some very important information, and I didn't want to arouse any unnecessary concern with your secretary."

The younger Tompkins seemed immediately concerned but didn't overreact. He took Fuller's identification, looked at the photograph, and handed it back.

"Well, I appreciate your consideration. You're right. Obviously my secretary doesn't run into an FBI man every day, and word would have gotten around. But what kind of information are you looking for?"

Fuller didn't answer until he had placed the identification back into his breast pocket. He wanted eye contact with Tompkins when he spoke.

"I need information about your mother and father."

Tompkins's reactions were split-second but were what Hal wanted to see. The first was surprise. It brought the man's hands down to the desk as if to support his weight. The second was concern. He settled slowly into his leather chair and leaned forward, his hands supporting his chin. His voice was quiet and he spoke slowly.

"What's happened to them? Are they all right?"

Fuller answered quickly.

"We don't know yet. When was the last time you spoke to your father?"

"About a month ago. Is this about him? What has he done?"

"We don't know that he's done anything yet. Right now it's very important that we locate him, though."

"He's in Florida. Miami. I've spoken to him there."

"When did he leave for Florida?"

"Last May. They left rather abruptly, without telling us in advance. My mother has severe arthritis, you know, and I guess they just decided to get into a warm climate."

Fuller was taking notes on a small pad.

"So they left just like that."

"Yes, I was very concerned, but we got a call from him three days later."

"What did he say?"

"He said they were in Miami and were in the process of buying a house. In the meantime he gave me a post-office box to write to if we wanted to contact them. Mother was fine and feeling better in the warm climate."

"Did you speak to your mother?"

"No."

"Have you spoken to your father since?"

"Three times. The last time he said they were enjoying their new home and that Mother was much better."

"When was that?"

"Like I said, about a month ago. He called me."

"How did he sound?"

"He sounded a little tired but other than that, fine."

"And you haven't heard from them since?"

"Oh, yes, we've gotten two letters. In fact my mother even wrote one that was quite amazing. Her arthritis has kept her from writing for over a year now."

"Do you have their address?"

Tompkins hesitated again. Fuller sensed that something was bothering him.

"Funny you should ask that," he began. "The address has been a post-office box ever since they moved into their new house. I always thought that kind of strange."

"Have you tried to call them lately?"

"Only once since Dad called. I wasn't able to reach them. I kept getting a busy signal."

"And you haven't tried to call them since?"

"No."

"But you did get two letters."

"Yes."

"And you wrote back?"

"Only once. I got very busy with a difficult project and was working long hours. I guess I got so involved for a couple of weeks running that I wasn't really thinking about them that much. Besides, from the letters I got, they seemed to be pretty well settled in and enjoying themselves."

Fuller studied Tompkins carefully. He was dressed casually in a corduroy sport jacket, solid slacks, and penny loafers. He wore a college ring over a wedding band. Next to his phone were three pictures of his family. One was a simple studio portrait with him and his wife posed behind two smiling, freckled children. Another showed them in front of a ski lodge with a Christmas tree in the window. The last one was a shot of them running on a beach, probably in the Caribbean.

On a shelf behind his desk were some architectural awards in simple black frames. Next to them was a picture of his parents. Based on the last government picture Fuller saw, he guessed it to be about fifteen years old. The rest of the office suggested a very busy person. There were piles of blueprints scattered over

a drawing board with telephone messages taped to an overhead
lamp. Fuller got the feeling that Tompkins was juggling a lot at
once; a demanding job and the active social life that went with
it. However, he looked like he was ready to help, and Fuller
needed all the help he could get quickly.

"Mr. Tompkins, what I'd like to do is take a look inside your
parents' house. Do you have a key?"

"Not with me."

"Can you get it?"

"Certainly. It's at home."

"Good, but before we do that, I'd like to try to call your
father in Florida. Do you have the number?"

Tompkins reached for the Roladex file near the phone.

"Yes, I have it right here, but I'd like to know what you
think my father is involved in. I hope it's nothing serious."

Fuller came right to the point.

"We believe he may be involved in a counterfeiting
operation. A very big one."

The younger Tompkins leaned back in his chair and smiled.

"My father involved in counterfeiting, Mr. Fuller? I really
doubt it. He is the straightest man you will ever meet in your
life. In over forty years of driving, he never got so much as a
parking ticket. His income tax was accurate down to the last
penny. If someone gave him too much change, he'd return it.
Besides, he considered working for the Bureau a sacred
calling. To him, it was an honor to be able to use his skills to
make currency. His mark was on every bill printed, and he was
proud of it, at least until they cheated him out of his retirement
and let him go practically overnight."

"That may be so," Fuller said, "but your father may have
been forced to work on counterfeit plates."

"What do you mean?"

"I'm not sure yet. Try to call him."

Tompkins dialed the number. "It's busy, the same as it was
the last time." He handed the phone to Fuller, who listened for
a moment.

"That's what I thought," Hal said, and hung up.

Fuller met Tompkins the following day, and they drove back
to Hartford to his parents' house. It was raining and took them

almost two hours before they pulled up to the small frame house.

They unlocked the front door and went inside. There was a musty smell from the house not being open to ventilation for a long period of time. Fuller checked the first floor. There was nothing unusual; the house was neat, except for some dishes that had been left in the kitchen sink.

They went upstairs. At the top of the stairs was a hallway. The bathroom was on the left. Fuller noticed a dripping faucet in the sink, which he tightened. There was a small guest room across the hall that had an ironing board folded against the wall and some clothes lying over the chair. Mrs. Tompkins apparently had used it for a sewing room.

The master bedroom was at the end of the hall. The door was closed. Fuller opened it, and Tompkins came in behind him. Immediately they noticed the empty closet to the right of the room. There was nothing in it but two woolen dresses pushed to the side and two pairs of dress shoes.

Fuller opened the closet to the left. It was full of the elder Tompkins's clothes. He checked the dressers. One was full of men's clothes, and Helen's was half empty. There was nothing but a few heavy sweaters, skirts, and dressy blouses left behind. He found an unopened jewelry box in the bottom drawer.

He looked up. Tompkins was rummaging through the top of his father's closet. He was taking everything off a shelf and putting it on the bed. There was a metal box, a 35mm camera, a shoe box full of canceled checks, a hot-water bottle, and an old top hat. Whatever he was looking for, Fuller knew he hadn't found it. He looked like someone had drained the color out of his face.

"You said you thought my father was involved in making counterfeit plates?" he asked.

"I said that was possible, yes," Fuller answered cautiously. "Why do you ask?"

Tompkins looked down at the items on the bed.

"Because my father's engraving tools are missing. He always kept them on the closet shelf. They were there for years, ever since I was a kid. He'd bring them home to sharpen them on a wheel he had downstairs. I remember watching him doing it, then carefully putting them back into a special box he made. Then it would go on the shelf until he went back to work the next morning. When he retired, it went up there permanently. I saw him put it there myself. It's not there now."

"Maybe it's somewhere else in the house," Fuller said, looking around the room.

"No, he always kept it in this closet," Tompkins said vehemently.

Fuller closed the dresser drawers and walked over to him. Some things were beginning to fall into place now. First of all, he doubted that the elder Tompkins had just upped and left for Florida with his wife. Why was Mrs. Tompkins's whole wardrobe gone and her husband's left behind? It looked to him like she knew ahead of time that she was going, but that Tompkins had left very abruptly. Another thought came to mind. If they had been taken hostage, it must have been at different times. Maybe because she was an invalid and offered little resistance, the intruders had time to take her and her clothes, while Tompkins had fought them and had to be taken quickly. At any rate, he felt now that he had the right man.

Fuller looked at the engraver's son. Bill seemed to know what he was about to say.

"I think your parents may have been taken hostage. I also think they're in different places. Your mother's clothing is gone, your father's is here. Since they've gone, you've spoken to one, but not the other. They've got to be in separate places."

Tompkins nodded.

"But how do you explain the letters? Both of them have written from Florida three or four times. And what about the calls I got through to Dad? He seemed calm enough and happy at the time."

Fuller shrugged his shoulders. "I don't know yet. Letters can be written in one place and forwarded from another. Telephone calls can be relayed to other locations. As far as sounding happy, he may have been forced to act that way."

The younger Tompkins looked at the items on the bed. He was shaking his head in disbelief over the whole situation. Finally he looked up and asked, "Where do we go from here?"

"We check their friends and neighbors. Maybe they can tell us something."

• • •

They spent the rest of the afternoon talking to the few friends the couple had. Almost all of them said the same thing. Bob and Helen had left unexpectedly for Florida without saying anything beforehand. It was assumed that Helen's condition had gotten so bad that they had to get to a warmer climate. Most of them had received either a letter or a postcard, but nobody had spoken to them by phone. The stories were pretty much all the same, until they got to a Mrs. Gilroy, who lived across the street.

She recognized Bill immediately, although she hadn't seen him in quite a while. They were ushered into a small living room that was cluttered with antique furniture. Mrs. Gilroy, who looked to be about eighty, sat on a Victorian-style sofa with lace doilies on the arms. She was pouring them mint tea from a silver teapot. Her dog, Penny, was lying at her feet on a floral-patterned throw rug.

"I remember your children playing on the front lawn, Bill. Your father was always telling them to play in the backyard because they were digging up the lawn." She waved a ringed finger at him and added, "You were out there playing *with* them, too, weren't you?"

Bill looked at her sheepishly and took a sip of his tea.

Fuller attempted to get her to the point of their visit. Bill had introduced him as a real-estate man interested in selling his parents' house. He said he was showing him around the neighborhood.

"Were you a very close friend of the Tompkinses, Mrs. Gilroy?" he asked innocently.

She smiled at him over her bifocals.

"Oh, yes," she said. "Helen and I met regularly twice a week for lunch at her house. I don't know if Bill told you, but she wasn't well, you know . . . arthritis, poor dear, but we managed to enjoy our little lunches. I'd bring a small gelatin salad or something and we would talk."

"And Mr. Tompkins?" he asked.

"He's a bit of an old fuddy-duddy," she said, winking at Bill. "Everything had to be just so around the house, you know. But he's been wonderful to Helen, has done everything for her since she's been sick."

Bill took a slight nod from Fuller as his cue and asked her if she had heard from either of them since they'd gone away.

"Oh, yes," she said excitedly. "I got two postcards from Helen in Florida. She's having a wonderful time."

"May we see them?" Fuller asked.

She got up and went over to a hutch that seemed to sag under the weight of the china that was displayed on top of it. After looking in two or three cluttered drawers, she took the postcards from one of them.

"Here they are," she said, returning to the sofa. She handed one to each of them.

Fuller looked at the card. It had been postmarked in Miami three months ago. There was a picture of a strip of beach on the front, and a short note written in a scraggly handwriting on the back.

> Dear Margaret,
> Bob and I are terribly sorry to have left so abruptly without saying good-bye. We've come here to look for a new home because the doctor says I must be in a warmer climate if I'm to get better. Please stay in touch. My address is P.O. Box 664, Miami, Florida 02910.
>   Love always,
>   Helen

He gave the card to Bill and looked at the other one. It also had been postmarked in Miami and had been mailed a month later. She said that they were enjoying themselves and that her arthritis was better. They were still looking for a house, but it was difficult. He handed the cards back to Mrs. Gilroy.

She reached down and petted her dog.

"I was so glad she wrote that first postcard, because I thought she had gone to the hospital."

"Why do you say that?" Bill asked.

"Because the day she must have left, I saw two men helping her into a car."

"What two men?" Fuller asked.

"I don't know who they were. It was dark and I was taking Penny for a walk. I saw two men helping somebody into a car. I thought at first that it was your father," she said, looking at

Bill, "but then I figured it must be Helen and they were taking her to the hospital."

"Did you get a look at the car?" Fuller asked excitedly.

"Oh, yes, it was a lovely Mercedes—black, I believe—but it was so dark, I couldn't be sure. Well, anyway, when I got the card a few days later, I knew everything was all right. It must have been a friend helping your mother into the car."

"Did you ever see the car again?"

She thought for a minute.

"No, that's the odd part. I never saw it again, and I'd never seen it before. Bob and Helen didn't have many friends, but I knew most of the ones they did have."

"You didn't by any chance see the license plate number?" Fuller asked on a long shot.

"Goodness, no," she said, adjusting her bifocals. "At my age, young man, I'm lucky I saw the car."

They talked for a while longer, but Fuller had heard enough to convince him even further that the Tompkinses had been taken hostage. The next step was to find where they were in Florida.

After leaving Mrs. Gilroy, they drove back to New Haven to Tompkins's office. It was after six and the offices were empty. Fuller sat down at a small table while Tompkins phoned his wife to say he would be late.

Hal took the pad that he had been taking notes on from his pocket and turned to the Miami address that Helen had given Mrs. Gilroy. Tompkins hung up the phone and sat down next to him.

He seemed exhausted from the day. The emotional strain of finding evidence that his parents had been kidnapped was beginning to show. Fuller had watched him carefully while they were in his father's house. Searching through the rooms had in a sense returned him to his childhood and the relationship with his mother and father. And Fuller judged it to have been a strong one, even though it may have faded in the past few years. But that love had apparently resurfaced. Now the son was concerned and wanted to do everything in his power to help Fuller find them.

"What do you suggest we do next?" Bill asked as he loosened his tie.

"I'd like to see that address you have again in Florida."

Tompkins retrieved it from his pocket and gave it to him. Fuller checked it against the one he had taken from Mrs. Gilroy. They were the same.

"I want you to write a letter to your parents in Florida tonight. It doesn't matter what it says, I just want a letter to be going to that post-office box. When it gets there, I'll be waiting for it."

"You mean, you'll be watching the box to see who picks it up?"

"Exactly. I'll leave for Florida in the morning after I call Washington and make arrangements for a stakeout in Miami. The letter should get there the day after tomorrow if I mail it first thing in the morning."

Tompkins reached for a pen and paper and began writing.

Fuller left for Miami the next morning. As the plane took off, he settled back in his seat and thought about his conversation with Davidson late the night before. Dave's trip to Buffalo had been a dead end. It turned out that Albert Snyder was now doing hand etchings of the birds of America and was making a fortune at it. A New York gallery had been exhibiting his work for nearly a year now, and couldn't sell enough of it. As a result, he was rolling in money and had traveled all over the world with his wife. Dave had also mentioned casually that his flight was two hours late leaving Buffalo because of a snowstorm.

When he told him what he found in Hartford, Dave was enthusiastic. He agreed that it sounded like Tompkins and his wife had been kidnapped. He also thought there was only a fifty-fifty chance that they were in Miami. The KGB wouldn't take a chance having them in the same location that the letters were sent from. However, he felt it was a starting point and had made arrangements for agents there to help with the stakeout. He would leave Washington immediately and meet him at the Bureau's office in downtown Miami. The agents there were to be told that this was just a routine stakeout to find the key man behind a small counterfeiting ring operating in the area.

The plane landed on schedule, and he caught a taxi outside

the terminal building. It was an unusually warm day for March, the temperature well into the eighties. He started to roll down the window to enjoy the warm air but saw the cabdriver shaking his head in the rearview mirror.

"I'm running the air-conditioning and you want to cool off the whole city, right?"

There were two people he had learned never to argue with, cops and cabbies. He rolled the window back up.

The cab pulled up in front of the federal building in downtown Miami. Minutes later he was in the Miami Bureau Chief's office where a briefing was already in progress. As he came into the room, he was surprised to see Davidson holding the briefing.

"What took you so long, buddy? We were about to stake this out without you," he said with a smile.

Fuller put down his bags. There were six agents who had been taking notes that were now staring at him.

"How did you get here so fast? I thought you wouldn't be in until later in the day."

Davidson took a puff on his pipe and blew the smoke toward the ceiling.

"When you've been in a cold place like Buffalo and you hear that you're needed in Miami, you get your cold ass on the first plane you can find."

Fuller laughed.

"Well, you'd better take it out to the beach this afternoon, 'cause from tomorrow on, we'll be inside a post office waiting for someone to open a box."

"Yeah, I know," Davidson said, reaching for a folder. "We've located the post office from the zip-code book, and Steve and his men here took a look at it this morning."

Steve Brenner, the Miami Bureau Chief, stood up from behind his desk and reached out to shake Fuller's hand. He was tall and thin, with a crewcut. His hands were huge. Fuller had read somewhere that he had been a college basketball star.

"Welcome to Miami," he said in a friendly voice. "Hope we can be of some help to you fellas in breaking up this ring."

Fuller looked at Davidson, who simply nodded. Apparently, as planned, he had only told Brenner the minimum, giving him just the information needed to carry out the stakeout. Brenner got up from behind his desk to introduce his men.

"Hal, meet Bob Harris, Tony Wald, Al Rivers, and Pete Foley. They'll be the team assigned to the post office. Tony was there this morning and talked to the postmaster. Also, he's got a floor plan of the customer area."

Tony Wald was a short, stocky man with a good build. He was sitting on the window ledge with a notebook in his lap and a rolled piece of paper at his side.

"The postmaster is the only one in the building who knows of the stakeout," he said. "He's aware that we're looking for the person who will open the box. Box 664 is registered under a Mr. Ross Anderson of 8 Crestmont Circle, Miami. That checks out to be a phony name with a phony address. Right now the box is empty. Mail has been picked up from it, though, because the sorting clerk remembers putting letters into it regularly."

He turned to the next page of his notes.

"Your letter, mailed from Hartford, should arrive tomorrow afternoon in the one-thirty delivery. By three o'clock it should be in the box. The post office is open until six P.M., and reopens again at eight-thirty in the morning."

"What's our cover, Tony?" Davidson asked.

"First let me show you the layout that Bob and I drew of the customer area," Wald said. "That'll give you a better idea of how the cover can operate."

Bob Harris, a thin black man in a three-piece lightweight suit, spread the drawing out on Brenner's desk. With a red pencil he traced out the customer area.

"There are two entrances from the street, both revolving doors," he began. "Once inside, the parcel-post area is off to your left; stamps, registered mail, and letter drops directly ahead. To the right are the letter boxes. There are three hundred and fifty of them. The whole customer area is about sixty feet long and eighteen feet wide. This is a big post office. It's staffed by about a hundred and fifty people and handles over one hundred thousand pieces of mail a day."

He drew two circles within the customer area with a red pencil.

"There are two armed postal guards stationed in these positions every day. We've arranged for them to be off for the next week. Tony and I will replace them. That'll enable us to watch the boxes closely."

"It'll also allow us to be openly armed," Harris added.

"What about the rest of us?" Fuller asked.

Harris looked at him with a sheepish grin. "How are you at sweeping floors?"

"You're kidding," Fuller answered, anticipating his assignment.

"That's your cover. There's a guy who normally keeps the area clean by sweeping up every hour or so. Goes around with a small broom and dust bucket. It's a good cover because you won't have to be in the area all the time. You can stay out of sight until either Tony or I see something suspicious. If we do, we'll signal with a beeper that we'll have inside our jacket pocket. That same signal will also go out to the rest of you."

Brenner spread a blown-up section of the city map across his desk. There was a circle around the post office located at Fifth and Center.

"The rest of us will be in two cars, out of sight of the building. Dave and I will be in the command car, parked in a Hertz garage on Seventh Street. Since Fifth is one way, Al and Pete will be in another car parked in the post-office garage on Center. That way we've got all directions covered."

He traced his finger around a large circle drawn over the adjoining area. "The Fifteenth Precinct will be available to us and will have extra patrols cruising inside this circle. If for some reason we lose the target, they'll be able to pick it up."

Davidson emptied his pipe into an ashtray and stuck it upside down in the breast pocket of his jacket.

"Sounds good to me. When do we begin?"

"Well, since the letter is due in at one-thirty tomorrow, I'd say we ought to get set up around noon to be on the safe side. We'll meet here," Brenner said. "By the way, where are you two staying?"

Fuller hadn't made any arrangements yet. He first wanted to coordinate with Dave.

"I was going to stay at the Fountainbleau," Davidson said,

"but I know my friend here can't afford much on his sweeper's salary. Guess it's the Sunset Motel on Sixteenth and Davenport."

The letter arrived on schedule the following day in the one-thirty delivery. Six days later it was still in the box.

So far there had been two false alarms. On the second day, when a man approached the box, Harris had signaled Fuller, who was having coffee in the back room. He came out onto the floor just as the man opened up Box 663. Two days later the same thing happened with 665 on the other side.

He and Davidson had begun to wonder if the letter would ever be picked up. Maybe Tompkins had been moved to another location recently and they weren't taking anything from the box. Or worse yet, maybe Tompkins and his wife were both dead and the whole thing was a waste of time. Both of them agreed, though, that they had to stick it out until something proved them wrong.

Washington was in constant contact with them at the motel. Dillon continued to apply pressure nightly by quoting new figures as to how much counterfeit was in the economy. He also reminded them that every day was another opportunity for word to leak out that nearly twenty percent of the currency in circulation was counterfeit. If that happened, the economy would come crashing down.

It was one-thirty in the afternoon, and the post office was very busy. The lunch-hour rush usually lasted from twelve until two. Three stamp windows were open and had lines of ten to twelve people. The parcel-post line was even longer.

Harris and Wald were at opposite ends of the postal boxes. Fuller was sweeping around the letter drop, occasionally glancing at Box 664. He turned to sweep up some cigarette butts when he bumped into an elderly lady about to put a letter into the general mail slot.

"Excuse me, I'm terribly sorry," he said as the letter fell to the floor. He bent over and picked it up. "Are you all right?" She took the letter and deposited it in the slot. "Oh, yes, it's nothing at all," she said.

He watched her as she walked away. She was very old, probably around seventy, dressed in a neat black suit, white blouse, and low-heeled shoes. Just a few feet away, she appeared to have forgotten something and stopped. From her leather purse she took a pair of glasses and something else he couldn't see. She put the glasses on and walked toward the boxes. She headed straight for the 600 section and inserted a key into 664.

Instinctively he hit the beeper in his breast pocket, but Harris and Wald had already seen her. They were rushing through the crowd toward the box. Fuller got there first, just as she was taking the letter out and putting it in her purse.

"Ma'am, I'd like you to come with me quietly," he said, showing his Secret Service identification. The two uniformed agents were now standing beside her. Wald was holding her arm, and Harris started to take her pocketbook. The crowd turned its attention toward them.

"What are you doing? Let go of me," she said, pulling her purse away. "What's the meaning of this?"

"We're federal agents and we'd like to talk to you privately," Fuller said quietly.

"I've done nothing but take a letter from a box," she shouted angrily. "What's wrong with that?"

The crowd gathered around. Some were visibly annoyed at what seemed to be police officers harassing an old lady.

"We have this particular box under surveillance, ma'am, and we'd like to talk to you about the letter you took from it."

"I don't know what you're talking about," she said loudly, aware now of the supportive crowd. "It's never been under surveillance before when I've picked up letters. Why should it be now?"

"You pick up mail from it often?" Fuller asked.

"Of course," she said, taking the letter from her purse. "I pick it up for a friend."

"What friend?"

"My friend is blind," she said indignantly, "so I pick up the mail for him whenever I come here. I've been doing it for over three months now. If you want to talk to him about it, I suggest you go out those doors. He runs the newsstand right outside."

Fuller and Harris turned and bolted for the revolving doors, leaving Wald behind with the woman. As they came outside,

Davidson and Brenner were pulling up to the curb. In front of them was the newsstand. There was no one in it.

Twenty minutes later a man carrying a white metal cane and wearing dark glasses got off a bus in North Miami. As usual, the driver let him off in front of his house rather than at the corner bus stop. He only had to walk a few feet to avoid being spotted by the hundreds of police cars searching the street armed with his description.

Once inside the small cottage, he put his cane in the hall closet and took off his dark glasses. Without bothering to remove his jacket, he bounded down the steps to the basement. He turned on a light over a workbench and took a key from his pocket. Quickly he unlocked the top drawer and slid it out. Inside was a small shortwave radio. He unhooked an antenna lead wire from a portable TV set and clamped it into the top of the transmitter. With a screwdriver he tightened two screws around the wire, then turned on the power. There was a loud hissing sound as he adjusted to the correct frequency. Finding it, he picked up a microphone and spoke softly into it.

"Falcon One calling Base One. Come in."

A voice crackled over the small speaker.

"This is Base One. Go ahead, Falcon One."

His message only contained seven words, but he knew it was what Yuri Vladislav was waiting to hear in New York. He spoke them slowly.

"The Eagle has come to the nest."

10

Bonn, West Germany, March 31, 1991 (Reuters)—

WEST GERMAN CHANCELLOR HANS ZWEIGER FLEW TO WASH-
INGTON TODAY FOR A MEETING WITH PRESIDENT TURNER.
ZWEIGER WOULD NOT DISCUSS THE AGENDA, BUT IT IS
RUMORED THAT THE MEETING WAS TO DISCUSS THE RECENT
BUILDUP OF SOVIET TROOPS IN EAST GERMANY.

SOURCES CLOSE TO ZWEIGER REPORT THAT THE CHANCEL-
LOR IS CONCERNED ABOUT RECENT DOWNTRENDS IN THE U.S.
ECONOMY, WHICH COULD PREVENT THE UNITED STATES FROM
MILITARILY SUPPORTING WEST GERMANY AGAINST THE
RUSSIANS.

Treasury Department Memo #947 (Top Secret)

From: Secretary of the Treasury Allen Dillon
To: John Cristaldi, Undersecretary for Monetary Affairs
Subject: Inflated Money Supply

Dear John:

Reports handed me today show an even more drastic situation in
the money supply than anticipated. Latest figures show $1 billion
in currency now flowing into the economy daily. This amount
exceeds Bureau of Engraving figures by twenty to one.

It is imperative that the situation be kept top secret until the CIA
or Secret Service find the source. Any disclosure of these figures to
the public will be disastrous.

Please keep me informed of any information you receive daily.

March 31, 1991
Moscow

VASILY GAGARIN WAS sleeping soundly when the phone beside his bed rang at three A.M. Reaching into the darkness, he groped for the receiver to get it off the hook before his wife awoke.

"Hello, who is it?" he whispered, knowing it had to be the Ministry of Finance, since they were the only ones with his private number.

"It's Dworkow, sir." The voice sounded embarrassed at having to call at such a late hour. "We have just received a message from Falcon One, relayed through Base One."

"Yes, yes, go ahead," he said impatiently.

"Falcon One reports that the Eagle had come up to the nest."

Gagarin stared into the darkness of the room and smiled. It was the message he had been waiting for but hadn't expected this soon. The plan was ahead of schedule. On the other end of the line, his aide was waiting for a response from his superior.

"Sir, do you understand the message?"

"I understand perfectly. Thank you very much."

He hung up the phone and got out of bed, feeling his way across the room to his closet. He managed to find his robe and put it on over his pajamas. Then he stepped into his slippers and quietly left the room to go down to the study.

As he came into the room, he noticed there were still some embers smoldering in the fireplace from a fire he and Irena had enjoyed earlier in the evening. He opened the firebox and took out two logs, which he laid over some kindling. Immediately the small pieces of wood ignited. Flames lit the room, casting eerie shadows over the dark walls. He warmed himself for a few moments, then opened the drape that went along one entire wall. It had begun to snow outside. The flakes sparkled against the light of a full moon as they fell to the ground. He stood there motionless, looking out on the scene.

He thought about the message he had just received. Although brief, it contained an enormous amount of information. First of all, it meant that the Americans had discovered an inordinate amount of currency in their economy. They also had determined that it was counterfeit and were in the process of tracking down the source of it.

Good, everything was going according to plan.

Actually he hadn't expected the call for another week or so. His economists had calculated that the U.S. Treasury wouldn't recognize the influx of counterfeit until it reached the $200 billion mark. Apparently the Americans had a more sensitive pulse on their economy than he thought.

Also, their Secret Service had operated very efficiently. They had begun to track down the government engraver responsible in a very short time. His own KGB could learn a lesson from them.

Now they must be terribly frustrated. The post-office box in Florida had been their only lead to Tompkins. With the Secret Service reporting failure of the mission to Washington, the administration would be in a state of panic.

He poured himself a brandy at his small bar and returned to look out the bay window. The snow was coming down more heavily and was beginning to drift against the side of the house. He pulled his robe around his neck, feeling a cold draft coming through the frosted pane.

The warmth of the brandy felt good inside him. It never failed to calm his mind in critical situations when he needed to think clearly.

The question facing him now was what to do with the American engraver. If the Treasury Department had actually found any counterfeit money, he wouldn't be needed any longer. It would have meant that the bills weren't perfect, after all, and the government would be able to withdraw them from the economy. Apparently that wasn't so. The amount of counterfeit had gone into the billions before the Secret Service had attempted to track down Tompkins. No, they knew counterfeit bills had to be coming into the economy, but they hadn't actually found any.

Also, no one had reported any counterfeit being passed through the California bank. Geisler had assured him of that. The money was perfect, and he would see that it remained so. He still needed Tompkins alive to insure that, at least for the time being.

Geisler, himself, was another matter. The man was power-hungry and bore watching. Right now he was a necessary link to the international financial community, but eventually his power-hungry nature could cause problems. However, the banker was being observed closely, and that made him feel more secure. Welte, with the help of KGB Agent Nina Praeger, was doing an excellent job of keeping Geisler under surveillance. Also, their information on Walter Schein had enabled him to eliminate the only opposition to Union Suisse's involvement with his plan. As long as he could continue to monitor Geisler and the people around him, he would be successful.

With that success he would have achieved what was thought to be impossible: the destruction of the United States. Not with weapons costing billions of rubles but with the enemy's own dollars. What had his government's defense budget been last year? Over one hundred and fifty billion rubles. Rubles spent on weapons that if deployed would not only destroy the United States but themselves as well. It was impossible to achieve military superiority to such a degree that they would not be destroyed by a retaliatory strike. His plan would enable them to defeat the enemy without firing a shot.

He thought of the rewards. His reputation within the Party was impeccable. Over the past three years he had moved steadily up the ranks of the Politburo, amassing more and more power. As the architect and executor of this plan, its success could eventually put him in line to be Premier.

The snow was coming down even more heavily. A cold wind was blowing it across the lawn, and it drifted against the carefully pruned shrubs along the house. Tomorrow the Secret Service would be looking for a blind newsstand dealer in sunny Florida. They wouldn't find him, though, because he would be on a plane heading for New York to report to Vladislav. The only lead to Tompkins had disappeared. Within a week, news of the inflated money supply would be leaked to the press. Once that happened and the financial world found out that over half of the U.S. currency in circulation was counterfeit, with millions still pouring in daily, the economy would begin to collapse.

Outside, he noticed a small evergreen that he and Irena had

planted in the fall. The snow was beginning to cover it so that the top showed. By tomorrow, billions of tiny snowflakes would fall and smother it completely.

He smiled and went back to bed.

11

KGB coded transmission 509, Moscow
Headquarters to Base One, New York City, April 1, 1991

Proceed to acquire necessary Treasury figures for release on or about April 3. Stop. Transmit all information to us by 2300 hours your time.

Washington, D.C.
April 1, 1991

THE PARK NEAR the Lincoln Memorial was crowded for a weekday. Vacationers were milling about, enjoying the warm spring air and taking pictures of each other in front of the massive monument. Others were fishing in a stream that ran through the wide green lawn and spilled into a small lake. Cherry blossoms were in bloom everywhere. Washington was beautiful this time of year, and people were willing to travel hundreds of miles to see it.

Standing in front of the steps leading up to the statue of Lincoln was a tall man dressed in a knit sweater and jeans. He was carrying a leather bag with wide pockets that was slung over his shoulder. A rolled-up copy of the *Washington Post* protruded from it.

Others around him also seemed to be waiting for people. The monument was a perfect meeting place from which to go off and enjoy a picnic in the park.

He looked at his watch: twelve-thirty. Apparently, whoever he was waiting for was late. He took the paper out of his bag and sat down on the steps to read it.

A few minutes later a young woman carrying a briefcase came hurrying up to the monument. She looked around, trying to pick someone out of the crowd. The man lowered his paper and saw her. She looked like a typical Washington secretary, gray flannel suit, white blouse with a gold necklace, three-quarter heels. Her blond hair was pulled back into a tight bun and held by a piece of gold jewelry.

She saw him. Straightening her hair, she walked over to where he was sitting.

"Hi, I'm Jill," she said, looking down at him. She seemed nervous and unsure of herself. He stood up and took her hand.

"I'm Steve," he said. "I guess the *Washington Post* idea worked."

"Yeah," she said with a giggle. "I thought lots of people would be reading newspapers, but you were the only one."

He smiled and gestured toward the crowd.

"They're all Midwesterners. They don't read."

"Oh," she said again with a giggle, which seemed to be her way of ending sentences.

They stood looking at each other awkwardly, until finally he opened the top of his bag and turned it so she could see inside.

"I've got some cheese, wine, French bread, and fruit. Whaddaya say we find a quiet place and have our lunch."

She hesitated for a moment, then nodded her head in agreement. They walked away from the monument and turned down a black-topped path that led into a wooded area. There was an empty bench there, and they sat down.

She looked at the briefcase in her lap. It was burgundy-colored vinyl and had her initials, J. A. C., engraved near the handle.

"You know," she said softly, "I don't know if I can go through with this. These don't seem to be ordinary vault-cash audit reports. They've been making a big deal out of them for the past three weeks. I had a hard time even making copies."

"I knew they'd be hard to get," he said, taking the wine from his bag. "That's why I told you I was prepared to pay you an awful lot of money."

She put the briefcase on the ground beside her. Her eyes narrowed, and she spoke in what was almost a whisper.

"Look, this is weird. You call me at work and I don't know

you from Adam. Just like that, you want copies of confidential bank audits. How'd you know they were doing audits on a weekly basis now?"

He spread some paper napkins on the bench and put the cheese and fruit down on it.

"I make it my business to know."

She sat for a moment, studying him closely. Finally she said, "Can you tell me what you want the information for?"

"Sure, like I told you on the phone, if I can get these figures before anyone else, I can make a lot of money in the market; far more than what I'm going to pay you."

She accepted a paper cup from him and held it out while he poured some wine. She took a sip, then looked around her.

"Do you know what would happen to me if they found out I copied these reports?"

"You'd get fired," he said calmly.

"Under normal circumstances, yes; but these audits were suddenly classified as top secret three weeks ago. They never were before. If they knew I copied them, not only would I be fired, I could end up in jail."

He took a large manila envelope out of the bag and handed it to her. She held it gently, as if it were so precious that it would break.

"First of all, they'll never know you copied them. Secondly, you don't have to worry about being fired. Next week you can be lying on a beach in the Caribbean, never having to work again. One hundred and fifty thousand dollars is an awful lot of money."

She opened the clasp and looked inside the envelope. There were stacks of hundred-dollar bills each neatly held in a white band and marked $10,000. Quickly she closed the flap.

"I've never seen that much money in all my life. It's unreal."

He let the comment pass and ate some of the bread and cheese.

"Before you walk off with that bundle, I'd like to see what you have for me."

She handed him the briefcase and he opened it. As he had instructed her, the material was also in a manila envelope. He tore it open. By just glancing at the figures on the first page, he could see that they agreed with what Russian economists had predicted. Reports from ten thousand banks put bank-vault currency at $250 billion. There was a breakdown by denomination, showing high amounts of twenties and hundreds. It was more than ten times the normal amount. He turned to the second page. It contained Bureau of Engraving figures for the past six months. The third page drew comparisons of amounts of currency printed versus vault cash. There was a discrepancy of over $80 billion.

He smiled. This was exactly the information he needed, all neatly typed on Treasury Department stationery with the words TOP SECRET stamped across the top.

He took the envelope and put it in his bag. She had already put the money in her briefcase. Slowly he extended his hand to her.

"I think we have a deal here. You've gotten rich today, and I'll become rich tomorrow."

"I'm so nervous," she said. "I don't know if I can go back there."

"Sure you can. You don't have to be afraid. You've got enough money to do whatever you want now."

"Yeah," she said with a giggle, "I guess I do."

An hour later the KGB agent was at Dulles Airport, changing from his sweater and jeans into a three-piece suit taken from a locker. He made a quick phone call and then boarded the four o'clock shuttle to New York. The afternoon had been a successful one. He had gotten the report he wanted, and at the same time had passed one hundred and fifty thousand dollars worth of counterfeit bills.

At La Guardia he caught a cab into the city and by six-thirty was at Mid City Printing, meeting with Vladislav.

Later that night, copies were made of the stolen document to be delivered by messenger the next morning to Mr. James Trainor, Publisher of *The New York Times,* and Mr. Kenneth Wirth, Chairman of the New York Stock Exchange. A third copy was mailed to an office in Washington. Vladislav was pleased with the agent's work. Before midnight, he radioed a coded message to Gagarin: "Numbers better than expected . . . will be released in two days."

• • •

Jill Cummings switched on her bright lights as she drove her 1984 Honda along the dimly lit Mount Vernon Memorial Highway outside of Washington. The rain was coming down harder now, and she was still another three miles from the Alexandria, Virginia, exit. The nine-mile drive normally took about fifteen minutes, but tonight it had taken almost a half hour. She looked at the digital clock on the dash. The green numbers read 8:10. It was seven hours since she had met with the man called Steve in the park, and she was still shaking.

Her imitation leather briefcase was lying on the seat beside her. One hundred and fifty thousand dollars. That was more money than she had ever seen in her whole life. It was so much, she hadn't even thought about what she would do with it. The initial shock of just having it hadn't worn off yet.

After she left Steve, she went back to her office and locked herself inside. Within an hour she had counted the money three times. It was in all new bills, clean and crisp, neatly stacked in five little piles. Steve must have withdrawn it from a bank the same day.

Suspicions had plagued her the whole afternoon. What if they found out she had taken the copies of the audits? Had anybody seen her at the copying machine? Why had her friend Cheryl been looking at her that way? Was she suspicious? By the time five o'clock had come, she was emotionally drained. A quiet dinner alone in a small coffee shop near her parking garage had helped settle her down.

Now her thoughts turned to Steve himself. He was so blasé about the whole thing. Wasn't he worried about her? She may not know who he was, but she certainly could identify him. And she might have to if those M1-A reports were as important as they suddenly had become and she found herself trapped.

She came down the exit ramp and passed through the small town of Alexandria. At Grant Place she made a left onto a dead-end street. Moving slowly, her headlights found the reflector arrow marking the entrance to the parking lot in the rear of her building. It was one of three ten-story apartments that formed a semicircle around a cul-de-sac. The driveway was narrow, and she slowed to a crawl as she made a sharp turn around the end of the building. Her designated parking spot was now on the left. Someone was in it.

It was a black Corvette, the only one facing outward in the long row of cars. Somebody had probably just run inside for a minute and would be coming out shortly. There wasn't any sense in looking for another space. At this time of night the lot would be full. She waited.

Through the rain-spattered windshield she could see a figure approaching out of the darkness. As it came closer into the light, she saw that it was a man carrying a shopping bag. He headed straight toward the car, then turned abruptly toward the rear entrance door. He opened it and went inside.

Now the lot was empty. She became very aware of the rain beating down on the roof of the car. Her cigarettes were tucked in the sun visor. She took one and lit it with the car lighter. The glow of the light circled the dark silhouette of her head. From fifty feet away she was a perfect bull's-eye.

The electric window on the passenger side of the Corvette had begun to lower as soon as the man with the shopping bag had entered the building. Now a 350 Magnum, equipped with a silencer, protruded through the opening. There were two muted pops, and two holes formed an inch apart in the glass next to Jill's head. As both bullets entered the left side of her brain, she fell forward onto the steering wheel. There was a long, steady blare from her horn as the Corvette's lights popped up and the engine started. With a screech of its tires, the car roared out from the space, sped down the driveway, and disappeared into the night.

Allen Dillon sat at his desk in the Treasury Building thinking about the previous night's meeting with Davidson and Fuller. The two men had met him at his home in Maryland late in the evening, having just flown in from Florida where they had continued the search for Tompkins.

He had desperately hoped that the one lead they had would pan out, but instead, they were up against a dead end. Having determined the identity of the engraver meant nothing unless he could be located. Even then, he might not be able to help them at this point; but at least they would have something. Now they had nothing except a situation that was worsening daily.

He looked at his watch: nine-thirty. He had a meeting with

President Turner at ten. The President wanted answers. He didn't have any.

The phone rang. His secretary came on the intercom.

"Mr. Secretary, it's Mr. Trainor of *The New York Times*."

"Put him through, Harriet."

Jim Trainor was an old friend. Dillon had known him for over twenty years, ever since Trainor had run for Controller of the City of New York. At that time Trainor had been a financial writer with the *Wall Street Journal*. They had gotten to know each other and had stayed in touch over the years.

He picked up the phone.

"Jim, I thought publishers never got to the office before noon, much less made phone calls. What can I do for you?"

Trainor was usually a very animated personality with a quick wit, and always had a quip to make at the beginning of a conversation. However, there was a long pause before he spoke. When he did, it was straight to the point.

"Allen, I received some information this morning, and I'd like you to verify it."

"Sure, if it's something you can give me over the phone, I'd be glad to."

"No, it's not."

"It's not what?"

"Something I can give you over the phone."

"I see," Dillon said, puzzled by Trainor's tone of voice. "Can you at least give me the subject of the information?"

Again Trainor hesitated, but he finally said, "It has to do with an audit your agency recently conducted . . . on bank-vault currency."

The words went off like a bomb inside Dillon's mind. What he had feared over the past two months was finally happening: Word of the inflated currency had leaked. Beads of perspiration began to form on his brow, and the receiver trembled in his hand. He wanted to scream out in alarm, but he managed to say in a relatively calm voice, "You can't print anything concerning those audits."

"Well, I think we'd better talk about that," Trainor replied tersely. "This information has already gone beyond you and me. The Chairman of the New York Stock Exchange has also been copied."

"Oh, my God" was all he could say. It took him a few moments to regain his composure before he could ask who had sent Trainor the figures.

"I don't know," Trainor answered. "They arrived here this morning by special messenger. It had to come out of your office, though, because it's on official Treasury Department stationery. Again, I won't give you any figures over the phone, but I suspect you know what they are."

"What if I tell you I can't verify the accuracy of those figures," Dillon said, grasping for straws.

"Then we would have to check them out ourselves. It'll take a few days, but you know we have ways of determining their accuracy."

Dillon's mind was reeling. Every sentence seemed to be another damaging blow.

How had those figures gotten out of the Treasury Department? He thought he had taken every security precaution possible, but the information had leaked, anyway. If Trainor printed what he already knew, the economy would be doomed. Oddly enough, he had been the one to warn against a breach of security at the meeting weeks ago with the President. What he'd said then had been absolutely true: As long as nobody knew the counterfeit was coming into the economy, they had time to find the source of it. Well, unless they could silence Trainor now, time had run out.

"Jim, you've got to come to Washington tonight for a meeting with the President. Promise me you won't show that report to anyone until then. You've got to promise me," he said, shouting into the phone.

"All right," Trainor replied, surprised at the suddenness with which a meeting with the President could be arranged. "You're sure you can arrange a meeting that quickly?"

"Yes, I'm sure," Dillon said immediately. "Nine o'clock in the Oval Office. You'll be there?"

"I'll be there."

"Not a word about the report until then."

"Not until then."

Trainor hung up.

Dillon put the receiver down and wiped his face with a handkerchief. It was dripping wet. The powder keg they all knew they were sitting on was about to explode. It would be an explosion far greater than any bomb the Russians could drop, unless he stopped it. He had to act, and he had to act fast.

By the time Trainor arrived at the Oval Office, the President; his financial adviser, Eric Nietsche; Secretary of State Patterson; and Dillon had already met for over an hour. Only Patterson had to be introduced; the rest of the group had known Trainor for years. He was barely seated when the phone on the President's desk rang. Dillon answered it. New York Stock Exchange Chairman Kenneth Wirth was waiting outside. Dillon had him sent in immediately, and the tall, distinguished-looking chairman of the world's most powerful trading exchange was introduced.

Patterson filled in the two men on the situation, beginning with the government's discovery of a large influx of money in the economy and ending with Davidson's losing the lead to Tompkins in Florida. Both men sat silently, listening to an incredible chain of events that were part of an ingenious plan by the Russians to bring down the U.S. economy.

Patterson finished describing what had occurred over the past six months and leaned back in his chair. He poured himself some water from a pitcher on the President's desk. Trainor and Wirth looked at each other in disbelief. Finally the newspaperman spoke, his question directed at the President.

"Are you sure the money is counterfeit?"

The President shrugged his shoulders. It was a question he had asked the men around him many times.

"We're convinced that it has to be, Mr. Trainor. I know we don't have one single counterfeit bill to point to, but we're talking about billions of dollars here, billions more than the Russians could afford to put into the economy."

"Well, what *about* the Russians?" Wirth asked, interrupting. "Has anybody spoken to them directly?"

Turner directed the question to the Secretary of State.

"I met with Foreign Minister Sarandov two weeks ago in New York. They freely admit to being behind what's happening, and they're proud of the fact that we can't do a damn thing to stop them."

"Are they admitting to printing counterfeit money?" Wirth asked.

"What counterfeit money?" Patterson answered, his arms outstretched in a sign of resignation. "They claim they don't know anything about counterfeits. In fact, Sarandov went so far as to say that their official statement will be that *we're* printing counterfeit money. That we're printing more currency than we can back up to cover up mismanagement and spiraling inflation. That we're covering up a capitalistic financial system that doesn't work."

Trainor looked at the group of men around him. They were silent. Even the President seemed at a loss for words. He studied Turner closely. The man had just been elected by a narrow margin eighteen months ago. At forty-nine, he was one of the youngest men ever elected to the office. Already the job had aged him considerably. Like the President before him, he had tried to launch a new economic program aimed at creating jobs and stimulating the economy. So far he had failed. Congress hadn't passed many of his administration's proposals, and inflation was higher than it had been in three years. The Russians couldn't have picked a better time to attack the economy. It was practically killing itself.

As governor of Alabama, Turner had done a brilliant job. His programs had revitalized the state's dormant manufacturing areas. New companies had been drawn into the state, replacing those that had moved elsewhere in search of tax incentives and cheap labor. Because of his leadership Alabama now offered incentives competitive with anybody. But Washington was something else. He had come on strong in the early months; too strong. Many senators and congressmen were alienated by his aggressiveness. Trainor wondered how he would survive this crisis. If there was any chance at all of coming through it successfully, Congress would have to be involved, and Turner would need their support.

Trainor was about to ask the President what his plan was at this point, but Eric Nietsche, the President's seventy-year-old economic adviser, spoke first.

"I'm afraid, gentlemen, that we're all reluctant to say that the Russians have us where they want us: backed into a corner. There's nothing we can do to stop them until we can prove to the world that they're involved, but first we've got to put a stop to the flow of counterfeit money. It may even be too late for that. There may be too much in the economy already. Our only hope is to hide the facts a little longer, until we can at least stop the flow. That's why you can't print this, Mr. Trainor. We need more time if we are to save the situation."

"I understand that, sir," Trainor answered, "but the information has already leaked. I don't think you have any more time. People besides the Russians now know of the situation."

Secretary of State Patterson slammed his hand down on the President's desk. "The Russians leaked the information. That should be very obvious," he said to Trainor.

"That's true, Mr. Secretary, but someone at the Treasury Department provided them with the figures. Once information like that leaks, there's no way of stopping it."

Turner got up from his desk and paced in front of the large windows, now spattered with rain. He stared at the drops sliding down the panes, his back to the men seated around his desk. Finally he turned to them.

"The point is that this story can't be printed now. We have to buy time to rid the economy of this counterfeit money and bring it back to full strength. Then we can expose the Russians for what they've done before the World Court. We need that time, Mr. Trainor. I know that as a newspaperman you have a right to print the facts. In your mind you might even think it a moral obligation. But I say that morality now rests with protecting your country from an insidious plot by its enemy. That's your moral obligation."

He looked around the room for agreement. He found it with Wirth.

"I agree, Mr. President. If word of this got out now, the market would plummet within a few days. An overrun of currency like this would make the Crash of '29 seem like a minor recession. The dollar would be devalued so quickly that everyone would become a seller. Billions would be lost in days, not because of true inflation but because of Russian-induced inflation."

Trainor held the copy of the audit in his hand.

"But you can't hide these figures. You have to report M1-A in a week. What are you going to do then?"

Nietsche answered quickly. "M1-A won't reflect as bad a situation as our audit. It will take time for the decreased demand for cash from the Federal Reserve to take effect. It could take weeks yet before M1-A slips enough to be a factor. And those are the weeks we need to find the counterfeit."

Trainor put the paper down in front of him, absently pressing out the folds running through the columns of damaging numbers. Every man in the room was watching him carefully.

"Gentlemen," he began, "every part of my experience tells me that when something has leaked this far, it's fatal. If what you say about the Russians is true, you can be sure they won't stop until this information is made public. It has to be an integral part of their plan. All the counterfeit in the world isn't going to affect the economy unless the financial world knows about it. Only then does it affect the value of the dollar. Believe me, these figures are going to be printed for the world to see. It's just going to be a matter of who prints them first."

Turner answered him in a loud voice. He was beginning to become frightened with the reality of what Trainor was saying. "Don't you see, though, that every day we can buy will give us a chance of finding the source of the counterfeit?"

"You don't have any new leads," Trainor replied. "You lost track of your man Tompkins in Florida. You're starting from scratch again. There isn't any time left. I think you'll find that within the next two or three days the figures will be made public. The Russians aren't going to give you any more time. They've got enough money out there to raise hell with the economy; why should they wait?"

No one answered. Trainor's last few remarks had hit home with the sudden reality that the disclosure of the figures was inevitable. The room was quiet. Suddenly the phone rang on the President's desk; it was as if a siren had gone off. Startled, Turner reached over and picked up the receiver. He spoke a few words, then handed it to Trainor.

"It's for you . . . your office in New York. They say it's important."

Trainor took the phone. He listened for a few moments without saying a word. Then he handed the phone to the President.

"It's my editor in chief in New York. He's going to read you an article that will appear tomorrow in *Pravda*. I want you to hear it with me. I'll pick up the other phone."

"I see," Turner said quietly. "We might as well all hear it over the conference speaker."

Trainor went across the room and picked up a white phone on the coffee table. He cradled the receiver on his shoulder and took a pad from his breast pocket.

"Go ahead, Tom. I've got the President on the other phone."

The voice of an experienced professional came over the line as Turner held the receiver to his ear. It was calm, almost matter-of-fact, as if describing what might have been something as mundane as a weather report.

"I have in front of me, Mr. President, the lead article that will appear in *Pravda* tomorrow. Pictured over three columns of the front page, running one hundred and thirty lines deep, is a U.S. Treasury report on bank-vault currency from a recent Treasury audit. The headline reads: GOVERNMENT DOCUMENT REVEALS HIGHLY INFLATED U.S. MONEY SUPPLY. Subhead: SECRET DOCUMENT SHOWS OVERPRINTING OF U.S. CURRENCY. Are you ready for the first paragraph, Jim?"

"Go ahead," Trainor replied.

In a modified kind of shorthand, Trainor scrawled the headline on his pad as it came over the phone. Turner closed his eyes, anticipating the destructive words that would follow.

"'In an official document obtained by TASS, the Treasury revealed the results of a secret audit conducted during the past three months. Over 10,000 of the country's 16,000 banks reported a total of over $285 billion in vault currency, over four times the normal amount on hand. Because of mismanagement by the Turner administration and rampant inflation, the U.S. government has resorted to printing billions of dollars to sustain the economy. However, this currency does not have the backing of U.S. Treasury assets. It is worthless paper that will bring about devaluation of the dollar on the world market. Calculations by economists contacted by *Pravda* show that the dollar will be devalued by as much as twenty percent in the next few days. When told of the startling figures, Vasily A. Gagarin, Deputy Minister of Finance, was quoted as saying that, "This was another example of the capitalist system of government's failure to control inflation.'' He predicted, however, that international financiers would quickly reconsider their positions and convert their dollars to other currencies.'

" 'Gagarin went on to say that he was surprised by the Turner administration resorting to underhanded economics. Had *Pravda* not uncovered the reckless overprinting of currency, the administration would have continued not only to dupe the American people but the financial world as well. He said that Soviet Foreign Minister Sarandov was preparing immediately to meet with the Turner administration to strongly suggest they take a "more responsible financial position." '

"He goes on to discuss the figures of the report in detail," the editor said. "Do you want me to read on?"

"No," Turner said quickly, "I've heard enough. I think we all have. Apparently we can read the rest in tomorrow's *Pravda.*" He hung up the phone. Trainor thanked his editor for the information and his promptness in contacting him. By the time he rejoined the group around Turner's desk, Secretary of State Patterson was pacing the floor, shouting at the top of his voice.

"The nerve of those sons of bitches. Sarandov is preparing to meet with us to suggest a more responsible position. The bastard was gloating over flooding the economy with counterfeits a week ago in New York. They've completely turned the whole story around."

"You've got to admit that they've done it cleverly, though, don't you," Nietsche said. "And with the photograph of that report giving them credibility, the financial world is going to react. You can be sure of that."

"They'll react, all right," Dillon said, putting out his third cigarette. "It'll be an immediate recommendation for the devaluation of the dollar. And you can be sure it'll be a hefty one."

"Never mind what'll happen *outside* the country," Wirth said quietly. "I don't even want to think what will happen in the market tomorrow, once that story is read."

"That story can't be the only one read," the President said. He was still standing behind his desk, and now he looked directly at Trainor.

"I guess you're right, after all, Trainor. It seems now that the true story will have to be printed. At least, then the American people will know why the money is flooding the economy, and they'll know who is responsible for it being there. If we're being attacked, and I consider this as much an attack as a military one, they damn well better know who the enemy is."

There was complete agreement from everybody. Trainor could see that they were fired-up now, responding to the audacity of the *Pravda* report. He sensed a relief on their part that they would no longer be hiding something from the American public. Now it would all come out into the open and they would be free to deal with it. He put the notepad into his pocket and looked directly at the President as he spoke.

"I'll print the true story as it exists, Mr. President, but I'm afraid that doesn't include naming the Russians."

"What do you mean?" Patterson said, looking over his glasses. "You heard me say that Sarandov was gloating over the fact that they were attacking the economy."

"I know that," Trainor said quickly, "but that's hearsay at this point."

"Hearsay! Are you saying that you wouldn't take our word over the Russians'?" the President said, raising his voice for the first time.

"I'm not saying that at all, but as a newspaperman, I can only print the facts that are in front of me. They are that there is an overflow of currency in the economy, far more than the Bureau of Engraving shows, and that it is *assumed* that the currency is counterfeit, although no counterfeit bills have been found."

"Well, goddammit, we're getting that from *Pravda* tomorrow. Whose side are you on, anyway, Trainor!" Patterson shouted.

"That's not fair, Fred," the President said before Trainor could respond. "I'm afraid that the facts Mr. Trainor states are accurate. We don't have any actual proof that the money is counterfeit or that the Russians are behind anything. Five minutes ago I was prepared to ask Mr. Trainor—and, if necessary, order him—not to print anything. The phone call from his editor eliminated that option."

He turned to Trainor.

"I do think we must counteract the *Pravda* article in that the money isn't coming into the economy because of mismanagement or irresponsible printing of currency. We can prove that. But I think you must say we suspect the Russians are behind the counterfeit. Mr. Patterson's conversation with Sakarov *did* exist."

"All right, I'll agree to that," Trainor said quietly.

Turner sat with his hands folded in front of him. His body was hunched over, as if he were preparing for the tremendous weight of the situation to fall on him suddenly. He seemed to be looking for a solution to the problem, or at least a direction to go in, but it was obvious now that nothing more could be done. Without looking up, he said, "I'm afraid we've lost round one, gentlemen. The result of your article will be devastating, Trainor. What was described earlier as happening in the market and on the foreign exchange will occur just as the Russians planned it. As you said, their plan was to force us into revealing an overage of currency. They've accomplished that this evening. Tomorrow's reaction is also part of the plan. Right now they're winning, and they're winning big."

Another forty minutes passed before Trainor finally left the meeting, along with Cristaldi, Nietsche, and Wirth. It was almost midnight. Patterson and the President were alone in the Oval Office. They had moved to the other end of the room and were seated in two soft chairs next to a coffee table. An attendant brought in coffee, poured it from a silver pot, and left it on the table. Turner took a few sips. He rolled up the sleeves of his monogrammed white dress shirt and loosened his tie. Patterson was seated on the sofa, jotting down some notes as he spoke into a telephone. Finally he hung up, dropping the receiver into its cradle.

"How bad is it going to be?" Turner asked.

"Bad. The market will go down to six hundred at least. We'll be lucky if the dollar doesn't fall more than eighteen points. It's going to be as bad a situation as 1929, maybe even worse."

"How much time do they say we have before the whole thing collapses?" the President asked.

Patterson adjusted his glasses while he turned some pages on the pad. "My chief economist says three weeks. If we don't find the source of the counterfeit bills before then, it'll be all over."

"Where do we stand on that?"

"Cristaldi says Davidson has found the blind newsstand owner's house in Miami. As he expected, the guy's already left the place. Fuller is back in Hartford, talking to Tompkins's son. It doesn't look good, Pete."

Turner was trying to prepare himself mentally for the reaction to the next day's headlines. The news media would descend on his administration in droves. Most of their questions wouldn't have answers: Why wasn't the influx of currency noticed earlier? How do you know the money is counterfeit? Who is responsible for printing them? Do you have any leads as to where it's being printed?

The reaction internationally would be even worse. Every country dependent on American dollars for aid would be in a state of shock. Countries trading heavily with the U.S., such as Japan, Germany, England, and France, would be demanding instant devaluation. Just when he was beginning to have success with foreign policy, the bottom was going to fall out of it all. There had to be a way to avoid total collapse. If something wasn't done quickly to counteract the lack of confidence in the dollar, the Russians would win this "financial war" easily.

Turner looked at Patterson, who was now tapping the edge of his pad with a ballpoint pen. That night, the Secretary of State had lost control with Trainor. That was rare. It was the first time Turner had ever seen Patterson flustered. But they were all backed into a corner now and were reacting defensively. The Russians had surprised them with a financial attack that was more sudden and terrifying than any nuclear war. Oddly enough, a nuclear threat would have been easier to deal with. The enemy would be known to the world and defenses mobilized. But now the enemy was anonymous and there weren't any defenses. It was the ultimate frustration: to be attacked and not being able to do anything about it.

Patterson wrote something down and tore the page from the notebook. He folded it once, then held it up to Turner.

"What we need is help from the financial world to sustain the value of the dollar while we prove that the Russians are behind the counterfeit. Our only hope is with the Bank for International Settlements. They helped save the pound-sterling situation for the British in 1964, and helped Germany when they tried futilely to avoid devaluation in 1969." He waved the paper in the air. "This is the only man I know who can persuade the bankers of that organization to maintain confidence in the dollar and minimize devaluation. Not only that, he's a personal friend of mine who'll respond to us on a personal level. I'm confident of that."

He passed the piece of paper over to Turner. On it was the name of Karl Geisler.

The following morning, with the six-hour time difference between Washington's and Europe's major capitals, *Pravda* was in the hands of investors on the Continent long before the *Times*. In most cases the blazing headlines telling of the inflated money supply were taken as another propaganda campaign by the Soviets to discredit the capitalist system. Some, however, used the newspaper intelligently, recognizing it as a propaganda arm but also realizing that often propaganda was an extension of truth. Those people immediately made preparations to react, should the article have any credence. As a result, when the *Times* article broke in New York at six-thirty A.M., investors in the European exchanges were prepared to convert assets from dollars to other currencies. The article took up nearly half of the front page, the headline blaring across the top.

INFLATED MONEY SUPPLY REVEALED
MONEY IN CIRCULATION EXCEEDS BUREAU OF ENGRAVING
FIGURES BY $20 BILLION DOLLARS
MARKET DROPS SHARPLY

Washington, April 3, 1991—

IT WAS REVEALED TODAY THAT BANK-VAULT CURRENCY IN THE NATION'S 16,000 BANKS EXCEEDED THE AMOUNT OF CURRENCY PRINTED BY THE BUREAU OF ENGRAVING AND REPORTED TO BE IN CIRCULATION. THE DISCREPANCY WAS IN EXCESS OF $200 BILLION. TREASURY DEPARTMENT OFFICIALS SUSPECT THAT COUNTERFEIT CURRENCY IN LARGE QUANTITIES IS ENTERING THE ECONOMY.

THE NEW YORK STOCK EXCHANGE DROPPED DRAMATI-
CALLY AS THE NEWS DROVE DOWN THE VALUE OF THE
DOLLAR ON THE INTERNATIONAL MARKET. BY FOUR
O'CLOCK CLOSING, THE DOLLAR HAD FALLEN OVER 20
POINTS AGAINST THE GERMAN MARK AND 15.62 AGAINST
THE BRITISH POUND. THE DOW HAD FALLEN TO 580. THE
BREAK WAS ONE OF THE WIDEST IN THE MARKET'S HISTORY,
WIPING OUT THOUSANDS OF ACCOUNTS BOTH LARGE AND
SMALL. EFFECTS WERE FELT IN EUROPEAN AND JAPANESE
MARKETS AS WELL.

BANKS ACROSS THE COUNTRY REFUSED TO ACCEPT ANY
NEW CURRENCY FROM THEIR CUSTOMERS, OR TO EXCHANGE
CURRENCY WITH OTHER BANKS. PAPER CURRENCY WAS
FROZEN EVERYWHERE.

TREASURY DEPARTMENT OFFICIALS CONCEDE THAT THE
INFLATED AMOUNT OF DOLLARS IS DUE TO THE COUNTERFEIT
CURRENCY FLOODING THE ECONOMY. HOWEVER, NO COUN-
TERFEIT BILLS HAVE AS YET BEEN FOUND.

SECRETARY OF THE TREASURY DILLON COULD ONLY SPECU-
LATE AS TO WHERE IT MIGHT BE COMING FROM. WHEN
PRESSED ABOUT WHETHER RUMORS THAT THE SOVIET UNION
WAS BEHIND IT, HE COULD NOT COMMENT.

PRESIDENT TURNER IS SAID TO BE PREPARING A MAJOR
ADDRESS, TO BE BROADCAST THIS EVENING IN AN ATTEMPT
TO CALM THE NATION AND THE FINANCIAL WORLD. HOW-
EVER, IT IS REPORTED THAT MAJOR INVESTORS HAVE AL-
READY MOVED LIQUID ASSETS OUT OF U.S. BANKS AND ARE
CONVERTING TO OTHER CURRENCIES. ECONOMISTS PREDICT
THAT SHOULD THIS TREND CONTINUE, THE ECONOMY IS IN
DANGER OF TOTAL COLLAPSE WITHIN A MATTER OF WEEKS.

The news spread rapidly around the world. Exchanges in
London, Paris, Rome, West Berlin, Tokyo, and New York had
record high transactions. By eleven-thirty A.M., the New York
tape began falling behind. By two P.M., even with the latest
computerized electronics, it was twenty minutes behind. An
hour after the four o'clock closing, transactions for the day
hadn't all been tabulated. But everyone knew the losses were
staggering. By evening the TV networks were running file film
recalling the Crash of 1929, mixed with interviews hastily
arranged with Treasury officials. Many of them stood in front

of the Capitol building with bright TV lights shining on their confused faces. There weren't any answers or explanations to be given. Yes, it was true, there was an inflated money supply. Yes, the official administration statement was that it was counterfeit. No, they didn't have any counterfeit bills. No, they didn't know who was printing it. Who did they suspect? No comment. Was it the Russians? No statement could be made at this time.

By the end of the evening, most Americans went to sleep having heard a confused, defensive government unable to explain a crumbling economy or offer solutions for its recovery.

In Moscow, key members of the Politburo met to watch Western newscasts transmitted by satellite. After an hour of viewing, champagne was served, and a toast was offered in honor of Deputy Minister of Finance Gagarin, architect of the plan that would bring about the defeat of the United States.

12

New York, April 13, 1991 (*The New York Times*)—

WITH OVER 12,000 BANKS NOT ACCEPTING ANY NEW CURRENCY, BARTERING HAS REPLACED THE USE OF CURRENCY THROUGHOUT THE COUNTRY. WITH THE VALUE OF THE DOLLAR DECLINING EVERY DAY, PEOPLE HAVE TURNED TO TRADING GOODS FOR OTHER GOODS OR SERVICES. ONE OF THE LARGEST TRANSACTIONS RECORDED WAS THE SALE OF 50,000 HEAD OF CATTLE BY A TEXAS RANCHER IN EXCHANGE FOR 2,500 ACRES OF FARMLAND IN WESTERN KANSAS.

Houston, April 13, 1991 (UPI)—
CRIME HAS INCREASED IN THE MAJOR CITIES AS THE MONETARY CRISIS CONTINUES. SUPERMARKETS LEAD THE LIST AS THE DOLLAR FALLS. CHAINS HERE IN THE SOUTHWEST REPORT BREAK-INS AT OVER 400 STORES IN THE PAST MONTH AS PEOPLE BECOME DESPERATE FOR FOOD.

April 13, 1991
The island of St. Maarten

BOB TOMPKINS PUSHED his sunglasses back on his forehead to get a better look at a sea gull gliding overhead. It made a long, wide turn toward the beach where it picked up a warm current of air. Gently the updraft lifted the bird higher in the sky until it flew out of the airstream to begin a slow glide downward. It descended lazily, then turned into the current to repeat the process again.

He envied the graceful white bird. It had its freedom,

something that had become more and more valuable to him as each day passed. Almost a year had gone by since he and Helen had been taken hostage. There had been months of striking contrasts. The time spent working on the plates had been terrifying. He feared he would never see Helen again. Then they had been reunited, and that gave him new strength. Her arthritis was much better, and they made an attempt to find whatever happiness they could within the confines of captivity. The climate was pleasant, their surroundings luxurious, but they lived under the fear of his no longer being needed to work on the plates. God knows what would happen then. But as the months passed, the fear subsided until now it was replaced by boredom and anxiety.

He looked out from under the umbrella that protected him from the blazing sun. To his left was a wall of coral-covered rock that ran from the hill behind him into the sea. It provided a natural barrier between the beach and whatever was beyond. Even at low tide, it extended far enough out into water that was too deep and treacherous for him to get around.

To his right was over five hundred feet of white, sandy beach. At the end of it was a second hill, covered with bright red and orange bougainvillea high enough so he couldn't see over it.

He looked behind him. Two guards were sitting at a picnic table near the cottage he and Helen occupied. One was playing solitaire, while the other listened to a portable radio through an earplug. This was only one of the precautions taken that prevented him from getting any news from the outside world. He and Helen existed in a luxurious void; Adam and Eve in the garden of Eden, forbidden by Satan to go beyond.

Weeks ago he had given up calculating the amount of counterfeit money that would be in circulation if they were still printing. By now it could be in the billions. He tried to put it out of his mind, but it continued to gnaw at him. What terrible thing could be happening to the country? Had the Russians used the counterfeit bills to buy weapons? Or was it being used to buy into an economy like West Germany or the Middle East where Russia had ambitions of taking over the government? He thought it might even be used against the United States economy, but that seemed beyond the realm of possibility.

What frustrated him more than anything was knowing there wasn't any way to identify the counterfeit unless he could find a way to escape.

He thought back to the night at the printing plant when he'd overheard the men speaking Russian. He had become terrified at what he was doing to help his country's enemy. But he had found a solution, a way to alter the plates so they could be detected as counterfeit. The problem had been extremely difficult. He had to find a way to sabotage the Russians without risking Helen's life. The bills had to appear perfect when Vladislav tested them or they would torture her. And they were perfect. No one could detect them as counterfeit, no matter what test they put them through except himself. The plan was ingenious, maybe too ingenious. It may have protected Helen's life but had destroyed the country.

It was ten-thirty. Helen would be returning from her morning therapy session. He looked down the beach. She was walking toward him carrying a small beach bag. He wondered what was in it. Every day was such a routine that now she made little attempts at surprising him.

She sat down in the beach chair next to him and took off her white straw hat. He noticed that she had a new bathing suit on. It was a lemon-yellow one-piece with blue-striped trim.

They sat for a moment under the beach umbrella without saying anything. Conversation had become difficult lately. They were with each other twenty-four hours a day, with the same people, the same routine, the same experiences. It didn't leave much to relate to each other.

Finally she broke the silence.

"You didn't notice my new bathing suit."

"Yes, I did."

"Then why didn't you say anything about it?"

"Because it's the fifth new bathing suit you've gotten in three weeks."

"So?"

"So that's a little extravagant, isn't it?"

She looked at him, and he could see the disappointment begin to show in her eyes. However, she took his hand and smiled at him.

"Don't you know how many bathing suits three hundred and

fifty thousand dollars can buy? I'm going to have them buy me every suit in this stupid place and everything else along with it. It's all I've got to do."

He had almost forgotten about the money that Vladislav had deposited in a local bank for them. It bothered him to spend any of it. Spending it meant justifying what he had done to earn it. He couldn't come to terms with that. Maybe she had the right idea, though.

He squeezed her hand.

"You're right. It's all you have to do. It looks great on you. So do the others."

"You're prejudiced," she said, winking at him.

"I know."

She picked up the bag and held it in front of him.

"So what do you think is in the bag?"

He held up two fingers.

"Two piña coladas in a thermos with ice. Just like yesterday."

"That, my good man, is correct. But would you venture a guess as to what else is in here?"

He sat up in the chair and leaned over to get a look. She pulled the bag closer to her.

"A bathing suit for me," he said.

"Wrong."

"A *Playboy* magazine."

"Never."

"Then I give up."

She reached into the bag and took out a small box wrapped in a cut-up grocery bag.

"The paper's the best I could find. Open it."

He tore the paper apart and found a box. He looked at her curiously, then opened it. Inside was a 35mm Nikon camera. It was fully equipped with a motor drive, built-in meter, the works.

"I hope it's the right one," she said excitedly. "I tried to get the closest to what you have at home."

The camera felt good in his hands. He aimed it down the beach and focused the lens. It was a 50mm lens and seemed to be very sharp.

"It's fine," he said. "Even *better* than what I have at home."

She snuggled up against him, pleased with his reaction to the gift. "Now you won't be bored with yourself. You can get back into your old hobby again, taking pictures and developing them yourself."

He looked at her and smiled.

"Develop them myself? I don't have the equipment for that."

She looked up at him innocently, her brown eyes flashing. "You do now," she spoke quickly, imitating one of those TV game-show announcers. "You, Robert Tompkins, are now the proud owner of a new developing lab, complete with developing tank, chemicals, enlarger, dryer, mounts, even a complete instruction book courtesy of . . ." She hesitated. "Well, courtesy of whoever they are."

He put his arm around her.

"How did you get all of this, and where did you put it?"

"Well, since we don't have many clothes and our walk-in closet is empty, I thought it would make a perfect darkroom. So I asked Rudy to order everything and he did. Tom has been installing shelves for the past two days. They're finished now. Aren't I a genius?"

He took her hand and then kissed her on the forehead.

"Ya know somethin', kid? With you I think I'll make it through this yet."

For a moment he thought he saw tears in her eyes, but she quickly controlled herself and held them back. She looked up at him.

"Now, shall we have those piña coladas?"

"I'll drink to that," he said.

He spent most of the day tinkering with his new equipment. Much of it was slightly different from what he had in his tiny basement lab at home. The enlarger was a different model, the chemicals for the developer took different mixtures, and the mounts for the slides fitted together differently. He enjoyed reading the instruction booklets. A lot of improvements had been made since he'd bought his equipment years ago.

Some of the smaller items were still in the boxes. Again, the

KGB agents had been very careful. Each shipping label had been removed to prevent him from learning his location. Even the return addresses had been blacked out. Somehow, despite his dislike for them, he secretly admired their professionalism. Since the first night at the printing plant, they hadn't slipped once. Their English was perfect, their mannerisms very American, and their security very tight. They were professionals, and despite himself, he admired that. It surprised him later that night when he found that they had made their first mistake.

Helen had gone to bed and he was sitting in the living room reading the instructions for the assembly of the enlarger. He had most of the pieces in front of him, but the bulb was missing. Checking through the boxes around him, he found them all empty. Putting the instruction manual aside, he got up and went into his tiny lab in the closet. There were other boxes on a shelf. He looked through them again and found a small one unopened. Back in the living room, he sat down and opened it. Again, the outside label had been carefully peeled away. With a kitchen knife he sliced the tape open and spread the cardboard flaps apart. Inside, there was some crumpled newspaper around the bulb to protect it. He threw it on the floor and then realized what he had done.

He stared at it. It was a newspaper, the first newspaper he had seen in months. Quickly he uncrumpled the pages and pressed them flat against the coffee table with his fingers. He took off his glasses and cleaned them with his handkerchief to see the small print better. There were three pages. The first contained real-estate ads for condominiums. He focused in on one of them: "Condominium near sandy beach, 4 bdrm. liv rm. eat-in kitch. hi $80s." There were others mentioning beaches and water rights. Nothing unusual. Then he looked up at the top of the page and saw it. "The *Philipsburg Times*, St. Maarten ANVV." It was a local newspaper. He was on the island of St. Maarten.

His heart was racing. He turned the page over: more real-estate ads. The next page, local supermarket ads: "Oranges, 5 for $1; chicken cutlets, $2.29/lb." The other side: more of the same. He picked up the last page, and an article continued from another page jumped out at him. It was just a single paragraph. His hands trembled as he read the words.

"The financial crisis in the United States continued for the third week in a row. Counterfeit currency in circulation now exceeds $200 billion, and today the value of the dollar on foreign exchanges dropped another five points. President Turner has made another appeal to the heads of foreign governments to hold the value of the dollar until the source of counterfeit can be found."

His worst fears had come true. The Russians were using the money to defeat the United States financially. He leaned back in the sofa, the paper still in his hand. His whole body was shaking. What was he going to do? He had to escape from this island prison somehow. The fate of his country depended on it. Only he knew how to identify the counterfeit money, which apparently government experts had failed to do. But he knew months ago that that would happen. He had been forced to make sure the plates were perfect, or Helen would have been tortured or even killed. But he also had provided a way for them to be identified as counterfeit. Unfortunately he was the only one who knew how.

He looked at the bay window on the far wall. My God, the curtain was open. Quickly he shoved the paper under a cushion and went to the window. He looked outside; no one was there. Supposing they had seen him reading the paper. He closed the curtain, took the pages from under the cushion, and went into the bathroom. He turned on the light over the medicine chest and read the paragraph one more time as if he could change the words.

It was all his fault. There were times when he should have attempted to escape. All those nights in the printing plant. He knew he was in a city. What if he had just run out into the street? Somebody would have helped him. Or what about the trip down here? There were times when he could have just run from them into a crowd. The reason he couldn't was Helen. He knew that. She still prevented him from doing it.

They had to escape, but there was no way they could do it alone. They needed help. His only hope was to get word to somebody now that he knew where they were.

He looked at his reflection in the medicine-chest mirror. How had this all happened to him? It didn't make sense. He was just an ordinary guy who had worked all his life and wanted to enjoy retirement. But now he had become responsible for the defeat of the most powerful country in the world. His stomach felt queasy, and his legs were starting to get weak.

He took the antacid from the shelf and swallowed a few mouthfuls straight from the bottle. It helped a little, but he still felt sick. He looked at the newspaper pages in his hand and considered tearing them up and flushing them down the toilet. Something stopped him, and instead, he laid them carefully over the top of the medicine chest where they couldn't be seen. As he was about to leave the bathroom, he felt a retching in his stomach and he dropped to his knees to vomit into the toilet.

It was another twenty minutes before he could get enough control of himself to get into bed. Lying beside Helen, he tried to calm down and begin to think rationally. His thoughts all focused on escape. That was a certainty now that he knew the terrible results of what he had done. There had to be a way.

He thought about where they were: St. Maarten. What did he know about the island? A few years ago they had considered a vacation there but had decided against it. Still, he remembered going through some travel brochures. It was a big island, over twenty miles long, and belonged to both the Dutch and the French. What was the place they were planning to stay at? Mullet Bay, that was it, a large condominium resort on the ocean.

Outside of that, he didn't remember much else. It didn't matter, anyway. They would never manage to escape from the compound. The KGB watched them all the time, and at night there were guards at the gate. Even if they managed to get out, where would they go? It wouldn't take long to find them. They didn't know the island at all; the KGB knew it well.

No, they had to have outside help. He had to find a way to let someone know where they were. He had to get word to their son Bill. But how? They screened every letter he or Helen wrote very carefully. In the past they had been forced to eliminate any references to their true location. As far as anybody knew, they were still in Florida. There was no way they could say where they really were without the guards picking it up.

But then an idea came to him. Maybe they didn't have to write it; maybe they could show it. A plan began to form in his

mind. It was a long shot, but still it was a plan. He lay there for
over two hours. The more he thought about it, the more he
realized that it was the only chance they might have. Yes, it
might work. He was lucky that Helen had bought all that
photographic equipment.

The following morning he was up and about at six A.M. It
was going to be a beautiful, clear day. The sun was coming up
over the horizon, illuminating a deep blue sky. A perfect day
for taking pictures. He sat at the kitchen table with a cup of
coffee, loading the Nikon with slide film. There were twenty-
four exposures to a roll. He planned on shooting two rolls.

Helen came into the kitchen wearing her bathrobe. Her eyes
were half open as she took some eggs and orange juice from
the refrigerator. She set them on the table and came up behind
him, putting her arms around his neck.

"I see you're ready to go and play with your new toy," she
said softly. He slipped the film into the camera and closed the
back. With a few quick turns of the take-up knob he had the
film in place. Turning to her, he said, "Put on your best bathing
suit, kid, because I'm ready to shoot up a storm."

"I'll wear the new one I got yesterday, but I'll put a robe
over it."

He kissed her lightly on the cheek.

"Forget the robe, you look great without it. Besides, I want
to see if I can send some of the pictures to Bill so he can see
how better you are."

She sat on the chair beside him and poured some coffee from
the pot he left out.

"Do you think they'll let us send the pictures out?"

"I don't know," he answered, "but it won't hurt to find out.
Who do you think we should ask?"

She thought for a moment.

"I think it'll have to be Rudy. I'd much rather ask Tom, but I
don't think he has the authority."

He looked at her carefully. He could see her mood changing
as she sipped the coffee. The thought of Bill, Elaine, and the
grandchildren was kindling the longing she felt for them.

"We haven't gotten any letters in over three weeks now. Do
you think they've given up on us?" she asked.

"Nonsense," he said quickly. "They're probably holding the letters back from us. Anyway, that's why these pictures will be great. They'll see we're okay. Maybe they'll send some back."

"Oh, that would be wonderful," she said. "I'd love to see pictures of the children." She paused for a moment and then said in almost a whisper, "I don't know if I'll ever see them again."

He put the camera in the carrying case, along with the extra roll of film.

"You'll see them again soon. It can't be much longer now. They must have printed enough money by now."

Suddenly she stood up and was staring at him. Her hands were clenched at her sides. Tears were welling up in her eyes.

"Don't you ever say that to me again," she said, beginning to cry. "You've been saying that for over two months now. They must have printed enough now. They never will have printed enough, never. Do you hear me? Never. We're not going to get off this island. Don't you realize that if they've printed enough, they don't need you anymore and they'll kill you? They'll kill both of us. They're not going to come to you and say, 'Thank you very much, we've decided we've printed enough money and you can go home now.' They'll kill us. They have to."

He reached over and took her hand. She was sobbing uncontrollably. There was nothing he could say. If she knew the truth as he did now, it would make things even worse. He felt it was best to just let her cry it out. For months she had held it back, trying to hide her emotions by making full days interesting with little surprises and gifts, games they played, and false hopes. Now she had reached a point where the reality and the futility of their situation had caught up with her.

Gradually her tears subsided, and she looked up at him with red cheeks and eyes. He wiped away the tears with his handkerchief and held her face in his hands. He wanted to tell her of his plan but couldn't. It had so little chance of working that it would just be too much for her to bear if it failed. All he could do was take her in his arms and hold her tight, hoping that whatever strength he had would be felt by their closeness.

• • •

Rudy, the leader of the KGB group on the island, listened to their request politely. As far as he was concerned, they could send any pictures they wanted, but first he would have to check with Cutrone. He promised to radio him as soon as possible and then get back to them.

In the meantime they went to their cottage and just sat. Tompkins was so obsessed with getting permission to send the pictures that he could do little else. Finally, just before noon, there was a knock on the door. It was Tom. He had come to tell them that Cutrone had approved their request. However, they were to send no more than five pictures, and they all had to be close-ups. He would not allow anything that would reveal their location. There were to be no wide shots of the cottage exteriors or the beach. Everything was to be head shots with little or no background.

They spent the whole afternoon taking the pictures. It did a lot to lift Helen's spirits. She felt that at least a part of them was escaping the island prison to go home to their son and family. She smiled happily in all of them, wishing to portray as much of a happy feeling as possible.

Bob took a lot of time to compose each of the shots, so they would be acceptable to Rudy. One in particular, he seemed to take forever with. It was simply a picture of Helen standing in front of the cottage window. She was wearing her straw hat and had put some freshly picked flowers in the headband.

"Move a little to the left, dear. That's too much, back a little. Now lift your head . . . too much. Turn slightly to the right." He went on and on for over five minutes before he clicked the shutter. She was surprised to see him take four shots of that same pose.

Finally they took some pictures of the two of them with the electric timer. She laughed when he barely got into the picture before the shutter went off. When they finished the last roll, the sun was setting over the mountain in back of the compound. Tompkins was happy. He had gotten the one picture he wanted.

That evening they barely finished dinner when he went to the makeshift darkroom and began developing the slides. Helen, realizing that he was lost for the evening, went to bed and read a while before falling off to sleep.

Bob set about developing the transparencies very carefully. He selected a roll that had pictures of himself in front of their cottage to develop first. It would be a test roll to assure that he was mixing the developer properly. Carefully he put the strip of film into the tank using the red safety light in the darkroom. Then he added the developer and set the timer. Eleven minutes later he emptied the chemical from the tank and poured in the stop solution. He reset the clock. Three minutes. He emptied it out and put in water to wash the strip. He rotated the shaft protruding from the top of the tank to wash it evenly, then dumped out the water. As he opened the tank and removed the developed film, he could see that the exposures were nearly perfect. The light meter on the Nikon had worked well.

He hung the strip to dry and began the same process on three other rolls, saving the one with Helen in front of the cottage window for last. Satisfied with their quality, he put the last roll in the tank. Fifteen minutes later he had all four rolls hanging from a line he had strung to dry.

He went into the bathroom and took the newspaper page he had hidden the night before from the top of the medicine chest. Carefully he pressed it flat and taped it to the white, enameled bathroom door. With a black marker he circled the heading at the top of the page: *Philipsburg Times, St. Maarten ANVV*. Then he took two lamps from the living room, removed the shades, and hung them over the door on either side of the page. He turned them on, then set his camera in place on a tripod. Returning to the darkroom, he took his engraver's glass and looked at the pictures of Helen in front of the window. After examining them carefully, he selected one and cut it from the strip. Holding it to the light, he studied the composition through the glass, fixing in his mind the position of the window in relation to the thirty-five-millimeter frame. Back outside, he looked through the camera viewfinder at the newspaper clipping. With his eye on the finder, he picked up the tripod and moved it backward. The clipping became smaller in the frame until it was the same size as the window in the other shot and in the same position. He went into the darkroom to check it one more time, then shot twelve exposures of the clipping.

An hour later he held the developed roll of the clipping

against a light to select the best exposure. The third one down was perfect, and he cut it from the roll. Carefully he positioned it over the shot of Helen so that the clipping was hidden behind the darkened window.

Taking one of the cardboard mounts, he sandwiched one slide over the other, checked the position of each, and sealed the mount. He held it up to the light. Perfect. The window was dark enough to hide the picture of the clipping in back of it.

He selected four other innocuous pictures to present to Rudy, then put them in an envelope. Tomorrow would be a crucial day. If the KGB leader simply looked at them through a viewer, there would be no problem. However, if he projected them on a screen, there was a danger of the second transparency showing through.

The thought led him to how his son Bill would view them. Would he use a projector? Did he have one? Yes, he remembered seeing slides of a trip the family had taken two summers ago. He hoped he would use it.

Outside the darkroom, he took the newspaper clipping off the door. As he reread it, he wondered what was happening back home. Had the FBI or the Secret Service made the link to his disappearance and the counterfeit money? Were they looking for him? He hoped so, because then they would pay special attention to any communication with his son. They would examine the slides very carefully.

The first hurdle would be getting the slides mailed out tomorrow. Then they would just have to wait . . . and pray.

Rudy sat at a table in the main cottage, about to examine the five slides Tompkins had selected. He asked Tom to bring in a viewer, which he now put in front of him. He held each of the slides up to a light for a quick examination.

"Nice pictures, Bob. You're a pretty good photographer," he said, looking at a close-up shot of some fiery red bougainvillea.

"Thanks," Tompkins answered. He was nervous. The screen on the viewer was larger than he expected.

Rudy put the first slide into the machine. It was the one of the newspaper sandwiched behind the picture of Helen. The image came on the screen, enlarged over five times. Tompkins could feel his heart beating faster as he strained to look at it over Rudy's shoulder. He studied the darkened window. The clipping behind it wasn't showing through. He had been successful.

Rudy turned to him.

"I don't know about this picture, Bob. There's a reflection in that window. See it?"

He hadn't noticed it before, even through the engraver's glass. He held his breath as he searched his mind for an answer. But before he could speak, Tom came around to look at the picture.

"It's water," he said matter-of-factly. "So what. It looks like where they're supposed to be."

Rudy considered the comment for what seemed to be an eternity. Finally he took it out of the viewer and laid it on the table.

"Yeah, I suppose so. Let's see the next one," he said, putting it into the viewer.

After examining all five, he put them into an envelope and then dictated a letter to Tompkins. It would be sent with the photographs. It said that Helen's arthritis was still improving in the warm climate and that they had decided to take a trip to California. That's why the letter had come from there. In three weeks they would return to Florida. Both of them sent their love and promised to visit them soon in Hartford.

Tompkins was surprised at the letter. Apparently the KGB was going to have men in California to relay letters to and from Hartford. Also, the indication that soon they would be in Hartford was hopeful. Maybe they didn't have much longer to go before their release. Well, it really didn't matter. False hopes before had been shattered; this wasn't anything new. He had to escape as soon as possible.

Rudy put the letter in the envelope and sealed it. Taking a small notebook from the desk drawer, he copied an address from it and onto the envelope. Tompkins noted that it was a Los Angeles address. He decided to press Rudy about the change in location.

"Why are Helen and I taking a vacation in California? Isn't your relay working well in Florida?"

Rudy hesitated for a moment and then looked at Tom, who seemed to avoid his glance.

"We just want to keep whoever might be looking for you guessing," Rudy said, smiling.

"What about the promise of visiting Hartford soon?" he asked.

"Ah, well, we're just about finished printing the money now, Bob. Within three weeks to a month, you should be back in Hartford."

Tompkins wanted to tell them he never would be let off the island. Helen was right. As soon as they were finished, he would be killed unless he could get word to someone who could help them. It was their only chance. He wished he could tell them he knew what they were up to; how they were in the process of destroying the U.S. economy. He wanted to tell them of their carelessness with the newspaper, he wanted to tell them he knew they were Russian, and most of all, he wanted to tell them he had tricked them, that the money could be identified as counterfeit. Instead, he simply nodded his head and turned to leave, Helen beside him.

Rudy and Tom watched them walk down the beach hand in hand, a guard trailing behind them.

"What's really going to happen to them?" Tom said, putting the letter into a small shoulder bag.

"When I called Yuri last night to ask permission to send the photographs, he told me the order for their execution would come any day now. They've just finished printing."

"We'll keep them alive until then?"

"Not necessarily," Rudy answered, lighting his pipe. "The Secret Service is getting close now that they've traced Tompkins to Florida. Yuri feels that if he has to, he'll eliminate Tompkins and take a chance on the plates not breaking. The final decision, though, has to come from Moscow. In the meantime they'll 'relocate' Tompkins to California."

"That's to throw off the Secret Service?" Tom asked.

"Right." Rudy drew some smoke through the pipe and blew it into the air. "That's why he allowed the pictures, to let the Americans know they're still alive, but in California. That should send a flock of them there to turn the state upside down."

"Soon we'll have to get rid of them."

Rudy was still watching them. They had stopped to watch some sandpipers pecking in the sand in search of food.

"Yeah," he said softly, "and I hope neither of us has to do it."

13

Washington, May 5, 1991 (AP)—

TODAY THE GOVERNMENT ANNOUNCED IT WOULD IMMEDI-
ATELY PROVIDE FOOD STAMPS FOR THE AREAS OF THE NATION
HARD-HIT BY UNEMPLOYMENT. THE NORMAL THREE-WEEK
APPLICATION PERIOD WILL BE WAIVED, ACCORDING TO
STEVEN W. BROOKS, DIRECTOR OF THE PROGRAM. AREAS
THAT WILL RECEIVE IMMEDIATE ASSISTANCE ARE DETROIT,
CHICAGO, MIAMI, DALLAS, SEATTLE, AND NEW YORK.

IT IS ESTIMATED THAT UNEMPLOYMENT HAS NOW REACHED
21%, THE HIGHEST FIGURE EVER RECORDED. AND THE END
DOES NOT SEEM IN SIGHT. GENERAL MOTORS SAID TODAY IT
WAS HALTING PRODUCTION OF 1992 MODELS AND WILL LAY
OFF AN ADDITIONAL 65,000 WORKERS.

Zurich, Switzerland
May 5, 1991

HIGH OVER ZURICH, Air Force One turned to begin its final
descent into the international airport. The pilot received special
clearance to land on the main runway. All other flights were
being held until he was on the ground.

Inside the large jet, Secretary of State Fred Patterson
buckled his seat belt and closed the folder he had been reading
for the past two hours. He stared at the typewritten words on
the tan manila folder: "CIA Report 7-1000—Karl Geisler."
The words seemed to jump off the page at him. They now
represented the last hope of a nation on the verge of being
destroyed by its own currency.

The hope was Geisler. As chairman of the Bank for International Settlements, he was the last resort in getting the

187

organization to come to the country's aid. Already there were indications that a vote to be taken by the executive committee three days from now would not be favorable. Representatives of government banks, once thought friendly to the nation, were not about to lend any assistance. One by one the United States was losing friends. Israel realized that the U.S. could no longer aid her militarily and was reneging; France wouldn't help; Japan saw the situation as an opportunity to retaliate on strict import laws; and the Arab states were already converting investment dollars into other currencies. America stood alone, unless someone of Geisler's stature could convince them that the dollar could bounce back.

Patterson thought about the man himself. They had met over fifteen years ago at an international banking convention in New York where he had been asked to speak. His speech, entitled "The Government's Role in Banking," had impressed Geisler, who had just been elected president of Union Suisse. The banker made a point of coming over to his table and introducing himself. He remembered Geisler's words well. "That's the first time I've ever heard a government official admit that banks can operate more efficiently if government stayed the hell out of their way." He remembered the speech hadn't quite stated it that way, but yes, he did feel that government was exercising stifling controls over the industry.

They became friendly. Both of them had two more days in New York, and they spent their free time together. He found that Geisler loved sports, so they played tennis and squash at Patterson's club. Geisler was quite good.

From then on they managed to stay in touch, either through letters or when they found themselves in the same city, which was usually once or twice a year. Unfortunately, during the past three years the relationship had lessened somewhat. As Patterson had moved up in position, he hadn't found time to stay in touch with Geisler. Now he regretted not having answered letters that he continued to write up until a year and a half ago. The last time he had any contact with him was at his wife's funeral.

Because he had essentially lost touch, he asked the CIA to give him a report on his activities within the last two years. Since they had little reason to monitor his activities prior to that, the report was thin. However, they did find that his social life had picked up considerably. He was seen with younger women at night spots in Switzerland and throughout Europe. Physically he had changed, having lost over thirty pounds, so he appeared younger than his sixty years. Presently he was seeing a young German model, Nina Praeger, who had moved in with him.

The only other information of interest was that recently he had traveled to Prague. CIA agents assigned to cover the Russian embassy there had seen him arrive in the embassy limousine. Patterson found that strange but rationalized it as simply a business meeting that was not unusual for someone in Geisler's position.

He looked at his watch. Six hours had passed since he'd left Andrews Air Force Base outside of Washington. This would have been the end of the trip had Geisler's secretary not called the previous night to say that the meeting had been moved from Zurich. A sudden change in Mr. Geisler's calendar had meant the meeting would have to be held in Lucerne. Geisler had arranged for a helicopter to fly the Secretary and his aides there. The afternoon meeting would be on his newly purchased sixty-foot yacht, anchored in Lake Lucerne. Patterson was upset at the abruptness of the change, but Geisler apparently wanted to meet in pleasant surroundings.

The plane touched down on the runway and taxied to an area away from the main terminal. A twelve-seat Bell turboprop helicopter was waiting on the tarmac. The jet stopped next to it. Patterson and his three aides came down the steps of the portable boarding ramp that had been rolled up to the aircraft. They were met by a man in a dark suit. He recognized the Secretary immediately.

"Welcome to Switzerland, Mr. Secretary," he said, extending his hand. "My name is Alain Gerard, Mr. Geisler's personal secretary. He sends his apologies for the sudden change in plans. However, as you can see, the helicopter is waiting and we can be off to Lucerne momentarily. The flying time is just a half hour."

Patterson looked around the tarmac. He had expected the press to be there in force, as well as Swiss diplomats. Part of the visit had been to cause as much media excitement as possible. Publicity might pressure the BIS vote favorably. Gerard sensed his thoughts.

"Mr. Geisler also wanted to spare you the unpleasantness of a press conference here at the airport. The media people have been diverted to the main terminal building. By the time they find out you have landed, the helicopter can be in the air."

The helicopter engines started with a roar, its large rotors churning overhead. Patterson wanted to ask for time to meet with the newsmen, but Gerard took him by the arm and urged his staff to get aboard. He shouted above the roar of the engines.

"Please get on board the aircraft. The pilot has been cleared for takeoff and is ready to leave."

They boarded the helicopter reluctantly, and the doors closed. Once buckled in their seats, the craft rose quickly into the air and they were under way. Minutes later Gerard unbuckled his seat belt and moved through the small cabin to speak to Patterson.

"Our pilot has radioed Air Force One to let them know you have gone directly to Lucerne. They will relay the information to the press, which is waiting in the terminal."

"I wanted to speak to the press," Patterson said, showing some annoyance in his voice. "It's important that the people back home be kept abreast of our efforts to secure financial aid here in Switzerland. Also our ambassador was to meet us."

Gerard avoided Patterson's comment and looked at his watch.

"You'll be able to meet with both the ambassador and the press in a matter of a few hours, Mr. Secretary. Mr. Geisler has only one hour scheduled for your meeting. We will have you back in Zurich by five P.M."

Patterson couldn't believe what he had just heard. Neither could his aides.

"Did I hear you correctly, Mr. Gerard?"

"Yes, sir. My instructions are to land at a pad near the pier. A launch will take your party out to the yacht where you will meet with Mr. Geisler for approximately one hour. The launch will then take you back to the waiting helicopter, which will fly you back to Zurich."

Patterson was livid.

"Do you mean to say we've flown four thousand miles for a one-hour meeting? I've come to ask for help to save the United States from a financial disaster and he has only one hour to give me?"

Gerard remained calm. He spoke slowly, with a hint of arrogance in his voice.

"I'm sorry, sir, but Mr. Geisler is taking time out from his vacation to see you on very short notice. You must realize that—"

"Vacation!" Patterson was shouting now. "We were told there was a change in his calendar that made it necessary to go to Lucerne."

"That is correct," Gerard answered, turning to leave. "Mr. Geisler decided two days ago to take a short vacation on his yacht. He plans to cruise the lake for the next two days."

"That's when members of the BIS need to be convinced to give us aid prior to their meeting. That's when we need Geisler to help us."

"I know nothing of this," Gerard answered. "I am only giving you Mr. Geisler's schedule." He bowed slightly and returned to his seat. The helicopter banked to the left and began a slow, gradual descent into Lucerne.

Karl Geisler didn't look like a man about to meet the Secretary of State. Dressed in an open silk shirt and white slacks, he looked more like a wealthy man about to spend the afternoon engaged in some sport. In a sense, that's what he was about to do.

Standing on the deck of his sixty-foot yacht, he watched the Bell helicopter set down on the town pier through a long brass telescope. He saw the Secretary of State step off the craft. He looked worried. Geisler smiled. Of course he was worried; the man was coming to plead, actually beg, for the salvation of his country. Right now the U.S. economy was beyond hope unless he, Karl Geisler, could influence the most powerful bankers in the world. He was their last hope. He held the fate of the United States in his hands.

The Secretary of State wanted him to speak to a few key members of the BIS organization. A simple vote of confidence in the dollar, and faith in its ability to bounce back, would help

America's case with the organization. That's what Patterson was counting on, only it's what he wouldn't get.

He felt a sense of power building inside him; the power to destroy the United States. And this was only the beginning. He would share in the Russians' drive to dominate America and eventually all of Europe. With the U.S. removed as the prime benefactor of NATO, nothing would stand in the way of a military takeover by the Russians. In a matter of months, Soviet troops would move westward across the continent. There would be no stopping them.

He thought of the power that must have been felt by men throughout history who had attempted what this time wouldn't fail: Caesar, Napoleon, Hitler. They hadn't succeeded because they sought to dominate through military means. Finance was what ruled the world today. The Russians realized that. That's why he would be one of the most powerful men in a government that would use his expertise to eventually take over most of the Western world.

He reveled in the thought of it. Once he had the financial power of the United States in his hands, he would point all of its devastating force at England, France, and Germany. Then, with manipulation of funds, by simply moving numbers across columns, he would invade the financial structures of their economies. How civilized. No shots to be fired, just financial control leading to eventual defeat. There would be no suffering, no death, just submission to a financial force greater than anything ever known to man. And he would be the one behind it.

So far everything was going according to plan. The American economy was crumbling daily as more and more counterfeit dollars came into it. Little confidence remained in the value of the currency. Banks across the country would not accept any new cash; neither would shops and stores. A bartering system had sprung up instead—goods for other goods or services. It was the only way people could be sure of an equitable exchange. Yes, in another two weeks, whatever was left of the economy would cease to exist. Already the Politburo had approved his plan for the Russian takeover of Wall Street and the American banks. Once they were secured and the equivalent of counterfeit removed from the economy, the value of the dollar would be reinstated. Then the billions of dollars in the U.S. military budget would be directed against European economies. At the same time the Russian military would move across the continent. Without U.S. protection and U.S. dollars supporting their economies, country after country would fall like dominoes. He and his Russian colleagues would be victorious.

Nina came up behind him and put her arms around his neck. He could smell her perfume and the sweet scent in her hair as she nuzzled the lobe of his ear. "I saw you peeking through that telescope," she whispered. "You've spotted some delicious creature and are going over every inch of her body."

He laughed.

"What I've spotted are the Secretary of State and his entourage. They're in the launch and should be here any minute."

"Well, then, how do I look?"

She stepped back and turned around slowly so he could see her outfit. She looked magnificent. Her slender body fit snugly into a white lamé jumpsuit that hugged her tightly. She wore her diamond brooch with matching earrings and a gold bracelet. Black high-heeled shoes contrasted against the white suit.

"Don't you think it's a little too much for a meeting with the Secretary of State?" she asked.

"It's perfect." He looked at her for a moment, reconsidering the outfit, then repeated the word again. "Perfect. You look like an empress."

"I feel like one ever since I met you."

He smiled.

"This is only the beginning. There's much more to come."

"I don't know if I want any more. I have everything."

He held her hands and looked into her eyes.

"By next week you'll be an empress with the world at your feet. I'm going to be in a position where I will dictate the financial decisions for more than half the world with you beside me."

"What do you mean?" she asked with a surprised look.

"You'll know exactly what I mean very shortly, and so will

Secretary of State Patterson. I want you with me when I meet with him, Nina."

She backed away, appearing to be somewhat overwhelmed.

"I couldn't. You've got important matters to discuss. I really shouldn't be—"

"I want you to," he said, interrupting in a voice that was almost commanding.

She smiled as she thought to herself, *Of course you want me there, you power-mad fool. You want the pleasure of my seeing one of the most powerful men in the world grovel at your feet. You want me to watch you ascend to your throne. Of course I'll be there, awed with your power, swooning with desire. I'll be there to insure that you reject the pleas of the United States. I'll be there to fuel your desire for power so that you'll do the will of my government. That was my assignment from the very beginning, and now I'll see it to a successful conclusion. Maybe then the false admiration and feigned orgasms can come to an end.*

She came to him and wrapped her arms around his neck. Her lips parted. In almost a whisper she said, "If you want me, I'll be there, darling. I'll always be there."

He was about to take her in his arms when they both saw the motor launch approaching the yacht. As it came alongside, a crewman on the bow threw a line on board and the launch was secured to the larger boat. Aided by two men in white uniforms, the Secretary of State and his party stepped onto a white metal ladder that led up to the main deck. They climbed the steps to the gleaming deck and were surprised that there was no one to greet them. Alain checked that they were all safely aboard, then turned to Patterson.

"I'll take you to Mr. Geisler. Your aides are to remain here."

"Now wait a minute," Patterson said, interrupting. The Secret Serviceman beside him was already moving to the main cabin door to check it. Alain called him back. In a stern, almost arrogant voice, he continued.

"One of the reasons for selecting the yacht as a meeting place was because of the security it offers." He walked around the Secret Serviceman and then motioned with his hand to Patterson. "If you'll follow me, Mr. Secretary."

Patterson didn't move. He was appalled at the way he was being treated. Alain took a watch from his vest pocket and looked at it.

"I suggest you come with me directly. Mr. Geisler only has one hour."

"I really can't let you go in there without our checking it out first, sir," the senior of the two agents said.

"I'm afraid we'll have to accept the yacht as risk-free," Patterson said. "However, Mr. Gerard, I have brought Mr. Hazelton and Mr. Powers, two financial advisers. They're essential to this meeting. I want them in there."

Gerard stood firm.

"Mr. Geisler specifically asked that you meet with him alone. I cannot allow it."

Patterson stood staring at Alain, wondering whether to press the matter further. He was seething inside. The shabby treatment afforded him so far was unbelievable. He wondered what kind of game Geisler was playing. The change of location, the hasty departure from the airport, and the absence of Geisler to greet him were not typical of the man he knew. But apparently the only way he would get to see him was to play by the rules.

With a shrug of resignation he followed Alain to the cabin. Gerard led him down a flight of stairs to the deck below. The interior of the yacht was even more luxurious than the outside suggested. The hallway was carpeted in a rich royal-blue velour, and the walls were done in gold brocade fabric. The handles on the cabin doors appeared to be solid gold. At the end of the corridor, Gerard opened a white enamel door, and Patterson went inside.

The room was done entirely in gold-weaved fabric. Patterson found himself standing in a small foyer that overlooked a sunken oval area. Within the oval were seats made of gold brocade pillows on which Geisler sat with Nina sprawled beside him. Behind them was an oval glass wall in which they were reflected. The impression was of a king and queen in a throne room, and Patterson realized that it had all been carefully planned. He also knew that this meeting would be a failure.

Geisler stood. His white open-neck shirt and slacks, gold

neck chains, and sandals contrasted with Patterson's Brooks Brothers three-piece suit.

"How good to see you, Fred. Come in and sit down."

Patterson descended the steps and stood in front of his host. Geisler extended his hand, which he accepted.

"It's good to see you also, Karl, but I'd like an explanation as to why . . ."

"As to why your aides and security men weren't allowed into our meeting. Because I don't feel they are necessary. The yacht is obviously secure, and any financial discussion is strictly between you and me."

He turned to Nina. "I'd like to introduce Miss Nina Praeger. She will be with us throughout our little talk."

Patterson bowed but did not offer his hand.

"I thought we would meet alone. You understand the magnitude attached to what I've come to ask?"

"I understand completely, and Miss Praeger will remain. Now sit down, Fred, relax. What can I get you to drink?"

"Nothing," he said sharply. Then added sarcastically, "You apparently haven't much time so I'd like to get right to the point."

He sat down across from Nina. Geisler took a sip of his drink.

"Very well, then, let's get to the point."

Patterson leaned forward past Nina as if to put an invisible wall between her and the conversation.

"We would like you to use your influence with the BIS committee to prevent the dollar from being further devalued. We need to buy time while we find the source of counterfeit money coming into the economy."

Geisler placed a cigarette into a gold holder and lit it.

"I can't do that."

"Why not? You know we haven't generated that much currency ourselves and that it *has to* be counterfeit." Patterson opened his briefcase and took out a file. "Here, I can show you figures that—"

Geisler held up his hand.

"There's no need to convince me that the currency is counterfeit, Fred. I know it is. I'm the one who is putting it into your economy."

Patterson couldn't believe what he was hearing.

"You what?"

Geisler turned to Nina and smiled.

"You heard correctly, Mr. Secretary. My Russian partners and I have been feeding your economy with counterfeit currency. I believe over two hundred billion dollars to date."

"You're behind this?" Patterson said in what turned out to be barely a whisper.

Geisler put his hand on Nina's knee. She moved closer to him, her hand beginning to play with the hair on the back of his neck.

"Yes, I'm behind it," he said, smiling, "so I'm afraid that there's little I can do as far as the BIS is concerned."

Patterson could feel the fear rising inside him. The last hope of the country had not only disappeared but also had turned out to be the enemy himself. The country was going to die. If the BIS didn't move to help it, there wasn't any hope. The United States would be destroyed now. There was no hope left.

"Why are you doing this?" he found himself asking. His hands were trembling as he put the useless file back in his briefcase. Geisler leaned back into the pillows and stretched his arms outward.

"For the benefit of the world, of course."

"I'm afraid I don't quite understand that," Patterson said, trying to regain his composure.

"Well, then, let me explain," Geisler replied. "Right now a situation exists between the United States and the Soviet Union that can only result in a head-on collision. Both countries are spending large portions of their budgets on arms at the sacrifice of their people's standard of living. You know as well as I that this can't go on without it resulting in war, nuclear war. Rather than it being a military conflict resulting in millions of deaths, the Soviet Union has chosen a financial conflict instead where no lives need be lost. Within a week to ten days they will have won the war. They will have defeated the United States without a single loss of life on either side. Having accomplished that, they'll be able to move throughout Europe without the threat of U.S. intervention. Once Europe is under their control, a financial system can be put in place that will benefit the whole world."

"And what financial system is that?" Patterson asked cynically.

"Mine. A system that isn't based on rich nations getting richer but an equitable distribution of funds enabling all nations equal opportunity for investment. Specifically there wouldn't be any more national currencies. There would be one currency for all of Europe and the United States. There would be no invading of a country's resources by American dollars, no limits on trade, just one strong economy built on the strengths of everyone involved."

"What do you call this system? I call it socialism."

"Hardly. I would call it a free economic system. Free of the overwhelming U.S. influence that now rules world economics. Free of the U.S. wealth-bullying NATO, forcing nations to allow American military bases on their land. Free of U.S. economic support to some nations while others suffer as a result of it."

"And what makes you think this so-called system will work under Russian leadership? Any country they've dominated in the past has been doomed to economic failure. Poland, East Germany, and Czechoslovakia certainly aren't examples of economic prosperity."

"Because this time there will be a financial system that extends beyond national boundaries. It will be a system that uses the economic strengths of some nations to benefit all nations."

"And what's in it for you, Karl? What's in it for you personally?"

Geisler hesitated. He smiled at Nina, who was looking at him adoringly.

"Seeing a financial system that I've designed work for the benefit of mankind."

Patterson wanted to tell him what he thought the real reason was. The yacht, the room they were in, the woman Nina, they were the real reason. The man was power-mad. He probably had visions of eventually ruling the entire world with the Russians at his side. He realized now that he was dealing with a completely new Karl Geisler. The one he had known was a respected, old-line Swiss banker, sincere in his efforts to solve financial problems. This man wore gold chains, thought he was young and virile again, and thought of world conquest. He had to find a way of stopping him. He had to try to appeal to whatever was left of the old Karl Geisler.

"Karl, do you realize what you're doing by helping the Russians? You're destroying over two hundred million people. Think of that, two hundred million people of all colors—men, women, and children who'll be put under Russian domination. Think of all the suffering they've endured even now, as a result of this diabolical scheme: the unemployment, the poverty, the loss of homes and property, and for many the loss of human dignity. You've seen the American people. You've seen the spirit; the will to fight in two wars that helped save your country. And now you're about to ally yourself with men who would destroy them. For what, Karl? A system that you believe will help mankind?"

A smile came over Geisler's face. Again he looked at Nina, then turned back to Patterson. He spoke in a whisper. "A system that *will* benefit mankind. *My* system."

Patterson was beginning to perspire. He knew it wasn't the temperature in the room; it was the pressure mounting inside him. He was fighting for the life of his country. How could he convince this man who had seemingly gone mad to change his mind? He wondered how much Geisler knew about the counterfeit money. Was his bank involved in passing it for the Russians? It must be. That's probably what they wanted him for, anyway, not his plan for world financial domination. But that was beside the point. The future of his country now rested in the hands of a man possessed with the need for power. He had never begged for anything in his life, but now he was being forced to do so. It seemed the only course left.

He stared at the floor and said very slowly, "You're our last hope at convincing the men who can save our economy. Without your help there's no way our economic system can survive. I beg you, Karl. Don't go through with this. I beg you in the name of the American people not to destroy their country."

He looked up. Geisler was looking at Nina, and there seemed to be a glaze over his eyes. The man was enjoying this. He was in ecstasy. He was drunk with power, the power of having the strongest nation in the world groveling at his feet. Patterson sat in awe. It was as if Geisler had been transported off into another world. He spoke again, but the banker didn't hear him. His breathing became heavier. Then Nina reached over and touched the inside of his thigh. A shudder ran through his body, and Patterson knew that his country was lost.

Perspiration was rolling down President Turner's face as he leaned forward to make adjustments on his exercise machine. The rowing device was the culmination of a daily thirty-minute exercise routine that usually took place between six and six-thirty. It was now four A.M.

He was awakened earlier by an aide with an emergency call from Secretary of State Patterson in Zurich. Patterson was reporting on his meeting with Geisler. The fifteen-minute conversation that resulted seriously damaged the nation's chances of preventing an imminent Soviet financial victory. Geisler had been the key to buying the U.S. more time to stop the flow of counterfeit currency and prove Russian involvement. Now, without his support, there seemed to be no way out. And with him as the enemy, it was virtually impossible.

Turner wiped the sweat from his forehead and adjusted the tension on the rowing machine to maximum. The tougher the problem, the tighter he made the adjustment. The increased oxygen sent to his brain and the exhilaration of the exercise made his thinking processes sharper. When his heart was pumping at twice normal speed, he was able to get right to the core of a problem and see it from a new perspective. Problems that seemed insurmountable at Cabinet meetings found solutions on his rowing machine. He now kept a small notebook and a pen next to it to jot down ideas.

He pulled on the oars, the muscles in his arms and chest tightening against the strain. His legs pushed against the footrests, and his body slid forward and back in the movable seat. A rhythm developed: push . . . pull . . . breathe . . . slide.

Geisler, he thought. *Cocky, power-mad, behind the whole Soviet plot, their conduit to the world banks. The guy was openly admitting involvement with the Russians because he's cocksure we can't prove it.*

Push . . . pull . . . lean . . . bend . . .

There's gotta be a way. Who's the girl with him? Gotta check that. Who are his enemies? CIA has to get closer to his inner circle inside Switzerland. Got to get Ambassador Case in Zurich to identify people who might help us. Rollie's been there long enough to know most of the people Geisler climbed over on his way to the top. Have to start somewhere, but we're running out of time.

Push . . . pull . . . lean . . . bend . . .

Got to prove that Geisler is directly tied to the Russian counterfeit. If we can do that, the Swiss will be embarrassed into opening the Russian accounts that have to be in Geisler's bank. Got to be billions there. Once that's opened, the European banks will be forced to help us.

Turner quickened the pace. His body was moving in a fluid motion now. Oxygen to his brain increased; adrenaline was pumping through his system.

Where are the Russians printing the counterfeit? Has to be right under our noses somewhere. Too difficult to get all that money into the country. The engraver, Tompkins, he's the only lead to where the printing plant is. And if we're lucky enough to find it, some tough decisions will have to be made. They probably have him surrounded with KGB and won't give him up without a fight. That could mean killing Russians on our own soil, and we won't have much time to think about the consequences.

Push . . . pull . . . lean . . . bend . . .

Have to get a strike force together quickly. Once we find the Russians, we'll have to move in with people who know what they're doing. Professionals. The KGB will have their best on this one.

The rhythm continued. His thoughts turned to the worst scenario, but he didn't want to think about that now. He had to think positively. They would find Tompkins and he would lead them to the printing plant and the counterfeiter. It would take a lot of effort, but at this point it would also take a lot of luck. He never believed in luck because it wasn't self-motivated. It depended on outside events coming together without any real contribution on his part. Well, maybe this time there were enough pieces out there to come together. The KGB was good, but maybe they'd slip up and reveal Tompkins's location.

Maybe Geisler had an enemy who would come forward with some evidence. Maybe . . . all maybes.

Well, maybe it would have to be left at that. He would control what he could and let the rest happen. Gradually he reduced the rate of repetitions and then stopped. His T-shirt was soaking wet and his jogging shorts clung to his body. He felt his heart slowing down, and his breathing came easier. The notebook was on the floor next to him and he picked it up. On the first page he wrote, "TOMPKINS. Call Blackie. Assemble strike force." Blackie referred to General Otis Blackburn, Chairman of the Joint Chiefs of Staff.

He turned the page.

Across the top he wrote, "GEISLER," in large block letters. He thought for a moment, then drew a very crude sketch of the banker lying facedown in a mousetrap. The spring on the trap was set, and on the triggering mechanism was the bait: a pile of thousand-dollar bills. An idea was forming in his head. It was a real long shot, but maybe there was a way to draw out the person who could spring the trap. Yes, maybe he could do something to get the luck they needed. He would call Ambassador Case after breakfast.

14

New York, May 7, 1991 *(The New York Times)*—

THE INTERNATIONAL BANK OF SETTLEMENTS REPORTED TO-
DAY THAT THEY HAD VOTED NOT TO PROVIDE A $12 BILLION
LOAN TO THE UNITED STATES. CHAIRMAN KARL GEISLER
STATED THAT THE RISE IN U.S. CURRENCY AGAINST THE GOLD
RESERVE WAS CONTINUING AND WOULD PREVENT ANY
ASSISTANCE AT THIS TIME. UNLESS THE TURNER ADMINISTRA-
TION COULD STEM THE FLOW OF DOLLARS, THE BIS COULD BE
OF NO HELP IN THE IMMEDIATE FUTURE.

Zurich
May 7, 1991

PAUL WELTE SAT in the kitchen of his apartment reading the
morning newspaper. Sasha, his angora cat, was at his feet
eating hungrily from a yellow plastic bowl. Welte reached
down and petted the ten-year-old's soft fur as he scanned the
bold headlines on the front page. U.S. DOLLAR CONTINUES TO
FALL ON INTERNATIONAL EXCHANGE. Underneath, SECRETARY
OF STATE PATTERSON BRIEFS PRESIDENT ON BIS MEETING IN
SWITZERLAND. Farther down the page was an article by Franz
Boldt, a Swiss economist, entitled SWISS DISCRETION, AMERI-
CAN RECESSION. It reiterated a previous statement made two
weeks ago by the Swiss Banking Association that under no
circumstances would they reveal the identities of account
holders even if it threatened American interests. Welte scanned
the article and was about to turn the page when Sasha moved
against his leg and began to meow.

"Ah, Sasha. I almost forgot. Your warm milk." He rubbed

the back of her head with his pudgy fingers while the cat looked up at him with blinking eyes. The milk was part of her morning routine now that he found it tended to settle her stomach. "Let Daddy get it for you," he said in a childish voice.

He went over to the stove where the milk was warming in a pan. With his finger he tested it and decided it was warm enough. As he brought it back to the table, Sasha moved backward to let him pour it. With another quick pat on her back, he returned to his paper.

The Boldt article was continued on another page, so he reread the last few lines, looking for the continued page number. It was eighteen, but his attention was drawn to something else. It was a four-line filler at the bottom of the page, the kind that usually contains useless information and is there only to occupy space. It read:

T7486

It could be your winning number

for a ten-million-dollar prize.

555-6400

T7486. The numbers jumped off the page. It had to be; it would be too much of a coincidence otherwise. It was the account number of the holding company Geisler had set up for the Russians. Outside of Geisler, Nina Praeger, some clerical workers at Union Suisse and the California bank, Gagarin, some Politburo members, and himself, nobody knew that number. At least that's what he thought until now. He stared at the words again. "A ten-million-dollar prize." Somebody was offering money for information about the account. But who?

He rushed into the living room and picked up the phone. 555-6400 was a Zurich exchange. His hands were trembling as he dialed the number.

It was ringing.

A woman's voice answered.

"Good afternoon, U.S. embassy."

"Uh, hello. I, uh, seem to have the wrong number."

"That's quite all right."

"Sorry. Good-bye."

He hung up and stood motionless. A hundred thoughts came rushing into his head. The Americans were behind the ad. What did it really mean? He sat down on the sofa and lit a Turkish cigarette.

Geisler had met two days ago with Secretary of State Patterson. He knew that. But now the Americans knew that Geisler was involved with Moscow. That had been reported by Nina Praeger. They couldn't prove it, though. Without a direct connection between Geisler and the Russians, and access to T7486, they didn't have anything. Gagarin was only a week away from pulling billions out of the U.S. economy and . . . *My God, they've become so desperate, they've placed an ad with a huge reward for information.*

He thought about the other steps the Americans must have taken, and laughed to himself. They must have pleaded their case to the Swiss Banking Association. Ha, Geisler controlled that with an iron hand. Geisler's chairmanship of the BIS wasn't over until the following year. Union Suisse was one of the biggest supporters of the World Bank. No, wherever they turned to get at the counterfeit billions in that account, they would run smack into Geisler.

Sasha came into the room and jumped into his lap. She loved to lay on top of his ample stomach and stare up at him. He stroked her fur and leaned back, exhaling a long stream of smoke toward the ceiling.

"The Americans, Sasha. They need something only I can give them. We know what that is, don't we, old friend?"

The cat purred and looked up at him with blinking eyes.

"What do you think the Americans would pay for information about T7486, Sasha? They're offering ten million dollars. Now that's not enough for us, is it? What do you think saving a country, and possibly the whole world, from those bad Russians is worth? Fifty million, seventy-five million?"

He flicked the ash from the end of his cigarette.

That was an exorbitant amount compared to what Gagarin and the Soviet Politburo were paying him. What had he gotten so far? A couple of hundred thousand Swiss francs and the promise of some lucrative gold contracts that hadn't come through yet. No, Geisler would be the one who reaped the big rewards, not him. If the Soviets succeeded in defeating the

U.S., Geisler would be part of the inner circle of power, and he would get only a few crumbs.

But what if he sold his information to the U.S.? First of all, his life would be in immediate danger. If any link was made between Geisler and the Russians, they would eliminate anyone who knew about it. Then again, how secure was he right now? They could kill him at any time once his usefulness was over. And soon it would be. Within ten days the Russians would make their move and he would no longer be needed.

He had to think about it more. Selling to the Russians could be very dangerous, maybe too dangerous. His hands began to tremble again. Sasha sensed it and jumped off his lap.

If he were to negotiate with the U.S. embassy, careful plans would have to be made to protect himself. During the past month he thought he was being followed on a couple of occasions. He probably was. The KGB was watching him. That he could be sure of.

He stubbed out the cigarette in a glass ashtray next to his chair. A few sparks in the bottom of the tray remained. With a twisting motion of the stub he smothered them. Then he knew what he had to do.

May 8, 1991
St. Maarten

A thirty-foot sailboat headed into the wind, then tacked to start a new course that would bring it closer to shore. It was a bright, sunny day and the offshore breeze coming across Samson Bay moved the boat swiftly through the water. It was a typical spring day for the island of St. Maarten.

The sleek sailboat looked like many others in the bay except that when the sunlight hit the cabin windows from a certain angle, one could see that there wasn't any glass in them. Instead, a camera with a thousand-millimeter lens protruded through the opening, its long barrel shape searching the shoreline. Inside the cabin, Hal Fuller peered through the viewfinder while Davidson made notes on a nautical chart.

At the wheel was a trim, bearded man in his fifties. His long white hair blew in the wind, contrasting against his deeply tanned body, which was clothed only in cutoff jeans and sneakers. He rarely looked at the compass in front of him. These waters were as familiar to him as the back of his hand. For thirty years he had chartered boats on St. Maarten, long before the island had become a popular tourist spot. Nobody knew this island as well as Ted Wolk. For that reason the CIA had recommended him to search the shoreline for Tompkins.

Davidson took a single slide from a metal box and slipped it into a portable viewfinder. The picture that had shocked everyone two nights ago appeared on the screen. There was Bob and Helen Tompkins standing in front of a cottage with water reflected in the window behind them. If they could find that cottage now, there might be a chance to save both the engraver and his country.

Davidson thought back to the call he received from Fuller. Hal had just spoken to Tompkins's son Bill, who called from Hartford. A letter had come from his father, the first in over a month. There were some slides, pictures of his father and mother outside a small cottage. Would they be of help to them?

Bill, along with an FBI escort, had been flown to Washington on a chartered jet from Hartford. At a meeting with Secretary Dillon, present along with an expert from Eastman Kodak, the slides were examined. The sandwiched slide containing the newspaper clipping was found, and the President was contacted immediately. His orders were swift and decisive. They flew out of Andrews Air Force Base the following morning and had met Wolk the same afternoon.

"You still think the bay is the right place to be, Ted?" Davidson asked.

Wolk shook his head as he pulled in the sheet to draw more wind into the mainsail.

"Water's too calm to be the ocean, my friend. Gotta be the bay. We got breakers one hundred yards out all around the windward side of this island. You'd see them in the slide if it was the ocean."

"What about the leeward side?" Davidson persisted.

"Doubt it. You'd see signs of St. Bart's off in the distance, or one of the smaller offshore islands. No, it's the bay, all right; but that still gives us a lot of shoreline to cover."

Davidson ducked back inside the cabin and studied the chart again. For four hours now they had searched the bay for a white stucco building with black-slatted shutters that was near the water. So far they hadn't found anything resembling it. Dave had marked in red the fifteen miles of shoreline they had already covered on the chart. They had about ten left.

Washington was waiting. He was in constant contact with the Joint Chiefs via special radiotelephone relay from Puerto Rico. They were standing by for any news of the location. Once Tompkins's position was identified, they would act.

Davidson turned to Hal, who was adjusting the focus on the telephoto lens.

"See anything yet?"

"Nope, thought the white house we just went by might be something even if it didn't have any shutters."

"And . . ."

"It's set too high up on the hill. You'd never see the water reflected from there."

Dave looked at it through the binoculars and agreed there was no way the water could be reflected in the windows.

Ted turned the boat so that it fell off the wind and headed into a cove. Hal swung the camera around to focus on a group of buildings set back from the beach. Wolk called down to the others.

"Take a look at those houses. They could be something. The place has a chain-link fence going around the rear side, which faces the road. You don't see that very often on this island."

Hal looked through the camera. The buildings were white, but he couldn't see the front of them yet. Ted tacked the sail and headed across the cove. Slowly, the front of the buildings revealed themselves through the camera lens. Two of them, high up near the road, didn't have any shutters, but the one near the beach, yes, there they were, black metal shutters on all the windows.

"There it is," he said excitedly. "Black shutters, low near the water, a bay window in the front. That's gotta be it."

Dave looked through the viewfinder. There were three neat, white buildings. One was a small cottage, the other two larger. There were walkways connecting them through the well-kept lawn. In front was the beach. At either end were two high, rocky breakwaters affording complete privacy from the property on either side. He focused in on the cottage with the shutters. Hal was right. The bay window was low enough. He could see the sailboat reflected in it.

Checking the focus, he clicked off one roll using the motorized rewind on the camera. In the last shot he saw a man coming out of the larger building, back from the beach. He was wearing only jeans and sandals. Dave took three shots of him as he walked toward the beach. He called up to Ted. "We've got company. Can you drop the anchor here?"

"Yeah, but I'll need some help," Wolk answered.

Fuller went up on deck and worked the winches on the jib to get the boat headed into the wind. As it slowed to a stop, he went up on the bow and dropped the anchor into twenty feet of water. The boat moved backward as he paid out the line. With over a hundred feet out, he cleated it tight. Quickly he and Ted lowered the sails, and the boat bobbed lazily on the secured anchor.

Dave continued watching the man, who was now sitting on the beach under a thatched umbrella. He was reading a magazine. Occasionally he looked up, apparently keeping an eye on the boat. Dave watched him for a few minutes more, then joined Hal and Ted on deck.

"Let's get out the beer and lay around a little. There's a guy on the beach keeping an eye on us, so we'd better look like we just dropped in to lie in the sun."

Ted opened the cooler he had stashed in the stern locker and took out three cans of beer.

"What's this guy look like?" he asked, popping open the cans.

"Young, blond, mid-twenties. He's looking casual, but he's definitely watching us," Dave replied.

Fuller looked toward shore.

"How long do you think we can stay here without him getting suspicious?"

"A few hours, maybe. Beyond that, I think we'd be pushing it. Let's just look casual. If anyone else comes down to the beach, I'll go below and take some shots of them."

"What about radioing Puerto Rico?" Hal asked.

"Not yet. I don't want to risk anybody picking up our frequency. Besides, we don't know if Tompkins is in there or not."

"I think we've got the right house, though," Ted said, looking across the bay. "Where this bay opens up into the ocean is in a direct line with the cottage. That's why you thought it was a larger body of water in the slide."

Dave leaned against the cabin with his feet propped up on the cooler.

"I think you're right. We've got the house, but we've got to prove that Tompkins is in it."

An hour passed. It was three o'clock. The man on the beach got up, walked to the largest of the cottages, and went inside. Dave hurried below and watched him through the long lens on the camera. Moments later a second man, dressed in a polo shirt and shorts, came out, looked once toward the boat, then walked over to the cottage with the shutters. Dave focused the lens more sharply. The man knocked on the door. As soon as it opened, he went inside. Before Dave could see who had opened the door, it closed. Five minutes passed. He kept the camera focused on the door. Finally it opened and the man came back outside. This time he locked the door, looked once toward the boat, and went back into the other cottage.

Dave looked up from the viewfinder. He tried to piece together what might have happened. Were Tompkins and his wife in the smaller cottage? Maybe the younger man had reported the boat as suspicious and this guy locked Tompkins inside.

He took a pad from the chart table and made a sketch of the compound and the beach in front of it. If Tompkins and his wife were here, the Joint Chiefs would need a detailed description of the location.

Two hours passed. There was little activity, except for the three men who came out of the third cottage, got into a red jeep, and left via the road at the rear of the compound. Davidson took another look at the buildings. There wasn't anybody outside now. Slowly he scanned each of them until he came to the larger one. He stopped. There was something in back of the bay window. He sharpened the focus and then he saw what it was: a telescope. They were watching the boat. Quickly he took the long lens off the camera and went on deck. Hal was putting suntan lotion on his reddened chest. Ted was lying back, listening to a portable radio.

"Let's get ready to leave," Dave said quietly. "Nobody look toward the shore. They're getting a very close look at us through a telescope inside the large cottage. Just act normally. We've had enough sun and have decided to leave."

He turned to Ted.

"Use the engine to get us out of the inlet. Then while we're still in sight of the compound, raise the sails. That'll get us out quickly without it looking like we've seen them and are running away."

They moved slowly, keeping a conversation going between them as they took in the anchor and headed out of the inlet. At the mouth of it Ted raised the mainsail and began a tack that would take them back to his marina.

"Well, whaddaya think, Dave?" Fuller asked as he pulled the jib sheet tightly around the winch.

"I think they're in there, but it's going to be tough to prove it. If they're suspicious enough to watch us through a telescope, they're not going to let Tompkins out of that cottage."

"Do you have enough to convince Washington that they're in there?" Ted asked.

"No way. We'll need absolute proof. We'll need photographs of them."

"You know," Hal said, looking back at the inlet, "I just had a terrible thought. Suppose the whole thing was set up by the Russians? Suppose they put two slides together so we'd think Tompkins is in there when he's not? Suppose they're just trying to sucker us into attacking the place to provoke something the country could least afford at this point?"

"That's why the President is demanding that we see Tompkins with our own eyes," Davidson said. "If we don't, they won't do anything."

"How are we going to do that? As soon as they see us, they'll lock Tompkins inside. Besides, if they get frightened enough, they might just kill him, and the whole thing will be over."

Davidson tried to light his pipe with some book matches, but the wind was too strong.

"I know it's going to be tough," he said, throwing the

matches overboard, "and we'll need some luck, but I think there's a way."

The following day it rained, which was unusual for the island in May. But the next morning's dawn came early, at five A.M. As the sun came over the horizon, a dark figure moved through the water, his black wet suit and fins blending into the blackness of the rocks offshore. For a moment he looked toward the beach, adjusted the scuba tanks on his back, then quietly disappeared underwater. When he surfaced again minutes later, he was behind the rock jetty that ran in toward the beach. Two large coral-studded boulders hid him from the buildings.

Around his neck was an underwater camera with a special waterproof cover, which he now removed. From a pouch on his belt he took a telephoto lens and attached it to the body of the camera. Then he waited.

The sun rose higher in the sky, narrowing the shadows on the jetty. He adjusted his position slightly to stay within them. His arms and legs were starting to cramp as he crouched behind the boulders.

The digital numbers on his watch read 8:30 before there was any sign of life within the compound. A young man, dressed only in a bathing suit, came out of the large cottage and went into the water. He dived in quickly and started swimming out in the direction of the frogman, forcing him to submerge instantly. The uncovered camera lay on the rock. Underwater, the frogman watched the turbulence caused by the swimmer's kicking. He was heading right for him but suddenly turned back toward shore.

The frogman surfaced. The camera was still lying on the rock. Had the swimmer seen it? He looked over the coral edge at the shore. The young man was drying himself with a towel, which he spread on the sand, then he laid down.

The frogman's attention shifted to the small cottage. The door had opened. An old man was standing in the doorway, dressed in brown slacks and a T-shirt. He looked like he was checking the weather. He rubbed his eyes, then put his hands down to turn back inside. The door closed. It was Tompkins.

During the brief moment he was standing in the doorway, it

was impossible to get a shot of him without being seen by the other man on the beach. He would have to wait for a better opportunity.

It came almost two hours later. At eleven o'clock, Tompkins and Helen emerged from the cottage. The frogman positioned the camera between two rocks that hid it from view of the shore. He watched as the young man motioned for them to come forward. He apparently was granting them permission to come on the beach. As they came across the sand, the frogman cocked the camera manually. Through the viewfinder he saw Tompkins and Helen clearly. He clicked the shutter once. Helen was smiling. He waited; she was partially blocking Tompkins's face. She fell behind, her steps a little shorter than his. The shutter clicked again and again, four shots in all. Now they were next to the young man, talking to him. The frogman had enough. Quickly he covered the camera with the waterproof case, put the scuba mask over his face, and slid into the water with pictures of the man the world was looking for.

Tuesday, May 10, 1991
Zurich, Switzerland

The U.S. embassy on Friedrichstrasse was alive with activity. Chauffeur-driven limousines drove through the open wrought-iron gates as Marine sentries waved them through. The eighteenth-century mansion was aglow with light, streaming through the colorful lead-glass windows. Music and laughter came from inside as the bronze front doors were opened to receive the arriving guests.

Rolland Case, U.S. Ambassador to Switzerland, and his wife, Rachel, stood at the head of a receiving line greeting the thirty-five bankers and their wives who had been invited to the black-tie affair. These were the leading figures in Swiss banking. And they were a tight-knit group.

For the most part they were elderly, many in their late sixties and seventies. Almost all had served in the Swiss Army Reserve, and a good many during World War II, guarding, as they loved to say, "Swiss neutrality." They had been high-ranking officers who were comrades forty years ago and carried that camaraderie with them today. With each other they were free and open, laughing and telling "in" jokes. With outsiders they were wary. The stiff Swiss banker facade quickly surfaced.

That was the reason for the party. The invitations had gone out three weeks ago, when Case saw he was getting nowhere with the BIS or the World Bank. Neither would help the United States get out of its financial crisis, nor would they assist in pressuring the banks to reveal the identity of accounts allegedly holding billions of dollars in counterfeit currency. He tried every means possible. Threats of cutting off trade, even severing diplomatic relations, were unsuccessful. Nothing worked. He even began to suspect that the Swiss thought the Russians would be successful in defeating the U.S., and they didn't want to be on the losing side.

At any rate, the rational approach didn't seem to work. He welcomed Rachel's irrational suggestion. Why not throw a party? Get to know these old fogies better, and maybe when they've loosened up, you'll get some sympathy for the problem. He might never become close friends with them, but at least he might establish some rapport. There was nothing to lose.

They sent out the invitations and invited Geisler. He declined. Now Case knew why.

When the President called three days ago, he was shocked to hear that not only could Geisler not be counted on for assistance but, in fact, he was the enemy. It came as a total surprise. When he had arrived in Switzerland two years ago, Geisler was one of the first people he'd met. The man was a real social charmer and was more than willing to introduce he and Rachel to Swiss society. Beyond that, he suggested programs that ultimately resulted in better relationships between their countries. It was amazing what ambition and power could do to a man.

He couldn't remember when he had heard the President sound so shaken. Although he tried to hide it behind an optimistic tone, he had known Turner long enough to detect anxiety in his voice. There was no small talk. He came right to the point. After informing him about Geisler's relationship with the Russians, he gave him his instructions, which were twofold.

One: Use whatever contacts he had inside Swiss banking to find someone, possibly an old enemy, who could link Geisler to the Russians. (Thank God for the party.)

Two—and he thought this somewhat unusual—was to run a small ad in the Zurich *Tageszeiger,* which Turner dictated. If there was any link to Geisler outside Swiss banking, even possibly a KGB agent willing to talk for money, they might respond to it. When he kind of scoffed at the idea, Turner became irritated. "Do it, Rollie. It may be our last hope. Just do it," he said.

The ad had run for the first time the previous day. So far there was no response. Nor did he think there would be.

Rachel nudged him with her arm, and his thoughts returned to greeting his guests. Otto Krohn, Chairman of the Swiss Banking Commission, and his wife were next in line. After Geisler, he was probably the most powerful person in Swiss banking, also one of the keys to finding out who was behind account number T7486.

"Good evening, Rolland," the Chairman said, extending his well-manicured hand.

"Ah, Mr. Krohn, how nice to see you and your lovely wife," Case replied. Rachel took Mrs. Krohn's hand and smiled politely.

Krohn looked around the room, taking in the entire scene, then turned back to the Ambassador.

"For a country in serious financial trouble, you seem to be spending a lot of money for a party, Mr. Ambassador. Does your president know about this?"

"Yes, in fact, it was his idea," Case said quickly—it was a lie. "He felt it would be a good opportunity for us all to know each other better."

Krohn was known for his directness and was living up to the reputation.

"That would be nice," he answered. "As long as we are not forced to compromise any long-standing traditions."

Case thought to himself, *If only you knew about your trusted friend Geisler, all your Swiss banking tradition would go out the window.*

He simply smiled at Krohn and his wife, and they moved on into the ballroom.

Five hours later the party had moved to a large sitting room where brandy was served. As Case moved from group to group, he felt the subject of the conversations change abruptly. Apparently the American financial crisis was being talked about—until his presence was observed. Nevertheless, he tried to be as cordial as possible and was successful, he thought, in gaining the sympathy of some for his country's plight.

It was one A.M., and he was about to move to another group when his chief aide, Charles Brower, hurried over to him. In an unusual move Brower took his arm and eased him away from the group.

"Mr. Ambassador, I must speak to you privately," he whispered.

Case excused himself and followed Brower to a large, arched doorway at the end of the room. Brower whispered softly as two waiters passed with dessert and coffee.

"Rolland, I have a call holding on the library phone. It's a man. He won't say who he is, only that he must talk to you."

Case turned toward the guests.

"Charlie, I'm right in the middle of trying to ingratiate these guys and—"

Brower interrupted. "He has information about T7486."

"He's answering the ad?" Case asked quietly.

"Yes."

They hurried into the library. Case went to the phone with the receiver off the hook. Brower picked up the extension and took a notepad from his pocket.

The Ambassador took a deep breath and spoke into the phone.

"Hello, this is Ambassador Case. May I help you?"

"No, Mr. Case. It's not a question of your helping me, it's what I can do to help *you*."

The voice was low, the accent Swiss, authoritative, yet a little frightened.

"I'm sorry, I don't understand. Who is this?"

"That's unimportant. I need to talk to you."

"About what?"

"About Union Suisse account number T7486."

The voice was confident, more assured now.

"As you know, T7486 is the key to the survival of the United States. Not just for what it contains—although I can assure you that it's in the billions—but if the Swiss are forced to open it, the world's banks will have to follow suit and return the counterfeit currency they're holding. So far you haven't been able to get them to do that, have you?"

"Go on," Case said calmly, "I'm interested."

"Good, then I'll be brief. I don't have much time, Mr. Ambassador."

"All right, then get to the point," Case said sharply.

"The point is that I have what you need to open the account."

"What do you have?"

"I have Karl Geisler."

Case heard the words clearly, yet couldn't believe them. This was no crank call. The man had all the facts and was laying them out, one by one. He was establishing credibility with each word he spoke. His next question was barely a whisper.

"What do you know about Geisler?"

"He met with your Secretary of State on May seventh aboard his yacht and told him that he was involved with the Russians. He explained in detail how his bank was being used to accept counterfeit currency to reinvest back into the United States. Unfortunately this can't be proven by Secretary Patterson to the world."

"And you can prove it?"

"Yes, I can prove that Geisler and the Russians are coconspirators and are behind the Swiss holding company. In short, I have what you need to save your country."

Case still couldn't believe this was happening. Could this man have what the whole financial world was looking for? He started to feel weak as the gravity of what he was hearing took on real meaning. The most powerful country in the world was on its knees, and here was a man on the other end of the line giving every indication that he had the means to save it.

"What do you have that can prove this?"

The man hesitated, then spoke very slowly, enunciating each word so that he would be heard clearly.

"I have audio tapes that prove Geisler's involvement with the Russians."

"Who is on them?"

"Geisler."

Case looked over at Brower, who was making quick notes on his pad.

"You mean to say, you have actual recordings of Geisler?"

"Yes."

"How did you get them?"

"I have had several meetings with Geisler over the past eleven months and took the liberty of recording them. They have everything on them you need."

Case answered quickly, afraid of frightening the man and losing him.

"You realize the enormity of what you're saying. If you have those tapes, they could change the entire future of the United States."

"I realize that, and so do others," the voice answered. "That's why my life is in danger. The tapes are as valuable to the Russians as they are to you. I could sell them either way."

"What do you want?"

"Fifty million dollars and asylum in the United States once the deal is consummated."

Case hesitated. "How do I know—"

Again the voice interrupted. "You don't know anything, Mr. Ambassador. But the money is a small price to pay to save your country. Asylum merely requires your signature on a few documents and making some precipitous arrangements."

Case looked over at Brower, who was still taking notes.

"Very well, what do you want me to do?"

The man replied quickly. "The entire fifty million will be deposited into the Swiss National Bank this morning by ten A.M. It will go into account number R5718. I'll check with the bank by eleven A.M. to confirm the deposit. Then I'll have it transferred one hour later to an account known only by me.

"At one o'clock sharp you will come to the Kunsthaus Zurich," he went on. "There's a Rembrandt exhibit on the third floor for the remainder of the week. To the left, at the far end of the gallery, *The Nightwatch* is on display. You'll meet me there . . . alone. Don't worry about recognizing me, I'll recognize you. We'll view the exhibit for five or ten minutes, then leave together through the main entrance. You'll have a car waiting outside with an armed guard to drive us to the embassy. Once I'm safely inside, you can play the tapes. Within a week I'll expect to be relocated in the United States with proper citizenship papers and whatever other documents I need to begin a new life. Agreed?"

"Agreed," Case replied. "I don't think I have any other choice. But why do we have to meet at the Kunsthaus? Why not come directly to the embassy?"

"The embassy is watched. I can't risk it. This way, if anyone is watching, you'll have met a friend at the gallery and simply brought him back to the embassy with you."

Case sensed the man was about to hang up. He wanted more assurance that the tapes would be delivered after the money was deposited.

"How do I know you'll show up at all once the money is in the bank?" he asked.

"You don't, except for my word. I'm afraid there can be nothing more. If I'm still alive by one o'clock, I'll be there."

The line went dead.

Case put down the receiver and turned to Brower. For the next fifteen minutes they discussed what they had heard. Within the hour Case was talking to President Turner, determining how they would handle the situation at the Kunsthaus.

Vasily Gagarin was alerted to the call made to Ambassador Case within thirty minutes. The telephone tap installed by the KGB six months earlier in the embassy had finally paid off. Replacement of wiring in the basement for a new washer and dryer had offered the perfect opportunity for their newest listening device to be put in place.

Gagarin listened to a tape of the conversation in a communications room inside the Kremlin. The voice of Paul Welte was identified by experts within an hour, and Gagarin ordered his execution immediately. The Americans had begun to close in, and all avenues leading to Soviet involvement had to be closed.

They had to make sure that Case didn't get that tape. They were only days now from withdrawing the notes from U.S.

banks that would destroy their economy. Failure at this point was unthinkable.

Gagarin stared at the now silent recording machine in front of him. He would have to act swiftly. What happened in the next seventy-two hours would be crucial. They must get Welte before the Americans did. If that tape had anything near what he thought was on it, it would be undeniable evidence in the World Court.

His thoughts turned to Geisler. It would not be wise to eliminate him yet, as long as there was still a chance for achieving success. He would be too valuable in gathering international banking support for their new world plan. But should the Americans get the tapes, he would have to die swiftly.

Tompkins was no longer of any use. They had all the counterfeit they needed. The St. Maarten operation would be closed down immediately. It had to be done flawlessly so that no connection could be made between them and the compound. He would order Vladislav to supervise personally the evacuation and the execution of Tompkins and his wife. Those orders would go out in the morning.

15

Wednesday, May 11, 1991

KGB CODE 673
GAGARIN TO ZURICH   0100 HOURS
TRANSMISSION INTERCEPTED, U.S. EMBASSY. TARGET IDENTI-
FIED.
ORDER TO TERMINATE TARGET IMMEDIATELY. DETAILS TO
FOLLOW.

KGB CODE 674
GAGARIN TO NEW YORK   0130 HOURS
AGENT VLADISLAV TO EAGLE LOCATION IMMEDIATELY.
TERMINATE SUBJECTS AT LOCATION.

CIA TRANSMISSION 2184
WASHINGTON TO ST. MAARTEN
COMMENCE OPERATION WINDWARD.

St. Maarten

THE FOLLOWING EVENING, an Eastern 727 touched down at
Princess Juliana Airport. Slowly it taxied up to the terminal
building, its wing lights blinking against the darkening
Caribbean sky. A portable staircase was pushed up to the
aircraft and an Eastern employee scampered up it to knock on
the fuselage door. A stewardess opened it from the inside, and
the fifty passengers filed out, stepping into the warm tropical
air. Most of them paused at the top of the stairs to breathe in the
warm eighty-degree breeze, a far cry from the forty-degree
temperature they'd left behind in New York.

Custom officials checked the group through quickly. They were typical American tourists. The men wore bright-patterned short-sleeved shirts and loud-colored trousers. The women— polyester knit pantsuits with high heels, bright scarfs, and costume jewelry they would never wear at home. Cameras were slung over their shoulders, and tennis racquets protruded from artificial leather carry-ons. The custom agents had seen it all before. With just a casual glance to match faces to passport photos, along with a quick check of registration cards, the group was whisked through.

In the baggage area the luggage from the Eastern flight came onto a carousel. Bright yellow tags hung from each bag, identifying the group as Windward Tours in large red letters framed by an abstract palm tree. The baggage handler, a burly black man with biceps that bulged under his sweat-stained khaki shirt, noticed the inordinate amount of sports equipment carried by the group. Every third or fourth bag was a golf bag or one of those long canvas shoulder bags used to carry fishing rods. Also, there weren't any small suitcases, which usually contained children's clothing. In fact, when he had unloaded the first batch of luggage and had a chance to look around, he saw that there wasn't a single child in the group.

Having gotten all their luggage, the tourists moved outside where two Mercedes buses marked "Mullet Bay" were waiting. The doors opened and the anxious vacationers scrambled on board.

Three porters began loading luggage into the first bus. One took a new set of golf clubs and threw it into the hold. The owner, who was watching from inside the bus, winced and yelled through the open window.

"Hey, go easy with those clubs, will ya, buddy? I just bought 'em two days ago."

His friend, who was sitting next to him, leaned over and said, "Yeah, he plans to win enough money in the casino next week to finish paying for them."

The porter looked up and smiled, then threw a canvas bag filled with fishing gear over the clubs.

Finally the buses pulled out of the airport. They made their way up a winding road, which at the first turn afforded a magnificent view of Samson Bay. The sun was setting over the horizon in a kaleidoscope of bright oranges and purples. The entire bay glistened, with reflected color dancing on the water. Many tourists shot pictures through the windows as the buses moved over the crest of the hill and began their descent into Mullet Bay.

The lights of the resort were spread out below. Mullet was the largest resort on the island, with eighty two-story condominiums capable of housing fifteen hundred people. There were five restaurants, a PGA golf course, ten tennis courts, and a beach that stretched for half a mile.

Slowly the buses entered the compound, passing the main office. They turned onto a road that paralleled the beach and started along it. It was dark now, and the drivers turned on their headlights. A mile farther, they reached a group of buildings at the far end of the property and stopped. The doors opened and the passengers got off. Everyone milled around as the drivers opened the cargo hold and emptied the luggage onto the sidewalk. A tour director from each bus, using a flashlight, read down a list of names and handed out keys to the condominiums. The group then picked up their luggage and disappeared into the buildings.

Once inside, a transformation took place. Small talk and laughter came to an abrupt halt, and a group of seemingly carefree tourists turned into a fighting unit.

Small submachine guns were unpacked from golf bags. Automatic weapons were taken from the canvas bags used to carry fishing gear. Radios were unpacked from suitcases, along with jumpsuits, boots, helmets, and wet suits. Women unpacked medical equipment and began setting up a small infirmary in one of the suites.

Within an hour the group began filtering over to the larger condominium where Davidson and Fuller were waiting for them.

They greeted each person as they came into the room. Some were people they had worked with before; others they were meeting for the first time. The furniture had been moved against the walls, and folding chairs were set in the center of the room. A large map of the island hung from a bookcase.

With the group seated on whatever chairs were available and

the rest of the floor, Davidson took a pointer and stepped up to the map.

"I'd like to welcome 'Windward Tours' to the sunny island of St. Maarten."

There was some laughter from the group. They settled down, and cigarettes were lit.

"Kidding aside, that is the name under which we registered you with customs and checked you into Mullet Bay. I'd like to compliment you all on playing out our little charade. You were perfect tourists. We don't believe any suspicions were raised at the airport with either customs or airport personnel. It was very convincing.

"I wish I could welcome you all as vacationers to this lovely island, but what we're here for is far from being a vacation.

"Since the group was assembled practically overnight, I would like to introduce the various units here in case you don't as yet know each other. We have the First Special Forces Platoon from Fort Hood, Texas; the 104th Communications Group from Baltimore, Maryland; the Secret Service Undercover Team from Washington, D.C.; and the young ladies over here are from the Fifth Medical Emergency Squad stationed in Richmond, Virginia."

A few whistles came from the back of the room.

Davidson continued.

"As you may have guessed, we're here because of the financial crisis that exists back home. The situation is becoming worse every day now, and the economy is very near a state of total collapse. The newspapers have speculated as to how the money supply has tripled in the last six months and who is behind it. The consensus, of course, is that the money is counterfeit and that the Russians are behind it. Both are true. The Russians who are responsible, and the man who made the counterfeit plates, are on this island."

Davidson paused as the group took in what he had said. They whispered among themselves for a moment, then became quiet as he tacked two large photographs over the map.

"You've seen these pictures hundreds of times, so you know who these people are: Robert and Helen Tompkins. Both were kidnapped by Russian agents last year in Hartford, Connecticut. We have strong evidence that he was forced to work on the engravings. Four days ago Tompkins managed to give us his location. The President then ordered this mission. These people must be taken alive. They are the only—I repeat—the *only* link we have to the counterfeit money that is coming into the country.

"Study their faces. Copies of these photographs will be distributed later."

He turned to the map and pointed out a narrow peninsula that jutted out into Samson Bay.

"They're being held about three miles directly across the bay. We estimate a force of about twelve KGB agents guarding them in a small compound with three buildings. Hal will show you aerial photographs later."

Davidson traced a line along the middle of the peninsula.

"This is a narrow dirt road that runs along a ridge. It passes in front of the compound. Half the attack group will be taken over that road in a tour bus to a point just above the compound. The second group will come in from the beach. We have two motor launches to take them across the bay.

"Unfortunately we're a large group that can't be hidden very long without being detected by the KGB, which knows this island inside and out. Therefore we'll attack tomorrow. Hal will fill you in on all the details. Again, I can't stress the importance of this operation. It is probably one of the most important missions our country has ever fought or ever will fight. Good luck."

Davidson handed the briefing over to Fuller. Hal went over the entire operation, explaining assignments in minute detail. The lights were then turned off, and slides they had taken of the compound from the boat were shown.

In the dim light of the projector Davidson studied the faces of these professional soldiers who had been assembled just forty-eight hours ago with no knowledge of where they were going or what their task might be. And now they were being asked to rescue two people they had never seen before from a highly trained enemy who had the advantage of familiarity with the terrain. The whole thing was frightening.

Earlier in the day he had phoned his wife, Ellen, from a pay booth in downtown Philipsburg. He laughed to himself as he remembered the call. She didn't know anything about Russians or hostages or anything. In fact, she had kidded him about a reconnaissance mission in St. Maarten being a boondoggle that he and Fuller had concocted.

As he stood on Front Street talking to her, he was surrounded by tourists rushing to buy their Seikos, Sonys, and bottles of Chivas Regal in shops that lined the narrow street. The sound of the honking horns from cars trying to get through the sea of people made it nearly impossible for him to hear. Ellen was saying something about the car not running and missing her turn to drive in the car pool. He had laughed. The irony of the whole situation suddenly came into focus. He was about to risk his life on a mission that might very well determine the future of his country while he talked to a wife that was worried about her car pool. This was all in the midst of his countrymen trying to crowd into stores to get a good deal on booze. It was crazy.

And what about Tompkins? He had managed to reveal his location, but it could have been only to save himself and his wife now that his usefulness to the Russians had come to an end. Freeing him might not solve anything. No one as yet had discovered any counterfeit bills. Treasury Department figures said the money had to be counterfeit, but nobody had actually found one. That could mean the plates were perfect and it was too late to do anything. The only thing that could be said for Tompkins was that he was a link to the Russians, the only link they had. For that reason they must get him—if he was still alive.

Five hours after Davidson's "tour group" had left the St. Maarten airport, a Learjet touched down and taxied to the now darkened terminal building. The fuselage door opened, and a metal ladder was dropped to the ground. Two crew members jumped to the tarmac and assisted a third man down the ladder.

The waiting room was empty, except for a workman buffing the tile floor and a young man who sat in the corner reading *The New York Times*. He wore a white open-necked shirt and a pair of jogging shorts. After a year in the Caribbean sun, he looked like a typical islander.

Every few minutes he lowered the newspaper to check the door across the room marked CUSTOMS, PRIVATE. The passenger from the Lear would be completing his custom check any minute now. Just as he was about to turn to the sports section, the door opened and Yuri Vladislav walked into the room.

The young man got up immediately as his superior walked toward him. He noticed that Vladislav looked worn and tired. Slowly he put down his suitcase and shook the young man's hand.

"Dimitri, it's good to see you again."

The agent was one of his favorites. He was one of the first sent to New York when the printing plant was being set up.

"How was your flight, Comrade Vladislav?"

"It was tiring. I wasn't able to leave New York until late in the day because of a message expected from Moscow."

"Did it come?"

"Yes, it did. I'll tell you about it in the car."

Outside in the parking lot, Dimitri put the bag in the trunk of a battered Volkswagen and got into the driver's seat. He waited until Vladislav had lit a cigarette, then started the car.

As they turned onto the dark main road, Vladislav settled back in his seat and leaned against the headrest. He seemed deep in thought as he looked out at the moonlit bay. Dimitri wanted to question him about the message but hesitated to disturb him. Finally Vladislav spoke.

"The message from Moscow was from Gagarin himself. It said that we've finally printed enough bills in New York. It is not necessary to print any more."

"That's good news. It means we'll be leaving to go home soon."

Vladislav was still staring out the window.

"Yes," he answered, "you'll be leaving within two days with most of the others. A few of us will have to stay behind and see to the details of closing down the compound."

Dimitri shifted the Volkswagen into a lower gear as they started up one of the many steep grades leaving the airport.

"And what about Tompkins and his wife?" he asked quietly.

Vladislav took a long drag of his cigarette and blew the smoke through the open window.

"They will have to be killed before tomorrow morning," he said, without looking back at Dimitri.

There was a long silence as the car moved along the dark

potholed road. Having driven the route many times, the young agent knew where the holes were by heart now. The car swerved occasionally as he turned to avoid them. Finally he broke the silence.

"You know some of us have grown to like Tompkins and his wife over the past year." He said the words almost apologetically, knowing what Vladislav's feelings would be. However, he felt he had to make his own feelings known.

Vladislav flicked his cigarette out the window and turned to him. "We have a job to do, Dimitri. Personal feelings can't enter into an assignment of this importance. When I get my work confused with my emotions, I tell myself that sometimes a few people have to be sacrificed for the benefit of many. That's what happened here. We can't leave any evidence behind that will connect our country with the U.S. financial collapse. And that collapse, my friend, will benefit millions of our people. It'll save them from another war, which you can be sure the United States will eventually start.

"Within the scheme of things, the Tompkinses are incidental, meaningless. They were simply a means to an end that will benefit not just our country but eventually the entire world."

Dimitri started to interrupt, but Vladislav continued on.

"I know some of you have let your personal feelings overcome your sense of duty. Comrade Gagarin may have suspected the same thing, and that's why I was ordered here. So don't worry about who will do what needs to be done. Now it's my responsibility. I will do it."

The car turned off the main road and headed into the compound. Dimitri parked near the main cottage and took Vladislav's suitcase from the trunk. Together they walked to the main cottage. Vladislav paused to look at the lights in Tompkins's cottage before he went inside.

He found the entire KGB group assembled in the living room. Some were watching TV, while others played cards. They looked nothing like Soviet agents in their tank tops, shorts, and sandals. As Vladislav came in, they all rose to greet their leader. Over ten months had passed since he had come to the island to check on Helen. There was an undertone of sternness as he greeted each of them. He felt they had grown too lax in the Caribbean sun. For the next few days they would have to return to being sharp and alert. That tone had to be set right again. He sat them down and immediately issued them their orders.

They would start closing down the compound tomorrow. All weapons and communications equipment were to be packed and taken to the airport. There it would be put on the Learjet. In a few days the plane would take himself and two other agents back to New York. The rest would fly commercially. New York agents would be advised of their arrival time in the morning.

, The men were happy to be leaving. Most of them had been on the island for over a year now. Loved ones had been left behind in Russia, and they were anxious to see them. Life on the island had been boring. Once they got over the initial pleasure of being in a warm, sunny climate, boredom set in. They longed for the change of seasons again, the freedom to travel outside their little area, and, most of all, to return to their homeland. Vladislav told them they would come home heroes. They would be personally honored by the Premier once the American capitalist system was crushed.

The meeting lasted about an hour. He went over each step of their withdrawal from the compound. He stressed the importance of gathering up the smallest personal belongings down to used Russian razor blades that might not have been properly disposed of. Every man would be held personally responsible for making sure his area was "clean." Finally he got up from his chair and walked to the door.

"Now, I think we should get started packing equipment. If you all will return to your quarters"—he addressed the agents by their American names—"Bruce and Tom will stay to speak to the Tompkinses."

The agents left the cottage, and Tom went to get Bob and Helen. Vladislav checked the .357 Magnum he had in a holster under his jacket. It was fully loaded. He and Bruce said nothing. Each sat and watched the door. Finally it opened and the Tompkinses stood in the doorway. Tom was behind them. They seemed very surprised to see Vladislav. "Please come in," he said politely, "we'd like to talk to you."

They came into the room and sat together on a sofa near the bay window. Helen smiled nervously.

"I guess we're glad to see you here," she said, holding her husband's hand. "We *thought* we might be going home soon."

Tompkins remained expressionless. He seemed to be sizing up Vladislav, studying him very carefully. Helen went on.

"When you made us write our son to say we were coming home soon, we became very hopeful. I knew it would—"

Tompkins interrupted her. He stared at Vladislav.

"Have you finished printing the money?"

"Yes," Vladislav said, trying to avoid the engraver's eyes.

"And you're going to let us go now." The words were posed more as a statement than as a question.

Vladislav looked up at him. Helen had moved closer to her husband and was squeezing his hand. She looked so small and frail. Tompkins looked defenseless. These were people he had known sitting across from him, not dark shapes in the night that he had been ordered to kill in West Berlin and Warsaw. He turned to look at the men they knew as Tom and Bruce. Both were staring at the floor.

Then it happened.

His indecision had brought Helen to her own conclusions. She turned to Tompkins and began sobbing uncontrollably.

"He's not going to let us go!" she screamed. "He's going to kill us!"

"No, that's not true," Vladislav heard himself saying. He couldn't go through with this now. His plan had been simply to take them outside and kill them on the beach. Just like that, in cold blood, as he had been trained to do. Well, he couldn't do it now; he couldn't stand in front of these two old people and pull the trigger. He would wait until early morning. Then he would go to their cottage and do it while they were sleeping. He wouldn't have to see their faces; he simply would fire at dark shapes, as he had done many times before.

He finished the lie for Helen.

"We're closing down the compound tomorrow. Most of us will be leaving, including both of you. We'll release you in Hartford within a few days."

"Oh, thank God," Helen said, tears streaming down her face. She fell into her husband's arms. He held her close and whispered something that Vladislav couldn't hear.

Tompkins looked at the man across from him—the man

known to him as Anthony Cutrone but in truth a nameless KGB agent. He wasn't going to let them go, he knew that. He could see it in the way the Russian continually avoided his glance. They must have succeeded in printing all the money they needed. Now they had to destroy the only real witnesses to what they had done. The man was lying; he had come to kill them. The question was when.

He took his handkerchief and wiped Helen's eyes. Vladislav got up from his chair and walked across the room. He stood in front of the window, looking out over the water, and said, "Take your wife back to the cottage and start packing. Then get a good night's sleep. You leave at noon tomorrow."

Tompkins helped Helen to her feet and they walked to the door. Bruce opened it for them and they left.

As they walked arm in arm down the moonlit stretch of sand, Vladislav watched them from the window and wondered why he couldn't carry out his assignment. What was stopping him? He heard the Premier's voice telling him two years ago that their plan would enable them to take over the United States without firing a shot. Well, that didn't turn out to be quite true. Unfortunately the only shots needed to be fired had to be fired by him.

Paul Welte hadn't slept more than two hours since he had called Case. It was now morning, and Sasha had already been left with a neighbor, with the excuse that he was going away on a hurriedly arranged business trip.

He stepped from the shower in an enormous red-and-white-striped towel. After drying himself, he went into the bedroom where his clothes were laid out on the bed. Quickly he put on the khaki pants, plaid shirt, and sneakers that he would wear to the Kunsthaus. The old clothes barely fit his three-hundred-pound frame, but at least they might serve to blend him into a tourist crowd.

He set about selecting what he might take into his new life. Narrowing down possessions acquired over many years to fit into five suitcases wasn't easy. It took him the better part of two hours. As he squeezed the last of the bags shut, he looked at the clock on the nightstand next to his bed. It was time to check with the bank. After several minutes of being transferred through the bank's bureaucracy, he finally reached someone of authority. Yes, the money had been deposited. He jotted down the information and hung up. So far, so good.

Time seemed to creep by. There was still over three hours before he was due at the Kunsthaus. He walked across the living room and looked out into the street below. A feeling of nausea was beginning in his stomach again. He needed something to fill up the remaining time; anything, just as long as he had something to do.

The tape. Suddenly he felt he had to play it again. He took it from the antique rolltop desk he used to work at home and held it in his hand. Maybe it wouldn't play. Maybe something had happened to it, and when he got to the embassy, it would be blank. That was ridiculous, but he had to hear it one more time.

He took the eighth-of-an-inch cassette and slipped it into the Swiss-made player. There was a loud hissing sound as the leader passed under the sound head. Then Karl Geisler's voice came over the small speaker.

"Hello, Paul . . . Karl."

He heard his own voice. It startled him.

"Good, I was hoping to hear from you."

"Yes, I've just returned from Prague where I met with your client."

"What was the result of the meeting?"

"The result was that there's a far greater need for my bank's services than I expected. Also, a much larger sum of money is to be funneled through than I thought. American money. Four billion dollars."

"So? That means large commissions for your bank."

"That's beside the point. There's a number of questions I must have answered. Why is there such a large initial funding for two holding companies that I'm to establish, and why is it to be in American dollars? I want to know their motive, Paul. It certainly is more than just expanding their economy into the international system. They're out to put pressure on a single economy, and I want to know whose."

"Karl, I'm sure you're overreacting. Of course large sums of money are involved. Nobody should have to tell you that the use of American dollars is the simplest when it comes to international conversions of currency. There's probably a logical—''

Geisler interrupted. "I don't want a discourse from you on basic banking, and I don't want to discuss this any further on the telephone. They're hiding something, and I want answers before I make any further commitments." Already he was beginning to feel better. This was what the President of the United States wanted to hear. These were the words the *world* was waiting to hear. He pressed the fast-forward button to get farther along on the tape. The voices squealed as they passed through at high speed, but then he heard the familiar thump of a car door closing and he stopped the tape. This was the section he had recorded in Riesen Park in the back of Geisler's limousine. He remembered that the recorder had been hidden in his briefcase.

He pressed the play button, and again he heard his own voice.

"I came as soon as I could, Karl."

"I appreciate it. I didn't want to call on the phone with what I've got to say."

"I understand. We can go for a drive while we talk if you like."

"That would be fine."

There was the sound of the glass partition sliding back, and he heard himself asking the chauffeur to drive around the park. The motor started, and the car could be heard pulling into traffic.

"What is it, Karl?"

"I want you to contact the Russians and tell them I accept their offer. I want you to do it immediately."

"Then you must have received positive answers to your questions."

Geisler's voice was calm. "Just tell them I've received detailed evidence of their intentions and have found it to be satisfactory. I understand their objectives completely, and Union Suisse will be happy to serve them in the manner prescribed in Prague."

Welte heard the surprise in his voice.

"That's wonderful, Karl. I'll contact the Russians immediately."

He stopped the tape, and again the enormity of what he was hearing shook his whole body. When the Russians ordered him to record the first meeting with Geisler at the Exchange Club restaurant, it had merely been to record evidence that could possibly be used in the future. Nina Praeger was ordered to do the same. But once he saw that the Russians weren't about to reward him with anything substantial, he began to make copies. Each week he received tapes from Nina, copied them, and forwarded the originals to Moscow. It was all rather routine, until he saw the tapes taking on more and more importance. Now they were the key to survival for the United States. He was the one who would be wealthy and powerful beyond belief, not Karl Geisler.

He pressed the fast-forward button again. There was one section he had to hear one more time.

From the very beginning he wondered what was Geisler's real motive in joining the Russians. Money was not the reason; he saw that after the second or third meeting with him. But when he heard the tape recorded by Nina's people, he copied it not once but twice. This was the real reason a man of Geisler's stature sought even more power than he already had. President Turner would find it of great interest.

He turned the machine back on. There was the sound of the take-up reel turning, then the sound of movements in a bed. There were moans from a man and a woman. Suddenly the woman cried out in ecstasy. The man's breathing came faster. Then he seemed to gasp for air as he said the same word over and over in the throes of passion.

"Power . . . power . . . power . . ."

The voice was little more than a whisper, but it was unmistakably Geisler's. Now the world would know what drove the man not only to sell out his own country but also the entire free world. He ran the tape back to the beginning and played it again in its entirety. Yes, he was convinced the Americans would find it well worth what they were paying.

He checked his watch. It was time to call the bank again. After verifying the amount in the other account, he asked that the money be transferred into one with a different number. There was some difficulty in doing this, but he succeeded when he gave Ambassador Case's name as a reference.

Satisfied that everything at the bank was in order, he moved the packed suitcases into the foyer where they could be picked up later by the embassy. Standing over them, he wondered if he had forgotten anything important. The phone rang.

It was probably the bank checking on some last-minute detail. He crossed the sunken living room and picked up the receiver. As soon as he heard the voice on the other end, he knew that his life was in immediate danger. It was Nina Praeger; KGB agent Nina Praeger.

Why was she calling now? Saturday was her day to report in with information for him to relay on, not today. Every Saturday morning she phoned in information on Geisler using a sort of code they had established. Her greeting was always the same: "It's such a nice day, I thought I'd call to see if we could go out somewhere." That meant nothing was unusual and she had no news to report. Further discussion of the weather ranged from "Rain forecasted"—I have information or tapes forwarded to you by mail or messenger, but they aren't urgent—to "You can never trust the weather forecast," which meant she had important information that would be received the same day. Some other code words were inserted into their dialogue which either expanded or clarified the message he was to pass on to the KGB in Moscow.

But this wasn't Saturday, and her greeting wasn't in code. He began to tremble again. The KGB. What did they know?

"Paul," she began, "I'm glad I found you at home. I just got in from Lucerne to spend a few days shopping. Perhaps we could meet for lunch while I'm in town."

His mind struggled to come up with a quick excuse.

"No, I'm afraid I can't. I was just about to go out for the day." He stumbled over the words. They knew. They had to know.

"Well, I just thought that since we're always conducting our little business without seeing each other, this would be a nice time to get together. Can you make it tomorrow?"

There was tenseness in her voice. He sensed it more with each word she spoke. He was beginning to lose control, which caused him to speak very rapidly.

"I can't, I'm sorry, I have to meet somebody, maybe Friday. Are you still going to be—"

"Oh, Friday's bad," she said, interrupting. "I've got to go to the hairdresser in the morning, then right to a fitting for a new evening gown. I'm having it made for me by Talanos. Do you know him? He's a marvelous new designer who moved here two months ago, and he's gotten just fabulous reviews in the . . ."

Her words trailed off inside his brain, which was now racing for survival. Why was she calling? Why wasn't it in code? Suddenly it hit him. It was to buy time to keep him on the phone. Already they might be coming for him. He put down the receiver and ran to the window overlooking the street. He opened the blinds. A black Citroen had pulled up in front of the building. Two men were jumping out of it.

He ran to the bedroom, threw on a light jacket, and took the tape from the dresser. It was in an envelope which he stuffed into his inside pocket. Then he ran into the hall. They would be using the elevator. To his left was a door to the fire stairs that led directly down to the garage. He used his weight against it, and it opened easily. Bounding down the three flights of stairs two at a time, he was gasping for breath as he entered the underground garage. The sound of the heavy door slamming behind him echoed through the cavernous garage as he ran for his Mercedes, parked against the far wall. Why did he always lock it? It was taking precious time now to get into the car.

He slid his huge frame behind the wheel and started the engine. The car sprang to life. There was a loud screech of the tires as he threw it into gear and headed for the ramp leading to the street. Coming up into the sunlight momentarily caused him to squint his eyes as he got to the top of the incline. Instinctively he looked to his right to check the oncoming traffic, and then he saw them.

The two men were running back to the Citroen. Now there was an opening in the traffic, and Welte sped out into the street. Through the rearview mirror he saw the men jump into the car, and it began to make a U-turn.

It was about six kilometers to the Kunsthaus through the center of the city. The safest way was to stay in the mainstream of traffic. He headed in the direction of the Bahnhof Bridge. Ten blocks later he checked the rearview mirror and didn't see the Citroen behind him. Maybe they had lost him.

Coming off the bridge, he sped down Hirshengraben toward the Neumarkt public-transport stop. The street was wide enough for him to maneuver past the slower-moving vehicles. Ahead was the intersection where four streets crossed in front of the Zentralbibliothek, the central library. The light was red. He stopped. As the traffic to his right moved through the intersection, his fingers drummed nervously on the steering wheel, waiting for the light to change. It seemed to take forever. There was only one car left in the line moving through when the light finally turned green; a black Citroen.

For a moment he froze. They had caught up with him. The cars in back started to honk for him to move. As he was about to frantically make a U-turn, the driver of the Citroen rolled down the window and waved him to go forward. It was an elderly woman with an old gentleman next to her. He had lost the other Citroen.

He floored the Mercedes down the wide boulevard. Weaving in and out of traffic, he sped by the Neumarkt stop. Heimplatz and the Kunsthaus were just ahead. With one hand he reached inside his jacket and felt for the tape. He needed reassurance that it was securely in his pocket. If he made it to the plaza, he would have to make a dash for the gallery.

He just made it through the next intersection before the light turned red. As he pulled out to pass the car in front of him, he checked the mirror again. The Citroen wasn't there.

Even with the car no longer following him, he found himself roaring down the final block to the gallery. He pulled up to the curb nearest the main entrance and sprang from the car. Running up the steps as fast as his three-hundred-pound body would go, he wondered if he would ever leave the museum alive.

Once Welte came through the Neumarkt area, he had entered a ring of CIA surveillance that encircled the Kunsthaus. Although operating on very short notice, agents from as far away as Bern had joined those in Zurich to form a cordon around the museum. There were ten unmarked cars, three vans, and a helicopter in the area, all in communication with the embassy. Two agents were inside the museum. It was considered too dangerous to have any more near the Ambassador.

• • •

Twenty minutes earlier, Case had entered the Kunsthaus.
The gallery was not new to him. He had been there many times
and was familiar with the layout. Although much smaller than
the Metropolitan in New York, the interior reminded him of it.
The classic modern pillars and the marble floor gave it an
elegance that underlined the quality of the work displayed
within it. He liked to come here during the week, just before
closing when it was quiet. Often he was the only person
standing in a room among the paintings. The sound of his
footsteps on the marble were magnified by the stillness around
him. Each loud click of his heel gave him the sense that he was
walking back in time, actually living among the scenes above
him on the walls.

But now the gallery was crowded. The Rembrandt show had
been highly publicized during the past month. This was the
first time the painter's work had been assembled to travel
throughout the world. The first stop for the exhibition was
Paris, where it had been a huge success. Just two days ago it
had opened in Zurich.

Case made his way toward the staircase to his left. He
practically had to push his way through the confusion of people
asking for directions and programs in five different languages.
Slowly he climbed up the three flights, pausing at the second-
floor landing to help an elderly woman. At the top of the stairs
a guard stood in front of the entrance to the exhibit casually
observing the crowd. Case hoped it wasn't one of his security
men. The guard seemed more intent on studying the good-
looking women than anything else.

As he entered the first room of the exhibit, *The Nightwatch*
was off to his right. The huge painting was the center of
attraction for the crowd that filled the small area. There were
art students busily sketching on folded pads, trying to dissect
the master's compositional technique. Others discussed the
history of the work, but for the most part, people just stood and
stared, admiring Rembrandt's wonderful use of light. It seemed
to glow from within the ornate frame as if it were illuminated
from behind.

Case moved around the edge of the crowd, trying to pick out
his contact. He tried to remember the voice on the telephone. It
was deep, with a slight accent. Was it German or the lighter,

less guttural sound of the Swiss? Was the man heavy or thin?
He decided heavy.

His age . . . he would guess in his fifties, probably well
dressed, very precise in his manner, shined shoes.

The man said he would recognize him immediately. Who
was noticing him now? He scanned the crowd. No one that he
could see was paying any particular attention to him. He
decided it was useless to speculate blindly. Moving to the far
side of the room, he picked up a program from a wall holder
and waited for the contact to come to him.

In the middle of the crowd studying the painting, another
man was waiting. Nobody paid any attention to the raincoat
that was draped over his arm, even though it was a clear day
outside. He held the coat close to his body, as if he were
concerned it might fall. Preoccupied with the paintings,
occasionally he glanced over in Case's direction. The Ambassador was studying his program and didn't notice.

Case looked up to check his watch. It was ten after one. He
began to feel queasy in the pit of his stomach. Where was this
man who possibly held the fate of the country in his hands, this
man he wouldn't even recognize? His nervous stomach was
getting worse. He scanned the crowd again. The only thing he
noticed was someone leaving the group in front of *The
Nightwatch* as a number of other people entered the room.

The man holding the trench coat had spotted his target.
Along with other KGB agents, he had spent over two hours
listening to the conversation from the embassy tape. After
careful study of the voice and consultation with agents in
Moscow, the caller had been easily identified. Now he was
entering the room just a few feet in front of him. The agent
smiled at the ridiculously obvious attempt made at disguise.
When someone weighed nearly three hundred pounds, it was
very difficult to blend into a crowd. Nevertheless, the target
was wearing a peaked cap, tan windbreaker, jeans, and white
sneakers. A camera was slung over his shoulder.

Paul Welte looked around the room, then started toward
Case. The KGB agent shouldered his way around a French-
speaking couple to intersect the path of the target. Welte was
no more than an arm's length away now. He was keeping his

eyes on Case, apparently afraid of losing him through the
crowd. The agent's fingers tightened around the Magnum
hidden under his raincoat as he moved closer to Welte. With
one quick motion he pressed the automatic into Welte's huge
stomach, the silencer boring into the flabby flesh. He fired
once, and then again. Two muted cracking sounds were lost in
the din of the crowd.

Welte doubled over, his hands clasping his midsection. As
he fell forward, his gaping eyes searched for his assassin. As if
in slow motion, his body slid down between the people
crowded around him, finally collapsing on the floor.

The agent's movements were made to appear as if he simply
bumped into the man and moved on through the crowd. But
now he responded to their shocked reaction and doubled back.
Case was standing on his toes, straining to see over the
confusion in front of him.

Quickly the agent pushed back through the crowd.

"Let me through, I'm a doctor," he shouted. Out of respect
for authority and sheer helplessness, the people parted in front
of him.

"Move back, give me room," he continued as he knelt
beside the dying Welte. The gold dealer was gasping for
breath. His face was turning an ashen color. He was just
minutes away from death. "This man is suffering a heart
attack. Get help immediately," the agent ordered. Two people
near the edge of the crowd bolted for the exit.

With a series of quick movements he unzipped Welte's jacket
and undid his collar and belt. Then he reached inside his
jacket, feeling along the lining, appearing to examine the
chest. On the left side he felt something else. He outlined the
shape in his mind . . . a wallet. The tape was on the left.
Still appearing to examine Welte, he looked down beneath the
jacket. Blood was beginning to form a deep red stain on
Welte's light shirt. In a few seconds he would be forced to
execute the final part of the plan.

He gauged the distance to the crowd behind him . . .
about four feet, enough to get a running start through the
opening that still remained. From there it was about fifty feet to
the men's room in the outer corridor. He felt inside the jacket
again. With his right hand pressed to Welte's chest, he used his

left to carefully determine the size of the tape by squeezing the envelope between his thumb and index finger. It was very small. The whole thing would easily flush down the toilet.

Suddenly Welte's whole body contracted sharply and then relaxed. His eyes rolled upward and his head fell to the side. He was dead. The agent heard running footsteps entering the room, and then moving through the crowd to his right. He had to act now.

Pulling the envelope from Welte's pocket, he sprang to his feet and whirled around. The crowd instinctively moved back, still believing in his credibility. He took advantage of their confusion and lunged through several rows of people knocking some of them to the floor. The corridor and the men's room were straight ahead.

Behind him, he heard a man shouting, "Stop him. In the name of God, stop him."

Out of the corner of his eye he saw Case waving his hands frantically above the crowd. No one paid any attention to him. The whole thing had happened so fast that the people didn't know how to react. One minute the agent was a doctor helping a dying man, and the next, he was a thief stealing something from him. But what he had stolen was the proof a country needed to survive, and there would be no stopping him now. He would flush the only evidence left of the Soviet Union's involvement down a toilet bowl, even if he had to give his life to do it.

Finding himself clear of the crowd, he headed for the hallway. On the run, he discarded the raincoat, and now, with both hands free, he tore the envelope open and removed the small cassette. It was less than an inch long and about the width of a cigarette. The men's room door was just ahead. Using his shoulder, he pushed it open and sprang into the room. As he cleared the door, the heel of a shoe smashed into his face, breaking his nose instantly. He fell backward and tumbled toward the floor.

Instinctively his body reacted to years of training. As he fell, his left hand maintained a tight grip on the tape while the right gripped the Magnum tucked in his belt. His left shoulder dropped and reached the floor first, enabling him to roll over and come up into a kneeling position all in one fluid motion.

But his attacker had moved even quicker. He was already in a crouch position, both hands gripping a small-caliber pistol pointed inches from his head. (Earlier Case had noticed him as a uniformed security guard more intent on watching women than doing his job. But now he was a cool professional dealing with a determined adversary.)

"Drop it. Drop it now or you're dead."

The guard's eyes were cold, his hand steady. This was no ordinary gallery security guard.

"How did you know I'd come in here?" the agent asked calmly.

"We have somebody outside covering every exit, so when all the commotion started, I decided to try my luck in here. Give me the gun and then the tape."

The agent's mind was racing. Within seconds this CIA man, or whoever he was, would have help coming through the door. The bathroom stalls were just a few feet away. What stood between him and them was a small-caliber pistol. Even if he took a hit, even two, he still might make it.

"Now, throw the gun out in front of you."

He brought his hand back to toss it but at the same time shifted his weight to the balls of his feet. As the gun left his hand, he lunged forward, grabbing the guard around the ankles and pulling him to the floor. Continuing his momentum toward the stalls, he ran over the guard, his heel digging into the fallen man's chest and face. With his eyes fixed on the stalls ahead, his feet found the floor again, but the guard was rolling onto his back behind him.

The stall was about five feet away. He stretched his arms forward, the tape held tightly in his right hand. The shots would come any second. Suddenly he felt the impact of the first one, a burning sensation that pierced his back and then surged into his chest. *Hands outstretched,* he thought. *Keep them out ahead of you. Fall forward, keep your weight forward.* The second shot entered his back higher, between the shoulder blades, exiting through the heart's right ventricle. His feet fell out from under him, but his hands were over the bowl. He dropped the cassette into the bluish water and it sank to the bottom. With his body draped completely over the bowl, he groped for the handle. *Use your weight . . . flush it . . .*

push. He heard a loud whooshing sound, and then he died, not knowing whether it was the flushing sound or the last rush of air from his lungs.

May 12, 1991
St. Maarten

At daybreak the following day, two motor launches made their way across Samson Bay. In the lead boat, Davidson peered through binoculars at the shoreline, silhouetted against the early-morning sky. Ahead was the compound. The buildings were dark shapes against a hill in back of them. The only color was the bright orange and yellow bougainvillea that flowed down the hill in back of the buildings. All the shutters in the windows were drawn. Everything was quiet except for the hum of the inboard engines.

Davidson lowered his glasses and turned to the helmsman beside him.

"Bring her in behind those rocks to the right of the beach, Jim. It'll give the boats more cover while we wade ashore."

The boat slowed to a crawl as it moved toward the sea-worn rocks, edged with coral. Davidson turned to the fifteen men behind him and signaled them to crouch low. They lowered their bodies to the deck, cradling their weapons as though they were babies in their arms.

The boats were in position now behind the rocks, out of view of the buildings. Slowly the men went over the side, lowering themselves into water that was waist-high. With their weapons held above them, they made their way to the edge of the rocks toward the palm trees. Davidson was in the lead. From behind a palm tree, he scanned the buildings again through the glasses. There weren't any guards patrolling. It was very quiet, too quiet. He hoped they weren't too late. He hoped Tompkins and his wife were still alive.

Vladislav awoke.

The room was dark except for a thin ray of light that shone through the closed shutters. He looked at his watch: five A.M. Why was he still dressed? The events of yesterday came back to him: the orders to kill Tompkins and his wife . . . the long trip to St. Maarten . . . arriving at the compound. He cursed himself. He had done what all his training had taught him never to do—delay in carrying out an order.

The previous night he'd tried to rationalize why he had done it. Why had he felt compassion for these people who had to be killed to insure the success of his mission? His answer was because they were people he had known and spent time with, not just targets marked for assassination. But it was more than that. After they left, he went to his room and laid on the bed thinking. He thought about love, the love of another person. It was something he had never known. Somehow his profession had never allowed time for it. He thought about the family he had never had and the loneliness of every waking hour.

He had seen the strength of love between Tompkins and his wife. It was what had sustained them for over a year of torment and separation.

He had read all of Helen's letters to her husband. They were letters of encouragement, of hope, and, most of all, love. Each letter spoke of the wonderful times they had spent together and that soon they would be reunited. When he finally let Tompkins read them intermittently, they became a source of nourishment for his mind. Like food, it would sustain him for a period of time, and then he would have to have another or he wouldn't be able to face the next day.

His letters to her openly expressed his concern and love for her. Both of them fed on each other's strengths, giving them the courage to go on. This bond, this union of strength, was something he couldn't easily destroy. He lay there thinking about tomorrow, and then he fell asleep.

But this was another day, and now he would do what he had been sent to do.

He went into the bathroom and splashed cold water over his face. His image in the mirror looked tired and at least ten years older. He reached inside his jacket and took the Magnum from its holster and checked it. It was fully loaded. With one last look around the room he opened the door and stepped outside.

The coolness of the morning air hit him as he started down the walk to the Tompkins cabin. It felt good. He turned and looked toward the beach. There was a bright glow along the horizon that preceded the sunrise. The water glistened as the light danced over it.

But now there was a dark shape that was silhouetted in front of it. And then another and another. There were little flecks of light, but they weren't reflections from the water because they were exploding all around him.

Instinctively he reached for the Magnum and began firing as he raced for the cabin. It was no more than fifty feet away. Bits of concrete exploded out of the wall behind him as .30-caliber bullets tore into it. On the run, he hit the door of the cabin with his shoulder; it flew open and he fell into the room.

Tompkins, who had been startled by the gunfire, was out of bed and heading for the window. Vladislav rolled over on his shoulder, regained his footing, and leapt at Tompkins, pulling him to the floor. A burst of gunfire shattered the window.

He held the gun to his head.

"We're under attack. Stay down and do exactly as I tell you."

Helen was sitting up on the bed, staring at the shattered window, too startled to do anything else. Vladislav crawled over to the bed and with one hand pulled her to the floor.

Tompkins reached out to help move her to the corner of the room, but Vladislav shouted, "Stay back and lie facedown on the floor."

With Helen safely in the corner of the room, he moved to the window.

"What's happening? Who are they?" Tompkins said from his facedown position.

Vladislav didn't answer. He was pulling the curtain back to get a look outside.

Tompkins knew who they were. It had worked. His son had found the hidden slide and brought it to the authorities. They were there to rescue them. He turned to Helen, who was sobbing uncontrollably. Moving closer, he whispered, "Don't worry, everything will be all right. They've come for us."

She turned and looked at him, about to speak, but he put his hand over her lips to stop her.

Machine-gun fire was coming from the other end of the compound. More troops were coming up from the beach, and Vladislav could see that they weren't encountering any resistance. His men must have been taken completely by surprise.

How the hell had the Americans found them? They had maintained strict security on the island. How had it been broken? It didn't matter; there wasn't any time to think about that now. They were here to get Tompkins; that much was for sure. As it turned out, it was lucky he hadn't killed him the night before, because now he was his only means of escape.

Suddenly the gunfire stopped.

Vladislav could see through a corner of the window that men were moving toward the cabin and were spreading out to surround it. He heard the blare of a bullhorn.

"This is Henry Davidson of the United States Secret Service. We have the compound completely surrounded. You're holding two American citizens, a Mr. and Mrs. Robert Tompkins. We'll give you sixty seconds to release them or we will—"

"Or you will what, Mr. Davidson?" Vladislav yelled from the cabin. He threw open the shutters and pulled Tompkins and Helen up from the floor and held them in front of the window.

"Storm the cabin? I think not, because then I would be forced to kill them, and you can't afford to have that happen, can you?"

Davidson was behind a stone wall about a hundred yards from the cabin. He studied the KGB agent through the binoculars. The man looked calm and determined; probably the leader. Tompkins and his wife looked terrified. He had to act fast.

Fuller was behind the main building by the beach. He picked up a radio and called him.

"Hal, get some sharpshooters up on the roof of that cabin in back of me where they can't be seen. Sooner or later we're going to have Tompkins and his wife coming out of the cabin with the head KGB."

He picked up the bullhorn.

"All right, I won't play games with you. Right now you have the advantage, so it's your move."

Vladislav reached into the pocket of his trousers and felt for the car keys he had taken from Dimitri the night before. The car was parked in front of his cabin. If he could get to the airport, he would fly the Learjet out; to where, he hadn't decided. It wasn't important now; the first thing was to get to the car.

He shouted at Davidson, "I want your men to drop their weapons and stand up with their hands over their heads. I'm going to come out with Tompkins and his wife in front of me. If anyone moves, I'll kill them. Remember, I have nothing to lose, but you have everything."

Vladislav ripped two pieces of cord from the blinds. He tied Tompkins's hands behind him with one, and Helen's hands in front of her with the other. Then he loosely tied the two ends together. By holding the one piece of cord, he would be able to keep both of them close to him. He had about two hundred feet to go to reach the car. If this man Davidson was going by the book, he would have men with high-powered rifles back out of sight. They would fire only if they had an open target. Well, they'd better be good, because if they didn't kill him with one shot, he would kill Tompkins before he died.

Outside, Davidson was calling Mullet Bay. He gave orders for the airport to be covered and for a helicopter to be sent up. It would follow the car, which he knew Vladislav must be heading for. Since the President and the Joint Chiefs of Staff were standing by in Washington, he relayed everything to Mullet that had happened so far. When that was completed, he switched frequencies on the radio and got back to Fuller.

"Hal, did you hear my conversation with Mullet?"

Fuller's reply crackled over the radio.

"Every word."

"Good. We're going to have to go along with him. We've no other choice. Are those sharpshooters in position?"

"Yeah, Dave. One is on the roof, and the other is in the main building for a lower angle."

"Okay, now listen carefully. Keep them down and out of sight until they reach the car. At that point the Russian will be the most vulnerable. If they need to blow their cover to get off a shot, they're to do it. I have a feeling if we lose them here, we won't get another chance. It's all yours now, Hal."

Davidson put the radio down and passed the word to his men.

Inside the cabin, Vladislav was checking the Magnum.

There were three shots left in the clip. He turned to Bob and Helen.

"Our little charade is over now. Obviously the Secret Service hasn't come all this way to chase down some Mafia counterfeiters. My name is Yuri Vladislav, and I'm a special agent of the Soviet KGB."

Tompkins stood with his hands tied behind his back, staring at the floor.

"I know. I've known for some time."

Vladislav was noticeably taken aback. He pointed the Magnum at Tompkins's head.

"How long have you known?"

Tompkins's mind was racing. He may have said too much already, in his desire to defeat this man who had held them in captivity for so long, but he couldn't stop.

"Since I started to work on the plates."

Vladislav smiled.

"Then why did you work so hard to make them perfect?"

Tompkins glanced back at Helen, whose hands were tied to his.

"I had no other choice, did I?"

Vladislav cocked the Magnum, then pulled it away.

"No, you didn't."

The bullhorn blared outside the cabin.

"All right, my men have dropped their weapons."

Vladislav looked out the window. Davidson had lined his men up about fifty feet back from the walk. They stood with their hands on their heads. Their weapons were at their feet.

He turned to Bob and Helen.

"Now this is what we're going to do. Listen carefully, because your lives depend on it. I'll be holding the rope from your hands tight to keep you close in front of me. There shouldn't be any problem getting across the walk. When we get to the car is when I'll be most vulnerable, so we'll move in a precise manner. As we come up to the car on the driver's side, Helen will open the rear door and get into the car. Then, Bob, you will open the driver's door and let me get in first. I'll be holding the rope to your hands and will be sliding across the seat to the passenger side. You will then get into the car. I'll cut the cord from your wrists and you'll drive the car out. Any questions?"

Helen was trembling.

"Can I open the door with my hands tied?" she asked.

"I've tied the cord far enough back on your wrist so you'll be able to do it. There's one other thing you both should know. I can assure you that none of my men have been taken prisoner. I cannot allow any of us to be taken, either. If necessary, there are three shots left in the gun, one for each of us."

He opened the door.

The sun was up over the horizon, and it glared in their eyes as they stepped outside. Davidson's men looked like helpless toy soldiers as they stood with their hands over their heads.

Vladislav moved Helen and Bob quickly along the walk, being careful to keep them between himself and Davidson's men. Helen nearly tripped over Bob's feet because Vladislav was keeping them so close together. She felt the cord cutting into her wrists. They were almost to the car now. What was going to happen to them? Sooner or later this man would kill them.

So much had happened in the last few minutes. For months she had believed they were Mafia, involved in some sort of counterfeit scheme, but they were Russians. Bob knew they were. He had known for some time and yet had worked on the plates for them. But why? Because of her, that was why. She was the reason Bob had been forced to help the Russians make counterfeit money. What did this man Vladislav say? They were most vulnerable at the car. What was that flash on the roof over there? Vladislav hadn't seen it.

They came around the back of the car. Vladislav told her to open the rear door. She did, and he let go of the cord. Where the flash had been, now she could see a man with a rifle. This was their chance, probably the only one they would get. She got into the car and slammed the door behind her.

From inside, she could see the man again. He was aiming the rifle. Vladislav saw him, too, and now he was reaching to open the driver's door. Before he could, she leaned forward and locked it.

Vladislav tugged at the door, then turned to look back at her. As he did, he came far enough out from behind Bob to fall into the sharpshooter's sights. There were two shots. One bullet tore through his neck, and the other hit him just above the ear. The gun flew out of his hands, and he fell to the ground, dragging Tompkins with him.

The two men were lying face-to-face on the concrete pavement. Blood was streaming from Vladislav's mouth and neck. Slowly he raised his head and gathered his remaining strength to whisper, "It's too late. Your country is doomed, and you have made the perfect money that killed it."

Tompkins pulled the cord from his grasp and stood up.

"That's where you're wrong. The money isn't perfect."

Vladislav stared up at him and died.

16

THOUSANDS OF UNEMPLOYED WORKERS FROM DETROIT AND
NEW YORK MARCHED ON THE CAPITAL TODAY DEMANDING
THAT THE GOVERNMENT FIND THE SOURCE OF THE ALLEGED
COUNTERFEIT BILLS FLOODING THE NATION'S MONEY SUPPLY.
MILITANT GROUPS AMONG THEM DEMANDED MILITARY AC-
TION AGAINST RUSSIA, WHOM THEY CLAIM IS RESPONSIBLE
FOR THE PRINTING OF THE MONEY. POLICE ARRESTED FIFTY
OF THE GROUP WHEN THEY TRIED TO STORM THE BARRICADES
IN FRONT OF THE WHITE HOUSE.

VIOLENCE ALSO WAS REPORTED IN DALLAS AND ATLANTA
AS THE FINANCIAL CRISIS CONTINUED INTO THE THIRTY-
FOURTH DAY.

Friday, May 13, 1991
St. Maarten

THE HEADQUARTERS AT Mullet Bay was alive with activity.
Shortwave radio transmissions were being sent to Washington,
reporting the success of the mission. There had been just two
casualties in the attack group, both of them minor. Twelve
KGB agents had been killed. They apparently had been under
orders not to be taken alive.

Davidson and Fuller's main concern now was to get the unit
off the island quickly. Washington wanted to keep the mission
as quiet as possible without turning it into an international
incident. And the President wanted Tompkins in the capital as
soon as possible to debrief him. Then a press conference would
be arranged for the engraver to tell the world of his captivity.

Davidson had his own reasons. One, it was still possible that Tompkins could lead them to where the Russians were printing the counterfeit money. Two, Tompkins had given them some startling new information. From the moment they had gotten to him, he had been hysterical. He kept telling them over and over that the counterfeit bills weren't perfect. He said he had altered them and that they could be detected.

In the boat on the way back to Mullet Bay, Davidson and Fuller had filled him in on the financial crisis back home. He broke down and cried, saying over and over again that he couldn't help it, he had been forced to work on the plates; but he also insisted that he had altered them. He asked that they get some hundreds and twenty-dollar bills. Then he would prove it to them.

Davidson couldn't see how it was possible. Experts from the Treasury and Bureau of Engraving had done exhaustive tests on thousands of bills from every part of the country and hadn't discovered one counterfeit bill. Yet Tompkins persisted. He said he could prove it.

Finally Fuller suggested money be collected from the unit. When no hundreds could be gathered, what was later found to be a fortunate decision was made. They got the money from a casino. Fuller had just come back from there.

Hal put a small briefcase on the coffee table and opened it. Inside were stacks of hundreds and twenties.

Davidson fanned a stack of hundreds.

"How much is here?"

"Twenty thousand in hundreds from the casino, plus five hundred in twenties from our own people," Fuller answered.

"Good. We gave Helen a mild sedative. Tompkins is in the other room with her now. As soon as he comes out, we'll question him some more." He looked at his watch. "We've got another hour and a half before we're due at the airport."

Fuller poured some coffee.

"Dave, I really don't see how he could have altered the bills. There's no way it can be done."

Davidson was testing a Wollensac tape recorder on the coffee table. Satisfied, he turned it off and said, "I don't, either, but he's determined to try to prove it to us."

The bedroom door opened, and Tompkins came into the room carrying a small black case.

Davidson thought the man looked exhausted. What had been a feeling of excitement and relief for him just a few hours ago had apparently turned to dejection. Receiving the news of the financial crisis he had created by cooperating with the Russians was a severe blow to him. Although Davidson felt he must have known the money was being used to attack the economy, he probably never conceived of the result reaching such astronomical proportions. What the agent didn't want, however, was for Tompkins's guilt to prevent him from giving them any information he could about the Russian printing plant. Questions pertaining to that would be a priority. This notion of having altered plates might just be a figment of a panicked man's imagination.

Davidson gestured toward the sofa for him to sit down.

"Can I offer you some coffee?"

Tompkins nodded. He poured him a cup and handed it to him.

"Mr. Tompkins, before we leave for the airport, Hal and I would like to ask you some questions."

Tompkins nodded.

Davidson turned on the recorder. "Let's start from the beginning. If you can, I'd like you to tell us what happened when the Russians captured you and Helen."

Tompkins took a sip of his coffee and stared off into the distance as he recalled the event. He spoke slowly.

"They took Helen first. She was gone one night when I got home. The next thing I knew, I was in a printing plant. Where, I don't know to this day."

"Did you have any idea who had captured you?"

"They said they were Mafia and were involved in a counterfeiting scheme. They wanted me to work on engravings. They already had a hundred that just needed updating, but they also needed additional work on a twenty. I told them they were crazy, it was impossible to make perfect engravings, but they had paper and ink that were perfect."

Davidson stopped him.

"What do you mean by perfect paper? Did you examine it microscopically?"

Tompkins brushed the question aside with a sweep of his hand.

"I didn't have to; they did it for me. When they projected it on a screen, the fiber was perfect. The electronic frequency from the metallic fiber was even perfect. Crane, your government supplier, couldn't have made it any better."

"Did they threaten you?"

Tompkins seemed upset with the question. He stared at Davidson and raised his voice.

"Of course they threatened me. They had Helen. They said they would kill her if I didn't cooperate. I didn't know where she was or what had happened to her."

Davidson put his hand on his shoulder.

"I understand. Then what?"

"I created a new twenty. It was easy. Like I said, they had the best of equipment, the paper, the inks, they were all perfect. So was the engraving for the hundred . . . a German engraver had worked on it, a man named Schmidt, he—"

Fuller stopped him.

"Did you say Schmidt?"

"I think that's what his name was."

"Helmut Schmidt?"

"Yes, that's it."

Fuller turned to Davidson.

"Dave, do you remember Operation Bernhard?"

"Yes, it was a World War II operation. Germans counterfeiting the British pound, right?"

"The pound at first, but then a U.S. hundred that supposedly was perfect. They were supposed to have made three sets of plates, but none of them were ever found. Everyone thought the Germans had destroyed them, along with the man who worked on them . . . Helmut Schmidt."

Davidson turned to Tompkins.

"Do you know if Schmidt is still alive?"

Tompkins answered slowly. "He died a year ago. That's why they needed me."

"So you worked on Schmidt's engravings?"

"Yes, they were extraordinary. The man was a genius. Every detail in the engravings was perfect. I only had to upgrade the plates to incorporate changes over the years."

Davidson moved the tape recorder a little closer.

"All right, let's go back again. You thought they were Mafia, and they forced you to work on the engravings. Then what?"

Tompkins took a sip of his coffee.

"One night I overheard them playing cards. There was an argument, and one of them started speaking Russian. Vladislav stopped him immediately, but I had heard enough. I knew then that this was more than just some small counterfeiting scheme and that I had to do something. So I devised a plan where I could alter the bills without anyone ever detecting it."

Davidson went slowly now. "You said 'alter the bills,' Mr. Tompkins. Exactly what do you mean by that?"

Tompkins put his coffee down on the table. His eyes narrowed and he clenched his fists.

"You don't believe me, do you? I tell you, I altered them as soon as I found out they were Russian. But I had to do it carefully." His voice dropped to a whisper. "I couldn't risk Helen's life."

Davidson pressed him further.

"Didn't you have any idea what they were doing with the money? Didn't you realize they had to be using it to diminish the value of the country's currency?"

Tompkins's head slumped.

"Not until I realized how much money they were printing. They said it was one hundred million, but I had calculations that said it was much more."

"How much more?"

Tompkins hesitated and stared at the floor.

"Probably over seventy-five billion."

Fuller let out a slow whistle.

"But again, there was nothing I could do. They had Helen, and they had the plates to print as much money as they wanted."

Davidson calmed him with a slow gesture of his hand.

"I understand. You were brought here, and then what?"

"Then I found the newspaper clipping that told me of the financial crisis the country faced. I knew then that I had to risk everything if it wasn't already too late. I had to get to someone and tell them that the money I had created wasn't perfect."

Davidson reached over and snapped open the briefcase. He took the stacks of money from it and put them on the table.

"Mr. Tompkins, we'd like you to show us how you altered the bills."

Tompkins just stared at him, then he reached over and picked up the nearest stack. Slowly he leafed through the bills.

"Where did you get these?"

Fuller answered.

"From the casino here and the people who rescued you."

Tompkins opened the tool case beside him. Inside were various awls and punches, neatly arranged into slots cut into the leather. From a small pocket alongside them he removed a plastic card and a magnifying glass. He held the card up for them to see. It was full of tiny dots.

"This card is a one-hundred-twenty-line engraver's screen enlarged ten times. There are fourteen thousand, four hundred dots to a square inch. The dots form the halftone images that you see on printing every day."

He took some Scotch tape from the case and taped the transparent dot screen to the magnifying glass, enabling him to see through the dots. He began with the twenties. He took each bill and turned it over to the back side, examining it through the glass. Quickly he went through the first stack. Nothing. The second and third stacks . . . still nothing.

He put them aside and started on the hundreds.

One by one he examined the bills. It wasn't until he got to the third stack that he stopped and held up a bill.

"This one is counterfeit."

Fuller and Davidson were out of their chairs, leaning over his shoulder.

He put the bill aside and removed the dot screen from the magnifying glass. Then he handed the glass and another bill to Davidson.

"Now this bill is good. Look at the back of it through the magnifying glass. Position the glass so you're looking at the flag flying on top of Independence Hall. Do you see it?"

"Yes, I see it."

Tompkins picked up the counterfeit bill.

"Now, look at the counterfeit. Look in the same spot . . . at the flag."

He handed the bill to Davidson.

"It looks the same. There's no difference."

"Ah, but there is," Tompkins replied, "but you can't see it without this dot screen."

He took the magnifying glass from Davidson and taped the screen on to it.

"Look at the good bill again, this time through the screen."

Davidson repositioned the glass over the White House.

"It looks a little fuzzy, but I can still see the flag."

Tompkins handed him the counterfeit one.

"Now look at the flag on this one."

Davidson stared at the counterfeit bill, stunned. Without a word he handed it to Fuller. He took one look and his eyes widened. The words came out in a whisper. "Holy Christ, I don't believe it. Where the flag was, now there's a hammer and sickle."

Tompkins smiled for the first time.

"That's right, and the same would be true if one of the twenties were counterfeit. They look perfect until they're magnified under the screen because I've altered the flag ever so slightly. When the screen is overlaid the hammer and sickle appear."

Davidson got up from the sofa and walked to the window. He couldn't believe what he had seen. He never would have believed that a bill could be altered without it being detected. The man was a genius. The best engravers in the country hadn't discovered what he had done. If they had only gotten to him sooner. Now it was too late. Or was it?

He turned to Tompkins.

"If I hear you correctly, all the money printed in the plant could be detected as counterfeit if it was magnified under that screen."

Tompkins got up from the sofa and came over to him.

"That's right. If you see the hammer and sickle, you know they're counterfeit."

Fuller was still holding one of the bills in his hand. He looked at it through the glass again.

"But that would mean special equipment."

Tompkins was excited now and anticipated the question.

"Nothing more than a common overhead projector like they

use in business presentations. You know the kind. You put a clipping from a magazine over a light and project it on a screen. If you put the transparent dot screen over the lens, you've got it."

Davidson was thinking out loud.

"So if we demonstrated that to the world and could prove the Russians were behind it, we'd have taken a big step toward saving the economy."

Fuller put down the magnifying glass.

"You'd better believe it. Now that we can show how to detect the counterfeit, over a period of time they can be destroyed and replaced with newly designed bills. The confidence in the dollar would be restored, and the Russians would end up with egg on their faces."

"That's true, Hal, but there's still a few pieces missing. We've got Bob now and he'll tell his story, but we still need to shut off the Russians from printing more counterfeit. We've got to find that plant. It'll stop the printing and prove the Russians were behind it. We need definite proof."

Davidson took Bob's arm and led him back to the sofa. Fuller put a new reel of tape on the recorder and turned it on.

"You've got to remember everything you can about that printing plant, Bob. Even things that seem insignificant could lead to a clue. What about the sounds outside? Traffic, sirens, planes close overhead, a radio playing, anything at all."

Tompkins thought back over a year's time, sifting through his mind hundreds of events that had taken place. It was a few minutes before he spoke.

"There's nothing I can think of. They were very careful. I never saw a newspaper or listened to the radio. They screened everything that came in or out. They even screened their own conversations. Nothing was ever said that would tip off where we were."

"You're sure."

"There's absolutely nothing I can think of."

"Isn't there anything at all . . ."

"I'm telling you . . . nothing. What do you want me to do . . . lie to you?"

He was becoming aggravated again. Davidson could sense that his guilt in working on the bills would be hard to erase. On the other hand, some of that guilt was desirable. It might motivate him to speak out against the Russians when they needed him to.

He looked over at Fuller, and Hal gave a slight gesture with his hands that said they shouldn't press any further. Both of them were fully aware of an earlier conversation with the President by special telephone. Turner was elated that the mission had been successful. What he wanted now was both Tompkins and his wife off the island. He reported that the CIA and Ambassador Case were very close to linking Geisler to the Russians and the numbered account. That account had to contain billions of dollars, used to purchase securities to threaten the U.S. economy. And now that Tompkins could prove that the Russians had reprinted the counterfeit, a case was building. If everything came together, they would have an open-and-shut case, but they had to move fast. Intelligence reports now warned of a Russian withdrawal in just three days.

It would be a race against time. But with Tompkins in their hands, they had a good chance of winning. They would immediately inform Washington that Tompkins had altered the bills and then get him to a "safe house" being readied in Virginia. They would leave that afternoon. Fuller and the rest of the unit was scheduled to leave twelve hours later. As far as they knew, the Russians hadn't as yet learned of the attack. Communications from the printing plant to St. Maarten might still be sent to the compound. If any were sent, they would be waiting.

The break they were looking for came later that evening, after the Tompkinses, along with Davidson, had left the island. A coded message was received by two Secret Service men left to man the radio at the captured compound. The agents, Al Ross and Joe Helmsley, were having sandwiches and coffee when the radio started to crackle. Ross, the older of the two and an expert on Russian codes, quickly turned to a small computer, which contained fifty of the most recently broken Russian codes, and typed in the letter equivalents of the dots and dashes. Helmsley called Fuller at Mullet Bay on the other line.

The screen in front of Ross flashed the jumbled letters

intermittently while the computer scanned over ten thousand possible combinations of letters. Seconds ticked away. Too long a delay would make the Russians suspicious.

He hit the return key, sending the cursor jumping over to the left side of the screen. Then he typed, SCAN ONLY. That command automatically doubled the possible combinations, the disadvantage being that parts of the decoded words might still be jumbled. They were running out of time, and he had to take the chance.

The coded words stared at him while the computer's memory went through the combinations. Then, with a sweep of letters across the line, better than half of them were decoded. The line now read: HAR THC ASSAGRMINT REFERDENG THC HISTEGAS BAAN RERRAEDN IUT?

Ross's trained eye translated the rest: HAS THE ASSIGNMENT REGARDING THE HOSTAGES BEEN CARRIED OUT?

He typed the now completed line into the memory and then the words, AFFIRMATIVE . . . SEND.

The memory now knew the appropriate code and sent the word AFFIRMATIVE coded.

He waited. There was a long delay. Were they suspicious? Had he made an error in what he'd sent back?

Fuller was on the line now. Ross plugged a headset with a small microphone into the phone so he could code and relay the message at the same time. The second transmission began.

WILL BE EXPECTING YOUR ARRIVAL IN NEW YORK TOMORROW. GIVE FLIGHT NUMBER AND ARRIVAL TIME.

Fuller spoke over the phone.

"So they're in New York. Hold on, Al. Don't send anything back yet."

Ross could hear him put down the receiver and shuffle through some papers. Hurry up, goddammit, they're waiting. Finally Fuller came back on.

"Okay, send this."

Ross tapped out the words as he heard them: MEET AT KENNEDY . . . 1700 HOURS . . . EASTERN FLIGHT 17 . . . OUT.

They waited. Fifteen seconds . . . thirty . . . no return message. They had bought it.

Fuller's voice came through the headset.

"Let's hope it worked, guys. If it did and we're lucky, they may lead us to a printing plant in New York tomorrow."

It was four-thirty P.M., and Eastern's arrivals building was crowded. This particular Saturday had an unusually heavy schedule of flights returning from the Caribbean. Fuller, Ross, and Helmsley had flown in earlier on a two P.M. flight from St. Maarten. Upon arriving, they had met with New York police and set up a master plan where any precinct would be prepared to respond should the KGB lead Fuller and his men into their area.

The plan was based on three assumptions. The first was that someone would be at the airport to meet the KGB group that supposedly was returning on Flight 17. The second was that he could be identified. Number three was the long shot. It assumed that when the agent saw that his contacts weren't on the flight, he would either try to communicate with the printing plant or lead them to it.

Elaborate communications were set up from Kennedy to the precincts. Helicopters were in the air to follow the KGB agent if he left the airport. Unmarked cars were in touch with command headquarters at the 42nd precinct in Manhattan. Everything was ready.

The sign over the baggage carousel flashed, "Baggage from Eastern 17 arriving from St. Maarten."

Fuller and the two agents moved slowly through the crowd, matching every face to a mental file of known KGB agents. Once a month, picture files of the KGB were upgraded in Washington. They were required reading for Treasury and Secret Service agents. Remembering a face from those pages could save a man's life or, in this case, a country's.

It was Helmsley who first noticed the heavyset man standing near the Avis counter. There was something about him that triggered an image in his mind. He moved closer. The man was casually studying a rate brochure, apparently just killing time before the passengers came into the room. He looked familiar, but something was wrong. The mustache—that's what it was. Helmsley tried to imagine him without it. He took one last look, then turned and started working his way over to Fuller.

Hal was standing near the carousel with a *New York Times*

under his arm as Helmsley moved alongside him. In a low voice he said, "Watch the guy standing at the Avis counter while I check the paper."

Fuller handed him the newspaper, and he turned to the two pages they had inserted into the paper earlier. There, spread out before him, were thirty pictures of KGB agents known to be operating in the New York/Washington area. In the middle of the second page was the man he was looking for . . . without the mustache. He glanced at the caption as Fuller looked over his shoulder.

"Alexei Borshov, age 30. Russian embassy aide. 4 West 56th Street, New York. Photographic specialist. Aliases: Alan Papp, David Stroff."

Helmsley closed the paper and turned to Fuller, who simply nodded. Ross was moving toward them as the first group of passengers came into the room. The man at the Avis counter put down his brochure. He was up on the balls of his feet, straining to get a good look. Fuller and Ross started moving to the phone booths along the wall at the far end of the room.

As the area filled, the man moved away from the counter and into the crowd. Not having seen his comrades, he was searching more closely now. Where were they? All the passengers were in the room. Finally he turned and headed for the phone booths. Hurriedly he entered the last booth at the far end of the line. Fuller took a pad from his pocket and checked the numbers of all the booths he had written down earlier. Quickly he went into another booth at the opposite end of the line and picked up the phone.

"Operator Eleven, please."

Operator Eleven had been prearranged with New York Tel. She was the best they had.

"This is Operator Eleven."

"Code Eight is placing his call from ELdorado 8-6200."

"ELdorado 8-6200. I'll begin trace."

Fuller looked at his watch. She'd need a full sixty seconds, at least. He opened the folding glass doors a little and looked down the line of booths. The Russian was still inside. Fuller took a small radio from his coat pocket and called the agent in the parking lot, who was in touch with N.Y.P.D.

"He's in the booth. We're tracing."

Thirty-five seconds . . . just a little longer.

He looked across the crowd at Ross. He was reading the *Times* in a position where he could see both him and the KGB agent. Helmsley was at the exit door.

Fifty seconds.

Fifty-five . . . the door to the booth opened and the agent was heading for the exit door with Ross behind him.

Fuller was shouting into the phone.

"He's out of the booth. Have you got it?"

"One moment, please."

"Oh, Jesus, come on, will ya?"

The radio came to life in his hand. It was the agent outside.

"He's heading into the parking lot on the run. We're right with him."

He pressed the talk button.

"Stay with him. I'm still waiting for the trace."

The operator came back on the line.

"The call was made into the Murray Hill exchange. MU 8-4040."

"Who's the number listed under?"

"Mid City Printing, 147 West 23rd Street, Manhattan."

Fuller wrote the address down on the pad and ran out of the booth. Helmsley was waiting outside the exit door with the car. As he opened the door to get in, the agent tailing the Russian came back on the radio.

"Code Eight heading out of the airport for Grand Central Parkway, eastbound toward Long Island."

Fuller barked back, "The target is West 23rd Street. They've told him he's screwed up and is probably being followed, so now he's trying to lead us away from the nest. Stay on him and make it look like you're buying it."

Helmsley was bringing the car up onto the Van Wyck Expressway, which was now full of rush-hour traffic. Even with a siren, it would take at least forty-five minutes to get downtown. The raid had to happen now. The KGB at Mid City were probably on to them and would hide any evidence very quickly, certainly before they got there. He raised Radio Central so all precincts could hear.

"Fourteenth Precinct . . . the nest is in your area . . .

Mid City Printing . . . West 23rd . . . it's Code Three and it's now."

The reply came in seconds.

"This is the Fourteenth. We know the building. We're on our way."

Within minutes the building was surrounded with police cars. The first ones to arrive contained the attack force. The ten cars that followed stopped at key intersections along the way, halting all traffic into the area. Everything was cordoned off from 18th Street to 28th Street; from Eighth Avenue to Fifth.

Mid City was taken by storm. Ten policemen with Browning automatic rifles ran up the staircase. At the top of the stairs they stopped. A radio tuned to a rock station was blaring over the roar of printing presses.

Captain Mike Lilley, Commander of the Fourteenth Precinct, was the first one into the room. He saw no one. Two huge Miehle four-color offset presses were running at high speed, the paper spinning over the rollers and picking up impressions on its way to the stacker at the far end of the machine. The noise was deafening. Lilley motioned for his men to circle the room.

Quickly the men moved around the presses. As they came alongside the first color unit, a stunned pressman emerged from the access space under the roller unit. He was carrying a bucket of yellow paint and a spatula that was used to apply ink to the rollers. Upon seeing ten policemen with automatic rifles pointed at him, he stopped dead in his tracks and raised his hands.

Lilley shouted above the noise, "Shut off the presses."

The man put the bucket on the floor and moved a few feet to the main control panel. He flipped four switches, and the presses wound down to a dead silence. Immediately four other men appeared from the bowels of the machine with their hands up.

From the other end of the room, two policemen brought a pressman who appeared to be the foreman. He was the Russian agent that Tompkins had known as Sal. A plastic pen holder with different-colored ballpoint pens was stuck in his shirt pocket. He shook himself free of the two officers that were holding him.

"What the hell is this? What do you guys think you're doing, anyway?" he screamed at Lilley.

Lilley stood behind his Browning, still pointed at the man.

"What we're doing is stopping you from printing any more counterfeit money."

The foreman leaned back and roared with laughter.

"You gotta be kiddin'. Us printing counterfeit money? Angie, show the good captain what we're printing."

The short, stocky pressman nearest the skid containing the finished pieces grinned and took the top sheet from the pile. He held it up. The foreman pointed at it and said, "Care to buy some underwear for your wife, Captain?"

Lilley looked at the sheet. It was a counter card for a department store showing a woman wearing a bra and panties. The foreman stopped laughing and turned dead serious.

"If you guys don't have a warrant, I suggest you get the hell outa here."

"We'll have a warrant in twenty minutes, mister," Lilley snapped back. He turned to the sergeant next to him. "Read 'em their rights, Frank, although if they're who we think they are, it shouldn't be necessary. They don't have any."

Fuller and Ross arrived a half hour later. By then, four million dollars in counterfeit twenties had been found. They were mixed into the stacks of counter cards. When confronted with the money, they all refused to answer any further questions.

Fuller tried, anyway, for another twenty minutes, showing them the picture of the agent at the airport and identifying him as KGB. He explained that telephone company logs would show that this man had called the printing plant from the airport. They remained silent. At that point Fuller decided not to press them further. Tompkins would identify them soon enough.

They had to find out now where the counterfeit bills went from here. How were they passed into the economy? The farther along the route they traced the money, the closer they would come to tying in the Swiss. But they were running out of time.

Fuller planned to have the N.Y.P.D. book and hold the captured agents. Their instructions were not to reveal the men's identities to any newspapermen covering the precincts. This was to be just a small counterfeiting ring that had been broken up. If any more than that got out in the papers, the rest of the KGB operation would close up within hours, leaving the trail cold.

Within an hour Mid City Printing was empty, except for Fuller, Ross, and Helmsley. From the outside it looked like the night shift was in full swing. Lights were burning, presses humming. Fuller and his men poured themselves some coffee and prepared for a long wait.

At three o'clock the following morning, a truck with Nevada license plates made its way down Park Avenue South. The street was empty, except for a lone police cruiser patrolling the area. The truck passed it and made a right turn onto 23rd Street, then continued across Fifth, the driver and his companion both glad to be at their destination after a long eighteen-hundred-mile trip.

At the intersection of Fifth, Broadway, and Twenty-third Street, they could see the lights on the second floor of Mid City Printing. The guys were working late. The truck stopped just past an alleyway, and the man on the passenger side got out with a flashlight to direct the truck back. The driver shifted into reverse and backed into the alleyway, watching the flashlight in his rearview mirror.

The truck stopped inches from the loading dock; the driver turned off the motor and climbed down from the cab carrying two small overnight bags. He handed one to his partner, and they entered the building and started up the stairs.

As they passed the first landing and reached the second flight of stairs, Fuller and Ross stepped from the shadows and ordered them to turn around.

Both men acted instinctively. The driver pushed his overnight bag into Fuller's gun, causing it to go off as he fell backward against the wall. His partner took advantage of Ross's split-second glance at Fuller to push him against the wall, and brought his knee crashing into the agent's groin. Both men then wheeled around and ran down the stairs. One of them had picked up Ross's gun. They were halfway down when Helmsley stepped out on the landing and ordered them to freeze. They stopped, but the man with the gun fired. Helmsley fell to the floor, and the bullet ripped into the wall behind him. As he fell, he fired two shots, both aimed at the man in front with the gun. The first shot hit him in the chest, causing him to fall to the steps, while the second caught him in the shoulder as he fell forward. The bullet tore through cartilage and exited at the back, hitting the second man, who had ducked, squarely in the forehead. He fell forward into his partner, and both men tumbled down the stairs, landing at Helmsley's feet. Fuller and Ross rushed down the stairs in the hope of finding one of the men alive. Helmsley had only intended to take out the man with the gun, but unfortunately both were dead. There were no prisoners.

A search of the truck, however, produced a registration under the name of Catalano Carting, Las Vegas, Nevada, along with ownership papers under the name of Carl Ferrara, Las Vegas.

The following morning, the FBI, along with local police, raided Catalano Carting and found another five million in counterfeit bills. Five KGB agents were captured. After intense questioning, which used techniques not published in Secret Service manuals, two KGB agents were broken, and supplied information as to how the money was distributed. Within hours the Thunderbird Casino was raided. Elena Pryde and her fellow KGB agents were taken from behind the revolving cashier drawers and arrested.

The next day, the Atlantic City casinos were raided. An additional $780 million in counterfeit was recovered. FBI agents in California then moved in on the First National Bank and found not only large sums of counterfeit currency, but also the location to which the money was forwarded: Union Suisse, Zurich, Switzerland, account number T7486.

The entire Russian counterfeiting operation in this country had been shut down. What remained was to have Tompkins tell his story to the world and link Geisler and the Swiss to Moscow.

Karl Geisler was driving on Autobahn N-1 outside of Zurich. He hadn't slept in days. Two nights ago Otto Krohn of the Swiss Banking Commission told him about Welte's tapes, and then he knew all was lost. He would not become the powerful controller of the world's finances that he had envisioned himself being. On the contrary, he had been disgraced in the eyes of his peers. This morning's meeting with Krohn would be the final straw. He was sure it would result in his being publicly dishonored by the Commission. He would deny any knowledge of the money being counterfeit. Even the tapes that the Americans now had couldn't prove that, but in the end he would lose. That was certain.

So far the Russians hadn't been of any assistance in his defense. For days he hadn't been able to contact either Gagarin or any of his subordinates. None of his calls had been returned. Since he was the only one who could link the Russians to the counterfeit bills, he had wanted to coordinate the defense he knew would be needed in the World Court.

He was late for the meeting. Traffic was light on the Autobahn. Most of the rush hour was over. He stepped on the accelerator, and the Jaguar leapt forward. The speedometer read eighty miles per hour as the car came into the S-turn that led into the tunnel. Expertly he brought the car into the first turn, increasing the speed and using centrifugal force to bring it around. As he turned the wheel to the right to negotiate the second curve, he realized that he had misjudged the speed slightly. His foot went to the brake. The pedal sank to the floor. Despite the anti-sway bar and the excellent suspension of the Jaguar, the car could not hold the road. Desperately he pumped the brake, trying to get fluid up into the cylinder. He pressed again. Nothing.

The car crashed into the abutment of the tunnel at over a hundred miles per hour, the steering wheel crushing his body against the roof and killing him instantly.

Later, an investigation to determine the cause of the accident revealed two electrically timed solenoids positioned next to the brake cylinders of the rear wheels. Both cylinders had been punctured by the device, one that had been used in Europe before by the KGB.

There was a witness to the crash that the police never found. A woman had been only minutes behind Geisler on the Autobahn. She slowed down briefly to view the accident, then continued on.

Her name was Nina Praeger.

17

May 15, 1991 (UPI)—

A NEWS CONFERENCE IS SCHEDULED FOR NINE A.M. TOMOR-
ROW IN THE CAPITOL BUILDING. AT THAT TIME PRESIDENT
TURNER WILL PRESENT EVIDENCE THAT REPORTEDLY WILL
LINK THE SOVIET UNION TO THE AMERICAN FINANCIAL
CRISIS. ADMINISTRATION SOURCES REVEALED THAT ROBERT
TOMPKINS, THE RECENTLY RESCUED GOVERNMENT ENGRAV-
ER, WILL DEMONSTRATE HOW THE SOVIETS WERE ABLE TO
PRODUCE BILLIONS OF COUNTERFEIT DOLLARS AND HOW
THEY CAN NOW BE DETECTED. ALL THREE NETWORKS WILL
POOL THEIR RESOURCES FOR A BROADCAST SCHEDULED TO
LAST OVER THREE HOURS.

May 15, 1991
Washington, D.C.

A BLACK CADILLAC limousine made its way through the dark
back streets of Washington, D.C., its headlights piercing
through the pouring rain. Ahead of the car was a blue van, a
long whip-antenna protruding through its windowless side
panel. Following behind were two black Lincolns carrying
eight Secret Service men. The sound of a Bell turbo helicopter
droned overhead as it hovered over the small convoy.

Inside the limo, Bob and Helen Tompkins sat next to Henry
Davidson. Two stern Secret Service men faced them in the
jump seat, while Fuller manned the radio up front with the
driver. Davidson slid back the glass partition and tapped Hal on
the shoulder.

"What's the report from upstairs?"

"From what he can see through the rain, the streets are empty, except for a couple of cars and our guys at the corners."

"Good." Davidson looked at his watch. Three minutes to midnight. "What's our ETA?"

"About four minutes."

Dave closed the window and turned to Bob and Helen.

"We're almost there. In just a few minutes we'll be pulling up to the White House."

He saw Helen take Bob's hand and squeeze it tightly. The forty-minute trip from the "safe house" in Virginia had been an anxious one for both of them and the people responsible for their safety. Everyone was fully aware that these were the star witnesses against the Russians. They were not safe until they appeared in front of the television cameras the following morning, and neither was the country.

A plan was developed where they would move at night from Virginia to the White House, where President and Mrs. Turner would meet them. They would then be briefed and stay for the night under the tightest security. Information had been leaked that they would be moved to Washington in the morning and go directly to the Capitol Building where the press conference would be held. The three major networks would find out at six A.M. that it would be held in the Oval Office.

Bob Tompkins looked through the rain-splattered window at the streetlights reflected on the slick pavement. How far he and Helen had come. A year ago they were just an elderly couple trying to live out retirement. The next day, they would stand before the world. A nervous feeling passed through his stomach. Could he handle all this? Helen was far more articulate than he, and probably much more in control of the situation. He decided, though, that he wouldn't be nervous. Anger had replaced nervousness. Anger at the way the Russians treated them, anger at them literally trying to starve the U.S. From briefings in Virginia, he knew now that they weren't the only ones who suffered at the hands of the Russians. Hundreds of thousands had lost jobs, fortunes, and futures. The country had come very close to falling into their hands. Yes, he would be angry. He would tell his story and the world would know.

He looked over at Helen. She had taken away her hand and was opening her purse.

"May I have some light?" she said to Davidson.

Dave reached behind Bob and turned on the reading light mounted behind the seat. Helen took out a small compact and examined her makeup. Not satisfied, she dabbed some powder on her nose and cheeks. Clicking the compact shut, she noticed everyone looking at her.

"It's not every day that a girl gets to meet the President and his wife, now is it?" she said with her pixielike grin. "Have to look my beautiful best, you know."

She turned to Bob.

"Straighten your tie, dear." She adjusted the tie he had loosened earlier. "He always unbuttons his collar and the tie goes to one side," she said to Davidson.

"That's because this shirt is too small," Tompkins said as she squeezed the button through the hole.

"That's because your neck is too big," she answered.

The small convoy made its way down the final quarter of a mile to the White House. Two more intersections and they would be on the White House grounds. Fuller was on the radio with the helicopter pilot. He reported no unauthorized vehicles in the vicinity. The limo approached the South Gate, which was already opening. Two Marine sentries saluted smartly and waved them through. The van pulled to the side, and the remaining three cars drove up to the illuminated entrance. Davidson let out a sigh of relief. They were here, and now they were safe.

As the car made its way up to the South Gate, Bob saw that the White House was bathed in a soft, warm light. Every detail had been burned into his mind, having etched it thousands of times on twenty-dollar bills for the Russians. He looked at the seven two-story columns, winding staircases on either side of the portico, and at the flagpole, high on top of the roof. Here he had beaten the Russians with a thin line added to the flag that formed the hammer and sickle. Here he had won.

The car stopped, and another Marine sentry opened the door. He held an umbrella over Davidson as he jumped out and helped Bob and Helen from the limousine. Fuller followed.

Secretary of the Treasury Dillon greeted them under one of the protective awnings near the entrance.

"Welcome to the White House, Mr. and Mrs. Tompkins." He let out a deep breath. "I'm very, very glad you're here."

He shook hands with Bob, who said simply, "Thank you very much. It's an honor for us."

Dillon continued. "The President has asked that I bring you directly to the Blue Room, where he and Mrs. Turner would like to meet you. Then you'll be briefed for tomorrow's press conference. After that, we've arranged for you and Helen to stay overnight in the Jefferson Room."

He offered Helen his arm and added, "It's quite a room."

"I've seen pictures," she said, "but I never thought I'd ever, ever sleep in it."

She took his arm, and they went up the steps through the entrance doorway. Like most first visitors, they were struck by the elegant beauty of the seventeenth-century architecture, and the sense of history that emanated from it. As they stood in the Diplomatic Reception Room, Helen stared at the massive crystal chandelier that hung in the center of the oval-shaped room. She whispered to Bob, "It's beautiful, but I'd hate to have to clean it."

Dillon escorted them upstairs and stopped in front of a large wooden door just off the stairway. He knocked. The door was opened by the President of the United States.

Tompkins's heart was racing as he shook the President's hand and then the First Lady's. She clasped his hand in both of hers and said, "Thank God you've made it here safely. Please come inside."

They went into the room. Entering it was like taking a step back in time. It was done in eighteenth-century Federal style. There was a desk that Mrs. Turner explained had belonged to Dolly Madison, two original Chippendale high-backed chairs, and a large sofa that had been Daniel Webster's. On the far wall was a Gilbert Stuart painting of George Washington, framed by two brass wall sconces. Beneath it was a huge brick fireplace with an ornate hand-carved mantel.

The President gestured for Bob and Helen to sit on the sofa. He and Mrs. Turner sat across from them in two soft wing chairs. Tompkins and Fuller sat off to the side, near the door.

Tea and some light refreshments were served while the President talked about the historical background of the White House.

Finally he settled back and spoke in a soft voice that Tompkins thought very different from the dynamic quality of his television speeches.

"Let me just say," he began, "that I speak for the entire country in thanking both of you for your bravery. If you hadn't risked your lives to expose the Russians, the country could be in a dangerous position tonight. Instead, we're ready to prove to the world that they were about to destroy our economy. What you did was a brave act, one this country will never forget."

Helen smiled and thanked the President. Bob said nothing.

What he had done wasn't because he was brave but out of necessity. It was out of the need to survive. Bravery was when something was risked without regard for the consequences. He had acted because of *fear* of the consequences. All the praise they had received in the media was overblown, exaggerated.

For the past two days the papers had been filled with pictures of him and Helen. The press hadn't been allowed near them, but somehow they'd dug up old head shots of them.

They referred to him as "American Hero, Hero Engraver." He was far from being a hero. He was just trying to repair what he had caused, and the President should know that.

"Mr. President," he began, "I don't think we are brave at all in the true sense of the word. We did what we had to do to survive. When Helen was taken from me and I was threatened with her death, I was forced to do something that was wrong. I did it to survive. When I found out they were Russians, I did what they wanted in order to get to Helen. When I found out where we were, I managed to make contact in order to survive. I think that probably *survival* is the right word, rather than bravery."

Turner listened politely, occasionally glancing over at Fuller and Davidson. They had fully briefed him on the guilt Tompkins felt for what he had done. But if he was to be effective the next day, he would have to be free of this feeling. That was of prime importance.

He spoke slowly, with as much sincerity as he could muster. "I appreciate your modesty, Bob, but I've found that most heroes are survivors first. They have a will to fight, but they also have a sense of dedication for what they are fighting for. In your case, you could have gone on completing your work once you found out that your captors were Russian, but you risked your life and Helen's to alter the bills. If you hadn't, the country would now be lost. That's the difference I'm talking about. I've decorated many brave men during my time in office and have talked at great length with them. Believe me, Bob, they were all survivors first and heroes second."

Helen moved closer to her husband. It was her way of telling him that everything was all right. He did feel better now, because he had heard from the only person who could excuse what he had done: The President.

Now Helen would have something to say. The light had gone on in her eyes again. This was hold-on-to-your-seat time because he could feel that she was about to interject something unpredictable.

"I think," she started, emphasizing the *I*, "that what is important here tonight is that we are all safe and that the country is safe. Also, I'm thankful for these two men." She pointed to Hal and Dave, who lowered their eyes into their coffee cups. "They're the real heroes. *And*"—she emphasized the word with outstretched hands—"I'm thankful to be seated on Daniel Webster's sofa, which is inspiring me to talk so much, and"—she paused to look at Bob—"to sleep in Thomas and Martha Jefferson's bed, which may just simply inspire us."

Everyone laughed, and the President took the opportunity to get up and go to a small desk at the opposite end of the room. From a drawer he took a small square box and brought it over to Bob. Tompkins stood up, and the President handed it to him.

"Please accept this token of appreciation on behalf of the people of the United States."

Tompkins took the box and opened it. Inside was a leather case with the words, "Robert L. and Helen T. Tompkins" stamped in gold on the cover. He lifted it, and a small viewer snapped into place. There was a slide inside that illuminated automatically. It was the picture of Helen and himself on St. Maarten that had been sent to his son. Only this time it was superimposed over a flag furling in the wind. The slide was in a gold mount with an inscription below it: "To Bob and Helen Tompkins, from a nation forever grateful."

He accepted it with a simple "Thank you." Helen stood and they embraced. They spoke with the President and Mrs. Turner for a few moments, then Fuller opened the door. There was applause. Outside were members of the Cabinet, along with key members of the Senate and the House. They were the men who would brief him for a press conference that would defeat the Russians in a battle they had almost won.

Epilogue

Moscow, May 16, 1991 (AP)—

TODAY TASS, THE SOVIET NEWS AGENCY, DENIED ANY DIRECT INVOLVEMENT BY THE RUSSIAN GOVERNMENT IN THE COUNTERFEITING OPERATION THAT ALMOST DESTROYED THE U.S. ECONOMY. OFFICIAL STATEMENTS FROM MOSCOW INDICATE THAT CERTAIN MEMBERS OF THE POLITBURO WILL BE CENSURED TODAY BEFORE THE FULL COMMITTEE. THOSE SCHEDULED TO APPEAR IN A CLOSED HEARING ARE VASILY A. GAGARIN, DEPUTY MINISTER OF FINANCE, ANDREI P. GORKOV, MINISTER OF DEFENSE, AND MIKHAIL R. VENEDOFF, MINISTER OF INTERNAL AFFAIRS.

London, May 16, 1991 (Reuters)—

THE LONDON EXCHANGE SHOWED THE DOLLAR GAINING OVER FIVE POINTS IN THE FIRST HOUR OF TRADING. EXCHANGES IN PARIS, HAMBURG, AND ROME SHOWED EQUAL ADVANCES. LORD HAMILTON, CHAIRMAN OF THE EXCHANGE, PREDICTED THAT THE DOLLAR WILL RETURN TO ITS HIGHEST POINT OF TWO YEARS AGO WITHIN SIX WEEKS. HE WAS QUOTED AS SAYING, "THE DOLLAR HAS RECOVERED, AND SO HAS THE U.S. ECONOMY."

May 16, 1991
Moscow

VASILY GAGARIN PICKED up his briefcase and walked into the foyer of his home outside Moscow. His wife, Irena, was standing there between two KGB agents, his hat in her hand. He went over, took it from her, and placed it on his head.

277

Turning to a full-length mirror mounted on the inside of the closet door, he made final adjustments by squaring the hat and his tie. If they were going to throw mud at him today, they would at least have an impeccable target.

Irena came and stood behind him in the mirror. She knew what was ahead for him, and how it would affect their final years together. His bid to eventually become Premier had been lost. Instead, he would be censured, along with two other members of the Politburo, for plotting the financial overthrow of the United States. They were to be scapegoats before the world for the failure of the entire Politburo. The younger, aggressive members would now have the opportunity to exile the traditional party-liners into early retirement.

Besides her husband's disgrace before the world, tangible things in their lives would be lost. This house would go, along with the servants, chauffeur, and summer house on the Black Sea. The next years would be spent in a small apartment with a pension that would essentially return them to the middle class.

Gagarin turned and kissed her lightly on the cheek. One of the KGB men opened the door, and they went out into the bright spring morning. He handed his briefcase to one of the agents and walked over to some evergreens beneath his study window. There were three different varieties that Irena had experimented with the previous fall. One was a very small yew that stood between two larger junipers. He knelt down and examined the underside of the needles carefully. They were a healthy green with new sprouts beginning to form.

The first snowfall of the past winter now seemed a long time ago. At that time it looked as if he would succeed in smothering the American economy with billions of dollars in counterfeit. He remembered seeing the small yew and then saying to himself that "billions of tiny snowflakes would fall from the sky and smother it."

He stood up and stared at the healthy plant. In a soft voice not heard by the waiting KGB men, he said, "I misjudged. It was a lot stronger than I thought."

Bestselling Thrillers —
action-packed for a great read

___ $4.50 0-425-10477-X **CAPER**
            Lawrence Sanders
___ $3.95 0-515-09475-7 **SINISTER FORCES**
            Patrick Anderson
___ $4.95 0-425-10107-X **RED STORM RISING**
            Tom Clancy
___ $4.50 0-425-09138-4 **19 PURCHASE STREET**
            Gerald A. Browne
___ $4.95 0-425-08383-7 **THE HUNT FOR RED OCTOBER**
            Tom Clancy
___ $3.95 0-441-77812-7 **THE SPECIALIST** Gayle Rivers
___ $3.95 0-441-58321-0 **NOCTURNE FOR THE GENERAL**
            John Trenhaile
___ $3.95 0-425-09582-7 **THE LAST TRUMP**
            John Gardner
___ $3.95 0-441-36934-0 **SILENT HUNTER**
            Charles D. Taylor
___ $4.50 0-425-09884-2 **STONE 588** Gerald A. Browne
___ $3.95 0-425-10625-X **MOSCOW CROSSING**
            Sean Flannery
___ $3.95 0-515-09178-2 **SKYFALL** Thomas H. Block
___ $4.95 0-425-10924-0 **THE TIMOTHY FILES**
            Lawrence Sanders

Please send the titles I've checked above. Mail orders to:

BERKLEY PUBLISHING GROUP
390 Murray Hill Pkwy., Dept. B
East Rutherford, NJ 07073

NAME_____

ADDRESS_____

CITY_____

STATE_____ ZIP_____

Please allow 6 weeks for delivery.
Prices are subject to change without notice.

POSTAGE & HANDLING:
$1.00 for one book, $.25 for each
additional. Do not exceed $3.50.

BOOK TOTAL	$_____
SHIPPING & HANDLING	$_____
APPLICABLE SALES TAX (CA, NJ, NY, PA)	$_____
TOTAL AMOUNT DUE	$_____

PAYABLE IN US FUNDS.
(No cash orders accepted.)

LAWRENCE SANDERS

"America's Mr. Bestseller"